CANDLELIGHT AND YOU

This Valentine's Day, three Arabesque authors offer you stories that you'll fall in love with and cherish forever. Join Leslie Esdaile and newcomers Melanie Schuster and Linda Walters and be swept away by the power of love.

ARABESQUE BOOKS are published by

BET Publications, LLC
c/o BET BOOKS
One BET Plaza
1900 W Place NE
Washington, D.C. 20018-1211

All Kensington Titles, Imprints, and Distributed Lines are available at special quantity discounts for bulk purchases for sales promotions, premiums, fund-raising, and educational or institutional use. Special book excerpts or customized printings can also be created to fit specific needs. For details, write or phone the office of the Kensington special sales manager: Kensington Publishing Corp., 850 Third Avenue, New York, NY 10022, attn: Special Sales Department, Phone: 1-800-221-2647.

First Printing: January 2003
10 9 8 7 6 5 4 3 2 1

Printed in the United States of America

CONTENTS

VALENTINE'S LOVE

Leslie Esdaile

DEDICATION

"Valentine's Love" is a dedication to the concept of "hope springs eternal," and to encourage readers to never lose the faith—or hope—that good things can happen . . . sometimes with a little divine intervention. Haven't we all wished we had an angel on our shoulders, guiding us, clearing the path, and drying our tears? Well, here's a secret—we each do. Sometimes they also show up in the strangest ways, at the most surprising times. Enjoy their miracles!

With love to my sister, Lisa Jessie Peterson, my daughter, Helena Marie Esdaile, and my parents. Special acknowledgement to Chandra Taylor, my editor, who is always in my corner and an angel on my shoulder, as well as to The Evening Star Writer's Group of Philadelphia. Thanks for always pointing out the magic of life, and for reminding me not to detest small beginnings.

One

She had sworn to herself that *this* holiday, she would not let the fact that she was still unattached get to her. "Denise Blake, you just stop the pity party right now," she told herself in a firm tone as she turned the key and opened the door to her small floral gift shop and then stepped in. She loved her flowers.

Immediately, she felt at ease as the fragrant air from the blossoms in the back workroom wafted through the bright little shop to surround her. Ever since she was a child, and had spent time in her grandmother's backyard, sniffing the delicious array of honeysuckles and roses that her nana tended, she had been hooked on floral scents. Her nana went out every spring and summer morning and, for her, flowers represented God's way of keeping beauty in the world. They came in so many varieties, too, like people, her nana had said, and that was also why people shouldn't fight about differences—just look at the flowers.

Denise closed her eyes for a moment and breathed in, remembering Nana Blake's words. *Should the rose scorn the orchid, or the wildflower fuss with the tulip, because of its color or where it needs to grow?* Wise words from a wise woman. She dearly missed her nana, but was thankful to be able to still claim elements of the family sage amid the flowers she now offered to her customers. Denise opened her eyes and let the lights of the shop chase away the cherished memory.

By rote, she lit an incense stick to blend the fragrance of that woody scent in with the others filtering throughout the small space, and flipped on some music. Calm, Native American flutes drifted from the speakers and mixed with the sounds of nature behind it on the CD. Calm. Today she would be calm, she reaffirmed, as she went to add water to the small, trickling tabletop water fountains she had strategically scattered throughout the store. Harmony. When her customers came here, she wanted them to feel like she did, as though they'd stepped into a haven.

Relaxation began to return to her as the eclectic fusion of beautiful colors, sweet scents, and gentle sounds blanketed her. Yes. This was the way one should start the day.

Nana had taught her this, and so much more in her backyard while hanging linen on the line. If Nana were still here on earth now, certainly she would know how to gently chase away the holiday blues with good smells from her kitchen, too. Scent . . . that was her grandmother. A woman whom she could envision just by comforting aromas.

And then, there was her mother—a woman very different from Nana.

The newfound calm began to slip away from her as she thought about her mother. Ernestine Blake was not as easygoing as Nana, and was much more direct and aggressive with her words. Denise loved her mother, but wished she wouldn't constantly harp about it being time to get married. In fact, she wished her mother would just stop harping period.

"Okay, kiddo, give it a rest." Denise shook off the momentary sad thoughts and made her way to the counter. She had work to do. All this introspection was simply a waste of time, and had only been spurred on by the fact that it was Valentine's Day. Plus, her mom had asked the million-dollar question again last night, inquiring whether her daughter, *her only child,* would get some flowers from someone special this year. No, she wouldn't.

Instead, she had to remember what her mother had also told her: She was blessed to be able to have her own business, doing what she loved, at only age thirty-two. Yes, she had to remember that. Where was that tablecloth? She had to set up a special area for all the flowers for the day's promotion, and didn't have time for these thoughts.

Busying herself with the task of straightening up the displays and getting the register ready to open, she surveyed all that she was fortunate enough to have. Yes, abundance had indeed been visited upon her from hard work. True, the years as a floral designer for others had paid off, not to mention her long hours working two jobs in order to bank enough to open a tiny shop of her own.

So there was no reason to feel down, and there was no reason to feel a pang of wistfulness each time she prepared a dozen roses to go out to some lucky woman. She just had to get herself together and stop thinking about the male voices that had called, giving her tender endearments to put inside the cards that went with those shipments. She should be joyous that all her close girlfriends had special plans tonight, and that their boyfriends had thought enough of her to patronize her store . . . and she'd labored over those flowers to make the arrangements extraordinary, because after all, they were going to her best friends.

Denise worked at readying the store as her mind reflexively went back to the subject she'd been trying to shake. She used her mother's words to reinforce her goal—her mother didn't do pity parties and didn't suffer feeling sorry for oneself. Mom was right: Not many people her age got to have a budding enterprise, nor could they fill it with beautiful cards, knickknacks, and tiny stained-glass objects all of their own choosing.

Focus. All she needed to do was to focus. Plenty of women hadn't had a date in a year and a half, and they didn't have all these other good things to keep them occupied. So there was no reason in the world for her to become morose just because it was Valentine's Day.

Plus, she was done with the Hallmark holidays, on a personal level, despite the fact that these holidays were her bread and butter. She no longer believed in the concept of Mr. Right anyhow!

When the shop doorbell sounded and an elderly patron came in, Denise smiled. It was force of habit. She didn't feel like smiling. But this seemingly sweet old lady didn't have a thing to do with her somber mood.

"Hi. Welcome to Denise's Delights," she intoned cheerfully, moving toward the customer. "May I help you?"

"Oh, thank you, baby, but no. I'm fine. I just came in to browse. Don't waste your time on me."

There was something so melancholy in the woman's voice, even though she had smiled when she had spoken to Denise, that the woman's statement pulled at Denise to come to her side anyway. Odd, but she had just been thinking about her grandmother, and now someone else's grandmother was standing in her shop. The Lord works in mysterious ways, her own nana would always say. Well, if she could cheer up somebody's grandmom today, then it was all good.

Sidling up to her customer, Denise gazed at the lady as the woman patted her silver-blue hair into place and stared at the racks. Her worn black coat was somewhat wrinkled and had fabric burrs and flecks of lint on it. But Denise noted that this old woman smelled so wonderful, like roses . . . yes, rosewater. The old dolls wore that from an era gone by.

Denise studied the woman's bent shoulders that faced her, and tried to get her attention. "Ma'am, you are no bother at all. You can browse as long as you like, and if you need me, I'll be near. Just let me know."

She glanced at the woman's dark brown face that was etched with lines and held sad, but warm, eyes. She noted that extra moisture filled her customer's eyes, too. Something about this elderly lady made her want to just reach out and hug her.

"I like to come into the stores around the holidays to look at the cards."

"Look at the cards as long as you like. I'm just opening

up and getting started for the day." Denise began to walk away from her, but the lady's kind gaze held her.

"I like to think of the cards I would send to people who are no longer here," the woman said. "I have so many people that I used to send cards to who are just not here anymore. I know that's so silly, isn't it?"

"No, that's not silly at all, ma'am," Denise said in a soft voice. "I know they'd like whatever you mentally picked out." She started to move away from the woman, but her tender gaze again stopped Denise's retreat.

"You are somebody's gem, sweetheart. Thank you so much."

The look on the woman's face made Denise swallow hard and taste tears. Here she had been caught up in her own tiny little woes, and someone who had obviously endured real loss and was suffering put all that into perspective. She wanted to do something for this woman who no longer had people to dote on, or to dote on her.

"Just wait right here, ma'am. I have something for you, okay?"

The woman smiled, and her expression brightened as Denise strode away from her to the back of the shop. Allowing her nose to guide her, she picked out a beautiful, perfect pink rose, and found a little sprig of baby's breath to go with it. Snatching a bit of green tissue paper, she quickly wrapped it into an attractive single arrangement.

"This is for you," Denise said with a smile as she extended the gift to her customer.

"But I can't pay for—"

"Oh, my, no," Denise countered. "This is a gift for your heart. May those people in heaven now who love you be remembered. Maybe they put this in my shop just for you, hmmm?"

Tears filled the elderly eyes that stared back at her as the lady accepted the flower.

"I have something special for you, too, baby. Been keeping this for someone special. It's magic, you know."

Denise felt her smile grow wider, and she tried not to chuckle as the old woman rummaged in her pockets, finally producing a closed fist. She looked up at Denise, quiet mischief now sparkling in her eyes where tears had once been.

She took Denise's hand in her weather-beaten palm and closed her eyes. Her lips moved in what Denise could only assume was a prayer, and then she dropped something into the center of Denise's palm.

A tiny gold cupid angel sat in Denise's hand. The old woman giggled. So did Denise.

"You like him?"

"Oh, he's *so cute* . . . but I couldn't have you give up something so precious." She pushed the cherub around in her palm with one finger, delighting in the way its face seemed to grin and its eyes twinkled with an expression of joy.

"Fair exchange is no robbery, sweetie," her customer said, taking the cherub from Denise and pinning it on her tie-dyed shirt lapel. "He is for the young, and for those to be in love. I have nowhere to keep him happy now, and he just waits in my pocket. I'm old. He's for you. So you wear my little angel on your shoulder for good luck, and don't keep him in a jewelry box or a closet. Love needs the sunshine, just like the flowers do. Promise?"

This time she could not stave off her desire to hug the old woman. Compelled by sheer gratitude, Denise allowed her arms to briefly enfold her customer. "Thank you so much," she whispered. "You don't know how much I needed this today. I'll always wear him, especially when I'm working with my flowers. I promise."

"And you don't know how much I needed this hug right now, baby." The woman's hand touched Denise's face as she pulled away. "Nobody's hugged me in years . . . or given me flowers in longer than I can remember. Guess the Lord does answer prayers."

Denise stood in the middle of her shop as her single customer left it. Her heart hurt for the lady who had graced her presence, sadly browsing through the cards while caught up in remembering all the people whom she no longer had on the planet to give a card to. For some strange reason, what she'd just witnessed made her want to cry, and a tear found its way down her face. That lady should have a family, loved ones to dote on that sweet soul who was now alone. Denise sniffed, and the tear plopped onto her lapel, wetting her new little friend that her customer had just put on her shoulder. Her mother was right. Be thankful for what you have; many other people have so much less.

She wiped away the tear and drew a deep breath as she saw Bonita coming toward the store through the shop window. Calm and peace had just been banished. Denise smiled. Bonita was a trip.

"Hey, boss," her friend, who was also her cash register clerk, boomed out as she came into the store, breaking into Denise's thoughts.

"Hi, Bonita," she sighed. "You just missed the nicest old lady. She was so sweet. Look." Denise went over to her employee to show her the angel, while Bonita began pulling off her leather coat.

"Aw, now see. I told you this Valentine's Day was going to be different. You got a man, and he's all pinned up next to you, girl."

Both women laughed.

"Yeah, and it's time for me to stop daydreaming, too. In about a half hour, Plaza Mall is going to be a madhouse. Half of Cheltenham Philly will be in here."

"No lie," Bonita said with a chuckle. "But you're all ready for the hip-hop lover's holiday. Got your tie-dyed and fly shirt on, with some sassy jeans, chickee. However, at your height, you need to put on some heels. And why don't you have on red—like they said to wear to get a free rose from The Love Master?"

Denise sucked her teeth and chuckled as she went back to the register. "Girl, I sell roses in here already, okay. I don't need one from The Love Master. I was simply glad to get this mall's contract to distribute them for the event. Plus, if I'm working in the back all day, flats are the only things going on my feet. And I don't care what the radio promotion calls for; my favorite color is purple. Besides, I plan to be out of sight as much as possible today."

"Suit yourself, Miss all-work-and-no-play, but you know all the malls will be loaded with da bruthas—trying to get their free rose on, and trying to give a shout-out to somebody. Girl, this promo is da bomb, 'cause normally they give the flowers to the sisters—but this time only the brothers can get a rose. Whoever thought that idea up is on it!"

"Whateva." Denise had to chuckle again as Bonita rushed about, finding a section of chrome shelving to spy herself in, and using it as a mirror while she primped her weave ponytail into place.

" Oh, girl, get with it," Bonita fussed. "You know the Philly Power Hum-V is going around to each mall at a different time of the day and will only be at each one for like an hour, so the rush is on. Me, myself, I'm just trying to get one of those slim goodies who roll in looking for a honey to give a rose to, know what I mean?"

Denise waved her hand at her friend, who made her smile despite her decision to remain peevish.

"You should have put that highlight in your hair, too, like I told you. Added a little gold to those basic brown curls, girl."

"Bonita, you know I like everything natural." Denise absently ran her fingers through her short corkscrews, staving off the tinge of insecurity her girlfriend's comment had sent through her.

"Well, you could have at least put on a little polish, and more than just eyeliner and a smudge of lipstick."

Now Denise laughed. "My hands would be a wreck with polish on—by the time I finished working with them all day, they'd be chipped—"

"Not if you got the acrylic tips, like I've been telling you. They hold the polish against almost anything, and—"

"Oh, yeah, right. Picture that. Me with acrylic tips. I suppose I should have gotten a reverse French manicure, and had red tips and gold bottoms, huh?"

"Would look great on you. Now you're getting with it." Bonita giggled.

"In your wildest dreams. *Pulleease.* And, by the time I finished all that I need to do, with deliveries and everything, makeup would just be smeared across my face. Skip it."

"Do as you like, but today, after I get off from work, I'm going to the club. I'm gonna shake it fast, show 'em what I'm workin' wit'." Bonita laughed, making Denise laugh again, too.

"How do I look?" Her girlfriend turned around in a slow, sexy circle, showing off her big butt in skintight black satin jeans and her busty form that was only held in by a precarious red tube top covered by a sheer red blouse. Then Bonita pointed down at her feet, making Denise laugh at her red glitter toenail polish that was peeking out from the exposed toes of her red four-inch spikes.

"It is *February,* Bonnie. You are going to catch pneumonia trying to profile up here in the mall for that crazy WKDZ Power Radio promotion. Not to mention, you are at work, and by the end of the day, you'll be crying in those shoes. But you look great, crazy as you may be."

"Why, thank you." Bonita smiled and went behind the register to relieve Denise, and plopped down on the tall stool. Her hand went right to the stereo, as she switched off the tranquil CD and tuned in to the hip-hop station.

Denise cringed as the radio blared to a throbbing beat. But, in one respect, she couldn't argue with Bonita about it. The store, by rights, should have on the radio promotion that was heading their way like a tornado—sucking up and delivering customers to go with it.

Ignoring Denise's sideways glance of discontent, Bonita kept up the merry banter. "I'll be happy to profile out here while you cut up the flowers, like you enjoy so much. And you can count on me to be sure to take good care of all the customers who walk in, and to give each one plenty of attention—especially da bruthas."

"Pulleease." Denise chuckled as she made her way to the back of the store.

"Now you just take your time, boss. We have to hand out ten dozen for the folks that hit this mall—not a bad little contract."

"How could I forget?" Denise called over her shoulder as she went toward the peacefulness of the workroom. The Hot Philly Broadcast Network had been blasting this crazy lover's shout-out thing for the last two weeks on WKDZ. Every flower shop in or near a major mall in the city was loaded with single roses from the huge radio station promotion. On the one hand, it was great for business. On the other hand, it totally got on her nerves. The whole thing was just so contrived. And why couldn't the brothers simply *buy* a rose? What, they needed to wait for a free one?

Denise sucked her teeth and began separating the large bunches of flowers on the worktable. This was why she didn't deal with this particular holiday. All this hype for one day? It didn't make sense!

But she had work to do.

Two

The promotion was on fire—and so was he! It had been a veritable promo coup. Brandon Thornton walked through the mall as women swarmed his favorite moneymaking DJ, The Love Master.

"You are handling thangs, my brother," Brandon said with a grin, receiving a fist pound from the DJ who pulled in ratings, thus creating bankable opportunity. He'd slipped into the easy neighborhood slang, keeping his demeanor in sync with the personality that siphoned client revenues to the station from other airwave competitors.

"Well, you know, you know. I aim to please," the DJ replied.

"Yeah, dude. The advertisers went nuts with this one."

"Fat bonus check coming your way offa dis?"

"What can I say?" Brandon opened his arms and shrugged.

"Just don't forget to break a piece off for The Love Master."

"Cool," Brandon said. "You know I got 'chu. But you're the one who is crazy paid, and needs to break off a little for your brother."

"Yeah, yeah," the DJ said with a wry smile. "But look at the side benefits," he added, drawing Brandon's attention to the good-looking women in the crowd.

"I hear you," Brandon muttered with appreciation. "But remember, the roses are for the brothers, right."

"Yeah, I know. But *daaaayum*."

"Let LaToya hand them out, and you just keep talking

smack to make the women come to the center of this mall. That's the strategy, man. Stay focused. The brothers will come because the ladies came to the roses like bees come to flowers—and our advertisers know that everybody is tuning in, listening to the live gig for the shout-outs."

"It's sorta hard to stay focused," the DJ admitted, chuckling. He tipped his head in the direction of another bevy of incoming beauties. "You feel me? Just look at *da lovelies* swarming, brother."

"Yeah, man. I feel you. But this is business."

"Aw'ight. Aw'ight. Just hit the shop over there and refill my rose supply. The Love Master is in da house!"

Brandon shook his head as he walked away from the DJ's setup in the center of the mall. Youth. If the brother would get focused, and stop messing up the King's English, figure out his future—invest, get a financial portfolio happening—then by the time he was his age, thirty-five, he could switch gears.

Brandon glanced over his shoulder as he nudged his way through the mayhem. He hated hip-hop, but it paid well to learn it, understand it, and to get a handle on the target audience it attracted. The demographic profile for that market segment was going through the roof. He knew it, so he'd made sure that his clients knew it, and the network of stations he represented paid him very well to figure out cutting-edge gimmicks to penetrate it.

Yeah . . . Jeff might be The Love Master, but he was definitely the advertising *doctor*. Brandon laughed to himself as he neared the flower shop. Hell yeah, the docta in da house.

What The Love Master didn't realize was that this fame thing was fickle and fleeting. By the time he hit thirty, The Love Master would be old news, and a new promotional draw would replace him. One had to keep moving, keep evolving, and stay sharp—which was exactly why he wasn't interested in focusing his attention on *da lovelies,* as his buddy called them. See one fine woman, you've seen them all. And they all played games. He'd been burned a couple of times by the species, and was all about da benjamins now. Bank. He liked Jeff Simms, though. Would school the young buck, once his pilot light started dimming. For now, he'd let The Love Master have fun, and they could both make a killing in the meanwhile.

One didn't get to be the top advertising account executive for a major market radio network by thinking with the little head all the time. He kept "Junior" strapped down, in his pants, where it needed to be. His goal was singular these days—make some money and get free of the madness. Getting caught up in a relationship had been pushed so far off his personal agenda, he could barely remember when he'd made a run at one. Brandon opened the door to the bustling shop and crossed the threshold.

A throng of patrons was at the register, but he needed to get past them to collect another couple dozen flowers. For a moment he just stood there and watched the insanity from a distant place in his mind. How could one day create so much chaos? This love thing was a buncha bull. A scam. A complete advertiser's gimmick to get people spending money for gifts, cards, and flowers that, if they truly loved a person, they'd offer throughout the year. But, he told himself, he was in the fray, swimming with the best of the sharks, too—helping his station get a payoff through the advertisers during this holiday, just like all the others.

"I'm from the WKDZ squad," he intoned, getting close enough to the sister who was vamping behind the register. "We need another couple of dozen roses from our order out there on the mall floor. You all still have stock, I take it?"

The woman appraised him with a wide grin and cocked her head to the side, slowing down the impatient line of customers as she stopped ringing up sales. Her unabashed appraisal made him nervous. He hated when women just undressed a brother, all out in the open without any hint of discretion. Impatient, and glancing at the customers who seemed to be becoming that way, too, he cleared his throat.

"Uhmmmph, uhmmmph, uhmmmph," she finally said. "Yeah, brother. We got more stock in the back. We got anything you need in here."

Okay, enough. Could he just get his flowers, or what?

Before he could say a word, the cashier turned her head and opened her mouth, sending a deafening bellow through the store.

"Yooooo! De-nise! We need more flowers out in the mall!"

Her voice was like fingernails going down a blackboard.

"I'll just go back there and get them—you look like you're busy up here."

He didn't wait for the clerk to answer him. His legs propelled him forward in a swift gait toward the back of the shop. Anything to get away from another screech like that. His nerves were already fried, and the only reason he'd even come out on this promo was to get a pulse on how it was going. He needed to observe the progress of the promo for himself, to keep sharp. He was getting too old for this nonsense, though. However, he reminded himself that it was data he'd use for the next wacky thing he'd come up with, but the whole day was wearing on him. Knowledge had its price. He'd seen just one too many women poured into jeans with her boobs hanging out today. One too many glittered, eye-shadowed pairs of lids fluttering at him and his boy Jeff. And if he never saw another set of three-inch red talons or a nylon ponytail again in his life, it would be too soon.

He jettisoned himself through the beaded curtain and scanned the room quickly, and then stopped as his gaze hovered within the tiny confines. *Good Lord in Heaven* . . . what was an angel doing in the mall?

She looked up at him from her worktable, and gave him a slow, conservative smile. Time felt like it had stopped. Her hands were stained with green chlorophyll from the roses she worked with. Flowers framed her everywhere, and the scent of them with the sight of her momentarily eclipsed logic. Normally never at a loss for words, he found his voice stumbling as he tried to regain his equilibrium. *Daaayum* . . . Jeff wasn't lying. The lovelies had definitely come out today, but this delicate flower had been hiding in a back room, like Cinderella . . . working away, and naturally gorgeous.

"Uh, er, uh . . . the girl, uh, lady, I mean, at the front said you had more stock for the promotion."

Oh, my God. Denise quickly gathered up a bundle of roses as she tried to respond. She pricked herself on a thorn by accident, and put her finger in her mouth fast, then removed it. "Oh, yes, definitely. We were prepared for today's event. Uh. Just a second, and I'll put these in a box for you to take back out to the DJ's area. We really appreciate WKDZ's business, sir."

The way she'd brought her finger to those full, lush lips and kissed away the pain . . .

"We appreciate your being here," he said in a low octave, "and our station is committed to patronize minority businesses in the community."

The sound of his voice rippled through her, deep bass notes issued from a mouth that made her sip in a breath and hold it as she walked away from him. She had to keep moving, lest she make a fool of herself from gaping at over six feet of earthen-toned perfection. She rushed around, trying to find a suitable empty box, arguing with herself in her head as she did so. No. This was a customer, so she would not look at him any other way but in professional terms. Second of all, she didn't know jack about this man, other than that he'd flashed a smile so bright that it dimmed the fluorescent lights above her. She would not gape at that dimple in his cheek, or even allow her brain to wander over the formfitting, butter-soft black leather pants he wore, or to even notice the packed body beneath the turquoise silk shirt. Nope. If he was rolling with The Love Master, then he was a player anyhow.

He could only stare at the petite blur of motion before him. This was not what he'd expected to uncover in the back room of a flower shop. He had to be cool. Chill. Will his pulse to slow down. But everything on her was natural, soft, practically glowed from some sort of inner illumination. Eyes the color of cocoa brown, like her flawless skin, and a waist so tiny, he could probably circle it with both hands. But *daaayum* . . . baby had back, he noticed as she bent over to pick up a box. He argued inside his head to take his eyes off of her, but miserably lost the battle when she stood, turned around, and paced to him with a bright smile. Definitely her secret weapon. Megawatts.

Shell-shocked, he went for light conversation. "I see you're wearing an angel."

Damn, he could do better than that! What an opening line. A sister like this wasn't down for a club line. He groaned inwardly as her slender hand went to her lapel. He noted again that it was streaked with green floral blood as she fingered the little pin. He wrested his gaze from her pert bosom. No, this sister couldn't catch him appraising her like that. He looked at the flowers.

"Oh, this little guy," she said with a gentle chuckle. "I just got him today. A nice old lady gave him to me."

The easy timbre of her voice shot through his system and ignited it. High voltage. Be cool, brother. Be cool.

"An angel for an angel," he murmured, deeper than intended. Mistake. He'd given her another line, and she'd obviously processed it like one.

Her face seemed to lose some of its glow, and her tone became strictly business. "Yeah, well. It was a nice gesture. Maybe I'll start carrying them in the shop if customers like them. Here's your order."

He'd been dismissed. Damn it.

"Ur, my name is Brandon Thornton. And my client's name is . . . ?"

She issued a lopsided grin and extended her green hand. "Denise Blake. Thank you for your business, sir."

"Brandon," he corrected, accepting her hand. Silken skin slid against his palm and he lingered, holding on to it for probably a tad longer than professional decorum dictated.

"Thank you, Mr. Thornton," she repeated, putting him in his place—at a distance—and removing her hand from within his. "Our shop really needed a boost like your promotion gave us. We're new, and we appreciated your choosing us."

"Consider yourself a preferred vendor, then."

She raised one eyebrow, smiled, but didn't say anything as she slipped her fingers back into another bundle of flowers she'd previously been working with.

He could only stand there with the box of roses in one arm. Now what? All he was sure of was that he had to keep her talking, but he couldn't think of anything to say.

"Do you think that will be enough to tide you all over for a little while, or should I prep more now?" She hadn't looked up as she'd asked the question.

He could feel his window of opportunity closing.

"Uh, no, I think this will be good for the moment." Okay, she wasn't having it—the small talk. He'd detonated some invisible female distrust trigger. All right. Pace yourself, brother. You can come back later.

"All right. Just let us know if you need more." Still she wasn't looking at him.

"Thanks a lot. If we need more, I'll come back in."

"Thank you again. Good luck out there in the mall."

He nodded and left the back room that threatened to close in on him. He needed air, space, and time to process what just happened. She was the owner. She was the one his secretary had made arrangements with. If he'd only known, he would have come in and handled everything himself at this location.

The clamor out in the mall was deafening. Now it particularly got on his nerves.

"Whassup?" Jeff asked cheerfully, when Brandon dropped the box on the table next to the DJ for LaToya.

"Nothin', brother. This day is improving by the minute."

"Did you see him?" Bonita was in the back room whispering frantically once a lull in the shop traffic opened up.

"Yeah. Of course I saw him," Denise said as casually as possible. "You sent him back here to get a box of roses, didn't you?"

"Girl! Are you blind?" Bonita's response was so indignant that it forced a chuckle from Denise.

"Yes. I saw him. And?"

"And?"

"And."

"And, girl . . . you have got to be kidding me. You didn't see how fine—"

"He's a corporate customer. A *major* client."

"You are insane, Denise. Of course the brother is *major,* but I don't see what that has to—"

"It's unprofessional. That's why. You don't mix business with—"

"You haven't been on a date in a year and a half, and a tall, fine, chocolate—"

"My dating record isn't the issue—"

"Every woman should have chocolate like *that* for Valentine's Day!"

Both women giggled as the shop door chimed.

"Can you just go watch the register and the store to make certain we aren't shoplifted blind in here today, Bonita?"

Bonita left her to her thoughts, withdrawing herself from the back, all the while shaking her head.

Denise studied her hands, wishing for some odd reason that they hadn't been turned green. Bonita was so ridiculous at times. But she found herself glimpsing quickly into the chrome of the glass-paneled double door refrigerator, nonetheless. Maybe she should have put in a few highlights, or worn a red top? Nah . . . what was she thinking? All of this was stupid—silly. She was right where she was supposed to be. Working. One good-looking customer wasn't about to make her change her routine.

Besides, she didn't know a thing about this person. One couldn't judge a book by its cover. She'd dated good-looking men before, and they all had issues, baggage, drama. For now, she was perfectly content living her life in a serene, individualistic way. She didn't need a man to complete her. She did not need hot, sweaty nights of passion, especially when that only ended in tearful remorse when he'd ultimately hurt her— like the others. Why had she even gone there right now? She didn't need that mess in her life anymore. She'd sworn off the species. They were dangerous to a woman's self-esteem, her progress in life, and her ability to stay focused on her goals.

So what that the man had put tiny butterflies in her belly for a second or two? That was just a chemical reaction, nothing more than that. And one didn't start daydreaming on chemistry. She had a shop to run. Was blessed to have it.

But, damn, he looked good.

Three

"Girl, he's back in here, *again,* today," Bonita whispered with a conspiratorial giggle as she slipped into the workroom.

Trying to appear nonchalant, Denise kept her hands busy with the task of preparing a customer's order. "Then help the customer make a purchase selection, ring him up, and—"

"Five days in row, Denise, since Valentine's Day—save the normal day we're closed, and this man has been back in here—looking for you. Sweating your whereabouts hard, chile."

"You don't know that to be a fact. He was probably—"

"Girl! Quit it." Bonita stood firm, her legs in a wide stance with her hands on her hips. "The first day, you were making deliveries, and I told him so. The man piddled around looking at cards, then bought a handful, and finally left—*after an hour.*"

"Maybe he had a lot of people to buy Easter cards for, or family," Denise hedged, knowing her argument sounded contrived as she kept her gaze focused on the arrangement she was working on.

"Yeah, right. Then, the next day, he came in while you were delivering the hospital order, and he rummaged around and bought some incense."

"Well, good. I'm glad we're stocking the right merchandise for our clients."

"Tell me that you're not the least bit excited or interested?"

Denise refused to answer that one. How could she, with

Bonita's gaze boring a hole in her and threatening to let the little butterflies rush out of her system? The man was in the next room. Brandon Thornton was in her shop.

"Then, when he missed you for the third day in a row, he even decided to talk to me, and asked me all the questions he could without sounding like he was pushing up on you too hard . . . asking how long has the shop been in the mall, where did you learn how to design arrangements, did you pick out all this stuff yourself—blah, blah, blah. The man went on and on and on, and—"

"And I know you probably gave him my entire résumé, and even told him I hadn't had a date in over a year." Now Denise looked up, hoping that Bonita had had enough sense not to do that.

"Aw, struck a nerve." Triumphant, Bonita leaned in closer and dropped her voice. "No. I told him all the good stuff about your education and how smart and talented you were, and answered all his questions about the business that he'd asked, and when I could feel him hedging about your dating status, I just smiled and sold him fifty dollars' worth of candles. Then he left."

"Whew!" Denise let out an audible breath and peeked around Bonita to spy on what was slowly becoming her favorite customer. "Okay, then what?"

"Oh, but you're not interested . . . so I won't go on to tell you how he came in the following day, yesterday, and just flat out asked when you'd be in here. And, I guess I shouldn't mention that he left the shop with two fountains—ones that I told him were your favorites, huh? Won't tell you that the man has his MBA from Northwestern, and is the top account exec his age in the broadcast network. I know you wouldn't be interested in the little details about the fact that he's never been married, and has no kids."

"Seriously?"

Both women stared at each other. Bonita's sly smile widened.

"Seriously. You know me, girl. He was all up in your business, so I pumped him for his business—like you always say, fair exchange is no robbery, boss lady. Then he asked me about the CDs that are always playing in here, too. Brother had me write down the titles of those strange, New Age jaunskies. . . . What he needs to do is take you to dinner, put on some romantic—"

"Okay, okay, okay." Denise felt her face flush. "Give it a rest. Now you have wandered into the realm of sheer speculation. A guy like that has plenty of women. Plus—"

"A guy like that doesn't have to sweat a sister he's not interested in. Doesn't have to come in to buy little cards and knickknacks, and could have a secretary, or something, settle up with the account . . . but he didn't. He asked for you."

Bonita had a point. A strong and plausible one. Yikes.

"What should I do?" Panic made Denise's hands stop working, and she brought her arms around herself in a hug. "I mean, he's a client, and hasn't inferred . . . well, even if he had . . ."

"Go out there, and knock him dead. That's what you do."

Bonita was so dramatic. Knock him dead. Was she kidding? With what?

"All right. Since you have abandoned the front of the store, and there's no one on the registers . . ."

"I'm on my legally required fifteen-minute break, according to Pennsylvania law." Bonita smiled and then chuckled. "Go 'head, he won't bite."

If she could only be sure of that. Brandon Thornton suspiciously resembled a wolf in sheep's attire as she left the safety of the workroom to approach him. No longer in hip-hop fly gear, his conservative navy blue suit with a neat pocket handkerchief and white shirt that could be seen barely peeking out of it, sent the butterflies scattering through her bloodstream again. The deep hues of burgundy, burnt gold, and navy in the paisley pattern of his tie made the fluorescent smile he issued when he spotted her seem all the brighter. A glint of gold from his heavy watch and cuff links, the only jewelry that he wore, almost ricocheted off his million-dollar dimple. This was not good. Knock him dead—yeah, right.

"Hi," she said as calmly as possible. "May I help you?"

Oh, Lord . . . he had to turn it off. The smile and the intense stare made her nearly want to squint.

"You're a hard lady to track down. And, yes, I was hoping you could help me, as a matter of fact."

"Didn't know you were looking for me," she lied. Why was she playing games now? This man had a way of making her want to dash from her shop. "If you would have called," she intoned coolly, "I could have saved you a trip over here."

"No, I like browsing in your store better. You have a lot of wonderful things in here to chose from. Nice vibration, too."

The way his gaze traveled over her made her know that she was probably the merchandise he coveted. In his dreams. Nope.

"Thank you," she murmured, shifting her gaze to the card rack. She would not process any of this conversation as a double entendre. Nope. She was going to help this customer and go on with her day. She just wished that she wasn't so dressed down in a grungy pair of jeans and a cowl neck sweater.

He couldn't take his eyes off of her. He loved the way she seemed so comfortable in her skin, and God help him, she was wearing those jeans. The mauve color of her sweater added to the softness of her allure . . . and the way it draped her breasts.

"Uh, yes . . . I was definitely hoping you could help me."

"How so?"

She was smiling. Okay, okay, that was a good thing, he told himself.

"I was wondering if perhaps I could call you sometime, or convince you to have dinner with me one night?"

She could only stare at the man. Had he just asked *her* out? Oh, no . . . no . . . she was not prepared to start any mess like this. Not with a brother who would positively be her ruination. Just look at him. Okay, Denise, go for the gentle rebuff, because at least he'd been a gentleman.

"I, uh, generally don't date my customers, although thank you for the offer."

Silence surrounded them for a moment, but she could tell that he was working on a fast comeback. Truthfully, she wasn't sure if she wanted him to offer one or not. She was only good for a single no, especially with him standing there all fine and smelling so good. It had been a year and a half, and her body was beginning to remind her of that.

"Would you go out with me if it was just business, then?"

She smiled again. He was trying to come in from a different angle, and she had to admit that she was beginning to like it.

She'd smiled. Relief massaged his shoulders as they dropped an inch. This woman was so gorgeous. Soft spoken. Radiant.

"What type of business?" Denise glimpsed him from the corner of her eye as she began to distractedly straighten up the card rack.

Oh, *maaaaan* . . . he hadn't thought of that. "Uh, I come across all sorts of people in this line of work who might need a good florist. Perhaps, one day, I might be able to introduce you to some of those people?"

"I'd appreciate that."

He noted that her countenance had visibly stiffened and her voice was back to strictly business, and not all warm and mellow. He was blowing it again, he could tell. It was just that for the life of him, he wasn't sure why. What had he said wrong?

Pompous, arrogant ass. This guy was like the last man she'd dated. A social snob who thought that he could just introduce her to the right crowd, and throw around his platinum Rolodex, and then get her into bed. Why couldn't the brothers stop playing games and just come correct—honest. Why all the pretense?

"Okay, well, I guess I'd better let you get back to your business," he hedged as the door chimed. "I was just stopping by between client account calls."

"Thank you for stopping by," she said crisply, and went to wait on another customer.

Pure defeat claimed him as he strode through the mall and exited into the parking lot. Never in his life had he had a woman be so hard to read, or hard to get. Maybe she did have someone special. It was awfully presumptuous of him to think that a beautiful woman like Denise Blake wouldn't have someone. Her girl Bonita had been closemouthed about that aspect of his inquiries, even though she was kind enough to blabber everything else about Denise to him. Listen to him, already calling her by her first name. Damn, he had it bad for this woman!

Brandon slid into the driver's side of his Lexus. He hit the hands-free cell and speed-dialed his best friend. On three rings, Ralph's hospitality industry greeting poured into the speaker and filled the sedan.

"Hey, good brother, what's happening?"

"You, man. How's the station treating you?"

"Good, good. It's all good, dude." Impatience tore at him as he suffered the small talk that they exchanged.

As though sensing something amiss, Ralph chuckled. "You cool, man? Everything okay? You sound rushed."

"I'm cool," Brandon lied. "Just need to ask you a favor."

"Shoulda known. Me and the fellas have been starting to worry about you, ever since you dropped off the radar for a while."

"I've just been working hard, you know that. Besides, ever since you all got married, dropping like flies one by one, I can't get anybody to hang out with me."

Both men laughed.

"Yeah, guess you got a point. You know my wife don't play—and she's never forgiven you for what happened at my bachelor party."

"I told you not to confess." Brandon shook his head. "But it was the party of a lifetime, was it not?"

"That it was, that it was—so whatcha need, bro?"

"I need a hookup at the Radisson."

"Aw, buddy, buddy. She must be all that, huh? Damn, I remember the single days. Well, I can get you a comp room. We've been worrying about you, man. Don't seem like you've been stop, drop, and rollin' 'em like you used to—you've got a rep to maintain, and we need to live vicariously—"

"No, no, no. That's not why I'm calling. This one . . . uh, I don't need a room. I need flowers. A contract."

"Oh. My. Father."

Ralph was laughing so hard that Brandon turned down the volume with annoyance, and cranked the ignition and put his car into gear. He did not need this ribbing at the moment.

"All right, Ralph. But—"

"Uh-uh. You're not getting off the hook that easy, brother," Ralph teased. "Now, why are you calling the banquet manager at a major hotel for flowers, when you simply need a florist?"

Ralph was getting on his nerves.

"Man, I know where a florist is. I need to ask you to call in a marker for me, to maybe give a really nice sister, with a struggling new business, a lobby contract—for a week. Or to let her do one of your banquets. Something like that. All right?"

"Hmmm . . . this sister has my best boy calling in markers, but he doesn't need a room at one of the finest hotels in Philadelphia. Sure I can't get you a room, man?"

"No. It's not like that. She's just—"

"Playing hard to get and wearing your normally arrogant behind out. Good for her. I like her already." Ralph chuckled again. "Look, I can get her a small contract to do one of the upcoming banquets, but if I pull the existing lobby contract, which isn't even under my aegis, a lot of questions—"

"Cool! That's cool, man. I really appreciate this." Brandon threaded his vehicle through the traffic, trying to steady his nerves.

"Wow. Deep. Bingo. She got you, brother. Listen to yourself. And you ain't even tagged it yet?"

He would not dignify the question. "Can you do this or not?"

"Yes, given that we go way back, and you are always throwing the big station parties my way—which I appreciate. Okay, look, in a few weeks there's this big—"

"A few weeks?" He nearly had to slam on his brakes as the taillights of the vehicle ahead of him came up more quickly than anticipated.

"Oh, wow . . ." Ralph's voice crooned through the speaker. "Wait till I tell the fellas about this. The late, great Mr. Thornton, ex-superhero, just got taken out of the bachelors' circle."

"Man, this stays confidential, between you and me. It's just—"

"That in a few weeks you will be losing your mind. I can dig it. Gotta reel this one in fast-like. Okay. No sweat. Serious heavyweight marlin on the line, scared it'll snap, leaving you holdin' your rod."

Ralph was definitely getting on his nerves, for real, for real. And why the hell did the lights on City Line Avenue take so freakin' long to change?

"What's the plan? I'll stop messin' with you."

Brandon let his breath out hard. "Thought you could invite her in for a vendor's conference about a potential contract—that you'll give her. You all can have lunch, see what she likes to eat, ask her a few questions . . ."

"Like if she's married, seeing anyone, or what she thinks about you?"

"Well, yeah, but you have to be a lot smoother than that. Just casual, you dig?"

"I dig that you've got it bad. Why don't you just come out and ask her?"

Silence filled the car, save for the hum of traffic outside of it.

"Tried that, and she didn't take the bait." Ralph chuckled, answering his own question. "You will have to allow me my moment of amusement with this. But I'll do my best to hook a brother up."

Brandon rubbed his hand over his jawline. Fatigue from

adjusting to multiple adrenaline spikes was getting to him. The fact that he hadn't really slept well since he'd first seen Denise wasn't helping. "Thanks, man," he muttered.

"I just have one, itty bitty question, though."

"Shoot." Brandon let his breath out hard again. He needed to get to his appointment and to clear his head.

"Why don't you just call one of those tall, fine, long-legged chicks you always flash through an event with? You know, to calm your nerves, to take the edge off, while you wait to see what this one is about, or is going to do—or not do? You sound all stressed, like a married man and whatnot."

"I'm pulling up to my account now, Ralph. Catch ya later."

"Yup. Will do. I'll book a room here at the hotel—a banquet room."

"A banquet room?" He was losing patience with his buddy, significantly so, as he whipped the black sedan into a parking space. He peered up at the huge 555 City Line Avenue address and leaned his head back and rolled his shoulders.

"You know they book a year or more out, in this hotel, for weddings."

He didn't even answer as he slapped the cellular button, cutting off his friend's laughter in the process.

Four

Denise accepted the red-coated doorman's nod as he opened the heavy glass structure for her to enter. Crisp air chased her inside the building as she maneuvered her portfolio through the wide panes of the door, and moved her line of vision from his uniform that reminded her of something the guards wore to stand before Buckingham Palace. Slowly setting down her portfolio at her feet and juggling her purse, she removed her coat as she gaped at the room.

Casting her black velvet dress coat over her forearm, and slinging her black Coach saddle purse back over her shoulder, Denise allowed her gaze to absorb the exquisite lobby of the Radisson-Warwick Plaza Hotel. Awesome. She stooped and retrieved her portfolio, straightening herself, but clutching it as though for internal support. It was a breathtaking view.

The grand old structure's lobby hosted tall ivory-colored columns that had to range twenty-five feet in height against a majestic ceiling. She peered up at the gold gilding on the hand-plastered crown moldings above her, and then allowed her gaze to sweep around the well-appointed area, lingering on the crystal chandelier, and finally settling on the huge, four-foot floral arrangement that took center stage on an opulent marble table. Wow.

All of her reservations about accepting Brandon Thornton's offer vanished as she truly took in a floral designer's paradise. The hotel was so elegant that it could stand the dramatic arrangements that she very seldom got to try her hand at. Sketches of possible combinations raced through her brain as she waited for the banquet manager. She was just glad that Thornton had called, explained that a Mr. Ralph Simpson would contact her, and had left it at that—no strings attached.

Sure, she would send Brandon Thornton a thank-you card, and maybe a gift basket arrangement. But she'd made it clear that if there was anything else attached to this situation, then all bets were off. He'd been a gentleman and had complied, so he was due a basket. Period. Like she would offer any other customer who gave her a nice referral.

Soon a short round man was approaching her. He had a merry look on his face, and a broad, pleasant smile. This had to be Ralph Simpson. She stood, glancing at his gold name-plate on his black suit, and extended her free hand—leaning the portfolio against her leg.

"Miss Blake?" His brown eyes held a quiet mirth, and his deeper brown face was emblazoned with a grin.

"Mr. Simpson?"

"Oh, my pleasure. My pleasure. Do come to the restaurant. We can chat and chew over lunch, on the house."

Slightly taken aback by his ebullient insistence that they do lunch, she followed his quick paces while balancing her port-folio, coat, and purse as they walked. Even though he was only a bit taller than she was, he moved through the lobby like an elf rushing to get to an important destination. *Maybe it was because she rarely wore pumps?* She glimpsed herself in one of the long lobby mirrors as she passed, hoping that her un-derstated hunter-green pantsuit, pearls, and plain black heels would convey just the right level of conservative dignity to land her the floral job within a hotel like this one.

A maître d' immediately seated them in a far, cozy corner of the restaurant. Unhurried guests and executives never looked up as they passed. A slight tremor of nervousness ac-costed her. This was a substantial client, referred to her by another substantial client—and these fellas obviously rolled at the topnotch level. Regardless of Thornton's motives, this was all right. Okay. She could do this. She had to remember that she was very good at what she did, and her shop prided itself on solid customer service. Denise set her things down in an adjacent chair and tried to relax.

"Thank you for coming in," Ralph Simpson said pleasantly. "Please, first let's look over the menus, and get in our orders, and then we can talk."

She complied, noticing that she had been offered a menu without prices. She studied it hard, trying to affix a cost to the available selections, and trying to guess which choice would be reasonable—since her potential customer was picking up the tab. After a moment he closed his leather-bound menu and continued to beam at her. She followed suit and closed hers.

"All decided?"

"I think so."

She watched him nod, and just as quickly a waiter was at their side.

"I'll have the shrimp Caesar salad and an iced tea, thank you."

"Are you sure that's all you want?" Mr. Simpson seemed distressed as he asked the question.

"I generally don't eat a big lunch, but really appreciate your hospitality."

She wasn't sure what social blunder she'd made until he smiled.

"Okay," he said with a chuckle. "I know. Everybody doesn't eat like me—my wife tells me that all the time." He rubbed his thick belly and offered a wider grin. "Just that my people are from down South, and we eat. Don't want you to think you can't do that and still talk business."

She liked this man, and chuckled with him. His good nature came through without pretense, and she was deeply appreciative that he'd broken the ice.

"You sound just like my mother. She gets offended if you don't eat big at her house."

"Sounds like a Southerner to me." The banquet manager laughed again. "What part?"

"Virginia, by way of Richmond."

"Oh, that ain't the South. Not till you hit Georgia are you down South."

They fell into a companionable laughter, enjoying the meal, sharing tidbits about themselves and their family histories, and nearly dismissing the fact that they needed to conduct business.

"But I haven't even shown you my portfolio yet," she argued, as he foisted dessert upon her and would not be dissuaded.

"Must break bread, that's just Christian."

Again they shared a laugh.

"Okay, the cheesecake is calling me. And maybe some herbal tea."

"Good choice. It's the best in the city. We have a wide variety of teas that you can pick from the box when the waiter comes back."

Eventually Ralph allowed her to show him her work, and the look on his face as he complimented her made her feel fuller than the heavy dessert that had landed in the bottom of her stomach. This guy was so nice and so genuine . . . too bad his buddy wasn't as forthcoming.

But when Ralph's demeanor stiffened, confusion tore through her mind, and she followed his line of vision. A seemingly vexed woman was striding up to their table. She was short, plump, and pretty, but the look on her face said it all.

"Er, excuse me," Ralph said in a smooth tone, one that he obviously reserved for the rarely unhappy guests that he might encounter.

However, before the banquet manager could fully stand and slip away from the table to address the approaching female, she was at their side.

"Excuse me, miss," she said, her voice issued in a quiet hiss through her teeth. "I normally don't do this type of thing, but I need to have a word with my husband."

Uh-oh . . . what was up now?

Denise put on her most pleasant, stoic business response and nodded. "No trouble at all, Mrs. Simpson, we were just concluding our meeting."

"I'll just be a moment," he said in a controlled tone, and stepped away from the table, ushering his wife by her elbow.

Not sure of what else to do, Denise began folding the linen napkin on her lap and looked down at her open portfolio as she closed it. She took a very slow sip of her herbal tea and then dropped her napkin on the side of the table. What in the world could be wrong? It was obvious that this was a business lunch. Surely this woman didn't think that anything off the wall or shady was happening between them?

When Ralph returned, his complexion looked like it had a tinge of gray added to it. She wanted to ask if everything was all right, but thought better of that. Instead, she stood and extended her hand.

"I have taken up enough of your time, and appreciate the opportunity. I know you have a million things to do, so—"

"You have the contract," he said, accepting her hand, shaking it quickly, and then releasing it. "The apology is all mine. My wife works not far from here, and we, er, had a slight family crisis. But it's all resolved now, so . . . Well." Ralph's gaze went back to the restaurant exit as though he might be expecting his wife to barrel through the door again. "You set a price for the work we've outlined, and if it's within the budget range we discussed, consider yourself hired as a vendor to our hotel."

"Thank you." She didn't know what else to say.

Ralph pulled out a white handkerchief and blotted away tiny beads of perspiration that had formed on his brow. "I'll personally write you a letter of satisfaction, once we have seen your work—which might help you leverage future hotel placements for your arrangements. Again, my sincerest apology for the intrusion to what was otherwise a very engaging lunch."

"No apologies necessary," she said as upbeat as she could while gathering her possessions. "I'll have a proposal back to you in a day or so. Again, thank you."

He ushered her out to the lobby, this time his gait notably slower. What was that all about? She donned her velvet coat and braced herself for the chilly air outside.

* * *

"Girl, what happened?"

Bonita had literally body rushed her as she stepped through the door of the shop. Glancing around, and glad that there were only a few people milling about in the back, Denise came in close to Bonita.

"I haven't the foggiest idea. We were eating, going over my different arrangements, then this woman—the man's wife—came in all upset and angry, and the next thing I know—"

"Chile, she called the shop."

Denise found her hand releasing her portfolio and covering her mouth as Bonita pigeon-necked as she spoke.

"So, I was like, my boss ain't here, *okaaaay.* I knew it had to be some man's wife, 'cause that's how the heifer identified herself. *'This is Mr. Ralph Simpson's wife, and I would like to speak to a Denise Blake.'* I could tell right off this wasn't no basic customer call to order flowers."

She couldn't uncover her mouth. All she could do was stand there wide-eyed, staring at Bonita.

"Then she gave me this job number for you to call back. I was like, whateva. You should call that hussy and give her a piece of your mind. I know you ain't runnin' her husband. *Pulleease.* You ain't running even single men."

"Where's the number?" Denise whispered, finally finding her voice and picking up her portfolio again. "I'll take it in the back."

"I know you will, girl. I left it back there for you anyway. Lemme know what's up when you get off the phone. If she thinks she's coming in here to start some mess, she got an old-fashioned beat-down coming her way. Don't nobody mess with my girl! Hmmmph."

Denise's legs could not get her to the back of the shop fast enough. She dumped her coat, purse, and portfolio in a metal chair as she snatched up the number and tried to dial it with unsteady hands. Lord, why? The biggest possible hotel job, and one of the nicest ones in the city, and now there was some

mess. Rings pierced her ear as she held the receiver close to
her face. She glanced at her watch and prayed the woman
hadn't taken off early for the day or something. They had to
get this right, get all the confusion straightened out. This just
didn't make sense.

"Hello. May I speak to Mrs. Simpson, please?" Denise
nearly held her breath as she was put on hold and a new voice
answered the line.

"Mrs. Simpson here. May I help you?"

"Uhmmm . . . yes. This is Denise Blake, and you called my
shop?"

She could hear an exasperated rush of air come from the
woman on the other end of the line. But, oddly, when the
woman started talking again, she didn't sound angry, really.
Just very, very annoyed.

"Okay, let me tell you why I rolled up on my husband, first
of all—not that it's *your business* to know what I said to my
husband, but you have a right to know, I guess."

Denise forced herself to sit down slowly on the edge of an
empty chair. She promised herself that she would not say a
word.

"Well, my Ralph is a good guy, an innocent, actually . . .
but his rogue buddy, that dag-gone Brandon Thornton, gets
everybody's husband in trouble."

Denise felt the bottom of her stomach drop out, like she
had been on an amusement park ride—the one that releases
you from eleven stories up.

"Anyway, I was calling into the home voice mail to check
on my son, because he went to daycare today with a little bit
of a cold—normally I don't call home, but thought the doctor's office might have tried to reach me there about the
appointment I was trying to get set up. But there was this
message on the tape from Brandon. Why he remains my husband's best friend, I will never know."

"What did he say or imply?" Damn, and she'd promised
to let the woman talk.

"He told Ralph to remember to be smooth, to handle this

as planned, and to be sure to take you to lunch and stuff, and to call him afterward—and that the room wasn't necessary yet."

"Oh, my God . . ."

"Right. Well, I didn't like the whole thing—not from what I'd heard. And the thing that pissed me off was that my husband has a *good* job. He doesn't need to get caught up in any mess that will make him lose what he's worked so hard to earn. My feeling is that if Brandon Thornton has some sneaky woman-dealings happening, well then, he needs to leave my Ralph out of it. That's why I marched right up to the job, asked the girls at the front desk where his meeting was—like I belonged in it—and came to set him straight. You don't mix business with no mess. And you don't let your friends tangle up your job in no woman mess."

"Oh, my God . . ."

"Exactly."

Mrs. Simpson took a breath, and neither spoke for a moment.

"Listen," the woman on the other end of the telephone finally said. "You seem like a really straight-up sister. When I walked in there, I could tell you wasn't no hoochie momma, or nothing, and had your hopes all high for a contract with the hotel. Now, Ralph is probably still going to do that; if he promised you, he's a man of his word—and wouldn't give you a contract unless your work was good. But you watch yourself around his wolf friend. He's got more women than a flock of geese."

"Duly noted, and I thank you. . . . I also thank you for not thinking I was trying to do anything underhanded or anything. I honestly didn't know that he'd roped your husband into anything this convoluted." Disappointment seared whatever else she might have said to the woman in her throat. Denise swallowed hard and looked down at the floor.

"Figured you didn't, that's why I had to get this straight—nip it in the bud."

Denise only nodded and let her breath out in a slow sigh. "Thanks a lot."

"We women have to stick together, sis."

"Yeah . . . Well, my store is getting loaded, and I have to go."

"Call me if you need any more dirt on Brandon Thornton now, you hear. You have my number."

"Thanks so much, will do," Denise lied, knowing that she was never calling Mrs. Ralph Simpson again in her life.

She sat for a long while with her finger pressed on the OFF button of the cordless telephone, just studying the tops of her shoes. This is what she'd tried to tell Bonita all along. This was exactly why you didn't mix business with romantic interest.

And this was why she would read one Brandon Thornton when he came back into her shop.

Five

"Brother," Ralph whispered. "Take me off speaker in your office, man. This is 911, and it ain't good."

Brandon snatched the receiver off the hook and hit the button, pressing it to his ear. "Talk to me."

"I told you this was a bad idea—horrible, in fact, that's what happened—the worst."

"C'mon, how bad could a lunch—"

"Frannie called the house and intercepted your voice mail. You hearing me?"

Panic tore through him so fast that he spoke before thoughts could fully form.

"Oh . . . no . . ."

"Oh, yes! Why didn't you leave that message at my job number?"

"Because of the nature of the message. . . . Guess I got last minute jitters, wanted to be sure that . . . damn! You said if I needed to leave you any last minute details, to put it on voice mail so you could check it before the lunch to be sure we were in sync."

"I meant at my office number—*not at home*. I checked my work voice mail box five minutes before I came down to meet her. No message, so I thought we had a green light. But you are so messed up by this sister, and believe me, I can see why—but you ain't thinking like a double agent. Dag, Brandon, at one time your name used to be Bond—James Bond. But you almost got me killed today when Frannie came in and busted up the lunch. This is no longer fun, and done changed into some Secret Squirrel type adventure, and I'm out. Fini. Done."

"What!" Brandon was on his feet now. This was not a matter of panic, this was a code blue and he was about to flat-line. "Frannie?"

"Had me pleading with my wife to not just bust you out in a restaurant, or to mess up my gig by raising her voice— damned maître d' was giving me fishy looks, and the girls at the front desk were looking at me like *Boy, you in trouble now—we coulda had your back, but we don't cross wives.* Damn, man, up on my job and whatnot, and—"

"Frannie didn't say—"

"You know my wife, there's no telling what she said or did, and you, like a knucklehead, left the woman's shop name on there, her name with it . . . brother, this ain't good."

Brandon allowed his body to hit his high back leather chair with a thud as he sank into it. "I have to talk to her. . . . How did she seem when she left the hotel?"

"Cool, confused, a little dazed. But cool."

"All right, all right . . ." Brandon stood again and paced, dragging the phone system across his desk and nearly toppling several awards and the penholder in the process.

"Your best bet, if you really want to get next to this nice sister, is for once, do the only thing that a woman cannot argue with."

"Name it," Brandon said quickly and stopped walking. He was desperate. Salvation was on the horizon.

"Tell her the truth. Confess."

"Are you crazy?" Brandon began walking again. "And tell her what? Nothing I say is going to make sense, and—"

"Tell her the truth, man. That you walked in her store, she blew you away, but was hard to read . . . that you wanted to learn more about her, but she'd put up a wall. And that ever since you've met her, you couldn't get her out of your system, and that has you acting real stupid, like you're in high school. Apologize and—"

"That sounds so bogus . . ."

"You want her, then tell the truth. Women have guided missile systems that can find a lie and blow it up without even getting near the target. Ask me how I know."

"All right. Suppose I do this major bearing of the soul confession madness, as you suggest, and she tells me to take a hike?"

"Then you take a hike, and take your medicine like a man. New concept for you, I know, having a woman tell you to shove it, but on this one, I'd move heaven and earth to try to get her to understand before I walked."

For a moment, neither of them spoke.

"I'll think about it. That's all I can promise."

"Good. But think long, think wrong. The best way to deal with a sister is right when the BS goes down. The longer you let it fester, the harder it will be to come back in out of the rain—where the doghouse is located. This is pure truth, coming from a married man."

Brandon flipped open his Palm Pilot and checked his schedule for the rest of the day. Maybe he could slip by the mall that evening, just before the shop closed. But why did that seem like such a bad idea at the moment?

"Thanks, Ralph," he said in defeat. "I'm sorry for any trouble this caused for you on your gig, man—and at home. It wasn't supposed to be all of this . . . just a simple fishing expedition so I could find out more about her on the down low. That's all."

"Can't go fishing and play hooky without letting your woman know where you're at. That's another thing you'll learn, now that you're hooked yourself."

"Look, I gotta go."

"Yeah. And let me know how you make out. I still got'chur back—just from a spectator's seat these days now, though."

He'd rehearsed everything he was going to say, and had even said some of the words out loud in the car on the way over to Denise's shop. Inside the car, his voice sounded strong, sure, but as he entered her shop, and Bonita rolled her eyes at him and sucked her teeth, everything inside of his head simply went blank.

"Is she in the back?" He heard his voice ask.

"Wait here," Bonita said with an indignant huff. "I'll see if she wants to come out."

This was definitely bad.

Time was drilling a hole in his brain, too, further leaking coherent thought from it. When Denise finally walked out of the back room, he relaxed a little bit but remained on guard. Her tiny chin was thrust up, her stride was confident, and her gaze pre-warfare neutral.

"Bonita said you wanted to see me?"

Okay, her voice was even, not shrew-like. There was hope.

"I owe you an apology." He glimpsed Bonita from the corner of his eye when both women crossed their arms over their chests at the same time. "Can we step over to a more private place so I can explain?"

Denise let her breath out hard. What was this Negro going to tell her that she hadn't already heard? It was on now.

"Sure. Why not." She paced ahead of him to the workroom and parted the beads, allowing them to slap him as she entered the small space and then spun around, refolding her arms over her chest.

"Like I said, I owe you an apology."

"Yes, you do. I didn't deserve to be made to believe I was getting a major contract only to have that just be a ruse. If you don't respect anything about women, or me, you should respect that I'm a small business, and taking valuable time away from my shop for games was just plain not fair to me."

His chest cavity felt heavy as he looked at the clear disappointment that shone back at him in her eyes. Then he fully took in the suit she wore, and the pearls, and spied her abandoned portfolio. Oh, this was bad. She'd really gone all out to grasp this opportunity.

"Ralph Simpson is a man of his word," he murmured. "He would not jeopardize his position at the hotel if he didn't think you could handle the job. That's also why I recommended you—well, partly why. But that part was no game. The contract is yours, if you still want it."

She nodded and strode away from him and grabbed her portfolio, opening it for him. He accepted it and took her nonverbal lead to review it.

"I have worked so hard to build my business and good name on solid work. I didn't need this today—nor did I need Mr. Simpson's wife to call me and download your history with women. I try to keep my personal life very private, and very separate from my business. You had no right to be so manipulative."

She was driving a garden spade through the center of his chest. Albeit he deserved it, that still didn't do much for the pain.

"This is fantastic work," he murmured, closing the portfolio and handing it back to her. "I knew when I first saw you that you were talented, and someone very special." He glimpsed the angel that she still had adhered to her lapel. "An angel, and you don't lie to angels—but that's what I did. I'm sorry."

She just nodded and looked away, toying with the small pin as she did so.

"This is not an excuse, just the truth . . . I really wanted to get to know you better, and to take you out—hoping that you were available to date me. But then you wouldn't talk to me . . . there was a professional wall up, so I tried to scale it. And the way I went about it was all wrong." There. He'd said it. The truth was out.

She looked at him squarely, and he noticed that her gaze had softened a little. Ralph's warning to be honest filtered into his consciousness and propelled him to go on.

"I wanted to know what your favorite color was, what your favorite foods were, what kind of music you liked . . . and I wrongly asked my best friend Ralph to help me find out those things, and I messed up. It was stupid."

He held her gaze, which was distrustful, and he let his

breath out hard. "I don't know what to say, Denise. I hope I get another shot at coming back right."

"I really have to think about that, and this time, I'll be honest," she murmured. "Mrs. Simpson said a lot of things that just made me not want to take such a risk. I don't need to be a notch on your belt, or some trophy you won and can talk about. I've been treated that way before, and have had some very unpleasant dealings with men who played games . . . I guess I've just reached the age where I want to be treated with respect and honesty, and like I mean something more than a roll in the hay. So I'm not sure if I want to even *try* to get to know a man who has such a track record—and who went so far as to also concoct this fiasco today, too. I don't know."

She walked away from him and slowly went to the other side of the table so it stood between them. Her arms were hugging her waist, and in that moment as he stared at her, he wondered what fools had emotionally hurt and abused someone so precious. And, at the same time, he knew he'd been such a fool, too. Not just with the woman standing before him, but with those whom he'd treated as she'd just described. A sense of remorse and loss so profound filled him that there was nothing left for him to say. Truth had punctured and let the air out of his argument and lungs.

"I can understand that," he offered after a long pause. "You have every right to feel like you do. I don't have good character references; my credit record is bad with women. That's true. I'm just sorry that I ruined it before I met somebody as sweet as you."

He had to get out of there. Looking at what was now out of reach was too depressing. As he made his way out of the shop, he realized that it wasn't just her outer beauty that he'd miss.

In just a short time, he'd come to appreciate her smile and the warm genuine laugh that she had. Now because of a stupid male move, an unforgivable faux pas, he'd miss out on getting to learn more about the integrity that she displayed, and the keen intellect that could run a business, the wholeness of her that he sensed. He'd be banished from ever seeing her creativity in full bloom, and the thought of missing all of that was utterly sobering. He didn't even want to consider what other hidden treasures this jewel within the mall might possess.

He got into his car, angry with himself, and pulled out of the parking space, heading toward his Northern Liberties warehouse loft. He'd go into the Bat Cave and lick his wounds. It wasn't really what he would call home; it was his bachelor pad. The loft was where he crashed and sometimes burned. But the sad eyes that he'd pulled himself away from haunted him as he drove. They made him want a home, and that was frightening.

He reached for his cell and hit Ralph's number. When Frannie answered and gave Ralph the phone without a hassle, he knew he had been discussed before the call.

"You can tell Fran that she can stand down. Fran got through to the sister loud and clear. Denise Blake is done with this brother till the end of time. Tried being honest, but, like you said, that doesn't always work. Thanks for the assist, though. I'm tired. Going home. She told me to take a hike."

"So you just gonna give up like that?"

"C'mon, dude. I messed up big time. Let it rest. I'm out."

He could hear Frannie fussing in the background, and would have hung up, but Ralph's voice cut into his thoughts and held him.

"We got a plan," Ralph said quickly.

"We? Aw, Ralph . . ."

The other extension picked up, and both husband and wife bickered for a moment about who should be on the telephone and who should speak. This was precisely why he was committed to bachelorhood. Even though Ralph was his best friend, he was in no mood to have his friend's wife treat him like a henpecked husband; Ralph was the one married to her.

"Ralph has been fussing since he walked in the door—and I guess he has a point, once he explained everything—all he had to tell me was that you were serious about—"

"You didn't give the man a chance, or me a chance, to

explain nuthin', Frannie, before you beat his reputation down to that sister, and—"

"Well, Ralph, how was I supposed to know—"

"You weren't 'posed to know nuthin' and were supposed to leave man business between men!"

"Well, that's why I'ma try to right the wrong, okay? And I have a plan."

Brandon wasn't quite sure why he was listening. His gut instinct told him to just be done with the nonsense and accept the collateral damage from the fallout, but yet he was on the cell, listening to craziness, and hovering on every word. Oh, yeah, this relationship stuff was for the birds.

No wonder he'd avoided it for so long.

Six

"Girl, get in here! You are not going to believe who just called! Have I got *the scoop* for you, chile. You're gonna love this." Bonita rounded the front counter and practically pulled Denise into the shop.

Denise groaned inwardly as her employee and friend leaned in close. She had already been through an exhausting post-holiday cross-examination by her mother—who had called to thank her for the roses, but then had launched into a diatribe about the state of her personal life. Then there was the whole hotel contract fiasco, plus the mini-drama created by one Brandon Thornton. At this juncture, just three days outside of all that mess, the last thing she wanted to deal with was another twist of fate.

"Okay, might as well fire away." Denise hoisted the box of green tissue paper and supplies onto her hip. She sighed. She didn't have time for this.

"Remember that sister who called before about her husband?"

"Oh, no . . ." Denise let out a weary groan and began walking toward the back of the store. She was going to get tickets to the Philadelphia Flower Show, renew some of her business suppliers at a regional trade show she'd been eyeing, needed to get ready for another round of quarterly taxes—the last thing she was about to devote any attention to was some man-wife craziness.

"Hey, wait up," Bonita called behind her. "For a short person, you sure walk fast."

"That's because I do flats." Denise could feel her mood growing darker and stormier by the moment as she glanced up from her task of stowing supplies to see the merry twinkle of mischief in Bonita's eyes.

"The lady wanted to apologize."

"Well, she should have, and that's nice."

"Oh, c'mon, Denise . . ."

"What else do you want me to say, Bonnie? She called, apologized for getting me in the middle of something I had nothing to do with. Okay. Peace. I've let it go. She should, too." Denise's hands had found her hips. Just the mere mention of the situation still got to her. "You should let it go as well. Okay. Case closed."

"Well, boss," Bonita said with a hearty chuckle, "we might not be able to let it go."

"And why not?" Denise's voice had escalated a pitch, and now she could feel herself glaring at Bonita. Boy, this stuff got on her nerves!

"Because they offered us a big dinner party job."

"Fine, fine, fine," Denise muttered, dismissing the concept as she paced away from Bonita with the wave of her hand.

"For twenty dozen flowers."

Denise stopped and turned around slowly to stare at Bonita. If she weren't so stunned, she would have commented on her friend's unnecessarily wide grin.

"Ah . . . finally got your full attention, huh?"

Denise couldn't argue. A small shop like hers could not afford to discard a customer order of that size. "What did this woman say?" It was all she could manage, and it came out as a whisper, at that.

"Well, first she said all this stuff about how they were so very sorry to have upset you with their domestic issues the other day."

Denise just listened as Bonita prattled on. But she needed to sit down as this bizarre information began to take shape.

"Well, you know me. At first I thought that the woman was trying some mess when she said she wanted you to bring over some flowers for this soiree that she was hosting. I figured, she might try to jump in your face, in which case, I was going with you—'cause, if it was going to be some stuff, then I have your back. Hmmph!"

"Bonita, please. What did the lady say?"

"Well, she told me that she could tell I was a little wary, and rightfully so. That's when she put her husband on the telephone, and they both talked, so that's how I knew it was legit."

"Okay," Denise said in a rush of relief. "Then what?"

"She said that some of the things she said about her husband's friend were not all the way accurate. She said she said some of it because she was angry, maybe a little jealous, blah, blah, blah . . . about how she was just getting used to the idea of her Ralph still hanging with an unmarried buddy, so she was sorry if she upset you."

Denise sprang from her chair and began walking in a circle as she spoke. "I'm not upset. Was never upset. I don't know that man. Never knew that man. So who cares about that part of it? I was only angry that he wasted my time, and led me to—"

"Whateva." Bonita laughed and waved her hand at Denise. "Let me finish."

"Fine," Denise huffed, again placing her hands on her hips. "But I couldn't care less about that man."

"Yeah. All right. Here's the deal. In addition to the hotel contract—which Mr. Simpson says is still on the table for you; all you have to do is get him the proposal he requested . . . and he sounded serious, Denise. The man practically told me it was yours—if you would just act like you know."

"Yeah, I do owe him that . . . I just figured . . . okay." She had to get her equilibrium back. Denise leaned against the edge of the worktable. She *had* let her personal feelings cloud her judgment and ignore what a customer had said on a great contract. Mr. Simpson had told her it was still on, but she hadn't believed him. She would not make that mistake again, and would get it right.

"Well, boss lady," Bonita quipped after a moment, "you figured wrong. You might have even figured wrong about that tall hunk you sent out of the store with his tail between his legs—but that's another discussion."

"A much different discussion," Denise affirmed. "The flower job."

"Yes. Well. They are hosting this intimate dinner party in a warehouse loft down in Northern Liberties. The wife says that she has to get dressed, run a million errands, and they want not only the flowers—but also for you to design the arrangements. She said there's no time to really show you the space before next weekend—but she did give me the room dimensions and stuff. I told them your design fee, and they said fine, plus the cost of delivery and the flowers."

"What type of flowers?" Denise's mind scrambled to absorb this baffling information and to process it on the business side of her brain.

"They want wildflowers mixed in with tulips, calla lilies . . . but with an overall royal purple effect, ya know. They want dramatic arrangements, and the delivery to happen around four P.M. on Saturday. This is a serious job, boss. I'll close up the shop so you can go over there, and may I suggest you wear some nice slacks and a sweater—just in case some of the guests arrive early, or something."

"Wow. Some apology." She could only look at Bonita now.

"I'd say. You oughta get into a conflict with more of your major customers," her girlfriend laughed. "It's really been good for business."

"You think she'll go for it, Fran?" Brandon's gaze shot between Fran and Ralph as he sat on their living room sofa. "I don't know if this is a good idea, guys. She's already done with me for a ruse, and you said to be honest, and that women hated games, Ralph. This seems so—"

"Oh, *pulleease*," Fran said with a dismissive wave of her hand and a giggle. "Women hate games that trap or disrespect them, but a little assistance to aid a budding romance is standard practice."

"Seems Frannie has talked to her girls, and based upon a quorum of agreement, all our boys' wives want you off the streets as a bachelor. The only reason you're getting a female governor's pardon is because I told them the truth—that this is the first time any of us has ever had to help you get a date, and it's the first time you have ever acted this way about any woman. They smell a victory for their side in the offing . . ."

Humiliation warmed his face as he quickly stood and began pacing. "Look, I'm okay. The woman said take a hike, and I got the message. So we don't have to go to all this trouble." The fact that he'd been discussed, and now ganged up on by all the wives, with his best friends—all the fellas' assistance was just too much.

"Then, why, if this was so silly, and so not worth your time, and you are so disinterested in this sister, are you still here, walking in circles and babbling?" Fran giggled again and shook her head. "Ralph told me it was bad, but I had no idea. Ummph, ummph, ummph."

He shot a warning glare at Ralph. His best friend had turned him in to the female secret police. Brandon started to open his mouth to give Fran a rebuttal, and then decided not to—especially when his gaze locked with Ralph's, who issued a friendly, knowing wink. Something in his friend's eyes told him that this was a no-win situation. They were surrounded. Every man in their close-knit circle was dropping like flies. He was the last man standing, and had been ambushed. Now he'd become like the rest of them, a POW or a hostage.

"Trust me, brother, just go along with the program. It's easier this way." Ralph laughed and leaned back in his La-Z-Boy recliner and sighed.

* * *

The week had dragged as though time had forgotten to move the hands of the clock. Then, it seemed, the day had whizzed by.

Denise brought the shop van to a stop in front of a large warehouse, parking in the sidewalk carport. She looked up at the massive structure and began redesigning the way she would display the dozens of flowers she needed to arrange. She only wished that she'd been able to walk through the place first, to get a feel for everything. But, too late now.

She jumped down from the white van that had her logo on it, and glimpsed at the large purple script. Yes, she would outdo herself for this event. Her little business was finally turning the corner and getting in a steady flow of work. Her Easter orders were booming; life was good and abundant.

She rang the bell and waited, and hoped that there'd be an elevator in the building. If not, it would require at least four runs up the stairs. When Mrs. Simpson opened the door, they both smiled and began to exchange pleasantries. Denise relaxed immediately. Frances Simpson wasn't that bad—they had just met under very difficult circumstances.

"Here, give me one box, and I'll send Ralph down for one," Fran said as she paced around to the back of the van with Denise.

"Oh, no. You're a customer, and I can manage."

"Don't be silly," Fran insisted. "I have a toddler, and I'm used to carrying stuff, along with him, like a pack mule."

Both women shared in a friendly chuckle as they went back and forth to the van and loaded the elevator. Denise could feel a smile form inside her chest as they did so. For once, things were working out smoothly.

When the gate closed, Fran inserted a key and pulled the lever to take them up to the seventh floor. The elevator opened right into the most awesome living space that Denise had seen. Plus it smelled so good. Spices and garlic filled her nose, and she breathed in by force of habit as she entered. The delicious aromas made her stomach gurgle, and at that moment, she realized that she'd eaten like a bird all day—too busy and nervous to really have a decent meal.

Ralph Simpson immediately came toward them. "Hi, ladies. Let me get those and bring them in. Where do you want them?"

"Why not over by the coffee table? This way Miss Blake can work on them and figure out where to put everything."

"Thank you so much, and please call me Denise."

"Okay, Denise, only if you call me Fran."

"Done." Denise smiled and allowed her gaze to sweep the room, this time stopping to notice the details, while Ralph Simpson helped bring the flowers out of the elevator and into the room.

The couple before her fell quiet, as though sensing they were in the midst of an artist at work. In truth, they were. Denise could feel a slight current run through her hands all the way to her fingertips. One day . . . she'd move out of her little Cheltenham row house and do this. God, this was a fabulous space to create within.

Her line of vision took in the southern wall, which was completely made up of multipaned glass. "Wow," she breathed. "I'll bet you get fantastic light exposure with this."

"And a view of the city skyline from this direction," Ralph added.

"Mmmmm . . ." Denise began to study the decor, which was Swedish modern, minimalist with a heavy splash of cultural African art. "These pieces in here are absolutely fabulous," she said in a distracted tone, beginning to walk throughout the space, admiring the high ceilings, the exposed brick, and the exposed ductwork and skylights thirty feet above her head. Dramatic flowers would play beautifully in this place.

Everything was so open, even the modern kitchen with natural woods and black-faced appliances. Only a wide, curved, natural pine counter and eight black-lacquered ladder-back stools separated it from the open living room and dining area. African mud-cloth patterns were strewn over obviously re-upholstered antique chairs, creating an eclectic fusion with chrome and leather chairs, modern metallic studio lamps,

African fabric-designed throw rugs, tall masks, and hand-carved wooden room-divider screens that offered the only break to denote a seam between each room.

On one wall there was a low-profile, massive electronics unit that housed what she could only imagine was a ridiculous sound system—and that had several hundred CDs in black wire racks beside it. Immediately above it, hanging on the wall like a painting, was a huge, flat plasma screen television. Six-foot unframed paintings formed a gallery on the adjacent wall, and her gaze traveled up a black, wrought iron staircase that no doubt led to the couple's sleeping quarters.

The sights and the smells within the space held her captive. She should be paying the Simpsons for allowing her to create in here, she thought, as she let her gaze settled upon the long dining room table. The fabric that covered it was a spectacular, authentic Kente cloth, and the amber and mud-cloth design on the block-and-pyramid-shaped tall tallow candles made her stop. They looked so much like the ones she carried in her shop.

She glimpsed around and saw two fountains, both presented on four-foot wrought iron pedestals replete with Adrinka symbols in the ironwork. Again, the familiarity made her pause, but she kept walking, noting the black china and gold-toned flatware that had been set out along a side mahogany buffet on top of a mud-cloth center runner.

"Okay. I think I've got it," she said, her gaze still wandering. "I have some great brass vases, natural dark wood baskets, and a few modernistic marble-like bases in a variety of odd shapes that will play well throughout this fantastic space. This is a wonderful home, and I think you'll both be pleased and surprised by what I come up with."

"Oh, I know we will," Fran said, beaming.

"Well, we have to get to a few errands, and then get dressed. We'll be back a little later. How about if we just help you get the rest of your pieces in?"

"That will be fine, and thank you again so much," Denise murmured, practically swooning as her mind tackled the options.

"Oh, yeah," Ralph called over his shoulder. "Don't be alarmed if a friend of ours comes in a bit early. He's going to help with the cooking, and to get a few things done in here. So when you hear the elevator, don't panic."

"Will do," she said cheerfully, just happy to be able to get started.

Once alone, and with all her tools and displays at her feet, she laughed out loud, thrilled at the way her voice reverberated off the walls. These people knew how to live! But for the life of her, she couldn't fathom how they kept it clean, much less cared for a baby in a place like that.

Her eyes kept getting drawn to the items that were so similar to the merchandise in her shop, but she repeatedly reminded herself that it might not be appropriate to ask where the couple had gotten these items—even though she really wanted to know who else in the city carried her line. Working the puzzle within her head as her hands moved, a teeny nagging thought began to take root and grow.

What if all the stuff that Brandon Thornton had purchased had actually ended up here, at his good friends' home? That would be very plausible. And she could relent enough to give him brownie points for that . . . the Simpsons did seem like very nice people. The kind of good folks you'd want to do things for if they were your friends.

The sound of the elevator didn't startle her as she made her way into the dining room to set up her first creation. She stepped back from the table and walked around it, folding her arms as she studied it to be sure her idea could work as a high, dramatic centerpiece. Her gaze stayed fixed on the tall calla lilies she mixed in with deep purple tulips, Spanish moss, high irises, and elephant grass that she'd dotted with bloodred roses, stephanotis, and a profusion of wildflowers within a brass bucket.

She had to admit that it was gorgeous, and she smiled, pleased with her design as she leaned over to adjust the lilies and greenery so that it spread out nicely in a natural fan, but not so far that it would inhibit the guests' view of one another.

Then again, she wondered, maybe it was too high, and would look better on the side buffet, where the brass bucket would match the gold-toned flatware, and she could design something else lower, and less view obstructing for the main table.

Native American flute music wrested her back from her reverie and instantly broke her concentration. She'd forgotten that quickly that she'd heard the elevator, and she swiftly went toward the other side of the screen to greet the guest that Ralph Simpson told her was on his way over. The last thing she wanted to appear to be was rude.

It took a moment for her to collect herself, however, as she spotted the cook.

Seven

"Hi," he said with a sheepish grin, and hoisted up his grocery bag. "I just ran out to pick up a few more items."

Brandon Thornton is the cook?

She stood gaping in the middle of the floor as he walked away from her when he'd spoken, calling out information she wasn't the least bit interested in over his shoulder.

"Tonight I'm fixing a shrimp and scallop pasta Alfredo with steamed asparagus for the main course. I sautéed the shellfish earlier, but forgot to pick up arugula for the salad, and cheesecake from the Reading Terminal. Plus I needed a block of real Parmesan and Romano cheese. Can I offer you a glass of wine or some herbal tea while you work?"

Sensing a total setup, she paced behind him and slid into a chair at the kitchen counter while he unloaded his bags. She wasn't sure whether to be angry or to laugh. In truth, no man had ever gone to such lengths to get next to her, and a small part of her had to admit just how flattered she was by it all.

"I take it, then, there's no dinner party? Again, Mr. Thornton, we find ourselves at the crossroads of mistruth."

"No," he said with a chuckle, giving her his back to consider as he set up his cooking supplies and utensils. "My friends are hosting this party at my home. And they wanted beautiful flowers to add the right touch."

She stared at the back that was covered in a black turtleneck sweater, and looked away when he bent over for a large pasta pot. She would not go there, despite how easily his slacks gripped the rounded steel beneath it.

"Okay, then, an evasion of the truth." She stifled a smile as he turned around to face her. She was not going to allow his handsome smile to derail her argument.

"No. I told you how very sorry I was for all the trouble. I also told you how much I wanted to get to know you better— and you said you'd think about it. So, after carefully studying the habits of my target audience, you, I wanted to allow you to think about it while we broke bread, while I could possibly talk to you, and where we'd be chaperoned . . . to help you get to know who my friends are, and so that you can feel at ease and not stalked."

She laughed.

He laughed.

He loved the way she looked in dark hunter green, and the way her pants delicately fit her form. The jewel-toned silk blouse did something for her smoky eyes and the deep cocoa of her skin.

"Wine or tea, since you are at my counter?"

Her smile was warm and friendly, and he dared to consider it relaxed, even.

"How about tea, since I have about ten dozen more flowers to arrange."

"Consider it done. I'll bring it over to where you're work- ing when the water boils." He wanted to hold her there, to keep looking at her as they talked, but Fran had been adamant—give the woman space, and don't send her skitter- ing away again. So far, he had to admit that his buddy's wife was right. So he played it cool, wasn't about to blow it now.

She slipped off the stool and got away from him as quickly as possible. Her eyes looked at his space in a new light. This was like being in the Bat Cave from the comic books. This was definitely the player's lair . . . and she'd been invited in to dress it *with flowers?* Oh, this was not good. Plus, the man was an art buff, and could cook, and obviously liked a wide variety of music, and he had purchased all of that stuff from her shop, and had spent a mint on his little plan to get her here. Not to mention, he was going for the credibility factor by involving his friends—*a married couple,* at that . . . and Bonita had to be in on this. Her friend and employee had gone to the other side? Brandon Thornton was no common salesman; he was an ad exec extraordinaire, if he was able to get Bonita to relent!

None of it was lost on her. Not one single bit of it, as she busied her hands to keep from having a nervous breakdown. Sure, she'd been pursued before—but *never* like this!

The smells he was conjuring up in the kitchen were making her delirious with hunger. He'd brought her a cup of tea, and had set it down, then slipped away without a word. But she did catch him glimpse her from the corner of his eye. And the intense glance again released all those butterflies she thought had been securely netted. To her dismay, she also noted that this man, who was moving around at a distance, was having a significant effect on her libido. She'd thought that had been netted and put under glass, too, but realized that she was sadly mistaken as a warm sensation began to settle in her lower belly each time she snuck a peak at him.

He had to stop stressing, Brandon told himself as he'd walked away from her. Why on earth he had spent an hour in the health food store trying to decide what tea to get was beyond him. Rosehip was the choice, as he'd pressured Ralph to recount everything she'd consumed during lunch. His buddy was right—he was hooked, hooked bad. But his friend didn't have to tell him that, as he'd practically had to drag himself away from being near her so she could arrange the flowers.

Brandon glanced at his watch. Where were Ralph and Fran? The last thing he needed was for Denise to think he'd cornered her alone in his place. This was not the type of sister one rushed, or pushed up on. Had to keep things cool, move slow, but every time he glanced at her . . .

He saw her approaching from the corner of his eye, and he went back to the stove to try to be nonchalant. "More tea?" he asked over his shoulder.

"Sure," she said with an easy chuckle that he appreciated. "But first I want you to see what I did, and see if it meets your approval."

Wow. She was actually taking the lead on the conversation. With a broad smile, he rinsed his hands and followed her while she showed off his space to him like she was a real estate agent.

"Over here, I've placed an eye-catching arrangement on the side buffet. It is out of the way, but dramatic enough to draw people's attention through the room toward it, without overpowering the art on that wall."

"Impressive," he murmured, and meant it. What she had been able to accomplish was nothing short of phenomenal.

"Over here, in the center of the table, I have created a low, long spray, kept short so as to not obstruct the view of seated guests."

He nodded his approval. "Now, see, I would have put the big one there, never thinking of the logistics until we all sat down and had to lean around the arrangement to talk."

She smiled. "I almost did the same thing. A long table and high ceilings are seductive enough to make you want to place the biggest piece there—but one has to remember balance and functionality."

He swallowed hard. Seductive. She had no idea. But he wasn't about to comment on the various ways her statement could be employed.

"Then, over here, in the living room, I've placed a large, geometric block vase on the glass table. It won't obstruct the view as people talk, but it gives the room more color, texture. And, over there," she said, pointing, "I've scattered several smaller arrangements to soften some of the heavier pieces of art, and to brighten the heavy black foundation tones you're using."

"This is absolutely amazing . . ." He walked around the open spaces, truly marveling at what plants had added to his environment, as well as what her subtle touches and placements could achieve. "I can tell that this isn't just a business for you. It's a love of yours."

"Yeah," she murmured. "Ever since I was little, I've always loved flowers."

"Talk to me from a stool in the kitchen while you sip your tea, and I finish dinner?"

"Okay." This time she didn't wrestle with his offer. It had come on a note of genuine interest. She once again slipped onto a high seat and watched him work, bringing her empty teacup with her.

"Where did you learn how to cook, or about art? This place is fabulous, Brandon. Seriously."

She'd used his first name, and wanted to know about him—had complimented his home. This was good.

"My dad was in the military, so when I was little, me and my mom traipsed behind him all over the world. She worked, too, and I loved to eat, so at some point I began trying to replicate the different tastes I learned to enjoy from wherever we lived. I got better as I got older, and it stuck with me, I suppose. Guess I got the travel bug from him, along with the art. So every time I moved somewhere, or traveled, I'd pick up a piece."

"Your parents must love what you've done with it here."

"Maybe," he said, trying to chase the sadness from his tone. "They never got to see it." He paused and began making her tea. "Dad passed a few years ago, and Mom lost her battle to cancer last year. That's how I came back to Philly and also came by a lot of the art you see in here. Much of it's from their house. I was in Atlanta, then Baltimore, did New York, Chicago—working the radio network—but life has a way of making you take stock of what's important. So I came back to Philly, where we began and they'd retired."

Her eyes held an intense melancholy as he refreshed her tea before her.

"I'm sorry," she whispered. "I had no idea . . . I mean, I do know what that's like, in a way. I lost my dad five years ago, and my grandmother before that—but I still have my mom."

"Then cherish her while she's here," he said quietly. "I was always on the go, and they got on my nerves, always ragging about settling down, and now . . . Well, I wish I would have done what Ralph and Fran did, truth be told. My godson, their little boy, has grandparents on both sides that simply adore him."

He held her gaze as he told her the truth. "I didn't think putting down roots was important, never learned how when I was a kid, because we were always moving, you know. But when I came home, and all my homeboys from back in the day were here, and supported me through my parents' illnesses, I knew I did have some—and that they were very important."

She looked at this man for a long while, the silent understanding passing between them. She had been so wrong, had tried him without judge or jury, simply based on his exterior and what others had done to her in the past.

"My grandmother was that for me," she finally murmured while stirring her tea with the spoon he'd set by her cup. She added a bit of raw sugar, and looked down into the swirling pink liquid, caught up in the memory. "She was the family anchor. And I know what it feels like not to have one. But she always talked in metaphors, using the flowers and their differences to teach me things in her backyard. I miss her, too."

He glanced at her lapel. "Is that who you wear the angel for?"

"Oh, him? No," she said with a quiet chuckle. "He was a gift from an elderly customer who came into my store one day. She said love has to be in the light, and that I should wear him always."

"She was right, you know."

She cocked her head to the side, and he smiled, giving her another wondrous look at the dimple that hid when his expression was serious. "I don't follow."

"Denise, love should be in the light, out in the open, and not hidden."

He could not believe he'd just said that. Okay. It was time for a glass of wine. This woman had an intoxicating effect on him, and he needed to gather himself and go back to the stove before he bled all over the counter.

"She said, 'just like flowers'."

"You do beautiful work with the flowers," he evaded, struggling to open a bottle of chardonnay as his nerves shattered.

"Thank you," she whispered.

The sound of her voice threaded through his system and ignited something he couldn't define within it—this feeling went deeper, way past basic desire. He swallowed again and hunted for two glasses.

"Nana used to say that I was the family nose, and she would make me close my eyes and figure out what flower she was holding, then she'd let me arrange them for her table. That's how I started. Just associating love with the whole process, I guess. They always say, do what you love if you're gonna start a business, right?"

He could tell that she'd pulled back, and was trying to lighten the thick mood that had settled between them, but his nervous system was slow to react to the change. God, it had been so long since he'd been with a woman, and never in his life had he been with one like this. One that made him feel like this. She was so close, but yet so far. The cork popped, making him remember that he had the bottle in his hands.

"Then, everybody can't be wrong," he said quietly, pouring her a glass of wine and then one for himself. Where were Ralph and Fran!

He watched her take a sip and close her eyes, rolling the liquid over her tongue inside her mouth. The way the canister lights above shone down on her soft, curly tendrils of hair, giving it a golden highlight, and the way her throat moved when she tilted her chin up to swallow made him summon all the patience he could muster. Then she peered at him. That was positively his undoing.

"Can I tell you something, before my friends come back?"

She gave him a quizzical look and nodded her head. "Sure. What?"

"I am scared to death."

She looked at him with an odd expression and suddenly burst out laughing, covering her mouth with her hand. "Why?"

He had not planned on the truth—not like this, but he couldn't handle this whole thing. The dynamic was too intense. Brandon began walking back and forth behind the counter, and then stopped.

"You are scaring the bejeezus out of me, Denise. I'm a nervous wreck. I've never done anything like this before—much less ever told anyone I've never done anything like this before."

Her soft giggle connected to his spinal column and sent a current of desire through it.

"Listen. All my boys think I'm this player, okay. And, I'll grant you—it's easy to take someone out for a nice evening, or whatever . . . and, yeah, I did do a lot of playing. But getting close, coming in for a serious landing, is giving me white knuckles. I don't want to say the wrong thing, do the wrong thing, I just want everything to go perfectly—and now I'm standing in the middle of my kitchen babbling like a madman, and you now have three strikes against me." He walked away and leaned against the refrigerator, took a deep sip of his wine, swallowed it, and let his breath out hard. "There. I've said it."

It was the sweetest, nicest, most honest thing any man had ever said to her.

She smiled at him when he opened his eyes. "I think you're working with a clean slate, actually." She took a sip of wine. "And it might help you to know that I thought I would jump out of my skin when I saw you in the living room."

God, she was beautiful, inside and out. It gave him a sudden insane courage.

"Ever since I lost my mom, I've looked around, realized that I was thirty-five, had no brothers or sisters, and save good friends, I was alone in this world. My first reaction to it was sheer panic. Then I distanced myself from that, and got wilder than I had been in the past—sorta like trying to numb yourself, you know?"

She nodded, and he continued, bolstered by the soft gaze that she gave him, which transmitted understanding.

"Then I went through this phase of 'I don't need anybody.' And I focused on my career. But I would always find myself over a buddy's house, or making myself work late . . . I hated coming in here. All of a sudden it felt too big, too vast—so I stayed in the streets, or would get my friends in trouble by trying to get them to come out and play with me. Then I walked in that flower shop, and went—bam. That's it. Just like that."

While she could relate to all the things he'd said, she could not fathom the last part of it. His speech was sweet, but too hard to believe. It made her want to giggle, but she held that in check, polishing off her glass of wine in the process.

"You don't believe me, do you?" He chuckled and walked over toward her, refilling her glass as well as his own. "See, this is why I became a master of the one-liners. You can hide behind a line, but telling the truth just makes you give it all up. Leaves a brother exposed."

"You gave me a line when I first met you," she said with a sly grin.

"No, I didn't."

His face had gone stone serious, and it took her by surprise.

"I walked in there and saw an angel."

She fiddled with her pin, now looking at the wood grain of the counter. This man was on fast forward, and messing with every admonishment her mother ever told her—take it slow, he won't buy the cow if the milk is free. She could feel parts of her body awaken that should be asleep and well outside the realm of this conversation at the moment.

"I want something permanent these days. We're too old for me to hint around at that, Denise. I like you—a lot. I want to take you to do fun stuff, talk, and figure out if we want to go further than that. No games."

Nobody ever told her a man would come on strong like

this—why hadn't her girls warned her! "Uh, okay. What do you like to do?"

He laughed. This was not good.

"Do you like the movies?"

She, too, was glad that he'd veered off the taboo subject, because if he'd asked her, right now, she might have told him the truth, too.

"Oh, yes! Love them, but rarely get to go because of the long hours at the shop. Action adventures are my favorite, though."

"A woman after my own heart. So we do the movies, then."

"Okay, what's your favorite food, color, and music—since you've obviously already researched mine."

He laughed. "Seafood, electric blue, and jazz."

"All right. Biggest pet peeve?" She was warming to this game of twenty questions.

"Games," he said sheepishly. "I know, I know. But it's true."

She laughed hard. "Oh, go figure."

He laughed with her. "Okay. Favorite time of the year and thing to do?"

"Spring. And going to see the flowers."

"Sounds like a trip to the Philadelphia Flower Show . . . and maybe a drive to wine country—upstate Pennsylvania when it gets nice, so you can see them blooming in the wild. When's your birthday?"

"You would actually take me to the flower show?" Her voice trailed off, and she could only shake her head.

"When's your birthday?" He repeated the question and held her gaze now.

"May twelfth," she whispered.

"A Taurus woman . . . that accounts for your love of beauty."

She giggled, basking in his warm attention to the little details about her. "When's yours?"

"December tenth—yeah, yeah, I'm a Sag, wild, crazy, blunt, not good with games, and too honest for my own welfare." He chuckled as he continued to stare at her. "And, I also confess to be a bit of a hedonist."

"Oh . . ." she said in a soft tone. "Well, what you're preparing for dinner sounded, and smells, absolutely sinful."

"You have no idea of what I can cook in here. The kitchen is not my favorite room."

"Oh . . ." She swallowed hard, and added moisture to her dry mouth with a sip of wine.

"I'll remain a gentleman, though, until you tell me I don't have to be one."

She looked up at him and almost had to look away again. His gaze burned her this time. "Bet it's awesome in here with the candles lit, and a hard spring rain on the windows . . ." Was she out of her mind! Flirting this way, with this man, *this soon?*

"Why do you think I bought all the candles from your shop?" His voice had dropped a sexy octave, and it made her lock to his gaze. "A brother has to keep hope alive. I said I wanted to get to know you . . . that's an all-inclusive goal."

His statement had sent a mild tremor through her, and to her alarm, he seemed to notice it.

"Told you I was honest. And, with that said and done, I'm going to call Ralph on his cell phone to come to my rescue— before I put my own foot in my mouth."

Brandon paced away from her to the far end of the kitchen area and grabbed the wall-mounted phone. While he made the call, half of her was glad that he'd pulled back, the other half of her was left quietly smoldering as she wondered what type of lover this man would be. Was Brandon Thornton a slow, simmering, sexy lover, or a hard, intense, passionate one? Would he slowly devour her, when the time was right, or would he be the kind of guy to sweep her off her feet, literally, and crush her with fast, unbearable heat?

The thoughts he'd transmitted to her made a moist throb take root in her center, and she inhaled deeply through her nose to stave off the ache. But as she did so, she became aware of how gooseflesh was forming on her arms, and had spread to her breasts, making her nipples pebble and sting.

Damn, this brother was getting to her with his aggressive honesty.

"They were dealing with the baby, and getting him all settled in at the other sitter. They'd had him with one lady during the day, but another person was coming to stay at the house tonight while they came here."

All she could do was nod as he resumed cooking. Her body felt scorched as she watched him work from her perch.

"By the way," he asked out of the blue with a wide grin. "How many kids do you want one day?"

Eight

"Hi, Bonita!" She had practically sing-songed her greeting as she skipped into the shop.

"Oh, Lord have mercy," Bonita groaned. "Here comes Miss Sunshine again. You, know," she added with a peevish chuckle, "you two are going to have to tone it down for the rest of us. I mean, after two months of this, we're all so jealous, we could stab you, but won't only 'cause we love you."

"Oh, I'm not that bad," Denise scoffed, waving her hand at Bonita as she took off her light jacket. "But I do have one teensy-weensy little favor to ask you, though."

"Like you already don't owe me about fifty by now?"

They both giggled.

"First I had to suffer you coming in after he cooked for you. You were no good all day and just floated around sighing." Bonita imitated her dramatically as she walked around in front of the counter. "Then he started calling every day, and no matter how long the line of customers, you'd get all sigh-like again, and take an hour-long call in the back, then come out all messed up for the rest of the day. And, I swear, after the man took you to the flower show, I thought me and your mom were gonna have to scoop you up and pour you in a vase."

"I am not that bad," Denise protested. "But Mom likes him, I think."

"What's not to like? The woman nearly fell out when he

went to church on Easter with you guys, and then took the three of y'all to dinner. *Pullease.* Brotherman is big on grand entrances, and I'd say taking Mom to Zanzibar Blue for Easter—after church, mind you—was a serious move."

"You think so?"

Bonita sucked her teeth and walked away from Denise, as though refusing to dignify the comment.

"It was beautiful there, Bonnie. Oh, man . . . you should have seen it."

"Tell me all about it," Bonita said, giving her a scowl, then a slow smile. "I know you're dying to anyway."

"Yeah . . ." Denise sighed. "Oh, girl. It's fabulous."

"That's it. I'm calling the rest of the girls. We plan to jump you when the store closes tonight. Multiple stab wounds—expect it."

They both laughed hard and Denise gave Bonita a hug.

"Thank you so much for helping to get this thing started, lady. I was so crazy, wasn't I?"

"Out of your stubborn black mind, chile."

"But you think he's really, really serious, like permanent serious?"

Bonita held her back by both arms and stared at her. "You haven't given the man none yet? Oh. My. God. *Denise!*"

"It . . . it . . . it just never came up between us, I suppose."

"What!"

Bonita was circling her now, like a vulture on the serious hunt for information. Denise tried to dodge her by going between the card racks, but Bonita was on her heels. Her girlfriend spun her around, and allowed her voice to dip into a low, concerned hiss.

"Don't tell me he's got a problem . . . Oh, have mercy. No. Not that fine brother. Is there no justice, Lord?"

"No, no, no!" Despite her girlfriend's whisper, Denise found her voice escalating with alarm. "No, it just, well, he never, uh . . . well. There just wasn't time—the right time."

"What in the world are you talking about?" Bonita was now walking back and forth, waving her hands as she spoke.

"Y'all been to the movies, been to dinner, he done took you and your momma to church—she likes him, an endorsement if ever I heard one, 'cause your momma don't like nobody. And you've been out at his friends'—over their houses and stuff, to watch sports mess . . . met all the wives. Even took a covered dish or two with you when you went, like you was his real, solid woman. You don't take a covered dish to no wives unless you are *the woman*. Men don't letcha do that, girl!"

"I know, I know, I know." Her nerves were so jangled that Bonita now had her walking in a circle, too. "But each time we'd go out, he would give me this long, sexy kiss, smile, and step away, and leave me inside my door."

"You told him to be a gentleman, right?"

"Yes," Denise laughed. "And it's killing me."

"Kickin' your na'chel behind, is more like it."

"Wearin' me out, Bonnie." Denise put her hand over her heart, closed her eyes, and started laughing hard in earnest. "He calls at night, talking all low and sexy on the phone, asking me what I'm wearing to bed . . . and then after a while, says, 'Baby, I gotta go,' and blows me a kiss good night."

"You do know what this means, don't you?"

Denise opened her eyes wide as panic raced through her. "No, Bonita. What? You think there's somebody else, or that he doesn't find me attractive? Or, or, or, maybe he has a secret life, oh God . . ."

She'd turned around and around in a quick circle, until Bonita's swift tug on her arm made her stop and look at her.

"It means, silly, that he's really serious, I think. Like, this brother has been pressing to get to know you hard and fast— like bum rushin' you, ever since that dinner. I think he might have future plans for you."

"Oh, girl, stop it."

Denise shooed her away with a flip of her wrist. "He's just kissed me, and didn't even hang around to do more than that."

"He's shown you practically everybody that means something to him, even took you to a job function—and showed you to his work crew and *his boss*. And has spent all this time finding out your little ways, and stuff. *And,* he hasn't laid a hand on you—because you sent 'I'm not ready yet' signals, knowing you." Bonita strode away, snapping her fingers over her head in triumph. "That's 'cause you're *wife material,* girl. Ask him does he have a brother."

It was her turn to chase behind Bonita in the store. She couldn't come up behind her girlfriend fast enough to get her to turn around to talk to her. Bonita's statement was making her ears ring. *Wife material* . . .

"You heard me," Bonita said with a wry chuckle as she pretended to ignore Denise, fixing up the displays as she talked. "Brace yourself."

"No, no, it's waaaay too soon, and I do not want to get my hopes up like this."

"See, signals. You are sending the man mixed messages."

She stopped and listened as Bonita looked at her hard.

"Yes, mixed signals," Bonita repeated.

"Okay," she said slowly. "How?"

"You told him that you didn't want to be messed over, and probably told him about a few of the relationships that had gone wrong—am I right?"

She let her mind rip through the conversations she'd had with Brandon—over dinners, after the movies, over coffee, and on the telephone in their tiny, intimate world.

"Uh-huh," Bonita confirmed. "You just blabbered away and confessed about the doggish brothers in your life, didn't you?"

Initially, she could only nod. "But he told me a lot of stuff, too—about how he'd been in some bad stuff."

"And what did you say to yourself, or to him?"

"That I would never do those things," she shot back.

"Right. And why not?"

"Because I care about him, and the things those people did to him were foul, especially when he was losing his parents."

"Uhmmm-hmmm."

"Oh, what is that supposed to mean?"

Bonita burst out laughing. "Look at you. You're breathing hard. Oooooh, *girrrl* . . . you got it bad, don'tcha?"

Denise had to laugh.

"He's only doing what you're doing. You won't treat him like those bad relationship folks treated him, and he's probably vowed not to do you like you've been done—'cause you told him how messed up those brothers were. Follow?"

"Ohhh . . . no . . ."

"And," Bonita pressed on, "you asked him to show some commitment—without coming out and actually saying that, by the way you demand respect—which is a good thing. Problem is, though, now . . . you've turned the corner. Now you are more than ready—in fact, when the phone rings, you wet your draws."

"Oh, shut up. Not true."

"Yes. True." Bonita fanned her face with her hand, relentlessly teasing Denise as she tried to get away from her pinch range. "*Now* you want him to dog you good. Press up on a sistah, break her down, maybe half break her back, and—"

"Shut. Up. Bonita. Thank. You. Very. Much."

"Gotta send him the green light signal, sis—or there'll be no living with you in this shop. Do it for me, if not yourself."

Although Denise was laughing with Bonita, the words *green light* came flashing into her memory. He had said that . . . he'd wait for the green light from her. Dag, how did that crazy Bonita know so much!

"Change of subject," Denise exclaimed, trying to wrest back what was left of her dignity. "I have a favor to ask you."

"Red light," Bonita teased.

"Girl, shut up and listen."

"Okay, okay. Yellow light, 'cause I know you—I've already put in ten hours of overtime this week alone."

"Well . . . how about all day Friday and Saturday?"

Bonita looked at her bug-eyed, and then opened and closed her mouth. Then she covered it, stifling a scream. She paced away from Denise, and paced back, laughing behind her hand. "Details."

"He wants to drive to upstate PA to wine country . . . to look at the spring flowers. And said that if we get a little wine-silly and tipsy, it might make sense to, uh, maybe stay at an inn up there, and come back once we're less inebriated—to be safe. So—"

"To look at flowers!" Bonita boomed, cutting off Denise's words with a roar of laughter. "Oh, no—ain't nuthin' wrong with brotherman, don't worry. You took too long to turn on the *green* runway lights, and he's about to land a jumbo jet on the Pennsylvania Turnpike, hot damn!"

"Bonita, please," Denise fussed in a harsh whisper. "Lower your voice. This is major serious. I'm . . . I'm . . . Hell, I don't know what to do."

"Oh, yeah, this is major serious," Bonita giggled, "but it's like riding a bike. You never forget how to—"

"You know what I mean!"

"Yes, I know what you mean," Bonita conceded. "But you should hear yourself. If you were standing in my shoes, you'd just be shaking your head." Bonita sighed and then shook her head. "I will watch the store, only on one condition."

"Okay, what?" Denise said faster than she'd wanted to.

"I want every, single, itty-bitty detail." Bonita folded her arms over her chest and grinned.

"I—I—I—I can't do that. *No, girl.* No. I'll just have to close the shop, then."

"Whoah," Bonita chuckled. "I was just half playing. I've seen you drag your butt into this shop with the flu . . . You'd actually shut the doors to go up there with him? Uh-uh. I've changed my request. I do not want to just hear about this weekend—I want video."

Peals of laughter rang out in the tiny store.

"Shut up, you nut!"

He checked and double-checked his overnight bag. He checked and double-checked all his car fluid levels. He checked and double-checked the AAA maps. He checked and double-checked his reservations. He checked and double-checked his wallet. He checked and double-checked his outfit and his cologne. He had checked and double-checked until he had practically worn himself out. Damn, it never used to be this hard. Two dinners, if not one, and he was in.

But this had been two agonizing months. *Months.* And it all came down to this weekend. Either they were going to have a very tense time, and things were not going to click, or they would.

As he drove up to Cheltenham, he replayed the little disagreements that they'd had over and over again in his mind. Okay, so maybe a part of him was a chauvinist—but he was a moderate, not a right-winger. He liked to get her wound up, though, because he liked the passion it drew her to display. She was feisty. He smiled, amused at his own twisted humor. But she fought fair. He liked that. He chuckled out loud in the car as he thought about the most serious disagreement that they'd had so far—the one about her mom.

It still floored him that Denise had actually gotten angry with him because he'd defended her mother's position. "How's that for being put between a rock and a hard place?" He chuckled again, feeling quite jovial as he turned up the volume to feel the jazz in his bones. As the sound connected to his vertebrae, he wondered what she'd sound like. Smooth, mellow . . . or more like the older, brassy key of Thelonius Monk . . . experimental, or silent, R&B, or soul?

No. He had to let this weekend unfold naturally. Talk had to create the rhythm. Fun, the melody. Trust, the refrain. If her signals were right, he'd drop in heavy bass and percussion to bring out the vocals. But right now, all he could do was drive.

However, when she opened the door and smiled happily at him, all his intentions began to fade fast. She stood there, soft brown curls framing her face. He did his best to not reach out and touch them, but couldn't help himself this time. His hand cupped her cheek, and her skin felt so soft that he forgot they were supposed to be driving somewhere.

"You ready?" he murmured, hoping that she could read his statement in the second way.

"Yeah. I can't wait," she said. "Just let me get my bag and a jacket, in case it rains."

He stood just inside the door, processing the way she'd practically breathed her answer. Soft. She was smooth jazz. She was also wearing a soft lilac top and khakis. Yeah . . . . soft. Fixated, he watched her saunter away from him, just out of reach, to collect her bag and her jacket. He'd been so into staring at her that he almost forgot to take the heavy piece of luggage from her.

"Feels like you've got an anvil in here," he joked, trying to get himself together while she offered him the bag and she locked up behind them.

"Oh, I just packed a few things—just to be prepared."

He didn't say a word as he helped her into the car. This was going to be the longest car ride of his life, he could tell. Because in that moment when she'd returned to him to signal that she was ready to leave, he'd almost suggested that they nix the trip. Something in him had stirred hard—maybe it was the other signal that she'd given him.

Nine

"I want to show you something," he said, laughing, as they practically stumbled out of the old Tudor mansion that had been converted into the winery's main house.

"You sure we can make it?" She giggled as he held her waist. "These wines are fabulous, and this is the third vineyard we've been to today. One more, and I'm toast."

"That's why I think we'd better slow down and take a breather." He laughed again as he pulled her nearer, loving the way she leaned against him. "It's just up the road, and not far from the inn, either."

She followed his lead to get into the car, and gazed out the window with profound appreciation for all the beauty around her that now bloomed on the mountains. That appreciation began with the man sitting beside her, who had become her friend, also, in such a short time. Being near him created a level of comfort that, not long ago, she was sure would never be hers. Like the embers of a new fire, Brandon warmed her, and that warmth spread and caught on to everything in her and around her. Her fingers fiddled with the little angel that still clung to her shoulder, and as they wound down the scenic road, her relaxed thoughts drifted to the old woman who had given her the pin.

Odd, how she'd met Brandon that same day. Maybe the single tear that had splattered her golden cherub had awakened the magic the old woman had promised? Feeling giddy, she chuckled.

"What's so funny," he said in a mellow voice.

"An elderly woman gave me an angel to sit on my shoulder, and that very same day, I thought I'd met the devil himself."

He smirked. "Maybe you did. Who knows? That's quite a quandary—to have an angel on one shoulder telling you to do one thing, and a devil on the other, advising you to do the opposite."

"Mmmm," she murmured, amused. "Been struggling with that dilemma for a few weeks now." Even though she had come to the mountains with him while in her full and present mind, even with a little larceny in her heart, the wine had definitely loosed her mouth, and she covered it and giggled behind her hand.

"Well, I guess that makes two of us," he chuckled low in his throat, pulling the car to a stop on a grassy knoll. "But, c'mon, before I forget where I'm taking you. I want you to see something, and it's just a little hike from the road."

"A hike?" Again she laughed, and held on to his arm as he helped her out of the car and slipped an arm around her waist. "I've read up on you adventurous Sagittarian types. You like the outdoors, sports, anything unconventional."

"So you've been researching me, I see."

"I can research my target audience, too, you know."

Yes, she could, and the fact that she had researched something about him pleased him no end. He moved his arm to cover her shoulder, rubbing the top part of her arm as she leaned on him and they walked a ways. There was just something so right, so easy about being near to her. He lowered his nose to take in a whiff of the fragrance her hair produced, and chastised the spring blooms as they passed them for not comparing to the one he held beside him.

"What is back here?" she fussed as they had to go through a small section of bramble.

"You trust me?"

"Yeah, but . . ."

"No buts. Close your eyes and take my hand. I won't let you fall, I promise. It's beautiful, not dangerous."

"Brandon, honestly, this isn't some man-survival-camp-test or something, is it, where I'm going to hurl down a cliff?"

He laughed. "Why would I hurl you off a cliff?"

She grudgingly complied, and he set her in a giggling fit when he caught her peeking. To be sure she wouldn't ruin the surprise, he added an extra layer of security by covering her eyes with his free hand as he guided her.

"Okay. Look." He removed his hand and watched her face slowly open like the dawn.

"Oh, my Lord . . ."

"It's an old abandoned ski lift, and it blooms now with buttercups and other wildflowers that you can see for miles from the top of this hill."

Vibrant yellows and blues and aquas and fuchsias and purples spread out before her like a vast Arabian carpet, and she broke from his hold and ran, spinning and twirling like a freed butterfly.

He watched her run. The look on her face from such a small gift made it hard for him to breathe. Her dark brunette curls caught in the wind and bounced behind her. A glimpse of this hillside was his gift to her, but her openly expressed joy was a fair exchange of the shared offering. She looked like a majestic free pony, unspoiled by a harness, and as she laughed and kicked and jumped and ran about in the flowers, he knew that he loved her.

Seeing her that way also freed something within him, too. Soon he found himself chasing her in a game of dodge and dash, not really pursuing her, but rather enjoying how she sprinted away from his grasp, and then enjoying even more just watching her get away.

Finally, winded, they leaned on their knees with both hands—glancing up at each other, both grinning, and staying alert and poised, waiting to see if the other would give chase. When he stood up, she squealed and made a quick turn to get by him. He caught her by the waist, ending their game with a kiss.

But she broke it too soon for his liking, pulling him to sit down beside her in the flowers that were waist deep.

"How did you find this place? It's like you went up to heaven and brought a piece of it down with you."

Her gaze was cast out to the horizon like a wide net, not wanting to miss any of it. But his gaze was on her as she sipped in deep breaths after her run. The flowers and the perfect turquoise sky to frame her in his secret place were almost too much to stand.

"When I was a kid, my Dad put me in the Boy Scouts. Every year, for two weeks, until we had to move again, I got to go away to summer camp."

"You were not a Boy Scout." She looked at him, kissed his cheek, and pushed his shoulder.

"Was, too. Dad wanted me to know what it was like, in case I went into the military one day—used to say that, when he went away, while it was fun, by the end, he was ready to come home. I think that was just his way of making me feel safe. As a kid, I could relate to camp. So Dad was at camp and got to do all this cool stuff, and I was never scared that he would die or something. It took me a long time to figure out why the other military brats would be so upset when their dads had to go away."

Her hand found his face and he covered it, kissing the center of her palm.

"I never told anybody that little piece of useless trivia." He tried to laugh it off.

"How did you find this place, though? The campgrounds we passed were a long way back—I mean for a kid to walk."

He smiled and looked out at the seemingly endless slope before them, and leaned back on his elbows as he released her hand.

"You would be surprised how far a kid can walk when he's determined to go home. The older boys were teasing me and some of the younger ones; I was going to go get my father . . . was going to find my dad's platoon—hey, I figured his camp couldn't be far from my camp, right?" Brandon laughed. "Kid logic."

He shrugged and turned over on his side as she lay on her side next to him.

"Well, I got lost, and so I went off the road, and wound up here. And I sat on this hillside for a long time, wondering if my dad's platoon had just packed up and left—or worse. I prayed and prayed that wherever he was, he wasn't dead like the big kids had told me. And I started getting all upset, because I was hungry and thirsty and tired, and soon I realized how much I missed him. . . . Then I heard my camp counselor on a bull horn, sounding frantic. They had come in search of me, the older boys were in a lot of hot water, and my mom had been contacted, who contacted my dad—and they connected with him overseas when I got back, and put me on the telephone."

"You still miss him, don't you?" Her finger traced his jawline, and the soft pad of her thumb grazed his lips.

"Yeah, miss 'em both. They had something that people don't seem to be able to create, or hold on to any more. And, I can't define it for you."

"It's that quiet, sustainable glue. A friendship bond . . . saw it with my mom and dad, and after he was gone, she changed. It was as though the thing holding her together gave way, and she only saw fault with the world after that. Until you just said what you did, I don't think I really understood."

He gazed at her and closed his eyes, bringing his mouth near to the one he needed so much now in his life. Her lips parted and allowed his tongue entry, and he sipped a warm current of air from her mouth. When she deepened the kiss, his hand trailed down the length of her curvaceous side, and the change in texture from her shirt to her khakis left a scorching trail in the center of his palm. He tried to quench the burn by moving his hand to stroke the softness of her hair, and it felt like curly velvet, just like he'd imagined. But the texture of her hair was no comparison to the lush fullness of her mouth, and as she pressed to him more closely, he suddenly realized just how much of her he'd wanted to touch for so long.

He found himself sliding against her, and felt her hands at his shoulders pulling him closer, her now compliant form rolling onto her back as he blanketed her amongst the wild-flowers. As he did, a soft moan escaped her lips; yes, sweet, mellow jazz, fragrant and intoxicating. And he was the more strident chord, creating fabric friction that could be heard, as months compounded with daily interest in his groin, and her legs wrapped around his waist.

This was not how he planned it, not where he planned any of it. But God, she felt so good. He tried to shield the back of her skull from the ground with his hand, tried to not press against her so hard, but when she moved beneath him and clutched his shoulders, and tangled her legs within his, he had to keep moving. Then her voice entered his mouth, fused with his on a deep from the soul moan that traveled down his throat and lodged in his Adam's apple.

He pulled out of the hard kiss, and let his head hang back. Not here, not without protection, he told himself, he had to do the right thing, and get up.

"What's the matter?"

Her whisper entered his chest and sent another shaft of fire into his groin.

For a moment, he couldn't answer. His only response was to suck in a deep inhale. "If I don't stop now . . ."

"Let's go to the inn, okay?"

Sweet Jesus, she could also read minds.

He slowly peeled himself off of her, the warmth generated between them having created what felt like a vacuum seal. Disconnecting from her was pure agony. He forced himself to roll off of her, and then sat beside her for a moment, his arms around his knees, with his head painfully pressed against his forearms. "Yeah, just need a moment."

A soft kiss landed on his damp cheek, and his arms didn't consult his brain as he dropped them, straightened his legs and pulled her onto his lap. An intense spasm unlocked the words that had been trapped in his throat, sending them against the tender flesh of her neck in a rush. "I love you, baby."

It was foolhardy to prolong his own torture by continuing to touch her, but her breathy kiss had stunned his reason, paralyzed his nervous system. He couldn't take his hands off her.

"I love you, too," she whispered hard into his ear.

He wanted to say more, tell her how much, but her open straddle made him forget where they were when his lips found her collarbone. His hands were drawn to the fabric he'd wanted to touch all day, and the centers of his palms were teased by the hardened tips of her ripe mounds as he cupped them. Her quiet moan made him shudder, and her slow rhythm against his thickened lap almost made him cry out. The inn seemed so far away.

"Let's go to the inn," she repeated, her voice no longer holding the tone of mere suggestion, but had transformed into an outright plea.

"You're right, you're right." There he'd show her what his voice could not tell her.

But his hands continued to touch her, finding the edge of her sweater and slipping beneath it to connect to her burning skin. The whimper she released drew his mouth to suckle the tips of where he knew she felt pain, and it spurred her lazy rocking rhythm to press down in deep, hard circles against his lap. Her head was back now, her hands holding tight to his shoulders, her breathing coming up from her diaphragm, her circles becoming jerky thrusts. Part of him wanted to just flip her over and roughly remove her pants, but common sense snapped back to him as he heard a car drive by.

"The inn."

"Yeah."

"Right now"

"Uh-huh."

They both winced, parted, and stood. He helped her up and helped her brush some of the grass and flower petals from her hair. They walked together, quickly, she just ahead of him, brushing herself off the entire time, and peering around bashfully as they made their way to the clearing.

He didn't care that their pants and shirts were both marked with streaks of earth and grass stains. They hadn't said a word to each other as they entered the car, and he drove, solely focused on getting to the inn. There were no words or small talk exchanged as he signed in, and then waved away the bellman and took the bags himself. It was as though they were both in silent agreement that there was a level of immediacy to this evening, and that the room appointments would be fine. It only needed one piece of furniture—a bed, and that bit of information did not need to be conveyed to a stranger.

She had found his mouth as soon as they'd stepped through the door. He dropped the bags at either side of them, and filled his arms with her. From a single glance he had studied the layout of the room, and could get her to the one piece of furniture they needed without opening his eyes.

And they both worked at the task of making time hurry, both stripping off their clothes, fumbling while helping the other, then going back to complete the frustrating task of removing their own clothes, tangled in the fabrics on the bed.

When she stood and crossed the room, the cold air felt like it cut him, and as she gave him a posterior view when she bent to unzip her bag, his lids lowered to half-mast, carving what he saw into his brain. Immediately, the sound of metal rushing against metal unzipped his senses, and he shuddered again, knowing what she was searching for—his freedom to enter her.

She said nothing, just brought a large box out of her bag and tossed it on the nightstand. She hovered for a moment by the bed—watching him assess her. He could just suck in a shallow sip of air to acknowledge his eye's appreciation of what he saw . . . for in all of his life, never . . .

Cocoa skin like satin, small, perfect mounds that ended with a kiss of chocolate . . . curves to drive a man to his own ruin, slender legs that culminated in a brown profusion of tight curls, and a mouth and eyes that he'd surrender his soul for. All he could do was extend his hand to her for hers to fill it. There were no words.

His hand had outstretched to her like a dark beacon. What she saw lying before her had slowed her return to the bed, and for a moment all she could do was stare at him. He resembled one of the deep, walnut-hued pieces of art from his loft . . . chiseled perfection, every muscle carved and defined in his outstretched arm, his chest, abdomen, and legs. They way he held his hand out for her to take, was what they should have captured in the Sistine Chapel, and his half-closed lids, the way he barely breathed as he looked at her, released another warn rivulet of hot desire between her thighs. He was worth the wait. His intense gaze said it all, and her bottom lip trembled in anticipation of tasting his lips.

Her hand filled his, and his firm grasp accepted it. A force she could not describe made her body feel weightless as it slid against his, burned her, and then she found herself suddenly beneath him. Time had teased them long enough, and without opening her eyes, she grabbed the box. The sound of cardboard in her hand made him release a groan way down from within him, and it shook her with immediate force when it entered her bloodstream through the shaft of her ear.

Yes, she could read minds. Time had been playing with him. Foil never felt so good between his fingers as his hands trembled to release the latex.

"We have all night," she groaned as she moved against him. "I just can't wait any longer . . . I'm sorry."

He kissed the apology from her mouth hard as he grappled with the thin shield he had to put between them. Her body was like liquid fire. He knew all the things he should do, planned to do, was going to do to blow her mind, but she'd beaten him to the punch; she'd already blown a gasket in his brain. Later. The next time, God help him he couldn't wait.

"You sure," he panted, hovering inches above her.

"Yes . . ."

Her voice had broken and splintered into an elongated wail, and it drew him down like a magnet. Immediate, searing warmth connected him to her, sent a hard convulsion into his abdomen, and set the driving pace of their rhythm. Her hands raked his scalp, his shoulders, and his arms, and her legs encircled his waist, lifting her to greet him each time he moved away.

Oh, yes, she was a melody, and harmony, and rhythm, a deep vocal that called him and measured him out in lusty increments of pleasure. His voice only found escape from his body in guttural emissions, a bass line so deep that he could feel it reverb back to him through her skin. But then she scatted, called his name, stopped the R&B sound to give him Ella in 3-D, and it changed his whole song, hitting sharps within him, and a sudden flat, that came up from the bottom of his insides, rippled through her, and convulsed him so hard, he was sure he'd gone blind.

Moments turned into an eternity as he tried to catch his breath. For a second he thought he might have gone unconscious, until she stirred slowly beneath him. He had to allow her to breathe, he remembered in a sluggish awakening, and rolled over, glad that she'd held on and was still connected to him to lie on him when he'd moved.

She could hear his heartbeat through his chest, and her hands absently petted his shoulders. Sated and comfortable, and joined, she began to drift on the melody of his heart's rhythm. The glue.

"I had planned to take this a little slower," he murmured.

"Shhh . . ." she told him. "I would have lost my mind if you did."

He chuckled from deep within his chest.

"I still have plans. The night is young."

"I know, so do I—why do you think my bag was so heavy."

He felt his body stir. "Really?"

"I've done my quiet research on my hedonist, too. But, I'll only tell you this . . . it's a surprise, and there's candles involved . . . and some oils, and bath salts . . . and oh yeah, some rose petals . . ."

"Great minds think alike." His voice drifted. "Knew we

were going to taste and buy wine, but I have a bottle in my bag. And this room has a fireplace . . . and the inn has room service. But I bought something special."

"Knew you would, that's why I brought glasses."

"Always prepared . . ."

"You were the one who was a Boy Scout, right?"

He smiled again, and kissed the crown of her head and breathed in deeply.

"I want to do this forever."

She chuckled low in her throat. "Yeah, me, too."

"Think we can make this permanent?" He kissed her and drew back. "Oh, baby, you're messing up all my plans."

"What plans are those?" she whispered, kissing the center of his chest, and now peering down at him.

"To wait for your birthday to ask you what we both know I want to."

He held her gaze, and his face blurred as she studied his expression.

"Yeah, I'm serious."

She heard what he did not say, and two tears ran down the bridge of her nose and collided into one single drop that landed in the center of his chest.

"Say what you mean, so I know that we are talking about the same thing."

"Marry me, Denise. Please . . . even though you can read minds—and this has only been a little while."

When he kissed her this time, his mouth was slow and gentle. He wiped her tears away with a tender sweep of his mouth. Nothing in the world could have prepared her heart to expand to receive so much joy . . . not even the little angel that was now buried in her clothes on the floor.

Epilogue

Early fall . . . September . . .

She heard the door chime as she began to do a final tally just before she shut down the register for the evening, expecting Bonita to have returned with two sodas. Instead a friendly smile greeted her from the face of the older lady whom she hadn't seen in months. Sudden joy shot through Denise as she rushed over to the customer, whose name she never knew, and she touched the little angel on her shoulder as she walked.

She'd worried about this elderly patron off and on since she'd first met her, and every holiday since, she'd kept an eye out for her—always disappointed when the lady didn't come into the store to browse.

"Ma'am, how are you? I've missed you." Denise beamed. "I hope you've been well."

"Oh, I have," the woman chuckled. "Have been busy, not sick, and no I haven't gone to glory yet," she added, patting Denise's cheek with a gnarled hand.

"I'm so glad you're well." A sudden peace filled Denise as she studied the lady. "If you want to browse tonight, take all the time in the world. I'm just tallying up and straightening up a bit before we close."

"No," the woman said with a toothless grin. "Today I'm buying a wedding card."

"You are?" Denise could feel a giggle bubbling up inside of her. "Oh, someone close to you? That's so nice!"

"My angel worked, didn't he?"

Denise touched her shoulder again, and an eerie sensation wafted through her.

"Look at your hand. That rock wasn't there a few months back, was it?"

"Well, er, uh . . . no."

The woman clasped Denise's left hand and turned it over, oogling the three carat marquis that was rimmed with baguettes and platinum. "My angel did very, very well, I see. Next week are the nuptials, right?"

"Yes . . . how'd you know?"

"Word travels, just like prayers. Had me a vision, so I came to get your card."

Her mouth hung open.

The woman nodded. "Then it's time to pass that angel on your shoulder to the next dear soul that needs him."

"Ma'am?" She didn't know what to say or think, but was held transfixed by the old woman's knowing gaze.

"A pure and single tear, cried on behalf of someone less fortunate than yourself, releases all of God's miracles. Love. Pure love, the way it was intended to be. You had that in your soul . . . some call it magic, some call it mysteries untold . . . I'm just an old woman, what do I know? Now pass it on."

She could only stand in the middle of her shop as the old woman crept away from her, quickly selected a card, and brought it to the register.

"The card is on the house," Denise murmured. "Fair exchange is no robbery," she whispered in awe.

"Why, thank you, my dear. That it is. . . . I take it he's a nice young man?"

"Oh, ma'am . . . he's wonderful."

The old lady winked and stuffed the card into her ragged coat pocket. "My angel did well, then. See you at the wedding."

"But I don't know how to reach you." Denise watched her elderly customer leave, too stunned to move at first, then dashed to the door a moment after she exited, but stood very, very still when she could not find her.

An old woman who walked with a labored gait could not have simply vanished. Not thinking, Denise rushed out of her shop, glancing quickly in the row of neighboring store windows, and then ran down to the food stand, leaving her shop wide open, trying desperately to find the lady, and instead found Bonita.

"Girl, I was coming with your soda, just got hung up talking at the—"

"Shush. Forget the soda. Did you see an old woman, about four foot eleven, she had to be that short, she was shorter than me, wearing an old black coat, and—"

"Slow down, slow down, sis. What'd she do, shoplift us?"

"No, she made me hit the proverbial lottery! Oh, I have to find her and thank her right now. I didn't understand before. The big lottery—yes, I mean no, not the big number, but the lottery nonetheless. It's too confusing to explain—just help me find her!"

Bonita took her arm and ushered Denise back toward the store and into the shop. "You cannot leave the register open, the store open, running down the mall looking for an old woman who made you hit on a rub-off ticket."

Tears streamed down Denise's face, and she shook Bonita by both arms. Her girlfriend's expression went from amused to stricken.

"Bonnie . . . my angel. You take him. Wear him in good health. Promise not to take him off, and just believe in miracles." She removed the pin, handling it like it was worth millions, and found a thin spaghetti strap on Bonita's scant tank-top to adhere it to.

"Okay, okay—what happened? Did Brandon come in here and rock your world in the last five minutes, and this old lady caught you . . . What, are you having, some sort of religious experience, or somethin'?"

Denise twirled around and laughed, wiping her face with both palms. "Yes! I'd call it a religious experience."

"Oh, figures. You guys get on my nerves."

ABOUT THE AUTHOR

Leslie Esdaile is a native Philadelphian and Dean's List graduate of the University of Pennsylvania, Wharton Undergraduate Program. With many awards to her credit, Esdaile also holds a Masters of Fine Arts degree in Film and Media Arts from Temple University of Philadelphia, and she adds the dimension of filmmaking and visual media to her writing and other artistic and business endeavors.

After a decade as a corporate executive, Leslie Esdaile writes full time and enjoys being a wife, mother of a blended household of four children, and coping with an energetic Labrador named "Girlfriend." Always on the go, she stays involved in community activities, which keep her busy and well-fueled with dramatic content. She draws from life experience in her novels and adds a zany bent of humor to all her projects.

Ms. Esdaile lives and works in Philadelphia with her husband, children, and dog "Girlfriend."

WAIT FOR
LOVE

Melanie Schuster

ACKNOWLEDGEMENTS:

To Frankie Ann Powell, who somehow wasn't mentioned last time. Forgive me; you know it was an accident! To all my friends who continue to encourage me, especially Virgie, and Toni. To my sister-authors for your advice and caring, especially Bette Ford for keeping it real! To the REAL Janice and Curt who inspire me daily. And as always, for Jamil who is always, always in my corner. Thanks for being there for me and for a million other things.

Dedicated to my family,
For their unstinting support, especially my mother

One

"Yes, it *is* him!" the first woman said breathlessly.

"No, it *isn't!* If that were Curt Bowden, what would he be doing here in Detroit? He plays for Atlanta," her companion hissed.

"I think he got traded or something. It was in the *Free Press* or the *News* . . . wait a minute, here he comes!"

While they argued over whether the extremely tall, extremely well-dressed man was indeed the world famous basketball player, each woman unconsciously licked her lips, tossed her hair, and discreetly made sure an ample amount of cleavage was showing. It never hurt to be prepared, and even if this guy weren't the real thing, he was fine. No, make that *phoine*.

Curt Bowden was the kind of man who drew attention wherever he went. Anyone who followed basketball recognized him instantly, both from his outstanding career with the Atlanta Hawks and from the numerous ads in which he appeared. He even had a pair of expensive shoes named after him. Anyone who didn't follow basketball would still be captivated by his lean good looks and his towering height. Curt was always impeccably dressed, even when he was casually attired, as he was now. And as usual, he was oblivious to the women's scrutiny, the irony of which wasn't lost on his irrepressible cousin, Sasha Thomas.

Sasha watched the handsome hunk of man stroll across the restaurant as if he owned it, laughing behind her menu at the women who drooled in his path. Curt really had no idea how he affected the opposite sex. She was still smiling when he joined her at the table and kissed her on the cheek.

"So what time do we go meet this decorator or whatever she is?" he asked in a none-too-thrilled tone of voice.

Sasha perked up immediately. "Right after lunch, and she's an interior *designer,* not a decorator. She's got two degrees, one in art and one in design, and she's the best in town. You'll really like her; she's real down-to-earth and practical. You like my house, don't you?"

That was an understatement—Curt loved his cousin's home, which was why he asked her to hook him up with the woman who made the huge rooms so warm and vibrant. He was already beginning to regret buying the monstrous brick house in Palmer Woods. But due to his size, he was never comfortable in smaller houses; they all made him claustrophobic. Still, the house he purchased after accepting the offer to coach the Detroit Pistons was a bit much for a single man, and he expressed this thought to Sasha.

"Nonsense! You know you'll have family in and out, and I know you'll be doing a lot of entertaining," she rattled on happily, not noticing the look of panic that crossed his face. "That house is perfect for you! And who knows," she added coyly. "You might get married one of these days and then all that space will come in real handy."

This time she did notice his look of horror and wisely started talking about the menu. Sasha knew how sensitive Curt was on the subject of marriage. The women he met seemed to view him as a paycheck and nothing else. Now wasn't the time to be talking so blithely of marriage. She adroitly changed the subject and she kept talking until their lunch was served.

Finally, after a delicious lunch, a few discreet autographs for eager fans and a lot of handshaking, they were able to leave the restaurant and head toward the design center Le Coeur de la Maison. It was the premiere establishment of its kind in Detroit, and their work consistently won awards. Noelle VanHook, the designer who had worked such miracles in Sasha's Grosse Pointe home, was their lead designer, and her services were booked months in advance.

"If we weren't such good friends, I never would have been able to get her to do this on such short notice. But she's so sweet that she agreed to work you in, so be nice to her," Sasha cautioned as they maneuvered the streets of downtown Detroit.

Curt ignored the implication that he might act like a boor and asked the name of the paragon of design virtue.

"She goes by Noelle, but I think that's her middle name, 'cause her card reads J. Noelle VanHook," Sasha offered.

VanHook . . . damn. Curt didn't realize that he had spoken aloud until Sasha took a hand off the steering wheel to poke him in the arm.

"What's the matter with you? You look like you've seen the proverbial ghost, Curt."

Curt shook his head and smiled gamely. "Nah, I just knew someone with that name once. Back in college. But her name wasn't Noelle and she wasn't hardly nice. The exact opposite, actually."

"Oh. Well, *my* Noelle is an absolute doll. The kids love her to death and she loves them. She's become a dear, dear friend. Oh, here's the place now."

Heedless of the afternoon traffic, Sasha executed a masterful turn into the narrow alleyway that led to the tiny parking lot behind the salon. Chattering a mile a minute as usual, she led Curt up to the back door of the establishment and rang the discreet buzzer. They were immediately escorted into the main room of the elegantly appointed showroom and told that Mademoiselle VanHook would be joining them immediately.

Curt surveyed his surroundings with great interest, taking in the expensive and tasteful furnishings and accessories. He was examining an exquisitely austere chandelier, when an arresting fragrance aroused his senses.

"Hello, Sasha! Girl, I love that outfit! You look fabulous, as always."

Curt couldn't really hear his effusive cousin's reply because the sound of that voice left him momentarily unable to move. He finally turned very slowly to face the source of the low, melodic voice, which was unbearably familiar to his ear. *Damn.* It was the one person on earth he never wanted to see again. *Janice VanHook.* She was so engrossed in her conversation with Sasha that she hadn't looked at him at all. He was glad of that; it gave him time to get a good long look at his past.

She hadn't changed much in the twelve years since his junior year of college. She was still slender, although she had put on a few pounds in the most desirable places. Her skin was still the same silky pale cream, she still had the same glorious golden brown hair, but it was tamed into a smooth French twist. Those rosy lips were still as full and pouty as he remembered; the long neck and long graceful hands were exactly the same. Instead of the casually chic clothes she had worn on campus, she was wearing a black suit that probably cost a small fortune, and she had on some high heels that added about three inches to her height. Since she was already tall, she resembled a chic mannequin in some ultra high fashion boutique. Curt could barely breathe as he took in every inch of her, a vision of perfection. Then she directed her gaze at him.

Curt's stomach tensed as though he were about to ward off a lethal blow. In point of fact, Janice's weirdly colored eyes could deliver a knockout punch to the unwary, and Curt was anything but unaware of her dubious charms. He was therefore slightly surprised when her greenish blue eyes widened at the sight of him. *Don't tell me she actually remembers me.* He suppressed a look of amazement and forced himself to be cool.

"Curt . . ." she said breathlessly.

Before she could say another word, Sasha took over. "Noelle, this is my cousin Curt Bowden. Curt, this is Noelle VanHook, the wonderful woman who made my house a home," she said happily.

"It's Janice," she corrected quickly. "I use my middle name for business. I'm really Janice VanHook. Well, Janice Noelle VanHook. Well, anyway," she said, after taking a deep breath, "I actually know your cousin, Sasha. We went to college together."

Janice turned her big eyes to Curt confidently, waiting for his confirmation. Curt merely gazed at her beautiful face and her beguiling smile without saying a word. The silence grew so long as to be embarrassing, at least to Janice. Finally, without a scintilla of warmth, he replied, "Sorry. I don't remember you."

Some thirty minutes later, Curt and Sasha were leaving Le Coeur de la Maison by the back entrance. Curt was whistling a jolly tune while Sasha was surveying him as though a live chicken had sprouted from his forehead.

"Well?" she demanded. "Do you care to tell me why you were behaving like Attila the Negro back there? You couldn't have been ruder to her if you tried! What was that all about?"

Curt plucked the keys to the Mercedes from his cousin's hand; he'd had enough of her cavalier brand of driving for one day. He opened the door for her like the perfect gentleman he was, and after making sure she was seated, he practically danced around to the driver's seat. It was clear that he was in a fine ol' mood.

After starting the car, he turned to Sasha with a big grin on his face.

"Sasha, girl, that was the moment of a lifetime. That woman in there just got paid back for the meanest thing a woman has ever done to me in my life. It took twelve years, but revenge is still sweet, even when it's stone cold."

He then started singing the national anthem of all men, "I Feel Good," at the top of his lungs to Sasha's utter disgust.

He kept it up for several blocks until Sasha punched him in the arm and demanded details.

"Ouch! Okay, if you must know the whole story, here's

what happened. When I was a junior at Georgetown, Ms. VanHook was a freshman. And not just a freshman, *the* freshman; the one who made everybody drool and walk into walls and howl at the moon and stuff. I mean, you see how she looks now; imagine her at eighteen! She wasn't cute, she wasn't pretty—damn, she was *beautiful!* I had a crush on her so tough, I woulda committed a crime to go out with her."

Sasha turned to face him so that she could observe every expression on Curt's darkly handsome face. She was riveted in spite of herself.

"So anyway, I used to see her in the library, in the book-store, places like that. She was always walking around with her head in the air, always by herself, like Miss Anne or some-body. But she would always say hi, at least. We actually had a few little conversations here and there. I mean, she was the beauty queen and I was just this big dumb scholarship jock, but she was always nice to me . . ."

Curt's voice faded for a moment as he recalled those quiet little conversations, the way she had of looking up at him like he was the only man in the universe. He cleared his throat and went on.

"Well, I don't know what put the bright idea in my head, but I asked her to go to the Valentine's Day dance. Some Red and White Ball thing that the Deltas had every year. I was actually scared to ask her, Sash, I was scared she was gonna laugh in my face. I couldn't even look at her when I asked! I was looking down, stammering and shufflin' my big feet like a field hand! 'Uh, Miss Janice if'n it ain't too much trubble, Miss Ma'am, couldya kindly come to da big dance wit' me.'"

Curt stopped talking and shook his head to clear it, and also because Sasha had punched him again.

"That's horrible! I know good and well you didn't sound like that! And you mean she turned you down?" she asked in-dignantly.

"Nope. She said yes, actually. This is where the mean part comes in. She said sure, she'd be happy to go with me, and damned if she didn't actually look happy. All starry-eyed, just like a little movie star or something. We made plans to go, what time to pick her up, everything. Then, bam!"

"What bam? What bam? She stood you up? Hey, make a left here, where are you going?" Sasha pointed in the direction of her home.

"Hold on a minute." Curt guided the car into Sasha's long driveway and parked in front of the four-car garage before finishing the story.

"Okay, I'm all happy like a little kid because the most beautiful woman on earth is going to this dance with me. Then a friend of mine comes over to my dorm one day and says she has to tell me something. She tells me that Janice is telling everybody that she has no intention of going to the dance with a big country cornflake like me, she just told me that to see what I'd do. Janice was actually going with some other guy, some Alpha or Kappa, some big frat boy. And my friend Karla, that's what her name was, Karla didn't want me to get hurt. And I thank her to this day because she kept me from making a big fool out of myself."

Sasha was no longer looking at Curt; she was busy studying her fingernails. She didn't say anything right away but her entire body emanated the desire to blurt something out. Finally she spoke.

"So . . . you ended up not going to the ball at all? You just stayed home and licked your wounds, is that it? And you pretending that you didn't know her, that was some kind of payback?"

"No, I didn't stay home. I took Karla to the ball and we *had* a ball. It was a real nice evening. And yeah, acting like I didn't know who she was, that was payback. I enjoyed it thoroughly," Curt admitted, although he was starting to feel uncomfortable under his cousin's scrutiny.

"Well, I guess I don't understand the male mind, Curt. I mean, wasn't it enough when you showed up at the dance with Klara? Wasn't that enough to show her that you saw through her little ploy and you beat her at her own game?"

"It was Karla. Her name was Karla," Curt corrected her. Then he looked at her with a slightly puzzled frown.

"And she didn't come to the dance, come to think of it. She never showed up."

Two

The object of Curt's scorn was far away from Grosse Pointe at the moment. She was standing just inside the kitchen of her parent's huge brick home, knocking her head against the basement door. The soignée outfit of the salon was gone, replaced by jeans and a paint-spattered University of Michigan sweatshirt.

"Whymewhymewhyme," she chanted over and over. Her mother looked up with mild interest from the salad she was putting together.

"Janice, dear, don't do that. We just had the woodwork redone, it doesn't need any holes in it from your hard head."

Janice stopped tapping her head against the door and moved across the room to drape her long, lithe frame over her mother's.

"That's right, protect the woodwork and not your only daughter. You're a cruel mother," she moaned.

Pat VanHook laughed out loud at that. She stopped tossing salad long enough to give her daughter a big hug and cup her face in her hands.

"Okay, I'll bite. Obviously something traumatic happened—out with it. What's bothering my baby?"

Janice led her mother over to the breakfast table that was surrounded by ladder-back chairs cushioned in a colorful Provençal print. They sat down and Janice clasped her mother's hands tightly.

"Mom, you remember me telling you that Sasha's cousin

was coming into Maison today? Well, her cousin is . . . *him!*"
she said ungrammatically. "The one who broke my heart, destroyed my life, and ruined me forever." Janice dropped her
head and sighed dramatically.

Pat's eyes widened and she had to stifle a laugh. "You mean
that boy who stood you up for that little dance all those years
ago?"

Janice dropped her mother's hands and sat up, pushing her
now completely undone hair out of her eyes. Wincing at her
mother's jaunty tone, she haughtily defended herself.

"It was not *a* dance it was *the* dance, the Delta's Red and
White Valentine's Day Ball. And he was not *a* boy, he was *the*
boy, Curtis Vincent Bowden. He was tall, dark, handsome,
smart, sweet, the best basketball player on campus, and everybody was in love with him. Especially me. And he stood me
up and broke my heart and I've never been the same since.
You know that," she ended indignantly. "What're you cooking? It smells wonderful," she added as she went to inspect
the pots on the stove.

Pat cupped her head in her hand as she watched her beautiful daughter sampling the coq au vin that was simmering on
the six-burner range. Despite Janice's playful theatrics, she
had truly been devastated by that incident. Pat still nursed a
grudge against that boy for what he had done to her daughter.
Mothers never forgot any evil that befell their children.

"So he turned out to be Sasha's cousin, did he? What did
you say when you were introduced? What did *he* say? You
should have pretended like you didn't know him, that
would've fixed his little red wagon," Pat said brightly.

"Mom, how childish would that be? I said something like
'Udda dudda dudda doo,' I think. I was tongued-tied as usual,
and then I started babbling. Mom, he's even better looking than
when we were in school. He was this big, rugged, handsome
boy then, but now he's like . . . whoo-weee, mmm-mmm-*mmm!*
Indescribable. You know how I think Delroy Lindo is like the
finest man on earth next to Daddy? Think Delroy Lindo to the
ninth power, Mom. Dark, strong . . . and he's *bald*. You *know*

how sexy that is on a good-looking man." Janice sighed deeply and came back over to the table to join her mother.

"And the worst part is, he didn't know me from Adam nor Eve. I'm all 'We went to school together,'" Janice mocked herself in a chirpy singsong, "and he looked at me with all the interest one would show bird poop on the windshield. 'Sorry. I don't remember you.' That's all he said," she finished mournfully. "And I have to design the entire interior for that gigantic house he just bought."

Stifling a scream, she looked up at the ceiling. "Take me now, Lord. Now!"

"Take you where, Mommy?"

The curious voice was that of her six-year-old son, Justin. Janice forgot all her angst as she swooped him into her arms for a big smacking kiss.

"Take me to my babies, that's where! Where're your sisters?" Janice asked happily.

They were, in fact, right behind Justin. Stacey, the oldest at twelve, and Lisa, the middle at ten, walked into the kitchen followed by Janice's older brother Conrad, nicknamed Butchie. He had collected the girls from their dance class and Justin from his karate class and ferried them to his parents' house, where the family usually met for dinner on Wednesday nights. Butchie was at the moment taking some verbal abuse from his nieces.

"Mommy, Uncle Butchie's feet stink. I mean they *really* stink!" Lisa confided.

Butchie's indignant denial was drowned out by Stacey's agreement.

"She's right, Mommy. They smell terrible! I think Uncle Butchie has hyperhydrosis," she said sadly. "That's excessive perspiration," she added. "We had to ride in the backseat with his stinky shoes all the way here!"

Janice was torn between agreeing with her daughters and chiding them for hurting her brother's feelings. But Conrad needed no such defense. Impressed as he was that his niece had a word like *hyperhydrosis* at her immediate command, he was still out for vengeance.

"My gym shoes stink, not my feet. My feet smell like roses—wanna whiff?" he asked, whipping off his soft leather loafers.

The two girls screamed and ran from the room with their uncle dead on their heels, Janice calling after them to not rip and run through Grandma's house. Justin took off after them and so did Biscuit, Pat's little bichon frise, who was never far away from some member of the family. Janice sighed with happiness.

She went to the sink to wash her hands and begin setting the table for dinner.

"Dining room or kitchen, Mom?"

"Oh, let's eat in the dining room. We're having fancy food, so why not. And before you ask, there's plain baked chicken for the kids. You and your brothers wouldn't have eaten anything remotely like coq au vin when you were their age. And speaking of age, where in the world did Stacey get that word from? That child is way too well-read for a twelve-year-old."

"Her medical dictionary. Since she decided she's going to be a doctor, she reads that thing assiduously. She learns a new term every day. My little prodigy," Janice said proudly.

Janice worked silently for a few minutes, and then remarked that she actually owed Curt Bowden a big thank you.

"If he hadn't smashed my heart to pieces and weakened my resistance, I wouldn't have gotten mono and come home. And if I hadn't been feeling so miserable, I wouldn't have decided to transfer to school here. And I wouldn't have stayed here and found my babies. And my life would not be a fraction as wonderful as it is now. I don't know what I would be without my kids," she mused. "I'd be . . . who knows? Nothing. Crazy. Empty. Instead of a very happy and very hungry mom, which is what I am. Is Daddy in the studio? Can I go get him?" she asked in one of her lightning-fast segues.

Pat glanced at the clock above the kitchen window and

said, "He should be up in about two minutes. He has radar where food and his grandkids are concerned."

On cue, Cyrus VanHook entered the kitchen from his basement studio. "Yes, and where my beautiful bride is concerned, too. And don't you forget it, woman," he said loudly as he grabbed his still shapely wife and planted a noisy kiss on her willing lips.

In very short order everyone was seated around the dining room table saying grace. A stranger observing the charming picture they made might have assumed that it was a layout for a glossy magazine ad and they were all models. And the stranger would have been partially right, since Patricia Dayton had been a top model for years before marrying Cyrus Conrad VanHook, the virtuoso jazz pianist. She was one of the first black models to become a familiar name; she was the Naomi Campbell or Tyra Banks of her era. And Cyrus was handsome enough to stop traffic, which he often did while traveling in Europe. It was their stunning beauty that gave their three children such good looks.

Pat was tall, slim, and fair skinned with a wealth of wavy hair, which she had stopped coloring years ago. She wore her striking silver hair in a chin-length bob that showed off her timeless features and her arresting blue-green eyes, the same color as her daughter's. Cyrus, on the other hand, was so richly dark that he appeared burnished. His strong African features and full, chiseled lips still made Pat's heart skip a beat when he entered a room. That they were still madly in love with each other after thirty-five years of marriage was evident to everyone who ever met them.

Janice was an eerie replica of her mother, although taller than Pat. Conrad also resembled his mother's side of the family, with fair coloring and dark brown hair, which he kept cut close to his scalp. He was tall like Cyrus, both of them were about six foot three, as was the middle child, Randall. But Randall was slender and lean like his mother, whereas

Conrad was broad-shouldered, well-muscled, and taut. Randall, known as Randy, was a perfect blend of his parents, with coffee brown skin, long-lashed dark eyes, and black hair that was coiled in stylized twists. He also inherited his mother's fashion gene because he was the most clothes conscious of all the siblings.

Rounding out the group were Janice's three adopted children. All of them caramel brown with thick heads of healthy black hair, they strongly resembled one another, which was as it should be. Stacey, Lisa, and Justin were natural brother and sisters; everyone thought it was lucky that they were still together, but Janice always said that she was the lucky one. Tall, skinny Stacey with her amazing intellect; sweet, happy Lisa with her vivid imagination; and little Justin, the talker and the doer, whose curiosity was boundless: They were her angel babies. The funny thing was, in the way of adopted children the world over, they looked like they were blood relatives of the VanHooks, instead of being love relatives. And they certainly acted like VanHooks; Janice's family liked to play and teased one another a lot.

As soon as dinner was over, Janice took a quick glance at her watch.

"Okay, guys, we need to be clearing the table, loading the dishwasher, and hitting the road. We've got to get you guys bathed and in bed at a decent hour," she said, standing up and beginning to put actions to words.

Pat stopped her daughter by placing a hand on her arm. "Oh, leave that alone, Jannie. Your father and I can handle that. You do too much as it is," she said firmly.

"Mom, please, I didn't cook a morsel of this food, I just ate like a horse," Janice said cheerfully.

Pat shook her head slightly at her daughter. After suggesting that the children begin the process of getting their things together for the trip home, she patted the chair next to her.

"You just sit down, Superwoman. I want to know how you're going to handle this Curt Bowden person. Isn't this whole thing going to make you uncomfortable? Are you sure you want to take this on?"

The mention of Curt's name got an immediate response from Butch and Randy. Even though neither one of them were die-hard sports fans, they both knew who he was and why he was in Detroit.

"So what deal is Mom talking about, Jannie? Something going on that your big brothers should know about?"

This was from Randy, who accompanied the remark with a sardonic smile. Janice dropped her head into her hands and moaned.

"Look, you guys. I knew Curt Bowden while we were at Georgetown. He not only stood me up for some Delta dance, when we met today, he didn't know me from a can of paint. He's Sasha Thomas' cousin, and before I knew who he was, I had agreed to do his house. So now I'm stuck. Any sympathy and comfort you can offer would be welcome, any sarcasm, cheap jokes at my expense, or general laughter would be most unwise," she warned.

Butch and Randy looked at each other for about thirty seconds before bursting into loud shouts of laughter, which made Janice resort to the secret weapon of youngest daughters the world over.

"Daddy! See how they do me?" she said in exasperation, although she was trying not to laugh, too.

"This could be highly traumatic for me! It could make me neurotic or otherwise deranged. It could also make me a lot of money, but at what cost to my psyche?"

At the mention of money, both men stopped laughing.

"Now you know, sis, the man has got the bucks. He was one of the top paid players in the NBA for the last ten years. He was just made assistant coach for the Pistons, but he's probably just doing that for fun 'cause he definitely does not need the Benjamins," mused Butch.

"Charge him double your usual fee. Or triple. He should be glad you're taking the job on at all. Hit him where he lives and he'll not only pay for having the best-looking house in town, he'll pay for ruining your life and leaving you the bitter old maid that you are today," he added, and ducked to avoid the dinner roll that Janice aimed between his eyes.

Pat was disgusted with all of them. "Honestly, you children! I'm concerned about your sister's emotional welfare and you two are making jokes. And Cyrus, you aren't saying a word! What is wrong with you people?"

Cyrus looked at his wife with great affection before replying. "Dear, Janice is a consummate professional and I know she can handle her own affairs. She will do this project with all the skill and talent she brings to all her work, and that will be the end of it. The fact that she's going to charge him four times her normal fee is her business. And if he messes with her, the boys will see to it that the Pistons will be out one assistant coach."

Having made that pronouncement, he leaned back with a relaxed grin. "I don't think there's going to be a problem, do you?"

"Daddy, I am not going to overcharge that man. Unless he turns out to be completely obnoxious, which seems unlikely. I'm going to get in there, get the job done, and get out of there as fast as possible."

She turned to her mother and touched her cheek. "No worries, Mom. The only thing that will come out of this is a lovely new abode for Mr. Curt Bowden and a lovely fat check for me."

Janice smiled broadly and went to see what was taking the children so long. Her brothers looked briefly at each other before commenting.

"Yeah, well, if this moron tries anything, it'll be a lovely fat lip for him. Standing my sister up, who the hell does he think he is?" muttered Butch.

"And trying to pretend like he didn't remember her. *Please*. A blind man would remember her from the description alone," groused Randy. "He just better watch his back."

Three

Mornings at Janice's house were studies in organized chaos. She rose at 5:00 every day, to make sure that her children had time to wash up, dress, and have a proper breakfast. She also had to make sure that their daily activities were in order. In the breakfast area of the spacious condo, a large corkboard dominated the main wall, which was as it should be. It held the huge calendar that ruled their lives. Soccer practice, karate practice, dance recitals, doctor and dentist appointments, every move the family made was inscribed on it. Janice never made a move without consulting the board.

She was, in fact, perusing it when Stacey came into the kitchen bearing a comb, brush, and hair ribbon.

"Mommy, can you help me? I'm having a bad hair day," she sighed.

"It will be my pleasure," Janice replied, giving her a hug and a good-morning kiss.

As Janice brushed the child's long, thick black hair, Stacey pored over the morning paper. She was addicted to newspapers, CNN, the Discovery Channel, The Learning Channel, as well as anything that pertained to medicine in any way. Janice worried that Stacey was a bit too serious at times, something that was evident in Stacey's next remark.

"Mommy, do you ever wonder where our birth father is?"

Janice did a double take that Stacey couldn't see, since she was sitting in front of her mother.

"No, darling, I don't. Do you?"

"Not really. Not until I read that story about this man who had disappeared and then he popped up and wanted his kids back 'cause they had been adopted and he didn't know about it and . . ."

Janice stopped brushing her daughter's hair and tilted her head back so that Stacey could look directly into her eyes.

"That is not going to happen, kiddo. I've never tried to censor your reading material, but I think that you sometimes read things that are a bit advanced for you. Emotionally, not intellectually, that is. Please do not, I repeat, do *not* let that kind of thinking into your head, okay? I got this, all right?"

Stacey nodded her head with difficulty, as Janice still held her by the topknot of her hair.

"Okay. But, Mommy—"

"No buts. I'm the mom; I've got the car keys and credit cards to prove it. Let me worry about things that need to be worried about. Like what do you guys want for breakfast?"

Lisa entered in time to hear the last part. "Mmm, pancakes! With blueberries, please!"

Justin, who was barefoot and was having trouble buttoning his shirt, followed her.

"Mommy, did you sign my paper for the field trip?"

"Yes, I have your slip, honey, but a better question is where are your socks? And shoes? Lisa, can you help him get ready while I finish your sister's hair? And then after breakfast I'll do your hair and we will be out the door. It's our day to car pool, so we have to leave early."

Janice sailed through the early-morning rituals with her usual joy; nothing could upset her in the morning. Even the prospect of spending the rest of that morning with Curt Bowden held no terror for her. As long as her babies were fine, all was right with her world.

Janice truly loved her work. This was due to her more than congenial work situation, as well as her love of design. If she had searched for years she couldn't have found a more ideal place of employ. Le Coeur de la Maison was owned by Armand François, a tall, engaging Frenchman who hadn't lost his accent for all his years in the United States. His love for beautiful things and his unerring taste had never let him down in his pursuit of a career or a wife. He was married to a smart, stunning woman from Senegal named Amyanah, and they were the parents of two charming daughters.

At the moment, his newest client, Curt, was in the tiny office of his best designer learning how the process went.

"Well, Mr. Bowden, what I like to do is get to know my clients very personally," Janice said. "I feel that it's vital to understand what the client wants in terms of a home. Your interests, hobbies, likes, dislikes, and passions all go into designing the kind of environment that will make you feel most at home. To that end, I like to both talk to my clients a great deal in the beginning, as well as do some window-shopping, either in person or via catalog. Just to get a feel for their taste," she explained.

"How does that sound to you?" she finally asked. "I know it's a lot to take in, but I do get carried away sometimes. I hope I haven't overwhelmed you!"

Overwhelmed wasn't too bad a description; Curt was getting more uncomfortable by the minute. It wasn't what Janice was saying, it was the way she was saying it, with an over-abundance of charm. She grew more animated and lively as she continued to expound on her way of getting at the root of the customer's desires and bringing those things to life. Her eyes sparkled with anticipation and her smiles were very genuine. He hated to admit it, but she looked adorable. The next few weeks were going to be tricky. Just how much time was she talking about, anyway?

"Look, Ms. VanHook—" he began.

"Oh, please, call me Janice! Ms. VanHook is way too formal for me!" she admitted.

Curt was once again knocked off his stride. "Okay. Janice it is. And you must call me Curt. What I was going to say is, I don't really have a lot of time. The regular basketball season starts November first. We'll be doing exhibition games shortly and we'll be on the road a lot. In the meantime, we're already in regular practice, so my time is kind of limited. All this conversing and window-shopping . . . I don't see how I'm going to have time to do all that," he said frankly.

Janice smiled confidently. "Curt, I don't think that will be a problem. We need to meet at the house so we can go through it and decide on any structural changes you want to make. While we're doing that, you can give me some ideas on what you like and don't like, any special furnishings or concepts that you might have in mind, and tell me what you're looking for in a home. The rest of it, we can work out. Do you have a computer?" she asked.

At Curt's nod of affirmation, Janice smiled. "We can get a lot done via e-mail, Curt. Don't worry, you won't even know I'm around," she said cheerfully.

Curt felt a tiny tremor, like the earth shifting beneath his feet. Janice VanHook was nothing like he imagined. He kept getting flashes of the sweet, pretty girl who had captured his heart so long ago. She smelled wonderful; fresh, clean, yet sweet and delicious all at once. *How can someone who looks so innocent have been such a cow?* All of a sudden, Janice looked up and smiled. *Damn. That same smile, like I'm the only man in the world.* He could barely focus on what she was saying.

"Well, Curt, since it's the beginning of September now, we have a few weeks before the exhibition season starts. So if we get right to it, we can get quite a lot of work done before you get on the road. If you like, we can get started today. Do you have an hour or so to spare?" Janice asked offhandedly.

Curt agreed immediately. The sooner they got started on this project, the sooner it would be done and his contact with this woman would be over. Even after all the years since college, Janice VanHook still got to him. That kind of temptation was something he didn't need or want in his life at this point. Janice excused herself to get a jacket and let the receptionist know she was leaving. This gave Curt an opportunity to stare at her leggy figure as she left the tiny office, and to savor the essence of the feminine perfume that trailed her. *Nothing but trouble, nothing.*

Janice pulled the door to her office open so quickly that Lisette almost fell in headfirst. She worked at Maison part time between college classes. Ignoring the obvious fact that Lisette had been attempting to eavesdrop, Janice grabbed her arm and dragged her along into the ladies' room. The room was unusually large due to the fact that the building had undergone several incarnations before becoming Maison; it was little more than a toilet and sink surrounded by an ornate screen in the corner of an ample storeroom. To Lisette's utter amazement, Janice immediately splashed cold water on her face and began prowling the room like an edgy Siamese cat.

"I'm in trouble, Lissie, deep, deep, trouble. I can't do this. I thought I could, but I can't. It's not possible. He's too much. He's too tall, he's too fine, he smells too good, and who the hell does he think he is not remembering me, I mean, damn, it was a zillion years ago, but really, I mean, after all. Am I that forgettable?"

The last remark was made to the eighteenth-century gilded mirror into which Janice stared intently after muttering and circling around the clueless Lisette. She looked okay, a little flushed around the cheekbones, but okay. She was wearing some exquisitely tailored high-waisted slacks of wool crepe and a Thomas Pink shirt, which fit perfectly. Her hair was a mass of natural waves with a side part, and it framed her delicate face nicely. Her finely arched brows were raised in question and she did have a look of frenzy, but other than that she looked fine. Lisette seized the opportunity to get right into her business.

"Ah-ha! So there is something going on with you two! He is *way* too fine to be just another client," she mused, tapping her finger against her lower lip. "This could be extremely intriguing; Ms. Noelle VanHook, workaholic and *maman extraordinaire,* has finally met a man who can distract her from her goal of being the perfect mother! I gotta meet this brother—anybody who gets you this ditzy has gotta be off the *chain!"* Lisette said happily. She was reaching for the door to the ladies' room when Janice stopped her.

"I'll explain everything to you later, but you've got to come with us now. You must. Don't leave me alone with that man, not for five minutes, do you hear me? I swear, I'll make it up to you," she hissed.

Lisette was sorely tempted to tag along just to see what was transpiring between the usually unflappable Janice and the super-sized hunk of dark chocolate from whom she was hiding. Heaving a huge sigh, which was only part theater, she shook her head.

"As nosy as I am and as much as I want you to hook up with Handsome out there, I have a class in about forty-five minutes. But I reserve the right to hear the story behind all this drama. I'm impressed—I haven't seen this much emotion from you since Justin broke his arm in preschool! You go, girl!" And with that, Lisette left Janice to her fate.

"I'll get her for that. Hmmph. Okay, I'm grown, I'm a professional, and I am a strong black woman besides being a mother. I can handle him. Forget *me*, will you? I got your 'forgot' right here," she growled.

Thus fortified by her little pep talk, she marched out to meet the enemy.

They drove out to Palmer Woods in a guarded near-silence, Curt driving his big Mercedes sport utility vehicle even though he wasn't as familiar with Detroit as Janice, who knew it like the proverbial back of her hand. As he pointed out, he had to get to know the terrain sometime, and he may as well start now. Soon they were at the huge house. Curt pulled into the circular driveway and they looked at each other, then the imposing structure. Any awkwardness Janice was feeling completely disappeared when Curt gave her a sheepish smile.

"I think I'm in way over my head here," he confessed. "I

have no idea what made me buy this . . . barn. Do you think I can change my mind?"

Janice's heart just melted at his words. Nothing is more irresistible than a big macho man who needs help of some kind. She immediately reached over and squeezed his hand. "I think the first thing we need to do is take a look at the place. And I think that we can make it into a place that you will love calling home. Trust me!"

The smile that she gave him with those words made Curt feel like King of the World and King Rat at the same time. He regretted once again pretending like he didn't remember her from college. It was immature and futile, and she didn't deserve crap like that. After helping her down from the SUV and walking with her to the huge front doors of his new home, he turned to her to confess, but his words were stopped as she inserted the key he had handed over at their first meeting and threw open the double doors with the diamond-shaped mullioned panes of glass.

"Wow . . ." she murmured, looking around with awe. "Welcome home, Mr. Bowden."

They stared reverently around the huge foyer in which they stood; it was big enough to hold a Pistons' practice session. The walls were wainscoted in burnished oak and the vaulted ceiling was like that of a small cathedral. They stood there gaping for a few seconds until Janice recovered herself.

"Okay, let's take a look around," she said cheerfully. Then she looked at Curt with a wicked smile and asked if he had any bread crumbs handy. "We might have to leave a trail to find our way back," she pointed out.

That broke the ice for Curt and he laughed out loud at last. "Okay, Gretel, let's get going," he agreed.

It took almost an hour for them to scour the house. There was a divided staircase in the front, plus a separate staircase that led down to the kitchen. There were two formal parlors, a formal dining room with linenfold paneling, a butler's pantry, a breakfast room, and an enormous kitchen with the biggest stove Curt had ever seen, as well as double ovens.

There was also a greenhouse and a sunroom, as well as a room lined with shelves that looked to be a library, in addition to two powder rooms, and this was just the first floor!

Curt actually lost count of the rooms on the second floor; there was the obligatory master suite with its own bathroom and a dressing room that was the size of many studio apartments. Next to that was a nursery with a small maid's room that opened off of it, and so on and so on. They ended up in the basement of the house, a huge, dark expanse that made Janice wrinkle her nose.

"I'm not too fond of basements," she said darkly. "Not basements or the things that live in them."

She gingerly stepped out into the musty-smelling area and squinted around. "Hey, critter, critter, critter. If you're down here, you'd better stay out of my way," she said in a breathy singsong. "I have a big man with me who will stomp you."

With a sigh of relief she located the light switch and immediately turned it on, illuminating the big empty space. She was so occupied with looking around the basement that she missed the look of amused admiration that Curt was giving her.

She's something else, he thought. She wasn't stuck-up or full of self-importance, she was down-to-earth, friendly, and a little bit crazy in the best kind of way. This was the girl of his dreams from so many years ago, at least the way he remembered her from their brief encounters. He dragged himself out of his reverie as Janice was tossing questions at him.

"Do you play pool, Curt? This would be the perfect spot for a game room. In fact, you could put a whole arcade down here! It's huge! When your family comes to visit, you'll have lots and lots of room," she added.

"My family?" he answered slowly. "What makes you think I have a family at all," he challenged.

Janice stopped walking off the length of the main room of the basement and rejoined Curt with a smile on her face. "I know lots of things about you, Curt. You're from Gary, Indiana, and everybody was shocked that you didn't go play for Bobby Knight, but you really wanted to play for John

Thompson at Georgetown. You have three brothers and three sisters, your dad passed away when you were twelve, your mom remarried when you were fifteen, you're the middle child, and if you hadn't been a basketball player, you wanted to be a high school history teacher. And you eventually wanted to be a principal," she finished.

Curt's jaw had dropped open during this recitation and he looked nothing short of dumbfounded. "Where did you read all that? I know there's been a lot of stuff written about me, but where did you find it all?"

Janice's smile faded and she looked inexplicably hurt for a moment. "Let's go back upstairs, shall we?"

Suiting action to words, she hurried up the stairs with Curt right behind her. They were in the sunny kitchen when she turned to look him full in the face. "I didn't read those things anywhere, Curt. You told me those things. I know you don't remember me, but I really do remember you from Georgetown. We used to talk in the library sometimes and once in a while you would walk me back to my dorm. *I* didn't forget *you*," she murmured.

Curt was saved from answering by the irritating chiming of Janice's cell phone. She answered it and was speaking quietly to the caller while Curt collected his thoughts. *Damn, I'm a real jackass,* he berated himself. Why in the world had he decided to be so petty and childish? It was obvious that Janice had hung on his every word the same way he had on hers. However vain and selfish she had been in college, she had obviously matured into a really nice woman. He owed her an explanation and an apology.

"Curt, I'm sorry, but we need to head back to the salon. There's some kind of crisis that apparently only I can solve, although I doubt it's that serious."

They left the house by the back door so that Curt could take another look at the beautifully kept yard and gardens. What he was really doing was taking another look at Janice; her lovely, animated face, the riot of golden brown waves lit up by the bright autumn sun, with the crisp autumn leaves paying homage to her creamy complexion. She was the same sweet girl he'd had a crush on, there was no doubt in his mind. But how the hell was he going to tell her what a stupid thing he'd done?

Luckily, she kept up a steady stream of chatter all the way back to Le Coeur de la Maison, talking about colors and textures and styles of furniture. It made it impossible for Curt to get a word in, for which he was grateful. He was going to have to say something to her, and soon, but what and when he had no idea. He was just happy that they were going to be working together. This was a woman he wanted to know better—and fast.

In a short time they were back at the salon and Janice had no sooner opened the back door than she was greeted by Armand, who was in something of a tear. His normal Gallic calm was absent as he instructed Janice to go to his office immediately.

"*Mon Dieu*, that man is impossible!" he exclaimed, and continued to explain the situation in a combination of French and English that was impossible to understand unless one knew him well, as Janice did. She also knew the very client of whom he spoke; only one man could raise Armand's blood pressure in that manner.

"Oh, Armand, don't worry, it's probably just a misunderstanding. I'll get Mr. Chauncey settled down and everything will be fine, don't worry," she soothed.

At the very mention of the name, Armand blanched and groaned. "Hurry, *ma petite* Noelle, the man is insane. He will not be happy until I am in my grave!"

Janice smiled an apology at Curtis and took off. Armand sat down on a high stool and heaved a huge sigh of relief.

"*Pardonnez-moi* for the confusion, I am usually a very calm man. But this customer, he is so demanding, so unreasonable! But my Noelle will calm him. Noelle has a special gift with men, you know. She has them, how you say, eating out of her hand. There is no man who can escape the charm of my Noelle. Beautiful, brilliant, and charming. A devastating combination, no?"

Curt could barely reply, so fixed was he on Armand's assessment of Janice. *Eating out of her hand, huh? And I almost fell for it,* he thought savagely. Well, if little Miss Janice Noelle VanHook thought that Curt Bowden was going to be another one of her docile sheep led to slaughter, she had another thing coming. *So you can handle all the men, can you darlin'? Well, this is one man you won't be handling. I am* not *the one.*

Four

The next two weeks were like something out of a dream for Janice. To be more precise, it was her most dire nightmare come true. Curt Bowden was the worst client she had ever encountered. From the moment she had left his side in the rear of Le Maison to soothe the fluttery little Mr. Chauncey, he turned into the Customer from the Seventh Level of Hell. Nothing pleased him, he rejected all her ideas, he broke appointments; Janice was at her wits' end. She said as much to Lisette, with whom she was sharing a late lunch at the Greektown Fishbone's.

"He hates me and I have no idea why, Lisette. I absolutely do not see how I'm going to complete this project. He won't listen to a single thing I have to say, and I've had to resort to all sorts of subterfuge to get anything done. I make two drawings that I know he'll hate and one that I think he'll love just so I can get him to agree to something! I'm working way, way too hard on this," she muttered unhappily.

Before Lisette could respond, Sasha, of all people, turned up at their table. Fishbone's was, after all, a very popular place. Only Lisette heard the tiny whimper that escaped Janice's lips when she set eyes on Sasha.

"Well, ladies, how are you? Noelle, this is a coincidence. I've been meaning to call you and find out how things are going with Curt's house," Sasha said with a smile.

Janice looked down at her untouched crab salad and then

up into Sasha's friendly face. She was too honest to lie and too desperate to pretend.

"The only way things could be going worse is if the house burst into flames. Your cousin and I aren't communicating well. Well, that's not exactly true—we aren't communicating at all," she confessed.

Without waiting for an invitation, Sasha immediately sat down. Janice looked like someone had just stolen her puppy.

"What's the problem, Noelle? Curt is usually very easygoing. He's my favorite cousin because he's so sweet and kind," she added guilelessly.

Lisette and Janice looked at each other and burst out laughing. Lisette was the first to recover, although Janice's strained laugh ended on a hiccup soon after.

"Poor Noelle hasn't seen much of this kinder, gentler Curtis Bowden of whom you speak," Lisette said dryly. "She's only seen the autocratic, impossible-to-satisfy version."

Janice nodded unhappily. "One day he likes brown. The next day, no, it's green that he favors and why can't I remember that. One day it's antiques; the next day it's ultra modern. Not blinds, draperies! Not draperies, *shutters,* for heaven's sakes, why in the world would he want draperies!" She moaned aloud and massaged her tense temples with her fingertips. "I'm really on the verge of resigning, Sasha. And what I don't understand is how he got to be like this! He was so sweet in college!"

Only Sasha's burning desire to know more prevented her from pouncing on that tidbit like a ravening cougar on a prairie dog. With every indication of insouciance, she lazily asked how Janice actually knew Curt at Georgetown.

For the first time that day, Janice smiled. "Oh, honey, he was my very first crush. Sasha, I was so crazy about your cousin, I couldn't see straight," she admitted.

Sasha leaned back in her chair with a look of utter amazement. Flagging down the nearest waiter, she ordered a bottle of white wine. "And hurry, we're going to need it as soon as humanly possible," she instructed. "Okay, girl, get to dishin'. You had a crush on my cousin, hmm?"

Janice nodded, a faraway look in her eyes. "Picture it, girls; I was a sixteen-year-old bookworm freshman. I was away from home for the very first time in my life and I was so timid that any attempt at conversation paralyzed me. I was so shy that some of my relatives thought I was mute—no joke. That's partially why I went away to school. I graduated from high school at fifteen and I thought that if I went right on to college I would somehow magically lose the bashfulness. My brothers were in school on the East Coast, in fact, Randall was at Howard, which is why I picked Georgetown. Anyway, I'd only been there a few days when I realized that it wasn't the brightest idea in the world."

Janice stopped talking to take a sip of the wine, which had by now arrived. She also began to pick at her salad, a move that irritated Lisette, who wanted to hear more of the story.

"Okay. So here I am, tall, gangling, looking like Olive Oyl in a fright wig, knowing no one, and scared of my own shadow. And one day I bumped smack into the most handsome boy I'd ever seen in my life, Curtis Bowden. Only he was this big-time basketball star and I was this rickety-looking little freshman who couldn't say boo to a goose. I was pitiful," she said frankly.

"He was so nice to me, though! He picked up my books for me and he even talked to me for a few minutes. And then I started seeing him around campus here and there, mostly at the library. And he always took the time to talk to me and make me feel like I was, you know, *normal.* Not a goofy nerd, not a social misfit, just a real girl, you know?" Janice sighed briefly and sipped some more wine.

Lisette and Sasha were riveted as the tale unfolded. Janice leaned forward on the table and propped her cheek up with her long, slender hand.

"Well, it was the end of January and it was freezing in D.C. Absolutely frigid for some reason. I was coming out of the library at the same time Curt was coming in, and he turned around and started walking with me. He even took my arm, can you imagine? We went into this little café and got hot chocolate and we sat and talked. Honey, it was like being the prom queen, Miss America, and the *Playboy* centerfold all wrapped up in one! I was out in public with Curt Bowden, *the* Curt Bowden!

"And for once I was talking coherently, actually making decent conversation. I even made him laugh a couple of times. I also didn't drop anything or spill anything the way I usually did when I was nervous, which was always. Anyway, we were getting ready to leave and when we stood up, Curt took my elbow and looked down at me and asked me to go to the Delta's Red and White Ball on Valentine's Day weekend. I was so happy, I almost burst into tears, but I held it together. I did cry later on, when I was telling my mother about it. My first date!"

Lisette gave Janice a peculiar look. "You mean your first date in college, don't you?"

"No, I mean my first date *period!* I told you, I was extremely timid when I was younger. So much so that my parents took me to doctors because they thought I might be autistic or something. Seriously!" Janice gave a brief laugh at the expressions on the two women's faces.

"Nope, I never, ever had a date in my life. This was going to be my first time going out and it was going to be with the first boy that I ever liked, Curtis Bowden. I was so excited that I didn't sleep for days after he asked me. Daddy was touring in Europe and Mom sent me a beautiful white dress from Paris. It was bias-cut silk and it had a halter neck and a really low back, which was okay on me since I had the flattest chest in North America. Still do, actually." Janice looked down at what she considered her inadequate bosom and shrugged.

"She also sent me a fabulous black velvet cape with a white silk lining, and it was utterly gorgeous. I actually looked pretty in it with my hair up and everything," she recounted, her eyes going misty at the memory.

Lisette was really into the tale now, while Sasha was equally captivated but not saying a word. Lisette bounced on her chair and demanded more. "Well? What was his reaction when he saw you? Did you have a good time? Did you kiss him good night, what?"

Janice took a final swallow of the chardonnay before answering. "He didn't show up," she said sadly. "I finally took the gown off at midnight. I cried all night and got sick as the proverbial dog with mono the next week, which is another saga altogether. So that's my Curt Bowden story," she said bravely. She then looked directly at Sasha. "Please don't mention a word of this to Curt. He doesn't remember me, much less the whole incident, and I'd just as soon keep it that way."

Sasha was too stunned to speak at first, but she managed to agree to Janice's wishes. *Just wait until I get my hands on that moron cousin of mine! Men!*

Lisette's reaction was much more volatile than Sasha's; she was ready to string Curt Bowden up by his jewels in a public place. "Let him be an example to all the dogs, players, and lowlifes out there. What a horrible thing to do to a sweet young girl! Let's make everything in his wretched house paisley and plaid, that will fix him but good!" she sputtered. As always, her slight French accent became more prominent as her anger mounted, which always tickled Janice.

"Forget it, Lisette, it's ancient history. I don't bear a grudge and neither should you. I just wish he wasn't so combative and difficult about this job. I really don't think I'm the person for the job, Sasha. I'm going to give it one more week and then I'll have to suggest someone else take over," she said with finality.

"I'll talk to him, Janice. I know I can make him see reason. Just let me talk to him," promised Sasha. *And boy, do I have an earful for him!*

Lisette wasn't finished, though. "But you aren't shy now, at least you don't seem to be. When did you get over that," she wanted to know.

Janice smiled hugely at that and glanced over to Sasha for confirmation. "Honey, as soon as I became a mother, all traces of shyness left me forever. When you have children, they become the driving force of your life; everything else is secondary. I couldn't worry about what people thought about me or whether I would make a fool out of myself, I had to see to my babies," she said firmly.

Sasha nodded her head in agreement. She had always felt that Janice was a sweet, special person; now she knew it for a fact. And that dunderhead cousin of hers was going to know it, too, as soon as she got her hands on him.

Unfortunately, Sasha's decision to shake some sense into her cousin arrived at the same time as a nasty bout of stomach flu that worked its way through her four children. Once Curt was back in town from a round of exhibition games, she had no time to concern herself with anything but getting her family well. She couldn't suggest to him that he behave himself with Janice or lose the best designer in town, which is why he and Janice were still at odds.

At that moment, Janice was picturing the exact size and thickness of the stick she'd like to beat him with. The phone conversation had started out politely enough, but it went downhill immediately.

"Janice, I need to talk to you about those counters for the kitchen. I'm not sure they're what I had in mind," Curt lied in his deep, resonant voice.

Janice pulled the phone away from her ear and stared at it with hatred. She squeezed her eyes tightly shut as she brought it back to her ear and spoke in soft, measured tones so as not to scream.

"Well. You didn't like the granite that came with the house. We tried the slate but you didn't like that, either. We got the Carrera marble in from Italy and you thought it was too 'marble-y.' So now you don't like the Pewabic tiles, is that it? What would you like this time, Curt? Glass? Stainless steel? Plutonium? What would make you happy today," she said through tightly clenched teeth.

Curt chuckled to himself as he heard the unmistakable strain in her voice. *Not handling me too well, are you, darlin'?* "Well, I'll be off the road for a few days and I think we should meet at the house so I can show you what I have in mind," he suggested.

"Fine, fine, fine. Any day but Saturday works for me," Janice said immediately. Anything to get on with this job!

"Oh, but Saturday is the *only* day that works for me," Curt said silkily. This time he had to cover the receiver to keep from laughing at the outright dismay in her voice.

"But Saturday is . . . okay, but it has to be first thing in the morning. Be there at eight fifteen, not a minute later," she said in exasperation, and to her own surprise, she slammed down the handset. *That man is one of Satan's minions for sure! Why me, Lord? What did I do to deserve this?*

Saturday morning came all too soon for Janice. It was a bright sunny fall day but it could have been the dead of winter in the middle of an ice storm as far as she was concerned.

"Mommy, we're going to be late," Stacey said reproachfully. She looked at her oversized sports watch and back at her mother, who was easing the Aztek through traffic with the skill of a practiced soccer mom, which is what she was at the moment.

Lisa and Stacey were on their way to a soccer game with Janice and Justin as their cheering section. This was a semifinal match in their league and of the utmost importance; Janice had no intention of being late. They would be on their way to the game in mere minutes, as long as that irascible, capricious Curt Bowden was on time. *"Saturday is the only day I can make it." Huh, I'll bet he just did it for spite, the weasel.*

"Okay, kids, here we are. You guys are coming inside with me and you're going to do what?" she asked.

"We're going to sit still and be as quiet as mice," Justin and Lisa chorused. They knew the drill, having been thoroughly instructed that morning. They hopped out of the oddly shaped SUV, looking adorable in their dark green and navy soccer uniforms. Justin was clad in jeans and a Ralph Lauren rugby

shirt, and looked like a pint-sized magazine ad. They stopped
to admire the sheer size of the house before trooping in.

"Wow, Mom, this looks like a private school or a convent
or something. The man that owns this must be extremely
wealthy," Stacey observed.

"Yes, I'm sure he is. Now, sit here quietly and I'll be right
back, okay?" Janice glanced at her watch—it was already
eight-thirty and no Curt Bowden. She went into the dining
room and dropped her bag on the worktable that served as
an office for the various artisans who had been coming in and
out of the house for weeks. Despite Curt's lack of coopera-
tion, a few things were falling into place. Janice made a noise
of annoyance; she really wanted to complete this job—the
house could be so beautiful if he would just let her get on
with it! And where was he anyway—how dare he keep her
waiting!

She had made up her mind that she was leaving at 9:00 on
the dot whether he showed up or not. She wasn't about to risk
making her girls late for an important game because he
wanted to enact some power trip on her. She had just reached
for her ubiquitous Coach tote bag with her ever-present note-
book when she heard footsteps. It was Curt, looking better
than any man had a right to on a Saturday morning.

He was wearing well-worn jeans that nevertheless were
pressed to a knifelike crease, Italian loafers that were shined
to a high gloss, and a beautiful sweater that Janice knew immediately was a Missoni. The subtly variegated yarns in
softly vivid colors enhanced his dark satiny skin to great advantage and made Janice wonder once again how he had
gotten to be so mean. And he smelled like a million bucks,
too. *Why does he have to be so fine?* she thought grumpily.

"I was just about to leave you a note. I didn't think you
were coming," Janice said tersely.

Curt could sense the hostility radiating from her like lasers,
but it didn't make her any less gorgeous. He had never seen
her looking this casual, in jeans, Tod driving loafers, a crisply
pressed Ralph Lauren pinstriped shirt, and a sweater thrown

over her shoulders. Her hair was in a ponytail, her sunglasses were perched on top of her forehead, and she looked ready for action. And she smelled like she was ready for seduction; something fresh, slightly flowery, and spicy, just like her. For some reason he wanted to grab her and kiss her really hard, then take her out for breakfast, lunch, dinner . . .

He caught himself and remembered the role he was supposed to be playing. "Well, I wanted to make sure that the counters are just right. Let me show you what I mean."

He led her into the enormous kitchen, stepping over the paraphernalia left by the crew that had been working on the renovations. He was frantically trying to think of something to dislike about the Pewabic tiles that were being installed; he actually liked them very much. But he had to think of some way to see her again; she had been avoiding him like she was an insider trader and he was the SEC.

"Okay. Here we are, and here are the tiles. What's wrong with them and what do you want in their place?" Janice was totally fed up with him and his demands. She glanced at her watch. In fifteen minutes she was leaving with the kids, and he could take a flying leap as far as she was concerned. In fact, now was as good a time to quit as any. It was obvious that they simply were not *simpatico* and that they would never be able to collaborate on a home that was to his liking.

Curt hesitated. He opened his mouth but instead of the speech he was planning to make, what came out was, "Who's that?" He pointed toward the huge leaded glass French doors in the sunny kitchen that led out to the gardens. Three faces were staring into the kitchen, their hands cupped around their eyes for better visibility. "Whose kids are they and where did they come from?" Curt asked with amusement.

Janice sighed, walked over to the door, and opened it, beckoning for them to enter. "I have no idea who these children are," she said with asperity. "They bear a remarkable resemblance to *my* children, but that can't be because *my* children are sitting on the banquette where I left them, aren't they?" She tried to look stern, but was failing miserably.

Lisa and Stacey had the grace to look embarrassed, but Justin had no such compunction. He took one look at Curt and walked over to him with his hand outstretched. "How do you do, sir. My name is Justin Conrad. This is my sister Lisa and my sister Stacey."

Curt was both amused and amazed, as each child shook his hand formally. "Well. My name is Curtis Bowden. It's very nice to meet you all. You look like you're on your way to a game," he added, observing the girls' uniforms.

"Yes, we are, and we're going to be late, too," Stacey said anxiously, tapping her watch and looking at her mother beseechingly.

"Just two more minutes, Stacey. This is the only day Mr. Bowden could meet me here, so give us a minute, okay?" Janice said soothingly. She turned to Curt.

"As I said before, this is not a good day for me, so if you could quickly show me what's wrong this time, I'll have someone at Maison take care of it as soon as possible."

Curt tried not to let his emotions show on his face. He was feeling like the worst kind of heel in the world, besides being knocked off his feet by this development. He'd never given any real thought to what Janice did when she wasn't working. Somehow he'd just categorized her as some kind of artsy party girl who went around tantalizing men. Now it was obvious that she had a very full life, one that she enjoyed thoroughly. And one that she was very good at, to judge from the three attractive, well-adjusted healthy children in front of him.

He cringed inwardly when he thought of all the broken appointments and general chaos he must have been wreaking in her life, even though that was the general idea. Now that he knew that there were children involved, it seemed even more childish than pretending she was a stranger. Well, it was never too late to do the right thing; at least he hoped so. Looking at the three glowing faces of Janice's adorable children, he swallowed hard, hoping that the right words would come to him.

"Janice, I apologize for dragging you over here this morning. I had no idea that you had something this important to do today, or I would have never insisted. You guys go and have a good game, okay?"

The smiles on the girls' faces were reward enough, so it was a total shock to Curt when Justin asked if he would come along. Janice reacted immediately.

"Justin, sweetie, that's very nice, but Mr. Bowden has other plans for today. Let's get going, guys," she said hurriedly.

She was trying to herd them out to the car, when for some unknown reason Stacey got into the act.

"Are you really busy, Mr. Bowden? Will your wife mind if you come to watch us?" she asked innocently.

Curt was caught off guard by her comment, but rallied quickly. "I'm not married, Stacey. No wife, no kids. I'll bet you girls play a mean game of soccer," he added.

Stacey nodded, not in the least bit shy about her athletic prowess. "We're very good. Won't you come with us? It's going to be a good game," she promised.

"Yes, a really good game," Lisa added.

Curt smiled at Janice, who looked completely flummoxed by her children's persistence.

"How can I turn down such a nice invitation? Sure, I'll be happy to come to your game, if it's okay with your mother," he said.

Which is how Janice found herself in the last place she ever expected to be, which was watching her daughters play soccer on a warm October afternoon with Curt Bowden standing next to her. While it was plain that Justin was having a ball, Curt also gave every appearance of having a good time, cheering his heart out every time Stacey or Lisa scored. To her chagrin, Janice was so preoccupied with Curt's presence that she missed precious moments of play. *How did this happen? Why is he here? And what am I going to do with him when this is over?* she fretted. *And what could have possibly possessed these children?*

After the Friends School team handily won their match,

Stacey confided her reasoning to Lisa as they prepared to join their mother and brother. Stacey grabbed Lisa's hand and pulled her away from the crowd of their cheering teammates.

"Lisa, I have a good idea. No, a *great* idea! You remember that story I told you about the man who took his kids back after they were adopted?"

Lisa puckered her brow and nodded. "Yes, I do. I didn't like that story," she confessed.

"Well, if we had a dad, it would be harder for them to take us away. It would probably be impossible if we had the right dad. And I think Mr. Bowden would make a great dad for us!" Stacey whispered urgently.

Lisa's eyes grew huge as she pondered what Stacey was saying.

"He's way taller than Mom, which is good. He makes lots of money, so he can afford to have a big family. He's not married, he likes us, and most importantly, he likes Mom. A lot. If we plan this carefully, we could have a brand-new dad and live in that great big house. And no one could bother us, ever!" she finished triumphantly.

Lisa glanced over to the sidelines, where Janice stood with Curt and Justin. She looked him up and down and observed the way his eyes never left Janice's face. And he was also holding Justin's hand like he had been doing it forever. Stacey was almost always right about everything, but Lisa had to be sure.

"Are you sure he likes us?" she asked doubtfully. "And does Mom like him? She would have to like him a whole lot for him to be our dad," she pointed out.

Stacey looked over at their mother just in time to see her flash a beautiful smile at Curt. "Yep, she likes him, all right. Besides, we don't have too many alternatives. Do you want Phillip as a dad?"

Lisa's face immediately scrunched up at the thought of Phillip Wainwright as a prospective father. Phillip was the tame accountant whom their mother dated from time to time, and he was about as exciting as oatmeal. That did it for Lisa. Socking her right fist into her left hand, Lisa firmed her lips with determination.

"Okay, let's do it. Let's get us a dad," she said grimly.

Five

Janice found herself ensconced at a table in Pizzaopolis, the popular pizzaria in the Harbor Town strip mall on Jefferson. All the kids professed to be starving and had clamored for pizza. Since Curt had ridden in Janice's Aztec to the game, it seemed logical that he accompany them to lunch. Janice's feeble attempt at discouraging him was brushed aside as meaningless.

Curt was impressed at how polite the children were and how they immediately excused themselves from the table to go wash their faces and hands in the rest room.

"We'll take Justin with us, Mommy, and we'll make sure that there're no other ladies in the room while we're in there," Stacey offered.

Usually Justin protested at length about having to go into the women's room; it got him nowhere since Janice was not about to let him go to the men's room alone in a public place—or worse, ask a strange man to accompany him. He had learned to endure unless one of his uncles or his grandfather was along. But Lisa told him in the car that Stacey had to tell him an important secret, so today he went willingly, much to Janice's surprise. And to her discomfort, it left her all alone with Curt. It would have done her a world of good to realize that Curt was just as uneasy as she, but for a very different reason.

Curt sat silently for a moment, admiring the dainty way she picked up her bottle of San Pellegrino water in her slender hand; the way her short, perfectly oval nails gleamed softly in the light. Finally he spoke.

"Janice, I had no idea you were married. And you have three children. Your husband must be very proud of his family," he said awkwardly.

Graceless in her turn, Janice almost spat out the mouthful of water. Gasping a bit as she hurriedly blotted her lips with a napkin, she stared at Curt.

"I'm not married. Never have been. My children are adopted," she said proudly. "That is the single best thing I have ever done or will ever do in this life," she added.

Curt's surprise and admiration showed all over his face. "Wow. You're raising three kids all by yourself. How do you do it and work, too? I'm not a chauvinist or anything, but I know how hard it was for my mom after my father died, and I at least had older siblings to help out. But how do you do it all?" he asked.

Janice smiled happily. "Well, I have very good kids, for starters. They're very cooperative and helpful. I have great parents who live near me, as well as two very accommodating brothers who are extremely doting uncles even though they and my dad travel a lot. I have the best part-time housekeeper in the world and a job that allows me a lot of flexibility; I actually work from home two days a week. I have a very elaborate infrastructure that allows me to look like Supermom when I'm actually one step ahead of chaos. That's my little secret, though," she confessed.

"I am very, very blessed and I don't for one minute believe that most single moms have it like I do. But I have to tell you, I love every minute of it. I wouldn't change a thing," she added, as the children made their way back to the table and politely asked for money for the jukebox.

Janice was so occupied with digging out quarters that she didn't notice the giddy smiles between Justin and Lisa. Stacey was more composed, however, and waited patiently for the change, taking in every detail about Curt.

Janice triumphantly pulled out a handful of quarters. "Here

you go, kids. Nothing too weird, please. Come right back to the table when you're done, the pizza should be out by then."

Curt was concentrating solely on Janice, her warmth and sweetness, her obvious love of her children. Suddenly, Curt was seized with a desire to know everything there was to know about Janice. What she liked for breakfast, when she lost her first tooth, her favorite flower, her favorite anything. But before he could act on this new impulse, the children came back from the jukebox and he was surrounded by chaperones. The rest of the afternoon was pretty much a blur for Curt, mitigated by one overwhelming thought: he had to get Janice alone and as soon as possible. *Oh yeah,* he thought as he gazed at her laughing face, *I gotta get you into my life.*

Six

If Curt had known that "as soon as possible" was going to evolve into several weeks, he would have been better prepared to wait. Immediately after his delightful afternoon with Janice and her adorable children, he had driven over to Sasha's house in high spirits. This was actually the first time he'd spent any time with them since they had all been felled by the flu. After assorted noisy greetings from his small cousins, he joined Sasha in her enormous kitchen, where she was preparing her legendary lasagna.

"Sasha, you're not going to believe it, but today I had the best time I've had in a long, long time—with your friend Noelle. Although I call her Janice," Curt added.

If he hadn't been getting a glass of ice water, Curt would have noticed the odd expression on Sasha's face. Since he didn't see her glaring at him, he told her the whole story of how he had bullied Janice into meeting him that morning and how he ended up going to the soccer game with them.

"Sasha, you were right, I don't know what happened to turn her into the lady she is today, but she's a hell of a lot nicer than she was in college," he finished. Then he yelled as Sasha popped him on the back of the head with a handy wooden spoon.

"Hey, what was that for?" he asked indignantly. "What did I do to deserve that?"

Sasha was happy to enlighten him. "Just sit your overgrown butt in that chair over there," she said, gesturing menacingly with the same spoon, "and I'll tell you exactly what you did."

Without even a shred of concern for his feelings, Sasha went on to tell him the story that Janice had shared with her and Lisette. Curt could feel his dark skin flaming with heat as Sasha explain to him in excruciating detail exactly what Janice had gone through due to his actions in college.

"So. Not only was your little friend Clairol or whatever her name is *lying*, but since you didn't even bother to find out the truth, you hurt a very sweet, *very* shy girl's feelings and humiliated her. And to top it off, you've been treating her like a pariah for some twisted revenge thing, and I, for one, am ashamed of you. Just ashamed. You know you were raised better than that, Curtis Bowden. I should tell your mother," she threatened.

Curt's look of utter chagrin was enough to make Sasha relent. "Oh damn, Sash, I feel terrible. It just never occurred to me that Karla was making it all up. I mean, what the hell was the point? Why would she even do something like that?"

Sasha looked at her dearly loved cousin with pity. *"Duh!* So she could get you to drop Janice like a hot rock and take *her* to the dance, which is what you did, fool. Honestly, why can't men figure these things out?"

Curt felt his face flame up again. "If I'm gonna be truthful about it, Sash, I was about as shy as Janice. I always felt like a giraffe on roller skates unless I was on the basketball court. And if you recall, I wasn't particularly good-looking as a kid. Homely was the kindest word, butt-ugly was more accurate. You remember that big mailbox head with the Dumbo ears, don't you? And until I got braces, my teeth spread out like a garden rake. The only reason girls ever wanted to talk to me was because I was on the team. How was I supposed to know Janice really liked me?" he said defensively.

Sasha's tender heart melted at his humble words and she took pity on his hapless maleness. Curt was so handsome and polished now that it was hard to remember that he was once all arms and legs and no grace whatsoever. And she did indeed remember his mouth looking like the grillwork on a customized Cadillac for several years.

"Well, dearest, all I can say is, you'd better get to work, and work hard if you want to make it up to her. Especially after your latest tricks. I'd put in a standing order at a couple of florists if I were you. And if you like, I'll put in a good word for you," she offered.

Curt shook his head. "Nope, I got this, Sasha. I'm the one who was acting like a jackass, and I'm going to be the one to make it right. No matter what it takes."

Sasha's word were oddly prophetic. Even though Curt called Janice immediately, the result of the call was not the one he'd been seeking. Fully prepared to prostrate himself at her slender feet, Curt made what he hoped was pleasant small talk and then waded in with both feet.

"Janice, I know you're not going to understand this, but I owe you an apology. More like a million apologies. I've been acting like a total jerk and you certainly don't deserve to be treated like that. Can I please start making it up to you? Will you allow me to take you out and explain everything to you?" he said rapidly.

It was hard to say who was the more surprised at her answer, a firm "No." Curt was prepared somewhat for an initial rebuff, considering the way he had behaved, but Janice was surprised at the fact that she really meant no. She really did not want to go anywhere with Curt Bowden.

After explaining that she made it a rule to never mix her business life with her social life, Janice made a quick apology and ended the conversation rather hurriedly. Then she sat there and stared at the phone as if she wasn't quite sure what it was. The truth of the matter was that Curt had caught her completely off guard, at least that was part of it. The other part of it was that it felt a little bit too much like déjà vu. *Oh no you don't, Mr. Tall-Dark-and-Handsome. Been there, done that, had the heartache. I must look like my name is Boo-Boo the fool if he thinks he can just treat me any ol' way.* These and other uncomplimentary thoughts raced through Janice's mind. All at once she remembered how much it hurt to get stood up by Curt all those years ago and she was wallowing in the resultant rage.

If he remembered me, that would be one thing. But for him to not even know my name and still come up with the same-ol', same-ol'. . . ooh!

The only good thing to come out of the whole situation as far as Janice was concerned was an improved working relationship. Thanks to the fact that Curt was now being cooperative and pleasant, the mansion was taking shape beautifully. Even though Curt was on the road much of the time, he gave her carte blanche to make his house into a home. Of course, the flowers didn't hurt, either, she had to admit.

Curt had indeed taken Sasha's advice and Janice started getting regular floral tributes both at the office and at home. Sometimes an exotic arrangement, sometimes deliciously scented roses, sometimes potted plants glossy with health; at least twice a week Janet got something from Curt. Lisette stopped teasing her after the first week and just admired her skills.

"Umm, umm, umm. Still waters do run deep, don't they? C'mon, give! What did you do to bewitch this man? I have to know. I have my eye on a big, good-looking teaching assistant who has the decency to be single. I want to try this voodoo of yours," she pleaded. Lisette was known for her love of big men—she called them her teddy bears.

Janice just laughed her off. "Don't be ridiculous, Lisette! I think he's just trying to make up for being such a jerk when the project first started. That's all. Although I must say I've never had anyone apologize for so long!" she admitted as she gazed at that day's offering, a stunning array of bronze roses. The card read: "These reminded me of your beautiful hair. Be well, Curt." Janice had to admit that Curt was getting to her, despite her grudge. She smelled the rich, heady scent of the roses and fingered the greenery. These were going home with her that very night.

She was further delighted by an animated greeting card in her e-mail. Curt was getting quite handy with the computer, despite his earlier claim that he was hopeless. Over the past weeks Curt had gotten adept enough to e-mail her at least once a day, ostensibly to talk about the project but in reality to exchange little greetings, often in the form of an e-card. Today's was especially charming with a little song and a sweet message. Janice played it three times in the privacy of her miniscule office. She didn't want to admit it, but she could feel her guard slipping, and slipping fast. It was a good thing he was on the road so much, or she'd have been a goner. And having once been burned by the charms of Curt Bowden, she had no desire to submit to him again.

Surprisingly, Janice's continual brush-offs did nothing to deter Curt from pursuing her. He wasn't a vain man—far from it—but he wasn't unaware of his effect on women. He never, ever lacked for female companionship unless it was his choice. He was well aware that many of the women who flirted with him constantly and made it known that they were ready, willing, and available were interested only in the dollar signs that surround a professional athlete. Curt was acutely aware of how easy it was for someone in the public eye to be a target of the greedy and unscrupulous. His low-key personality made it easy for him to avoid the kinds of social events where he would be the center of attention, and Sasha, with her keen money acumen, had managed his business affairs ever since he turned pro.

Curt had never had a problem with dating anyone he chose, but Janice had changed all of that for him. And for some reason he liked it; liked the idea that Janice wasn't falling over herself to get next to him. She was, in fact, doing everything she could to stay away from him, not that he could blame her. Even when he was in town for a couple of nights and could take a look at the work being done on the house, she was nowhere to be found. He could see the results of her work in the beautifully painted walls the color and texture of rich parchment, in the handsomely outfitted kitchen with the new Sub-Zero stainless steel refrigerator and the six-burner Viking stove. But there was no Janice to compliment in person; he had to do it via voice mail, e-mail, and FTD. However, that was all going to change tonight.

"Trick or treat!"

Janice could still hear the joyous cries every time the front door opened to Sasha's annual Halloween party. She had sequestered herself in the small breakfast room that the caterers hadn't commandeered so that she could finally sit down and eat. She'd been dancing so much, this was her first chance to devour some of the magnificent buffet. She sank gracefully onto the padded bench that formed an eating nook and sighed happily. Her mouth was filled with an inelegant amount of a stuffed grape leaf when she realized that someone was standing next to her. She almost choked when she looked up into Curt's smiling eyes.

"Hello, Princess. Or are you a queen tonight?" he asked, taking in her tiara, full skirted gown, and the scepter that lay on the table.

Janice swallowed the mouthful of food in haste and took a quick sip of sparkling water. "I'm a witch," she said breathlessly. "A good witch. Addapearl, from *The Wiz*."

Curt smiled hugely. "I think you might be a witch, at that. I saw you casting your spell out there on the dance floor," he said in his deep, sexy voice.

Janice stared at Curt. There didn't seem to be anything to add to a remark like that, at least nothing she could think of. Besides, he looked so good, she couldn't trust herself to speak. He was wearing another sweater, this one a crew neck made of the finest cashmere. He was also wearing beautifully cut slacks with a double pleat in the front and a nice cuff that broke exactly where it was supposed to on his instep. The gray sweater and black pants would have been innocuous on anyone else, but on Curt they were extremely sexy.

"You're not wearing a costume," Janice pointed out inanely.

"Yes, I am," Curt insisted. "I'm the Man with the Broken Face."

Janice looked at him, puzzled. "The who?"

"The Man with the Broken Face," Curt repeated. He pulled out the chair from the end of the breakfast nook, turned it around, and straddled it. He laid one arm across the top and propped his head up with his other hand and sighed deeply. "Yeah, you won't go out with me, you keep rejecting me, bustin' my face every chance you get, so I had no choice. I had to come here just like I am, a broken man with a broken face."

Janice tried not to smile, but she failed miserably as she burst out laughing. "Curt, that's pitiful. You should be ashamed of yourself! Broken face . . . you need to quit!"

Curt reached over and took her long, delicate hand in his. "I don't want to quit, Janice, I want to get started. Will you please go out to dinner with me? I really want to take you someplace special so we can start getting to know each other," he said quietly. Then he pressed a soft kiss to the back of her hand.

Janice's eyes got huge and she stared uncertainly at Curt. He was so handsome, it almost hurt to look at him. He looked warm, sincere, tender, and eager; he looked, in fact, like the young man she had known so long ago. Two weeks ago, a week ago, even, she would have remembered why she was so angry at him and said no again. But at that moment, she could only think of how her hand felt in his, and how good he smelled, and how much she liked being with him.

"Yes, Curt. I'd like that very much."

In the doorway nearest the kitchen, three pairs of eyes lit up. Stacey, Lisa, and Justin had come searching for Janice, and what they found made them very happy. They immediately backed out of the doorway and took off for the family room, where they could express their exuberant joy. Stacey and Lisa gave each other high fives and Justin did his little happy dance. The Daddy Train was back on track, no doubt about it!

Seven

Due to Curt's hectic traveling schedule, it was a week before they could actually go out, but it was on a Saturday since the team had just returned from a series away and had a night off between games. Curt had procured reservations at what was arguably the finest restaurant in Detroit, the Whitney. This was the opportunity he'd been waiting for, planning for; this was his only shot at laying everything on the line for Janice and hoping she didn't knock him in the head. He wanted everything to be perfect tonight, and that meant he had to look his best. For some reason, though, his sartorial sense had deserted him. He couldn't find anything in his extensive wardrobe that was good enough for Janice.

The result of his indecision was evident in the number of suits that were strewn across his bed and the fact that he still hadn't decided what to wear. He was wearing a silk robe, standing in front of the huge closet, staring at it as though its contents could attack him at any moment.

"Damn, I thought women were the ones that went through this. I'm supposed to be all suave and laid back," he muttered.

"Ha. What've you been reading? Or smoking?"

Sasha's husband, Rob, stood in the doorway of the guest suite. Curt had taken to staying there until the house was ready to be occupied. Now that he was traveling extensively with the team, a hotel was the last place he wanted to spend any time.

Rob was obviously enjoying Curt's agitation. He came into

the room and sat down to watch with all the anticipation of an avid fan with courtside seats. Furthermore, he could very well relate to Curt's dilemma.

"Curt, we all go through this when it's someone we really care about. After Sasha finally said she'd consider giving me some play, I had tissue all over my face for the first six or seven dates. I was so nervous, I cut myself every time I shaved," he admitted with a laugh.

Curt looked at his cousin's husband with new understanding. Rob's narrow, handsome face was split in a huge smile, his green eyes full of laughter.

"Sasha finally suggested I get an electric razor. Or grow a beard," he added, fingering the blond goatee that matched his reddish-blond hair.

"She made you that nervous?" Curt asked in disbelief.

"Made? Don't use the past tense, cuz. My Sasha can still make me jump through hoops of fire without even trying. She's always had my nose open and she always will," he said calmly, taking a swallow of the Killian's Red Ale in his right hand.

Curt raised both eyebrows at hearing Rob's heartfelt declaration. "It's not like that, man. This is just a . . . just a date. Just dinner with an old friend from college. I just want to look good, that's all," he said in what he hoped was a convincing tone of voice.

Rob looked at him with something like pity in his eyes. "So that's why you're standing in front of the closet looking like a sixteen-year-old girl going to the junior prom. Sho' you right."

Shaking his head, Rob rose from the leather club chair and walked over to the enormous closet. In seconds he selected a midnight navy Armani suit, an ivory silk shirt, and from the rack of ties on the wall, an extremely expensive silk tie with an African-inspired pattern of blue, gold, and black.

"Here, Bozo. And no gators tonight, wear those black Cole-Haans and that lizard belt. You got to represent for the brothers, don't go out there looking like a chump."

Curt was always amused when Rob talked like a brother, which meant that he was always amused by Rob, since he had been doing it even before he and Sasha had hooked up. Rob had grown up in the inner city of Detroit and never forgot his roots. He was less amused when Rob started getting all in his business.

"Look, man, you know this is important to you, so don't try to play a used-to-be player. I knew I was dead meat the first time I laid eyes on your cousin, and it scared the hell outta me for about ten minutes. Then I realized that Sasha was the best woman I was ever going to meet in my entire miserable, unworthy life. It took me a few years of playing best friend to get her to trust me. After that it took a whole lot of serious beggin' to get to the next level, but it was worth every minute of the wait. I know the whole story of you and Janice. Don't you think ya'll two have waited long enough? Ain't it time to get this party started?"

Before Curt could formulate a sufficiently casual-sounding answer, Rob continued.

"And don't you think some matching socks would be more appropriate?"

Curt looked down at his feet, which were clad in one navy and one black sock.

"You can take the boy outta Indiana, but you can't take Indiana outta the boy. Get your country butt dressed and don't keep the lady waiting, cuz. And don't think I won't bring this up in my best man toast, either," he threw over his shoulder as he left the room.

Things were a bit calmer at Janice's condo; there was no question of what she was going to wear. After her mother's retirement from the runway, Pat put her years of modeling and innate sense of color and style to work as a clothing designer. Papillion was the result, a much admired and sought after line of clothing. When Janice mentioned that she was going to dinner at the Whitney, Pat presented her with a copper-colored silk jersey wrap dress. The dress was perfect for Janice; the color accentuated her fabulous hair, the mid-calf style enhanced her slender figure, and the plunging décolletage would have been downright indecent on someone else. With her small breasts, though, Janice looked innocently sexy, although she wasn't convinced.

Turning to the side once more, she surveyed what her brothers used to call the Pirate's Delight, her "sunken chest." "This is really sad. Even a Wonderbra couldn't help these poor little things," she sighed.

Lisette, who was baby-sitting the children, shook her finger at Janice. "Okay, since your *maman* isn't here to stop that sort of thing, I will. You look absolutely beautiful and you are going to knock that man off his feet! I'm still not convinced that he deserves to go out with you after his behavior, but if you're willing to let him slide . . ." Lisette's voice trailed off and she raised one shoulder and one eyebrow in a typically Gallic manner.

Janice laughed out loud. "Lisette, you sound like my mother! Mom is torn between being happy that I'm actually getting out of the house for a change and wanting to have Curt's head on a platter. Ya'll need to let it go! He's changed, I've changed, and we're two different people now. Really. I think he's a nice guy. And the children adore him for some reason," she added.

Even as she spoke, Stacey, Lisa, and Justin were waiting for Curt's arrival in the living room. They were trying to be nonchalant about it, with the exception of Justin, who had stationed himself by the front door of the condo to get a first glimpse of Curt. The entire front wall was made of windows, so he had an unobstructed view of anyone approaching.

"Justin, don't open that door when he gets here," instructed Stacey. "Let Lisette get it—you know Mommy doesn't like us to open the door at night. Then we can say hello and ask him to sit down."

"Okay," said Lisa. "Do we look all right? Should I put on a dress or something?"

Stacey shook her head. "We look fine," she assured her sister. They were all neatly attired in play clothes, which consisted of nicely pressed jeans, a Gap sweater on Justin and Petite Papillion tailored shirts on herself and her sister. Their hair was styled becomingly in long twisted braids to show off its shiny black abundance, and they looked just like what they were—happy, well-behaved children. The fact that they were cold-blooded conspirators wasn't apparent at all.

"Justin, remember to wait until after he's sitting down to invite him to Thanksgiving dinner. And do it when Mommy comes into the room so she'll have to say yes. She'll be all beautiful and she'll smell really pretty, and he'll look all handsome and they'll be looking at each other so much that they'll both say yes without even realizing it," Stacey said confidently.

Lisa was full of admiration for her big sister. "Stacey, this is going to work, isn't it? We're going to have a real dad and live in that great big house and Mommy will be so happy, won't she?"

Before Stacey could answer, Justin's eyes got huge. "I think he's here," he whispered. Sure enough, the doorbell rang.

Before the children could summon Lisette, she dashed down the hardwood floor of the hallway in her thick cotton socks, ending in a slide á la Tom Cruise in *Risky Business*. Taking a deep breath, she composed herself and opened the door.

"Hello, Mr. Bowden. Won't you come in? Janice will be ready in a moment."

Curt smiled and ducked his head slightly to enter the condo. "Thanks, but please call me Curt," he said. His dark eyes lit up on seeing the children standing winsomely by the door like a welcoming committee.

"Hello, Stacey, Lisa, and Justin. How're you guys doing?" He was surprised and gratified by their response.

"Hi, Mr. Bowden! You look very handsome tonight," Stacey said charmingly.

Lisa agreed immediately. She looked him up and down from the highly polished loafers to the top of his dark, smoothly shaven head, and smiled broadly. "You really look pretty when you're all dressed up," she told him.

Curt was so tickled by their effusive greetings that he was actually blushing. Justin noticed the festive gift bag he had in his large hand and immediately offered to carry it for him. Stacey and Lisa each took a hand and escorted him to the most comfortable chair in the living room, a sage green wing chair covered in cotton velveteen. Justin set the bag next to the chair and asked Curt if he would care for something to drink.

"No thanks, Justin, but it was nice of you to ask," Curt said with a big smile. He looked appreciatively around the living room of the condo, liking what he saw very much. The living room was done in soothing shades of cream and green, with un-expected touches of heather and antique gold. A large Diego Rivera print dominated the wall over the sofa. The focal point of the room was the French doors that led out to a fenced-in patio. The dining area flowed into the living room, creating an open but stylish space. Janice's deft touch had created a warm, inviting home, and the thought that she was doing the same thing for him was gratifying. Curt turned his attention to the children, observing once again what nice kids they were.

"Listen, guys, I brought you something. I hope your mother doesn't mind."

"I'm sure she won't," Lisa assured him with a big smile.

In the meantime, Lisette finally let Janice leave the bedroom. She had insisted that Janice make him wait a full ten minutes so he would fully appreciate the privilege of escorting her. Janice felt that was rude and tried to leave immediately, but Lisette told her she had lipstick on her teeth, something that wasn't true but had the effect of making her stop and check her final appearance. At least seven minutes went by while Janice fussed and preened and made sure that every hair was in place and all makeup was where it was sup-posed to be. When she was satisfied, she floated out of the room and down the hall toward the sound of her children's laughter. Lisette stayed behind in the bedroom to give them some semblance of privacy. She knew she could rely on Stacey to give her a review that was more accurate than videotape after the couple left.

Janice was so amused by the sight of the three of them in their new Detroit Pistons baseball caps that she missed the sharp intake of breath that came from Curt as he immediately stood. She didn't see the look of total amazement that came over his face when she entered the room looking like she had stepped out of a *Vogue* fashion layout. Her hair was a mass of curls twisted up off her long, slender neck with softening tendrils surrounding her face and the delectable nape of her neck. The copper silk jersey warmed her skin and made her slender figure look delicate and desirable at the same time. She was wearing a minimum of makeup and jewelry; only a small pair of earrings with a rhodolite hanging like a dewdrop, and a delicate eighteen carat gold lariat necklace with the same stones graced her body. When she entered the room, a faint scent like sun-warmed apricots and roses came with her; she smelled like a perfect summer day, only no day that Curt had ever experienced.

"Look how sporty you guys are! I hope you remembered to thank Mr. Bowden. That was very kind of him," she said in the low, sexy voice that was beginning to drive Curt crazy.

Justin immediately answered in the affirmative. "Yes, we did, Mommy. And we were going to ask him to come to Grandma's house for Thanksgiving, too. Would you like to come, Mr. Bowden?" Justin's sweet little face was the very picture of innocence as he uttered the words.

Before Janice could react, Curt immediately said yes. "I'd love to. It's been a long time since I've had a real Thanksgiving, what with traveling and all," he said with appreciation. It wasn't the complete truth since he usually went home to Indiana or to one of his siblings' homes for holidays, but Janice didn't need to know that, he reasoned.

Lisa and Stacey added their cheers to Justin's as Curt agreed to attend, and all three of them looked at their mother for her reaction. Surprisingly, she merely smiled.

"We'll all look forward to it. Stacey, can you get Mommy's coat? The silk one?"

While Stacey dashed off to get the coat, Curt recovered

from his reverie and remembered that he'd also brought something for Janice. He reached into the gift bag again and pulled out a ballotin of Godiva chocolates. His reward was the look of joy that immediately flashed into Janice's sea-green eyes.

"Mmmm, my favorite! How on earth did you know that?" she said happily.

Curt smiled and said a little bird had told him.

Janice looked up at Curt and gave him the first full smile of the evening, one that was so sweet and heartfelt, he was finding it hard to breathe. "Well, you just tell that little Sasha bird how much I appreciate her passing the word on," she said merrily.

By now Stacey had returned with the coat, a long, swirling length of bronze silk that was a perfect evening wrap. Curt assisted her in putting it on and was rewarded by a wave of that fantastic fragrance mixed with Janice's own pheromones. He didn't believe it up until that point, but knees actually could get weak. To compensate, other parts of his body seemed to gain remarkable strength right about then. It was time to get this date started before something really embarrassing happened.

The next two hours were the most wonderful that Curt could remember. Everything about Janice enchanted him; from the way she used her delicate hands while she was talking, to the low, thrilling pitch of her voice, to the way her incredible eyes never left his face while they were conversing. He enjoyed watching her eat, too, gratified by the fact that she seemed to be enjoying the exquisitely prepared food as well as the stately ambiance of the venerable restaurant. Curt would have also been extremely happy to know the kind of effect he was having on his date.

Janice felt like she was floating in a warm, incandescent haze. From the first moment she walked into her living room and saw Curt so beautifully attired, she couldn't form a co-herent thought, other than *Damn, he's fine.* Curt wasn't conventionally handsome, but to Janice his dark African features were absolutely perfect. His dark, penetrating eyes, his strong jaw line, the full lips that showcased his straight white teeth, even the deep furrow that ran between his eyes and gave him a look of intense concentration; everything about him was gorgeous in her eyes.

Janice had always loved the Whitney, even though she didn't go there often. The imposing three-story mansion on Woodward Avenue had only been a restaurant since the late 1980s but its service, decor, and cuisine gave it four stars in every restaurant guide that mattered. Frankly, though, she could have been eating at the Coney Island joint around the corner from Le Coeur de la Maison and she would have been just as happy as long as Curt was sitting across the table from her. He smelled so good and he looked so tasty that she could have made an entire meal out of him. She waited for the familiar hot rush of shame to envelop her when she allowed that thought to process and surprisingly, it didn't happen.

Janice smiled a secret little smile and took another small swallow of the very excellent chardonnay that accompanied her entrée. That little sip was probably what caused her to place her hand over Curt's free one and tell him what a wonderful time she was having.

"Curt, this is so nice. I'm having the best time with you. Thank you for not giving up on me when I said no the first time," she said sweetly.

Curt felt as though her soft hand had reached inside him and squeezed his heart. Her next words made the sensation even more intense.

"I have to confess something to you. I had a huge crush on you when we were at Georgetown. Obviously you didn't know I was alive since you don't remember me at all, but I actually used to dream about you," she confessed.

Janice's eyes got enormous as she realized what she'd just said. She stared at her glass of wine as though suspecting that it contained sodium pentothal or some other truth serum. Just as the dreaded hot rush of shame was about to make its scheduled appearance in earnest, Curt began speaking in his deep, captivating voice.

"The first time I ever saw you, you were walking toward the library on a sunny afternoon. You were wearing a pair of those pants they used to wear in the navy, the wide ones with all the buttons. You had on a white shirt and you had a big black leather bag on your shoulder instead of a backpack. It was windy and your hair was loose and blowing back from your face and you were holding a newspaper in one hand and a red pear in the other. You were the prettiest thing I'd ever seen in my life," he said softly.

"My cracker jacks," Janice said in an equally soft tone. "I loved those pants. And I still love red pears. But . . . you said . . ."

It was Curt's turn to take Janice's hand. "I know I acted like I didn't know you, I said I didn't remember you from college. I lied, Janice. I was trying to make you feel insignificant and unimportant. I was being a jackass because I wanted to hurt your feelings. I thought I had a reason to do that," he said slowly, and then proceeded to explain the entire situation and how he had been led to believe that she had been playing games with him.

"I'm truly sorry, Janice. I want to beg your pardon for all of that and hope that you can forgive me for my stupidity. Can you do that? Can you forgive a man for what a stupid boy did a long time ago?"

Janice had been perfectly still during Curt's entire recitation. Her facial expression and body language gave away nothing; it was as if she had been turned into a statue. She simply stared at Curt, as though he was speaking a language with which she was not familiar. Finally she spoke.

"I'd like to leave now, please."

Eight

Curt was sure his heart had stopped. Those words, spoken in Janice's seductive voice, were the last words he heard from her until they were in the car and pulling away from the legendary Whitney. For all he knew, they would be the last words she ever spoke to him, and who could blame her. Even while he was explaining his actions to her in the restaurant, he felt a deep sense of shame. Well, perhaps not shame, but utter stupidity. He should have thought his speech out better, practiced it on Sasha, something, anything. He'd given it his best shot and obviously blown his only chance to clear the air and make things right between them. Now what could he do other than accept the fact that she wasn't going to forgive him?

"Let's go to your house, Curt. I want to show you a few things and we can finish our talk," Janice said quietly.

Curt was glad for the darkness of the car; if there had been more light than the ones on the dashboard, Janice would have been able to see the utter gratitude all over his face. She was at least speaking to him; maybe all wasn't lost. He got to the huge house in record time and pulled into the circular driveway. In a very short time he found himself in the last place he ever expected to be, sitting in front of his own fireplace next to the woman of his dreams.

Janice hadn't said too much more in the car, but became quite animated as she showed Curt more improvements in the house, more pieces that had been added during his absence.

"You know, Curt, I think you'll be able to move in before the holidays," she told him as they admired a hand-woven wool area rug that graced the living room. "Once you've made a couple of decisions about the master bedroom, we can get that finished and the house will actually be livable while we finish the rest."

Curt nodded his head, not quite able to formulate a response. Janice seemed so calm, not angry at all. But she hadn't acknowledged his apology, either. They sat next to each other on the huge distressed leather sofa that was the very epitome of comfort; Curt had never seen a sofa so accommodating to his big body or so easy on the eye. It blended perfectly with the vivid, warm, yet masculine atmosphere Janice had created for him. He looked over at Janice, who was looking so gorgeous in the warm amber light that she hurt his eyes. He was trying to think of something to say to break the ice when Janice spoke.

"So. You do remember me from college and you were pretending that you didn't in order to hurt my feelings because someone told you some lies about me that you believed. Is that about the size of it?" she asked.

She used a normal tone of voice, which didn't give anything away, but she also wasn't looking directly at Curt as she spoke. When she raised her eyes to his, he didn't know whether to be relieved that she wasn't yelling at him or completely intimidated.

"I have to ask, Curt, why you believed that girl. Why would you think that of me? Did I impress you as being mean or hateful? Did I come across as someone who was thoughtless and callous?" she asked curiously.

"No, Janice, you really didn't," Curt admitted. "I think it was the fact that you were always so nice that made it seem like such a cold-hearted thing to do. It was like you had just set me up for the kill and I wanted to get back at you for thinking you could play me like that. It seems incredibly stupid now, but at the time, it was a powerful reaction," he said frankly.

"But Curt, this is what I don't understand. You didn't really know me that well, and someone comes up to you and tells you that I said this or that and you don't even come to me to find out the truth, you just assume that they're telling the truth and I'm a big fat liar. And you just admitted that I'd never done anything to make you think that I was a not-so-nice person. I don't understand," she repeated with growing frustration in her voice.

"Look, Janice, this isn't the easiest thing in the world to admit," Curt said, and then took a deep breath. "You were the knockout woman on campus. Everybody who saw you wanted you. And when you're that good-looking, people just assume that you're stuck-up and snotty. They just automatically label you as a bitch because they're jealous, or because they know you're way out of their league. So if you hear a rumor about someone like that, you naturally believe it because it makes the fact that you look so incredible easier to deal with," he said slowly.

Janice's eyes seemed to burn right through him, but he had to get it all out.

"Look, I know this makes me seem like a big fool, but I'm being as honest as I can. Almost anybody will believe anything bad about somebody who's gorgeous, rich, famous, whatever. It's not a nice characteristic of human beings, but it's the truth. I hope you can find a way to forgive me," he added.

Janice had been sitting perfectly still during this recitation. She didn't want to distract Curt in any way and she wanted to make sure she understood every word he was saying. Without realizing what she was doing, she started twirling a tendril of hair near her nape; it was a habitual gesture when she was deep in thought. Finally she spoke.

"I cried that whole night, you know. Once I got it in my head that you really weren't going to show up, I just cried like a baby. I made myself sick from it. Or I thought I had—it turns out I had mono," she said with a sardonic smile. "The point is, I went through a lot of misery that night, all because someone who wanted to go out with you made up a lie about me that you believed because you thought I was cute. Damn."

Janice sighed and shifted her slender body on the sofa. She stopped playing with her hair and slid her feet out of her Sigerson Morrison pumps and curled her long legs up onto the sofa's comfortable cushions. Instead of looking angry or hurt, she looked pensive, which Curt hoped was a good sign.

"Curt, I have to tell you that's the most amazing thing I've ever heard. I was the gawkiest, goofiest freshman on campus, and to think that people were plotting my downfall because they thought I was stuck-up or too pretty or something, that's just unbelievable. And you bought it—that's the part I don't get. You were the handsomest boy I'd ever seen, why in the world would you get all geeked up over me?" she asked rhetorically.

"You know, I come from a pretty good-looking family. My mother is absolutely drop dead gorgeous and my dad, well you know what he looks like, he's tall, dark, and handsome, just like you. My brothers are also very good-looking. I'm their sister and even I can see why women go crazy for them. But in my family we were always taught by word and action that the outside didn't matter, it was what was on the inside that counts. My looks are an accident of birth; I didn't have a thing to do with the fact that I come from handsome people. But how I act, how I conduct myself, how I treat other people is what matters, and I am totally responsible for that," she said seriously.

"What a mess. A lot of hurt feelings, a lot of lies and misunderstanding for nothing." Janice sighed briefly and looked down at her hands. Then she looked Curt full in the face and asked him a question.

"Let me ask you something, Curt. If I'd been what you consider an average-looking girl, would you have come and asked me about your little friend's accusations? Would you have believed them at all? Because you're showing me something I've always believed: It's better to be pretty on the inside than it is on the outside, at least people will give you a chance to prove yourself," she said sadly.

Not for the first time that night, Curt felt his insides twist.

He was still trying to get the picture of Janice crying herself to sleep over him out of his head. If he'd only had enough confidence in himself to ignore the gossip, none of it would have happened. Curt was preparing himself for a final apology and bracing himself for Janice's brush-off. But before he could formulate an appropriate remark, Janice did something that jump-started his heart; she reached over and took his hand. Running her thumb along the back of his smooth dark skin, she sighed softly, then looked at him for a long moment.

"We were kids back then, Curt. We're both all grown up now. I can let bygones be bygones if you can. What do you think?"

"I think you're letting me off the hook much too easily," he answered. " I think if you think *I'm* handsome, you need your eyes checked. And I still think you're the most beautiful woman I've ever seen. Inside and out," he added. "No one could have kids as nice as yours without being extremely wonderful."

"Thanks, I'll tell my mom you said so. I look just like her," Janice said with a smile. "And I'm trying to raise my children like I was raised. I have great parents and I learned a lot from them."

Curt enjoyed looking into her smiling eyes for a minute, then remembered where they were.

"So now what? Do you want to get coffee, dessert, go dancing, what? We're still on our date, aren't we?"

Janice moved closer to Curt on the sofa. "Yes, I guess we are. I don't really want to do any of those things, although you definitely owe me dessert. I planned on ordering that Chocolate Ugly cake back at the Whitney and I was so dumbfounded I forgot all about it. Imagine, making me forget *chocolate!*"

Curt laughed along with her.

"All I really want to do is talk for a while. But it's a little cold in here, so . . ."

Before she could say another word Curt had put his arm around her and pulled her even closer. "Is that better?"

"Mmm-hmm," Janice sighed. "Now let's talk about you. You know everything about me and what I've been up to over the past twelve years; it's your turn to tell me all about you."

Even though Curt could think of a few other things he'd rather be doing, he talked to Janice about his career and finishing his degree, about the injury that caused him to turn to coaching, his plans for the future . . . they might have talked for the rest of the night had it not been for the fact that Janice needed to go home and check on the children.

"I told Lisette we wouldn't be out too late, and I don't leave them with a sitter very often. You don't mind, do you?" she asked as she slid her feet back into the fashionable shoes and prepared to stand up.

Curt admired her legs for a moment before turning her face to his. "Yes, I do mind. I really do. I could sit here all night and look at you. I don't want this night to end, Janice. You're a very special lady, you know that?"

Janice's face lit up and before she could answer Curt started pulling her toward him, his intentions completely obvious. Janice flowed to him like a silken breeze on a summer day and stopped suddenly, bracing her hand on his chest.

"No!"

Curt looked as though she had slapped him. Janice stood and straightened her dress, then looked down at Curt.

"We can only have one first kiss, and I want it to be perfect. I've waited twelve years for this, so let's do it right. Stand up!"

Curt burst out laughing. "You're too much, Janice. Okay, let's do it right," he said agreeably.

He rose to his full six feet ten inches, straightening his tie and smoothing out his jacket front. He took Janice's hands and pulled her to his body. Cupping her face tenderly in his hands, he bent his head down and touched his lips to hers, softly and gently. Janice uttered a soft little moan of pleasure as the contact deepened. They kissed sweet kisses as their lips began to know each other. Janice raised up on her toes to get as close as possible to Curt, who obligingly slid his big warm hands down her neck, over her shoulders, and down her back until they were anchored around her small waist. Lifting her as though she weighed nothing at all, Curt brought her body into intimate contact with his at the same time he parted her soft, willing lips with his tongue.

Janice's arms went around Curt's neck and she hung on for dear life as she got the first real taste of passion she'd ever had in her life. Curt's mouth on hers awakened sensations she'd only read about in romance novels. The only sound to be heard was the soft plop of her right shoe hitting the floor, joined quickly by her left. Still, neither one of them wanted to break the enchantment brought on by their heated embrace. When Curt felt Janice's body begin to tremble, he regained his senses enough to slowly lower her to the floor. The supple jersey of her dress allowed her to experience every inch of his hardened and completely masculine form as he guided her down his body in a sensual slide as they continued to caress each other's lips with tongues hot with greedy desire.

When her feet finally touched the floor, Janice started ending the kiss with great reluctance. She never wanted to stop kissing Curt, but common sense prevailed. With a sigh that came from the very depths of her soul, she pulled away and laid her head on his chest, trying mightily to return her breathing to normal. She was gratified to know that Curt was at least as aroused as she; she could feel his heart pounding like a pneumatic hammer as he continued to kiss her hair, her brow, and her temple.

Finally they pulled apart enough to look at each other. Curt was too moved and far too aroused to trust himself to speak. Janice had never looked so appealing to him, her hair slightly mussed, her lipstick completely gone, and the air of a tousled siren all about her. He wanted nothing more than to scoop her up and carry this promising beginning to a very rewarding end, but the timing was wrong. It was too soon for a move like that, way too soon, although Janice had been right about one thing. Twelve years was long enough to wait. As far as he was concerned, the waiting was over. Still . . . he pulled her close within the circle of his arms and held her tightly. He tipped her chin up so he could indulge himself in one last, sweetly delirious mouthful of Janice.

"Sweetheart, it was a long time coming, but it was definitely worth the wait," he breathed into her ear.

Janice was too spent to talk, but in her heart she agreed with every word.

Nine

The next few weeks swirled by in a rush of sensation for Curt and Janice. After that auspicious beginning, they began dating in earnest, just slightly hampered by Curt's frenetic traveling schedule. When the Pistons were on the road, they stayed in touch by telephone and computer. But when the Pistons played home games, Janice and the children often sat at courtside to cheer on the team. On school nights Janice's father and brothers occupied those seats. They had accepted Janice's budding relationship with Curt and approved of him as a date. Pat's feelings were another story altogether.

Pat wasn't terribly impressed with the explanation Curt had given Janice for his behavior. She thought her daughter was a little too quick to forgive and forget. She also didn't like the way her grandchildren seemed enamored of him; they hung on his every word and delighted in his company. True, Curt appeared equally attached to them, but Pat found it hard to give up the grudge she'd nurtured for so long. Being the fiercely devoted mother she was, she was loath to give him the benefit of the doubt, something she made plain on Thanksgiving Day.

As far as everyone else was concerned, the Thanksgiving dinner at Janice's parents' home was a huge success. Janice and the children arrived the night before, as was the custom, so that Janice could help prepare the elaborate feast. Janice made the cornbread for the dressing, the potato salad, and the cranberry-orange relish, and then tackled the arduous task of cleaning the greens. While Pat was making pound cake, her special rolls and a pumpkin cheesecake, her obviously smitten daughter treated her to an unending litany of Curt's many virtues.

"Mom, he's so thoughtful and kind! Most of the time when we go out, it's to do something with the children. We've been roller-skating, we went to that indoor playland and played laser tag and arcade games, we go to the movies and for pizza afterward, and sometimes we just rent videos and pop popcorn. The kids just adore him and vice versa," Janice said happily.

"And he's a wonderful person, too. Did you know that he personally built five Habitat for Humanity homes when he was in Atlanta? I don't mean that he built them himself, but he funded them. And the charities he's involved with! He's just starting a foundation for scholastically gifted kids from inner city schools. Scholastic, not athletic," she emphasized. "He's very generous and concerned about others, Mom. He really is a sweetheart."

She was engrossed in concocting citrus vinaigrette for the red-grapefruit and spinach salad that was her father's favorite, so she didn't see the raised eyebrow and carefully neutral expression on her mother's face. Pat opened her mouth several times to speak but couldn't think of anything to say that wouldn't sound accusatory or small-minded. She was the only one who hadn't jumped on the Curt Bowden Express to the Land of Bliss, and she didn't want to appear shrewish. Still, she wasn't ready to queue up with his legions of fans just yet. Mothers find it hard to forgive anyone who harms their children, even when he's a tall, tantalizing millionaire with a devastating smile. Therefore, she was slightly put off her guard when Curt arrived bearing gifts.

Curt showed up right on time, dressed to the nines in an expensive suit with an Italian designed merino wool jersey shirt, and he had brought four bottles of Mondavi chardonnay, two bottles of nonalcoholic cherry spumante for the children, and

an incredible-looking sweet potato praline tart. It was the tart
that did her in after Curt acknowledged he had made it himself.

"I don't get the chance to cook much, but I've always liked
it," he admitted. "My mom always said anybody who ate as
much as I do better know how to prepare my own meals," he
added sheepishly.

Pat could see why her daughter was so smitten over the
man. His towering height, his dark good looks, his nice man-
ners, and easy charm would be hard for any woman to resist;
she had to admit that. Pat watched the two of them exchang-
ing ravishing smiles and suppressed her doubts for the
moment. But she was going to be keeping an eye on him, no
doubt about it.

Curt's eyes were closed as he lay back in his reclined seat
on *Roundball I,* the Pistons' private jet. The team was on their
way back home after a five-day road trip that had proved successful. If they kept up their momentum, they could end up
with a play-off berth. Curt smiled to himself as he thought
about the distinct possibility of the team gaining the NBA
Championship. He was also thinking about his relationship
with Janice and the progress they were making.

He got along famously with her father and her brothers,
and he had the feeling that her mother could at least tolerate
him. He'd never really thought about the importance of getting along with a woman's family before—his relationships
in the past simply weren't that serious. But now it was important to Curt that he got along with Janice's family because
they were very close. And he was getting closer to Janice,
which meant that he would naturally be around her family, especially her mother. But after the Thanksgiving Day
massacre, she was usually warm if not gushy on the few oc-
casions when they met. At least she wasn't trying to take his
head off.

As for Stacey, Lisa, and Justin, their adoration was completely mutual. They seemed to like him as much as he liked

them, and that was a definite plus for him. He'd never met a young mother as devoted as Janice. He suppressed a chuckle while thinking about some of their antics. Absently he fingered the latest tie in his extensive collection. It was a gift from the children for no particular reason, and they thought it was gorgeous; a silk tie with Bugs Bunny playing basketball on it. And yes, he had worn it courtside and dared anyone to say anything about it. Naturally, while he was doing all this daydreaming, he was thinking about being with Janice, which accounted for the dreamy look on his face, something that didn't escape his seatmates' attention.

"Check it out, man. Bowden's thinkin' about his woman . . . look at that big dumb grin on his face!" laughed one of the other coaches.

"Ha! That real fine sister that comes to the games, the one who looks like a model? That's who he's dreamin' about? Aww, he looks so purty. But I ain't mad at him, I'd be dreamin' about her, too." This was from Jerome, one of the team trainers, who had known Curt for several years.

Curt groaned inwardly. Once these guys got on your case, there was no way of getting them off. You had to just go with it.

"For your information, I'm not asleep. I was, umm, strategizing defensive tactics for the next game, that's all." He said this without opening his eyes—he saw enough of their ugly mugs on a daily basis.

"First of all, you're not the defensive coordinator, you're on offense. And second, the only strategizing you gon' be doin' is with that fine lady of yours. But if you need some help with your game plan, we can help a brother out," offered Jerome as he slapped high fives with the other coaches to a chorus of raucous laughter.

Curt opened his eyes at that and sat up; it looked like lying, signifying, and general snaps were about to take over. The plane was getting ready to land, however, so it wouldn't be long before he could make good on some of the daydreams he'd been having about Janice, but he wasn't about to let his crew know that.

He was thinking about Janice so hard that when he emerged from *Roundball I* and started heading toward the baggage area, he missed something vital. Out of the periphery of his vision he caught a glimpse of a tall, slender figure but it didn't register with him for a few seconds, not until he heard his name spoken in an unbearably sexy voice.

"Curt."

He turned his head to the left without breaking stride, then he stopped completely. It was Janice! He immediately put down his carry-on bag and embraced her, heedless of the passengers who had to walk around them.

"Baby, what are you doing here?" he asked inanely. Joy at her presence had temporarily addled his brain.

"I couldn't wait another minute to see you," she confessed. "I hope you don't mind."

His response was to kiss her tenderly yet fiercely, right there in the concourse of the airport. They were so involved in their passionate greeting that neither of them heard any of the pungent comments from assorted Pistons who were observing the tender scene.

"Baby, let's get out of here," Curt whispered. "Damn, I've missed you!" He looked around quizzically before asking where the children were.

"I missed you, too," she murmured. "The kids are having a sleep-over at Sasha's tonight. Where's your car? I can drive you to it and you can follow me home."

"Actually, I hitched a ride here. My SUV is at the dealer for a tune up, so let's get my bags and get outta here!"

And that's exactly what they did. Curt was a bit surprised when Janice drove directly to his imposing house in Palmer Woods. He turned to her with a question, but she shook her head.

"No questions, just come with me."

He did as he was bid and they entered the house, which he hadn't really seen for a couple of weeks. The transformation of the rooms was amazing, even to Curt's untutored eye. He was the first to admit that he knew little about art, but he certainly knew when something spoke to him, and his house was whispering "home." The entryway, which had been so intimidating, was now a warm, welcoming entrance. The walls above the wainscoting were now burnished amber, and the huge space was now the home of an ornately hand carved table from Africa, two leather side chairs and arts and crafts sconces that shed a mellow light on the area.

"Welcome home, Curt," Janice said quietly. She loved the look of utter peace that came over Curt's face as he surveyed his new home. Even though all of the upstairs rooms weren't furnished, enough of the house was done so that he could now live there. The foyer and living and dining rooms were completed, as was the kitchen and the breakfast room. The study was bare bones, as was the basement, which would be a screening room and game area. The guest bedrooms were painted and papered but devoid of furniture, but the master suite was all finished. Best of all, the furnishings that Curt had in storage had been moved in and artfully arranged so that it really looked like home to his dazed eyes. Janice and Curt went from room to room holding hands and talking. They didn't even remove their coats, she was so anxious to show him the newest improvements.

The master bedroom was magnificent. A massive panel bed dominated the room, with a copper silk duppioni duvet and an array of pillows in similar warm colors. The dressers were built-ins in the walk-in closet that led into the dressing room. That left an unusual amount of space for a seating area by the window seat, where Janice had placed a seductively comfortable chaise longue and a huge armoire, which housed a television. Curt and Janice had talked at length about whether or not Curt wanted a television in the bedroom.

"Well," she had told him, "I have one in my bedroom. You probably noticed there wasn't one in the living room, nor do I allow the children to have one in their rooms. There's one in the basement, which I converted to a family room. But when you have a television in your bedroom, you have to be prepared for Saturday morning invasions as well as total occupation when one of them has the flu or something. If I had it to do over again, I don't think I'd have opted for one in the bedroom."

Curt had given her a huge smile; she didn't realize that he was picturing the warm domesticity of the scene she was describing and liking it very much. He assured her that a television in the bedroom would be just fine. Besides, he loved the heavy mahogany armoire she had acquired.

Curt walked around the spacious room, basking in the warmth and sensuousness that Janice had created. Aside from the sheer size of the room, the thing Curt liked about it the most was the fireplace. Like many men, Curt was a true romantic at heart and somewhere in the back of his mind he had always nurtured a fantasy about making love in front of a fireplace. Just the thought of him and Janice in front of a fire, abandoning all inhibitions, wrapped in nothing but each other . . . damn. Curt felt the familiar urgency that seemed to overtake him every time he was near Janice for any length of time, and stifled a curse. He was trying to take it slow and easy with Janice, but just looking the way she looked tonight made it extremely difficult for him.

He tried to take in the other features of the suite, like the French doors that led to a small balcony, the beautifully swagged draperies that matched the duvet, the classic proportions of the furniture that were enlivened by touches of African art; it was no good, though. All he wanted was Janice.

"Baby, this is wonderful. I mean it. This is a room I'm going to love coming home to," he said slowly.

He was so occupied with trying not to ravish her, he wasn't paying attention to what she was doing. The smell of her perfume was driving him crazy as usual. The way she looked at him at the airport, the mere fact that she had come to pick him up, the way her mouth felt under his, the softness of her hand in his . . . all he knew was they'd better get out of the bedroom in a hurry or he wasn't going to answer for the consequences.

A soft whoosh drew his attention to the fireplace. The gas

jets had ignited as Janice pressed a button and the hearth was filled with gently flickering flames. The cognac leather chaise longue, piled high with leopard-patterned pillows, was facing the fireplace, and a low mahogany table next to it was set with two wineglasses, a crystal bowl of fruit, a tray of cheeses, a roast capon, and a variety of breads. Janice was standing near the fire with the stereo remote in her hand. She pressed the play button and the room was flooded with the sound of "A Night in Tunisia," one of Curt's favorites. While he watched her, she removed her black cashmere coat to reveal the most provocative dress Curt had ever seen, at least on Janice.

It was made of sheer silk georgette in a soft peach color over ecru, which made it almost the color of Janice's skin. It had an empire bodice and long sleeves that were off the shoulder, giving her an innocent but extremely sexy look. The mid-calf hemline of the loosely floating dress was an irregular handkerchief style and bordered with delicate ecru lace. Tiny silk rosebuds dotted the bodice, completing the sensual ensemble. Janice had already slipped off her boots and was standing before Curt with her long slender feet bare except for a soft rosy polish on her carefully manicured toes. Shyly, she reached up and removed a couple of strategic bone hairpins, which allowed her mane of curls to cascade down.

"I, umm, thought you might be hungry," she said breathlessly.

She and Curt looked at each other for a long moment while time ceased to exist. He suddenly flung his leather coat off and crossed the room to her in two strides, pulling her into his arms.

"I'm starving, baby, for you," he growled.

Janice's answer was a delighted smile and a kiss that drove him out of his mind.

"Listen, sweetie, do you want to take a shower? Because everything is ready for you if you do," she purred.

Actually, it sounded like a great idea to Curt. It would give him time to get his bearings and . . . something occurred to him while he loosened his tie.

"Janice, weren't you cold in that dress? There's not too much of it," he observed.

"I was freezing my fanny off! But I wanted to dazzle you. So I'm going to warm up by the fire while you take a quick shower. A really quick one because I'm hungry, too," she admitted with a sexy smile.

Curt's answer was to take off his shirt, giving Janice her first look at his smooth ebony chest with more rippling muscles than she had imagined. Without even thinking about what she was doing, she spread her hands against his smooth, enticing skin and sighed with pleasure as she stroked him up and down.

"Um, baby, you know there's plenty of room in that shower for both of us. And since you got a chill on my behalf, I'd be less than a gentleman if I didn't offer to warm you up," he murmured.

And it sounded like a perfect idea to Janice. Within seconds, it seemed, they were in the huge shower enclosure with the dual heads. The warm water pulsed over their bodies while they kissed wildly and passionately. Janice was amazed at the hard musculature of Curt's magnificent body. She couldn't stop staring at him, every inch of him, including the most male part of him, which was like nothing she'd ever imagined. As Curt lathered her body with Badedas bath gel, she returned the favor on every part of him, especially there. She was fascinated by the sleek, firm tautness of his skin, the heaviness of it in her hand. She was about to become more acquainted with his astounding anatomy when he suddenly pulled away from her.

"Hold it, baby, slow down," he entreated her.

Janice looked at him curiously. "Did I hurt you? Don't you like that?" she asked innocently.

"I like it too much, baby, that's the problem. Let's save something for dessert," he said with a smile. "In the meantime, how about this for an appetizer."

He bent his head down and gave her one of the long, sensual kisses that she craved every hour they were apart.

Running his big hands down her body, he stopped at her derriere and guided her until her back was flush against the slick tiled enclosure.

"You're beautiful," he breathed as he looked at her lissome form. They were both breathing unevenly, consumed with desire for each other.

"So are you," she said, sighing. She gasped as Curt kissed his way down her body, taking each blossoming nipple in his hot mouth and caressing it with his tongue. He licked and caressed his way down her trembling body, kneeling in the cascade of water while stroking her thighs with long, firm movements of his warm wet hands.

Janice's head fell back against the tiles as she realized the depths of intimacy that she was about to experience. Nothing in her imagination, nothing in her experience could have prepared her for the shock waves of ecstasy that rippled through her body as Curt devoted his lips and tongue to the most feminine part of her body. Her hands tightened on his shoulders and she moaned his name over and over as the ripples became a continuous, thunderous orgasm that left her weak and weeping with pleasure. As the last tremors began to slowly fade away, Janice felt like she was melting into the scented foam that was swirling down the drain. Curt held her up and kissed his way back up her body until their mouths were once again welded together, but it was even more exciting than before. Janice could smell her own feminine musk on Curt and she could taste the essence of her own body, heightening the erotic moment even more. Just when she thought she would surely die from sensation, Curt picked her up and carried her out of the shower stall into the bathroom.

He wrapped her in one of the big Egyptian cotton towels from the warming rack and took one for himself, wrapping it around his waist. Then he scooped her up and took her to the massive panel bed, where their lovemaking began all over again. The silk duvet was tossed on the floor, along with most of the pillows as Curt and Janice immediately divested themselves of the towels and dove into each other's arms. The feel of Janice's silky skin, the scent of her, the taste of her weren't enough; Curt had to be inside her, right now. He stopped long enough to realize he had no protection and looked around frantically for a solution. Janice correctly read the look on his face and rolled over on top of him to the nightstand that matched the bed. Pulling open the drawer she triumphantly pulled out a box of latex condoms and handed them to Curt with the sweetest smile he'd ever seen.

Curt sighed in relief and rewarded her with a huge kiss. "I love you, Jannie, I really do. Now, if you help me put this on . . ."

Janice was more than happy to oblige. He lay on his back while she stroked his tumescent penis with a soft, confident hand and then carefully rolled the protective device onto it.

"Now what?" she asked mischievously.

Curt looked at her golden beauty gleaming in the firelight as she knelt next to him. He reached over and pulled her to him, holding her tightly while he reversed their positions so she was underneath him.

"Now I show you how I feel about you, Jannie, and how you make me feel," he said in a voice thick with passion. And he did just that, sliding into her waiting body with all the tenderness and love he had never expressed to another woman. He was about to enter her fully when he stopped, realizing that something was amiss, or so he thought. Janice's eyes were closed in rapture and when he stopped moving, she started, wrapping her legs around his waist and pushing against the magnificent length that was filling her so completely.

Despite his misgivings Curt responded, rocking against her slowly at first, then more strongly as they established a rhythm that increased the pleasure for both of them. Janice was lost in passion. The heat of Curt's body, the musky scent that was emanating from their bodies, the damp flow of perspiration from him was driving her crazy, not to mention the incredible sensation of his body driving into hers. She felt as though she was going to explode into millions of stars, she couldn't hold out anymore.

"Curt, oh Curt, I . . . I, oh Curt," she moaned.

"Let it go, baby, just let go, I'm right here with you, I'm right here," he moaned in his turn and suddenly their bodies tightened and shuddered in a convulsive climax that seemed endless, like the fiery tail of an undiscovered comet circling their private universe.

Minutes later, Janice was still unable to speak. She was lying across Curt's sweat-slicked chest and trying to remember what normal breathing felt like. Curt was holding her like she was the most precious thing in the world and he, too, was utterly silent. Finally, he spoke.

"Why didn't you tell me?" he asked solemnly.

Janice raised her head slightly so she could look directly into his eyes. Tiredly, she brushed a long tendril of still-damp hair out of her eyes. "I'm sorry, Curt. I got caught up, I guess. I should have told you that I love you. Very, very much," she added and yawned sweetly like a little girl. Drowsily, she laid her head on his shoulder and started to drift away.

Curt was truly done in. Not only had she confessed to being in love with him, she had given him something she had never shared with another man—her body. As sweet as she looked lying there, he wasn't going to let her go to sleep just then.

"Listen, Jannie, I love you, too. I think I've been in love with you forever. But that's not what I'm talking about and you know it. You were a virgin. How did that happen and why didn't you tell me?"

But his questions went unanswered for the moment because Janice was at last enjoying the sleep of a very satisfied woman, being held tightly by the man she loved.

Curt sighed with pleasure and let her sleep. There was time enough to ask questions and truth be told, he was exhausted, too.

Ten

Janice hadn't been this happy since she adopted her children. She and Curt were totally, blissfully in love. After they made love, they slept for a few hours, and woke up starving for food as well as each other. By mutual consent they took a quick, utilitarian shower and dove into the light repast Janice had prepared, sitting naked in front of the fire and feeding each other with their fingers. And this time, Curt got an answer out of Janice.

"Okay, baby. Now you owe me an explanation of how you happened to be a virgin at your advanced age. You're thirty years old and still untouched. Fine as you are. That's just crazy," he mumbled as she slipped a piece of juicily ripe fresh pineapple into his mouth.

"Excuse me, but I'm twenty-eight, not thirty," she said indignantly. "I was only sixteen when I started college, remember? And I just never got around to sex. I was too shy to date for years and then when I got some backbone, I was too busy with my babies. And I wasn't about to start bringing odd men around my kids. You have to be really careful with how you conduct yourself, especially with young girls—you know that."

She stopped talking long enough to eat a big green grape from Curt's fingertips, licking his finger sensuously as she did so. She sipped her wine as she observed his dark beauty in the flickering light of the fire.

"Besides, Curt, I was never in love before. I've dated a

little bit, from time to time, but I always knew I was holding out for something big, something wonderful, earth-shattering like what my parents have," she said candidly. "Sometimes when I go over there in the evening, I can see them in the window before I get out of the car, and they're kissing like they're sixteen. After all the time they've been married, they're still happy to see each other every day. They like each other as much as they love each other," she said softly.

"I always wanted someone to look at me the way my daddy looks at my mother, like there was no other woman in the entire world for him but her. And I always wanted a man who would make me feel like his life was better because I was in it. Until I found that man, I wasn't going to have sex with anyone. Sex is too important to share with just anybody. At least, that's what I think."

Once again, Curt was knocked out. Janice's honesty, her integrity, and her ability to share herself with him were staggering. And if he understood what she was saying, her faith in him was humbling. Before he could ask for clarification, he was touched beyond measure when she knelt next to him and wrapped her arms around his waist. She kissed him on his shoulder, his chest, and the vulnerable dip beneath his Adam's apple.

"I waited a long, long time for you, Curt. You make me feel safe, secure, loved, and very special. I love you," she whispered.

Curt's heart caught in his throat and he found it difficult to speak. "I love you, too, Jannie. With all my heart. But baby, I'm not perfect, I'm not a knight on a white horse or anything. I'm just a big jock who got lucky," he cautioned her.

Janice laughed at that. "And who wants a knight on a white horse? Have you ever tried to polish armor? Then there's the matter of the horse. Do you know how much doody they produce? And what that doody smells like? And who gets to polish all that armor and clean up said doody while you're resting from slaying dragons? The fair maiden, that's who.

No, thank you! I'll take a nice assistant coach any day of the week," she said emphatically.

They both collapsed in laughter and almost immediately found better ways to occupy their time for the rest of the night. There were many more things that Janice wanted to learn about the art of making love, and under Curt's expert tutelage she proved an extremely apt pupil.

The Christmas holidays were especially joyful this year. Janice felt she had more reason than ever to celebrate since Curt had come into her life, a feeling that was shared by the children. They had insisted on including him in as many holiday activities as possible, including his attendance at their church Christmas pageant and going shopping with him as they purchased gifts for the family. And even though his game schedule made it necessary for them to delay their usual time to trim the tree, they all wanted to wait until he could be present to help them put decorations on the big blue spruce. As an added bonus, Curt's family spent the holidays in Detroit. Janice didn't realize how much she had been looking forward to meeting Curt's mother until the older woman gave her a warm embrace after looking her over from head to toe.

Althea Bowden Jackson, as she was known since her remarriage, approved of Janice very much. She was tired of dropping hints for her son to marry and produce some grandchildren. The fact that all her other children had notwithstanding, she wanted all of her children settled and married. She was wise enough to not utter a word, but she considered Janice's three as a lovely starter set. And if the loving behavior of Curt and Janice were any indicator, Althea would be a grandmother again very, very soon.

Immediately after Christmas, Curt was on the road again for a four-game series away from Detroit. Luckily, though, the team's schedule allowed for a three-day break before New

Year's Day, even though the first of January would be a travel day. That was fine with Curt; hectic though it was, his schedule wouldn't interfere with New Year's Eve. In the past the holiday had lacked much meaning for him, other than the fact that everyone he knew threw huge elaborate parties, which he generally didn't attend. This year it had special significance for him; it somehow symbolized the start of more than a new year, it was like a passport into a future with Janice. At least that was how he was going to treat it; he was going to give Janice an elegant celebration that would culminate in something extremely special. This was going to be a New Year's Eve that neither one of them would ever forget.

Several hours later, it looked as though he were right. The evening began with him picking her up at her condo, with her discreet weekender bag. He took one look at her in a vintage black lace Valentino dress and his heart melted. Janice always looked wonderful, but tonight she looked angelically sensual. He wanted to kiss her senseless right then and there, but he managed to restrain himself. They drove to his house with their fingers entwined and lost in their own thoughts; neither said much to the other. When Curt threw open the front doors, Janice was amazed at what she saw. The room that had been designated a study had been transformed into a sophisticated dining area complete with an intimate round table swathed in fine linens, set with crystal, exquisite porcelain, and silver.

Curt smiled broadly at the look of enchantment on Janice's face; he had spared no expense or imagination on this evening. From the pianist playing jazz selections in a secluded corner to the uniformed wait staff, the meal was perfectly prepared and elegant, and as well it should have been, coming from the Whitney. Curt didn't know which he was enjoying more, the fact that he and Sasha had managed to create a beautiful night for Janice, or the look of pure happiness on Janice's face. When the dessert cart was wheeled out and the Chocolate Ugly cake was revealed, Curt laughed at the sigh of rapture from Janice.

"Oh my," she said breathlessly. "You, this dinner, this dessert, just everything. Curt this is the nicest thing anyone's ever done for me."

She leaned over and gave Curt a brief kiss. "Can we have this in the living room? Next to the fireplace?"

"Absolutely, baby, anything you want," Curt replied.

In very short order they were seated in front of an aromatic fire. The catering staff had taken their leave, the pianist had gone, and it was just the two of them, bathed in the flickering light of the fire. The exquisite sounds of Cyrus Chestnut emanated from the Bose stereo and Janice was perfectly content. The billowing full skirt of the Valentino gown surrounded her and she looked like a ballerina in repose. Curt took a deep breath before asking her if she wanted more champagne.

"Yes, I would. Just a little, though," she answered.

Curt poured a small amount of a very rare and expensive vintage into her flute and handed it to her. Janice was looking directly into Curt's eyes as she took a sip of the softly bubbling wine, then gasped as something foreign touched her lip. She pulled the delicate flute away from her mouth and stared at it, puzzled. Holding the glass in front of the fire so she could see better, she put her long, slender forefinger into it and drew out the biggest ring she'd ever seen.

"Curt . . ." was all she could get out. "Curt, I . . . umm . . . oh my goodness," she murmured.

The mild anxiety Curt had been feeling turned into panic. "What's the matter, Jannie? Don't you like it? Don't you want it?"

Janice's hand immediately made a tight fist over the ring and she looked at him like he had lost his mind. He was sitting next to her with his long legs extended, his tuxedo jacket removed and the band collar of his shirt open, looking like an African king of a long-gone dynasty. Without a word she threw her arms around his neck and started laughing and crying at the same time.

"I want you, Curt. That's all, just you. Thank you a million times, but this could have been your class ring, a pop can pull-tab, a cigar band, anything. You're everything I want," she sobbed.

Curt's heart soared and he joined her in the laughter and the tears. He kissed her long and passionately, then cupped her face in his hands.

"Janice, I love you. You and Stacey and Lisa and Justin. I love you with all of my heart. Will you please marry me and be my wife, my family? We've waited long enough to be happy, Jannie, let's not wait any more. Marry me, baby," he said with all the passion he was feeling.

"It will be my extreme pleasure to marry you, Curt. I can't think of anything I'd rather do more. Except have some babies," she said sweetly, loving the look of happiness on Curt's face.

"Well then, don't you think you'd better put that ring on?" he asked with loving amusement.

"Oh!" Janice realized she hadn't really looked at the ring since she fished it out of the champagne. Opening her hand, which was still clenched around it for dear life, she screamed in pure excitement. It was an art deco ring in rose gold with an emerald-cut diamond flanked by seed pearls and pink rubies. The five-carat stone had a pinkish color, Janice thought, and Curt confirmed that fact as he slipped it on her finger.

"I hope you like it. It's an antique. Sasha took me to this really amazing place but I picked it out all by myself," he emphasized. "The big stone is a cinnamon diamond. If you don't like it, we can get anything you want, but I thought this one looked like you."

Janice extended her hand for a good long look at the ring she would wear for the rest of her life. "I love it, I wouldn't change it for anything. And I love you. Curt you've made me so happy tonight, I could just cry."

Curt put a finger under her chin and kissed away the vestiges of her earlier expression of joy.

"No more tears, baby. I never want to see you cry again,

even when you're happy. And I plan to make you happy for the rest of our lives," he said gruffly.

Wrapped in each other's arms while the old year faded away, they made plans for their future together.

Eleven

Curt had to leave town on New Year's Day to begin another road trip, but Janice wasn't nearly as upset about his absence as he was. She had a big wedding to plan and not a lot of time since they had decided on an August wedding. The day after New Year's, Janice was entertaining her mother, Sasha, Lisette, and Lisette's mother, Amyanah, in the family room of her condo. "Entertaining" was too loose a term for what was happening—it was more like a council of war to map strategy for a beautiful wedding. The large basement area had been cleverly converted into a laundry and utility room, as well as a cheery, inviting area for games, movie viewing, and the perfect place for wedding planning. Besides piles of bridal magazines and books of fabric samples, Sasha had procured videos and planning books galore, which the ladies could peruse to their hearts' content. At the moment, though, there was more happy chatter going on than actual planning. Janice had to recount every moment of Curt's proposal and show off her incredible ring before anyone could settle down to work.

Janice was sitting on the floor at her mother's feet with a dreamy smile on her face as she came to the part about retrieving the ring from the glass.

"There it was, this big beautiful ring, just sitting at the bottom of the glass! I almost broke that stupid flute trying to get it out, but I was trying to be all dainty, you know, and not look like a bear trying to paw honey out of a tree! I don't think I succeeded, though," she said, laughing.

Lisette snorted while she channel surfed on the big-screen television. "Hmmph. If it have been me, I'd have swallowed that ring—you know how I gulp champagne."

"Yes my darling, I do. I've been trying to teach you not to gulp since I stopped breastfeeding you," Amyanah said dryly. "Perhaps this will encourage you to make more of an effort."

"Okay, Maman, okay," Lisette muttered. "Ah! Here we go! There's always lots of bridal fashion shows on this time of year. So many people get engaged over the holidays and start planning weddings that there's always something good on. Although I wish Elsa Klensch hadn't retired," she sighed.

Everyone agreed that Elsa Klensch's late and much lamented program, *Style,* was indeed a watermark for fashion. But the wedding showcase that Lisette found on E!, the entertainment channel, was quite comprehensive. The commentator was going on about all the celebrity couplings that had occurred during the holidays as a lead-in to the show.

"Yes, Santa left quite a few carats in the stockings of some very happy ladies this season!" she chirped merrily. "The lovely and talented actress Tonya Moore and her longtime steady Rick Brooks of the Baltimore Ravens are saying 'I do' this summer. Popular songbird Chessie Wright and her producer Matt Stephens are putting an end to years of 'will they or won't they' speculation; they *will,* in a July Fourth extravaganza. And all of Atlanta is abuzz that former Atlanta Hawks forward Curt Bowden is tying the knot with his lady of long-standing, supermodel Nyesha Jones. No word on when they'll be tying the knot, but Nyesha assures me it will be very, very soon!"

The next thing seen on the television screen was the smiling face of Nyesha Jones, the so-called supermodel who once bragged that she didn't get out of bed in the morning unless an assignment was paying her at least $15,000. Her famous smile bracketed by her legendary dimples was in full effect as she gushingly confirmed the news.

"Curt and I have actually been engaged for some time, we just never announced it formally. But since we decided to set a date, we saw no reason to keep it a secret anymore! We're so happy and I feel like the luckiest woman in the world!" she purred as she flashed a hugely ostentatious ring for the millions of viewers to admire.

Janice immediately turned a pasty white and she broke out into a cold sweat. Her stomach started churning and her head was spinning. It felt as though her lungs had collapsed; she was finding it that hard to take a breath. She thought wildly that she was going to faint. How could this be happening? This had to be some kind of joke, she thought frantically. She couldn't look at the four women in the room with her, but she could feel their eyes on her, could sense the shared shock and anger. *How could Curt ask me to marry him if he was engaged to someone else?* Her breath became more shallow and strained as she fought for composure. Someone had the presence of mind to turn off the broadcast, but Janice was so deep in shock, she didn't realize it. *This isn't real,* she thought frantically, *it can't be real, it can't be.*

Curt's reaction to the news was more to the point. He caught the tail end of the item on an ESPN spot on the television in the visitors' locker room of Staples Center in L.A. His jaw went slack from shock and then tightened in fury. Only one person was responsible for this and he knew immediately who it was.

Curt stormed out of the locker room already punching the speed dial code for Janice's number. There was no answer on Janice's end, so he left a message on her voice mail. And on her cell phone. And at Le Coeur de la Maison. Eventually she would get one of his messages and he could explain everything to her. No harm, no foul. But there was someone who had to answer for this—the idiot who started the rumor.

Curt wasn't able to get Janice on the phone until after the game had been played, which made it an ungodly hour in

Detroit. But by now the story had taken on a life of its own; it seemed that every headline-starved tabloid talk show needed a piece of the action. There was a blurb on every channel about his supposed engagement. The most outrageous ones were from the Detroit stations, which showed footage of Janice cheering him on at courtside. Who is the mystery woman who was trying to steal Nyesha's man, one reporter asked coyly. Things were definitely out of hand.

When Janice finally answered the phone, Curt wasn't reassured by the sound of her voice.

"Okay, Curt, if there's an explanation, I'd love to hear it. It was all over the Detroit channels and my phone hasn't stopped ringing since the story broke. My girls cried themselves to sleep and Justin is ready to sock you in the knee the next time he sees you, so I hope there's a good explanation for this," she said tersely.

Curt was taken aback by the dry, inexpressive tone she was using, as well as by the fact that she needed an explanation. Didn't she trust him?

"Look, Jannie, it's really simple. Nyesha Jones is the little sister of a guy I played ball with back in Atlanta. When he got traded to the Golden State Warriors, I promised him I'd keep an eye on her. She's a little flirty and tends to run with a fast crowd, so I've had to bail her out of trouble a few times. I kind of run interference for her from time to time. If some guy is pushing up on her too close, I pretend to be her man and he backs off, that kind of thing. The little knucklehead must've gotten into something really deep for her to pull this one, though. She should have never made such a stupid, irresponsible remark to a reporter, and I'm going to tell her so when I see her again," he added casually.

Janice had been twisting the corner of her sheet during this recitation. Trying to get out of bed without waking the sleeping Lisa, Janice maneuvered herself carefully out of the covers so she could better express herself to Curt.

As she walked down the hall with the cordless phone in her hand, she was suddenly filled with resentment. She'd been put through a day from hell and he was going to give the guilty party a lecture?

"Curt, I'm glad you think this is some cute little prank, but I have three very upset children here. The man they love and adore and thought was going to be their father is all over the news as being some other woman's fiancé—how do you think it made them feel? How do you think it made me feel? I'll tell you, like the world's biggest fool, that's how! And you're going to give her a little talking to, is that it?"

Janice could not have cared less that her voice had become shrill and angry, that's just how she felt at that moment. Curt didn't seem to have an ounce of understanding about how this had affected her and the children.

"Hey, Jannie, I didn't say it was cute, not at all. I just know Nyesha very well and she would have never, ever done anything like this if she thought it would cause trouble for me. We haven't spoken in months, so she has no idea that we're engaged. She would have never tried to embarrass you or me if she'd only known," he said persuasively.

At the same time that he was offering this explanation, something in him was just a little hurt that Janice had to have things explained to her. Rumors, innuendoes, and gossip were part of being in the public eye, even when you were just an assistant coach on a professional team. Janice needed to have absolute faith in him or they were in for some bumpy times, but he wisely didn't express this thought to her.

They ended the call, but without all the warmth and sweetness they usually shared. Janice wasn't ready to forget her miserable day that quickly, not after seeing her children so affected.

The next day brought more stories as Nyesha seemed to be in front of every camera in America. The fact that she was the new spokesmodel for a line of luxury makeup probably accounted for why she was suddenly a media darling, but it was galling in the extreme for Janice. She tried to stay focused on her conversation with Curt and with all his assurances, but it was difficult. She even tried to watch the televised game, the second game in the Pistons–Lakers series. With her arms crossed and a troubled expression on her face, Janice watched impassively as the two teams battled it out on court.

Suddenly, a flurry of activity at the Pistons' courtside drew every camera. It was seconds before the half and just as the buzzer sounded, Curt was embraced by none other than Nyesha Jones, who wasted no time in letting the world know how happy she was to be with him. Even by Hollywood standards the kiss was remarkable; it looked as though it would never end.

Well, Curt, how are you going to explain that one, Janice thought as she quickly turned off the TV and flung the remote into a corner of the bedroom. For the first time since the whole ordeal started, Janice burst into tears as quietly as possible, so she wouldn't wake the children. Twisting her engagement ring off her finger, she tossed it into the top drawer of her nightstand. Tomorrow she would send it back to him via registered mail. Enough was enough.

Curt was beyond fury at this point. Grabbing Nyesha's arm he managed to get her past the phalanx of reporters and cameramen into an empty office near the locker rooms. Nyesha's sumptuous looks made no impression on him whatsoever; her flawless toffee brown complexion, perfect breasts, and legendary legs were nothing to him.

"Girl, what is wrong with you? First of all, I'm *engaged,* Nyesha. Engaged to be married to a woman who's barely speaking to me because of your big mouth. And second, what in the world possessed you to be so irresponsible? I know I told you I'd have your back, but what in the hell made you tell this big whopping lie? And why in the name of God did you show up here tonight for that stupid stunt you just pulled? I think that weave is too tight or something." By now Curt was shouting at the top of his considerable lungs, pointing his finger in Nyesha's face.

"Curt, let me explain. I just started as the spokesmodel

for Lotus Cosmetics and I need a lot of publicity. A *lot*—you can't ever let the public forget who you are. So since I'm supposed to be all glamorous and everything, it wouldn't hurt to make it look like somebody was madly in love with me. And the big ring was just perfect, they have this new scent coming out called Facets, and . . . and . . ." Nyesha's voice trailed off as she sensed Curt was buying none of it.

"Nyesha, that's a bunch of bull and even you know it. Cut to the chase and tell me what's going on," Curt growled.

Nyesha perched on the corner of the desk and crossed her long, well-insured legs. She cocked her head to one side and gave Curt her most winsome smile. "Okay, but you have to promise not to get mad. I've been dating this guy and he keeps dragging his feet about proposing, so I thought if he had a little competition, he might get it in gear. And I didn't actually tell anybody I was engaged, I just started wearing the ring, which is faux, by the way, and people started making assumptions. And people who had seen you and me together added two and two and got five, and I never corrected them. Then somebody wanted to interview me and I'd just had a big fight with Gerald so *then* I said, yes, we were engaged. And since I was already in L.A. for a shoot, my publicist thought this would be some good coverage. Are you mad at me?" she whined in a little girl voice.

Curt stared at her in disbelief.

"Hello? *Yes*, I'm mad at you, birdbrain!" He accompanied the statement with several taps on her forehead, to make sure the words were penetrating.

"And if this Gerald has any sense, he's mad at you, too. That was just off the hook stupid, Nyesha, and you know it. With my luck, everybody in the world saw you put me in that lip-lock and now I have something else to explain. Thanks a lot, nitwit."

Properly chastised, Nyesha lowered her head for a moment, then snapped her fingers and looked Curt in the eye.

"I can fix this, Curt, I really can! I have to be in Detroit next week for a photo shoot in the casinos. I'll meet with your fiancée, explain everything, and apologize! How's that?" she asked brightly.

Curt immediately shook his head. "No, thanks, Nyesha. That's not necessary. Janice and I are adults and we can handle our own business. Just keep your big mouth shut from here on out and you won't need to explain anything to anybody. And start making retractions about this fake engagement, you hear me? Don't make me have to start giving out interviews of my own," he said firmly.

"Okay, Curt, whatever you say," she said meekly.

"I'll see you after the game if you can behave yourself. I've got to get down to the locker room. Try to stay out of trouble for the next two quarters, would you?"

The next week seemed to be one eternal everlasting round of disaster for Janice. Even after Curt got home and Janice could see for herself that nothing had changed between the two of them, she was still uneasy. As she tried to explain to Curt, it was the fact that the children were so hurt that made her so unhappy.

"Curt, you weren't here. You didn't see how upset they were! They adore you. They've given their hearts to you, their trust, and for them to think you had betrayed them was devastating. I never want to go through anything like that again," she said with a faint glimmer of tears in her eyes.

Curt's heart twisted at the sight of her pain, but he had to say his piece. They were sitting on opposite ends of the sofa in her living room, trying to regain a semblance of normalcy.

"Jannie, I can't tell you enough how sorry I am that the kids were hurt. I know Nyesha is crazy and impetuous, but I had no idea she was that nuts. And I have a pretty good idea of how the kids felt; when I got home and you weren't wearing your ring, it was like somebody had kicked a hole in my gut. I thought we had something special, that we were going all the way with our commitment to each other."

Janice turned huge hurt eyes to him. "Well, of course we

do. That's why I was so disturbed by all of this." *And why I didn't send my ring back to you,* she thought ruefully.

Curt resisted the urge to crush her to him and offer all the comfort he had. "Well, Jannie, that means you have to trust me. All of you have to trust me and I have to trust in you. You can't believe the junk that's out there or we're never going to make it."

"I understand that, Curt, in theory. But you have to understand that I can't allow my children to be hurt like that by wild rumors and lies in the media. It's just not fair to them. They didn't ask for this, you know. I can't ignore my responsibility to them just because I fell madly in love with you."

Curt had more to say on the subject but the children, who were returning from an afternoon outing with Janice's parents, interrupted them. They had completely forgiven Curt and were noisy and affectionate in their greetings. Janice merely watched them hug and kiss Curt and wondered if everything would ever be back to normal.

Janice was feeling better but not completely back to her former joy when Curt left on his next road trip. He just wasn't home long enough to assuage her fears and doubts. She expressed this to her mother, who had dropped by Maison to say hello. Her atelier was nearby in the Harmonie Park section of Detroit and it wasn't an unheard of visit. It was a welcome one, however. Janice needed to talk.

"Mom, I feel like I should be more trusting or more understanding or something, but the whole thing is just making me crazy. You can't pick up a tabloid, a magazine, turn on the radio, or anything without seeing that woman! And Curt says she's going to issue a retraction, but I haven't heard any, have you?"

Without waiting for an answer, Janice went on. "I know Curt loves me, or he says he does, but what I know for sure is that I really truly do love him, Mom. It's so amazing, how I feel when we're together or even when we're apart, for that matter. Outside of my children, I've never had such an intense emotional reaction to anyone in my life; it actually frightens me, Mom. I don't know what I'd do if this all turned out to be a fake."

Before Pat could answer, the receptionist buzzed Janice's intercom.

"There's someone here requesting you, Ms. VanHook; shall I schedule her in for another time or will you be able to accommodate her?"

Janice looked at her mother apologetically. "Yes, Miranda," she addressed the receptionist. "Today is fine, I'll be right out."

Pat rose from her chair at the same time Janice left her small marquetry desk.

"I'll walk out with you, honey. We'll talk tonight. I know things seem really dire right now, but I think you two will work everything out," Pat said comfortingly.

By then they had reached the reception area of the salon and Janice turned to greet her caller. She and Pat both became statue still as the woman approached them; it was none other than Nyesha Jones.

"Well. You must be Janice, am I right? Curt's told me so much about you," Nyesha said breathily. She looked Janice over from her glistening hair to her designer pumps and took her time about it.

"Well, Janice, I'd like to get right to the point, especially since things are a little awkward. I'm sure you've seen some things on the news and read a few things lately that might require a little explanation, and that's what I'm here to do," she said.

Janice finally found her voice and was able to reply. "That would be nice," she murmured.

"Well, the truth of the matter is this. Curt asked me to come and see you and explain that . . . well, he and I are very much in love and he's terribly sorry he had to hurt you like this. He thinks this is for the best and he hopes you'll be able to forgive him in time."

"You did what?" Curt yelled so loud, he could feel his larynx about to explode.

Nyesha didn't even wince. After all, he was several states away from her; it wasn't like he could get his hands around her throat just then.

"Look, I said I was sorry before I started the conversation. I really was trying to do the right thing. I found out where your little girlfriend works and when I was in Detroit, I went there to apologize. You have to understand, Curt. I'm all bloated from eating a few measly peanuts on the flight in and she comes out looking like she was about to hit the runway of the fall Versace show in Milan and it just got to me. I guess I have PMS or something because I just lost it." Nyesha sniffed without any real remorse.

"As hard as I work to be this fine and she just wakes up in the morning looking like that! Don't tell me she doesn't, either 'cause I know better! My scalp is still hurting from that last twenty-five-hundred-dollar weave and she's standing there with that head full of blow hair. I haven't had a decent meal in months and she's got a nineteen-inch waist and probably eats like a horse. And to top it all off there was a woman with her who looked just like Pat Dayton and I just wasn't having it that day! I could work the rest of my life and never be another Pat Dayton! So I just snapped," she mumbled through a mouthful of food.

"You crazy heifer, I told you to keep out of this! You're insane, Nyesha, certifiable. Stay the hell away from my family and from me until you get some sense. And that means I never expect to see your crazy ass again because you'll never be sane."

Curt depressed the off button on his cell and threw it across the room. Now what?

Twelve

"Mom, I just don't want to. That's all, I just don't. Please don't ask me again," Janice moaned. She was slumped on an old ratty armchair in the back room of Papillion, watching Pat put the finishing touches on a sketch of a formal gown.

The last thing on earth Janice wanted to do was be in a fashion show, especially a Valentine's Day soiree. Why her mother couldn't see that, Janice had no idea, but then again, things had been so strange since New Year's, nothing really surprised her anymore.

She and Curt were no longer engaged, were in fact not communicating with each other in any way. No matter how Curt tried to explain, the fact remained that Nyesha Jones had confirmed to her face what the gossipmongers and rumor mills had started; she was Curt's fiancée and they were in love. And Curt had explained this to her over and over again until he got tired of defending his honor against a pack of lies with no basis whatsoever in truth. Their last conversation was more of a confrontation than anything else. Janice still felt the pain of every single word.

She had handed Curt her beautiful engagement ring and told him that they both needed time to think things through.

"Curt, I think part of the problem is that we rushed into this. We don't really know each other that well and we got caught up in the romance of the moment," she said sadly. "But I have a lot at stake here, Curt. My children were terribly upset over all of this, and I can't allow that to happen again. I have to put them first, no matter what we feel for each other. I think we just need some time apart to think about what we both want."

Curt had looked at her with so much pain and anger that Janice couldn't meet his eyes. "Jannie, you might need time to think, but I don't. I know what I want, and that's a life with you and the kids. And you might be Supermom but you're wrong about them. We sat down and talked about what had happened and how Nyesha started all this mess to get her man's attention and they understand. They didn't 'forgive' me, because I didn't do anything wrong. They understand what happened and they don't think it's that big a deal. You're the one who's using this to keep me away, Janice."

Janice shook off the memory and rose from the armchair. Wandering into the main showroom she went from mannequin to mannequin, not really looking at any of her mother's exquisite fashions, just brooding. She couldn't get Curt's last words to her out of her mind.

"I can only tell you what's in my heart, Janice. I love you, no one else. I want you to be my wife, not Nyesha or anybody else. I've explained this to you over and over again and it's like talking to a brick wall. I can't explain anymore. Either you're woman enough to trust me and stand by me come what may, or you're the little princess who can't deal with anything that isn't picture perfect. You've got to make the decision, Jannie. I can't convince you and I'm not going to beg you, so the next move has to be yours." And before she could utter another sound, he'd left her standing in her living room with the sound of the front door closing behind him.

The weeks since then had been tense and ugly. Janice hadn't been able to sleep, she'd been withdrawn and edgy and most of all heartbroken. Somehow, the confrontation with Nyesha had sent Janice back in time to a place where she was young, gawky, shy, and insecure. All the pain and misery of her first crush on Curt seemed to take over her conscious mind to the point where she couldn't think straight. Yet she couldn't rid herself of the idea that Curt was right about some things. Even her brothers had pointed out that there was more to the situation than met the eye. They had insisted on taking her out after she broke off her engagement. They were hoping to cheer her up and make her laugh for one thing, and for another, she was losing weight she couldn't spare. Nobody wanted to tell her to her face, but Janice was beginning to look truly gaunt.

Janice had succumbed to the tantalizing aromas of the Majestic, a café-cum-bowling alley in downtown Detroit that was known for its breakfasts. Many, many people had eaten away a massive hangover with a custom-made omelet at the Majestic. Maybe it worked for heartache, too, Janice mused as she stared at the contents of her plate.

Randy leaned toward his little sister, helping himself to a bite of her untouched omelet as he did so. "It wasn't Curt's fault, Janice. Are you so insecure that you're going to lose the love of your life over what basically amounts to gossip, or are you and Curt going talk this out?"

Janice's lower lip stuck out a little. They were supposed to be on her side, not Curt's! She was the injured party, why couldn't they see that? She said this to her brothers, expecting an immediate apology and some affectionate coddling. Instead she got a lecture from both of them.

"Look, Janice, it wasn't his fault that his little friend went crazy. It's not the first time somebody told a lie, and it won't be the last. Yeah, it was kinda crappy to see all that junk in the papers and see all that stuff on TV, but it was big news in Detroit for a hot minute. He's a new coach, the team is headed for the play-offs, she's a big name, of course it's gonna get a lot of coverage for a minute. But it was all hype, Janice. All that matters is how he feels about you and the kids, and you're just not hearing any of that, are you?" Conrad finished his spiel with a disappointed shake of his head.

"Yes, but Conrad, he's acting like it was no big deal. Like I shouldn't be upset or humiliated or like my children shouldn't be affected! It *was* a big deal, I assure you," Janice responded heatedly.

Randy leaned back in his chair, crossed his arms, and looked at his sister. "Janice, Curt was acting like it wasn't a big deal because to him it *wasn't*. None of it mattered to him because he knew what was true. It's kind of ironic, though. The reason you had all that heartache in college was because somebody told him a lie about you, and he didn't bother to check it out. Now somebody told you a lie about him and you won't even listen to him when he's telling you the truth. Strange, huh?"

Since that day Janice had been more upset than ever, but with herself and no one else. For the very first time she truly understood how Curt felt so many years ago when some jealous coed had told him all those lies. Now she knew exactly why he had turned his back on her so long ago and now, after all her big talk, she'd done the same thing to Curt. She'd allowed lies to drive her away from the man she loved. Randy had made her see the truth of the situation, that she was as culpable as anyone in her current misery. She had allowed other people's actions to lead her into a path of pain, and the only one who could get her over this was her.

She had tried contacting Curt several times and gotten nowhere. She could never catch him at home, his cell phone went unanswered, and she got no response to the heartfelt letter she had sent him. She had just taken it too far and there was no turning back. Curt had moved on. The love that was supposed to last forever was all gone and for this she could blame herself. Janice was thoroughly unhappy and all she wanted was to be alone to mourn. Unfortunately, her mother didn't agree with this method at all, which is why she was trying to get Janice to model in some society fashion show and auction on Valentine's Day. Getting busy and staying busy was Pat's cure for what ailed one.

"Janice, it's time you got yourself together, honey. Your father is concerned about you and so are your brothers. And I don't have to tell you what this is doing to the children, especially Stacey. You know what a worrywart she is. You need to show them that everything is fine with you and you can best do that by behaving normally. Being in this show would help a lot, dear. Besides, you're the only one who can pull off this dress," she wheedled.

While she was talking, Pat had the fingers of her right hand crossed behind her back. She wasn't exactly telling a lie, but she wasn't revealing the entire truth of the matter. She wasn't telling Janice about the long talk she and Cyrus had with Curt a couple of weeks before. And she certainly wasn't telling her the truth about the fashion show. Her conscience was clear, though; she was doing the right thing.

"Okay, Mom, I'll do it for you. For all the reasons you mentioned. But my heart won't be in it," she warned. *My heart will be wherever Curt is, even if he never forgives me,* she thought sadly.

Over the next week, the week before the event, Janice had cause to regret her decision more than once. The kids were so enthused over her modeling that she continued with the charade even though she wished many times that she was in Zaire or Bali or anyplace where the obnoxious red and white sentimentality of Valentine's Day wouldn't be visible.

February 14 dawned gray and slushy with thick wet flakes of snow falling everywhere. Dropping the children off at school was the only normal event of Janice's day. Everything else was like a comedy of errors. First, her mother called her on her cell phone to remind her about her appointment at Oasis for her hair. She slogged through the morning traffic congested by snow to arrive at the posh day spa in time to get her mane tamed into a feminine updo. While she was paying for her services, she got another phone call, this one from her father.

"Baby, do me a favor. Your mother's gift is at the jeweler's and my car is being serviced this morning. Can you run out there and pick it up for me?"

"Sure, Daddy. Where do I need to go?"

Janice swallowed hard upon hearing that the jeweler was in Somerset Town Centre, the fashionable mall at least twenty minutes from her current location, but she rallied nicely. At least she was too busy to think about how miserable she was, especially since she got another call, this one from Sasha.

"Hon, I know this is short notice, but I'm also in the fashion show tonight. Yeah, me with all the junk in my trunk," she laughed merrily. "Anyway, I'll pick the kids up from school if you'll do me a huge favor and pick up a package from Neiman's. Your dad told me you're going out to Somerset, so . . ."

By the time Janice made her way to the hotel where the fashion show was being held, she was about done in. She had fetched packages for her father and Sasha, picked up her brother's tux from the cleaners and loitered around her parents' house to accept delivery of a package from UPS. She hadn't had time to think about anything except running from place to place to place. She hadn't even seen her children since she dropped them off at school, and to top it off, she was starving.

She had just entered the lobby of the hotel and was about to ask the concierge which room was being used for the fashion show when she was practically accosted by Lisette and Sasha. They flew to her side and relieved her of her bundles.

"Ooh, you're finally here! Let's go, your mother is waiting for you!" Lisette exclaimed.

Before Janice knew what was happening, she found herself in a large dressing room standing on a white cloth while Pat adjusted the back of the beautiful long white dress she had just donned. Lisette and Sasha had body-slammed her into a chair and applied her makeup with the speed of light while making sure her hair was still perfect.

"Hold still, Janice," Pat said. "I've just got to get this last . . . okay, darling, you're all ready."

"I'm ready to eat, that's what I'm ready for," Janice grumbled. "Where are my children? Where's Daddy? Why is everyone in Detroit involved in this dumb fashion show? I know it's supposed to be for charity, but dang, Ma," Janice said fretfully.

Pat ignored the petulant tone of her daughter's voice and clasped her hands together. "You look beautiful, Janice. Just beautiful," she said with emotion.

Janice finally looked at herself in the wall of mirrors and gasped at what she saw. The dress her mother had designed was extraordinary; long-sleeved with a deep square neckline and a nonexistent back, a long straight skirt with an incredible bouffant train of silk georgette, and a cluster of silk gardenias at the small of her bared back where the train began. A fantastic pair of diamond earrings with a pearl drop was her only jewelry, but she needed no ornamentation other than the stars in her eyes. Even to her own critical eyes she looked wonderful. Suddenly she had the urge to cry.

Pat sensed the tears coming and announced it was time for her entrance. Before Janice could take a good breath, she was practically shoved through the door where she saw not a runway, but a huge, candlelit room full of people sitting in gilt chairs trimmed with scarlet bows arranged on either side of a central aisle that led to an . . . altar? Rob Thomas, Sasha's husband, was standing there, as well as three men she recognized as Curt's brothers. On the other side of the altar was Justin, in a darling tuxedo with a red vest, and Stacey and Lisa, wearing long white dresses and huge smiles on their faces and holding bouquets of red roses and baby's breath. And there were Lisette and Sasha, each wearing incredible red gowns and holding a sheaf of white calla lilies. Janice's rosy lips parted slightly as her overtaxed brain finally took in what was going on. This wasn't a Valentine's Day fashion show; it was a *wedding,* her wedding to Curt. Among the many faces of the guests she glimpsed Armand and Amyanah, Curt's mother and stepfather, and what looked like the entire Pistons organization. And in the doorway was Curt, holding out his hand to her.

Janice couldn't utter a sound. She took Curt's large warm hand immediately, but she couldn't manage to speak a word.

Curt could tell how overwhelmed she was and took her into the anteroom where the groom's party had dressed. He closed the door behind them and turned to her.

"Jannie, please don't say no. I went to talk to your parents a couple of weeks ago and the three of us actually sat down and talked about everything. It was your mom who pointed out that I was feeling like you were feeling in college when I didn't show up for the dance because of that mess that what's-her-name started. It was the first time I truly understood how hurt you were. And this just seemed like the best way to make it all up to you, sweetheart."

He stopped speaking long enough to kiss away the tiny tears that were forming in the outer corners of her eyes.

"Will you marry me, Jannie? Right here, right now, in front of God and our families and everybody?"

Janice took a deep breath and almost shouted her answer. "Yes! Right now, Curt, before you change your mind. I'm so sorry for the way I behaved, but I've never loved anyone like this before. I was so afraid of losing you that I pushed you out the door. I love you so much, Curt, I never want to be away from you again. I love you," she repeated, her eyes blazing with passion.

A gruff voice at her side made her look to her left. Her father was offering his arm.

"Is this what you want, baby? You can run if you want to, I got the car warmed up in the alley," he said cheerfully.

Janice smiled up at her father and said, "I want this more than anything, Daddy."

At her right side Pat sighed. "Well, let's get to stepping, we don't want to keep your guests waiting. Get back up to that altar, Curt, and let's get this show on the road. You children have taken years off my life with this," she reminded them.

She handed Janice a cascade of gardenias and dabbed the corners of her eyes with a lace hankie.

As her parents escorted her to the man whose love she thought she had lost forever, Janice was overcome with joy. Curt left the altar to take her from her parents, shaking her father's hand solemnly and kissing her mother on the cheek. Then he took Janice's hand and the two of them stood before the minister who had baptized her brothers, her, and her children. They never took their eyes off each other as Rev. Huggins said the words that would make them a family for all time. When he pronounced them man and wife, a cascade of happy tears escaped from Janice's eyes.

"I love you, Curt," she whispered.

"And I love you, Janice. Nothing's ever going to change that," he answered.

They were so blissfully wrapped up in each other, they didn't notice Justin, Stacey, and Lisa giving one another high fives and doing a victory dance at the altar.

Lisa smiled happily at Stacey. "We did it! Well, we didn't actually do much, but we got a dad! Now what?"

Stacey looked at their mother and new father kiss and smiled confidently.

"A baby brother, what else? I did the math, and if they keep this up, we could have one by Christmas," she added as the recessional began.

"You know what, Lisa? We're going to be a very happy family, all of us."

And being the exceptionally bright child that she was, she was absolutely right.

HAPPY VALENTINE'S DAY!

I've always loved the romance and sentiment that comes with the celebration of Valentine's Day and I took special pleasure in writing *Wait for Love* for that reason. I hope you enjoyed reading it as much as I enjoyed writing it.

Until next time,

Melanie
I Chronicles 4:10
MelanieAuthor@aol.com
P.O. Box 5176
Saginaw, Michigan 48603

ABOUT THE AUTHOR

Melanie Woods Schuster currently lives in Saginaw, Michigan, where she works in sales for the largest telecommunications company in the state. She attended Ohio University. Her occupations indicate her interests in life; Melanie has worked as a costume designer, a makeup artist, an admissions counselor at a private college, and has worked in marketing. She is also an artist, a calligrapher, and she makes jewelry and designs clothing. Writing has always been her true passion, however, and she looks forward to creating more compelling stories of love and passion in the years to come.

SEVENTY-TWO HOURS AND COUNTING

Linda Walters

DEDICATION

I dedicate this book to my family without whom I would not have acquired the patience, the perseverance, and the drive which helped to produce it. Thank you Niki, Lance, and Teylor for your continued support and energy. You are the wind beneath my wings and I am eternally grateful for your presence in my life and on the planet.

I love you guys, Mom

And to my three sisters, Gloria, Connie, and Delores and their families, I'd like to extend my love and gratitude. Thanks for taking the time to listen to my literary rambling, not to mention the mandatory readings of short stories, articles, etc.

Love ya, Linda Yvette

ACKNOWLEDGEMENTS

I'd like to extend a heartfelt thank you to my editor, Chandra Taylor, and the entire staff at Kensington Publishing. Thank you to the staff members of BET Books, especially Linda J. Gill and Kicheko Driggins.

Much gratitude goes out to Donna Hill, whose guidance and support I am eternally grateful for.

And most importantly, I'd like to thank God who makes all things possible.

Linda Walters

Day One

Majestic and just out of reach, the Catskill mountains framed the landscape surrounding each curve of Interstate 684. Directions were firmly suctioned to the dashboard, hastily scribbled notes as near to a lifeline as one could get.

Morgan Collins was thoroughly disgusted, somewhat off kilter, and not at all convinced that she wasn't lost. She tried to find something on the radio with a clear, audible tone without success; with each additional mile she put between her and the nearest signal, the more fuzzy, monotonous, and almost unintelligible everything playing on it had become. Turning her attention away from the highway that had faced her for almost two and a half hours, she quickly inserted a CD into the slot , resigned to providing her own listening pleasure. "Topaz," one of the most popular singles from the CD of the same name filled the car's interior. Morgan loved jazz. The Rippingtons, with their unique sound and dedicated following of listeners, were one of her favorite groups.

Glancing briefly at the other vehicles on the northbound side of Interstate 684, Morgan wondered how many of the occupants might also be on their way to the annual New York State Mortgage Banking conference currently in progress at Villa Novella Resort and Conference Center. Although the Catskill mountains were beautiful, she found herself silently praying that the number was less than zero. Perhaps if no one came, they could all turn around and go home. She laughed out loud at the thought and wondered if she was on the verge of either hysteria or insanity. Or maybe she was just nervous, dissatisfied with the industry, her job, and most of all, her life.

For what seemed like the tenth time that day, Morgan passed another farm with the requisite silo, barn, and a large acreage of rolling pastures with huge black-and-white cows grazing. It reminded her of an oil painting done by either Winslow Homer or Grandma Moses. The only thing missing was a marker to denote the distance that obviously stood between each country-like setting. She'd driven for almost twenty minutes this time before she'd even spotted what one would refer to as a "neighbor."

Downstate in West Hempstead where she lived, the tree-lined streets were quiet, clean, and tight; your nearest neighbor only several feet away and not very far out of your sight. You never visited without first calling, never dropped in without a reason, and never tried to cross that invisible border of next-door-neighbor without a firm and distinct invitation. The perceived distance was actually just as wide as the miles she now covered between each farmhouse dotting the landscape.

Why they hold these conferences way the heck upstate in woodsy owl country is beyond me. I mean, couldn't they have found an accommodating, interesting location somewhere within the confines of New York City; or for that matter, why not make it a real departure from the norm and hold it somewhere like Puerto Rico were her thoughts as she once again consulted the Hagstrom map in her lap. Morgan quickly realized that after the next turnoff, she'd almost be at her destination.

Opening the window as if to be heard, she shouted, "I'm almost there," almost as an affirmation, and then returned the window to its closed position, the rush of cold midwinter air sobering. The relief was welcome; she hated long, boring drives where the only thing allowable was a heartfelt monologue with oneself. It made for microscopic introspection, something she found herself avoiding lately. It made for microscopic self-analysis, something she found herself avoiding lately. It was too painful. Besides, she never seemed to be able to come up with answers that made any sense.

Morgan contemplated the two days ahead and realistically figured that perhaps the conference wouldn't be so bad after all. It had been a long time since she'd had to attend one of these gatherings. Her tenure in the industry had allowed her to "recuse" herself in the past, but with a new position as Area Manager with Town and Country Mortgage Bank, countless new challenges and changes were most definitely in order.

She wondered if any of the other attendees were having the same difficulties in following the directions, and locating the different points of reference at the same time as keeping their cars on the road. The sky darkened and it began to drizzle lightly. *Please let me get there before it gets dark,* she thought, turning on the windshield wipers. Her mind always seemed to operate with greater efficiency in daylight. Prescription reading glasses, which were in her briefcase in the trunk of the car, would have helped, but she rarely used them.

Morgan's mind reluctantly wandered to the topic she most wanted to avoid. Garrett. She'd wrestled with her feelings all morning as she'd packed, loaded the trunk of the Saab 9000, and during most of a mindless drive. Still, no solid decisions had even remotely been realized and she accepted the fact that she was no closer to understanding their relationship than she'd been twelve hours ago when he'd suggested that they drive separately. And although she knew he'd be there at some point during the three-day conference, he'd tried to play it down when they spoken the night before.

"I'll probably leave in the morning around ten, if I even show up. I really have so much work to do, I don't know how I can think of leaving. You go on ahead and I'll probably catch up sometime within the weekend."

"Yeah, well I plan to get there sometime in the late afternoon," Morgan replied as she moved around her bedroom, carefully selecting "casual business attire." The company memorandum had also outlined an agenda that included two days of meetings, product seminars, and carefully orchestrated cocktail parties, with business being the main event.

"Unfortunately, it's mandatory that I attend, especially since I only recently accepted the position with Town and Country Mortgage Bank. You know they pride themselves on having the most thoroughly trained mortgage consultants in the industry. We're also inclined to be pretty serious movers and shakers of the social scene as well," she'd added, laughing instinctively in an effort to cover up her disappointment.

"Well, they certainly hired the right one for that," Garrett responded. "I'm looking forward to watching you shake up the industry, babe. The move over to Town and Country was the right one. Look, let me finish up the rest of this paperwork so these loans can close sometime next week. I'll look for you whenever I get there, okay?"

"Sure, drive safe. Bye, honey." Morgan hung up slowly, mixed emotions plaguing her thoughts. So, he was looking forward to her creating some ripples in the old boy's network that the industry represented, yet he hadn't even suggested they take the drive together. Why not start removing old habits and clichéd attitudes at home, too? Damn him! And although she recognized that the conference was work, the setting would be relaxed, almost recreational just by sheer location alone. Mixing business with pleasure was an oxymoron but it was done all the time.

Feeling slightly guilty for questioning his motives, his policies, and his intentions, Morgan admonished herself lightly and switched gears. She acknowledged, realistically, she was fortunate to have Garrett in her life. Not only did he operate his own mortgage brokerage firm, but he also possessed the rare capability of delivering just the right touch of mentoring and guidance whenever she'd needed it. Although they'd made a pact never to discuss work during their private time together, they broke it often, laughing in an uproar at some unusual set of circumstances presented by a bank or a client.

He understood her, probably better than anyone, and for the most part, admired her drive and ambition without being threatened. His motivations matched her own a good deal of the time. They made a good team.

But there were times, like now, when Morgan realized that Garrett had purposely orchestrated a distinct and palpable space between them. And she couldn't help but wonder why and what purpose it served. The conference, due to run from February 12 through 13, was awkwardly scheduled just before what would be their second anniversary—Valentine's Day. Morgan was reluctant to admit it, but she'd been crushed when Garrett had failed to make any mention of the impending date, its significance, or how they would address it following the two days of business seminars and networking events.

Deep in thought, she failed to notice the black BMW 750 IL switch lanes abruptly. The driver cut in front of her in an attempt to move into the fast lane, narrowly missing her front bumper and causing her to brake sharply. She honked her horn, pounding the steering wheel, every instinct in her body becoming instantly alert .

"You jerk," she yelled, throwing one hand up in a gesture of frustration, making sure to keep control of her vehicle as it swerved around the winding roadway. Morgan could see that the driver of the BMW hadn't taken into account the S curves they were both handling, as well as the rain-slick pavement, accumulated oils and dirt having contributed their part to create a dangerous roadway. His car careened slightly as it took the curve. The brake lights flashed momentarily as the driver struggled to maintain control. His upper torso and arms strained to hold the steering wheel steady, while his entire body braced into the dramatic tilt of the car. She could just make out the barest outline of his head and neck, and found herself wondering what would prompt anyone to speed under the current weather conditions. He wore a black turtleneck sweater and horn-rimmed glasses, and seemed intent on either creating a significantly dramatic impression or leaving a lasting one.

Finally, out of the curve, and with a good, safe distance

between herself and the other vehicle, Morgan breathed an audible sigh of relief. Her heart was pounding.

The BMW speeded up and moved out of range, but not before she'd had a chance to notice his personalized license plates—BROKER ONE. She laughed then. *Damn fool. The industry is filled with arrogant upstarts,* she thought.

Morgan chided herself inwardly, feeling the need to calm down and concentrate on the remaining miles before her. In the next twenty minutes, she pulled off the road and into the entrance to Villa Novella and its visitor parking lot. It was almost dusk, the sun casting a brilliant glow as it settled low into the sky.

Registration was being handled at the front desk, with conference kits given out on the opposite side of the lobby. Several mortgage bankers, brokers, attorneys, and appraisers were already mingling at the bar in the lobby, ready to unwind after a three and a half hour drive that had been scenic, yet boring.

As Morgan approached the elevator bank that would take her to her room on the tenth floor, she looked up and was startled to see the driver of the black BMW, his back to her. She'd recognize that head, neck, and those shoulders anywhere. His horn-rimmed glasses were no longer in place, a sports jacket slung over one shoulder, Louis Vuitton garment bag resting at his side. Whoever he was, he was extremely well maintained, from his firm and toned body to the high-end clothing he wore; none of this was lost on Morgan in a quick once-over.

The elevator came just as she reached the doors to the right. He stepped aside with an exaggerated gentlemanly stance, allowing her to enter first.

"Thank you," Morgan said stiffly as she stepped into its interior. She wanted nothing to do with anyone who so obviously harbored a death wish and was a reckless hellion on the road. He looked at her then and cleared his throat.

"No problem. Floor?" he asked quickly, poised to press buttons, or anything else for that matter. What he really wanted to do was to punch someone or something, though his thoughts were actually a million miles away. Or maybe only two hundred or so miles with Oscar, who was back in New York City.

He had been through the wringer with his younger brother in the past six months. Legalities involving negotiations that would make the company they'd both created, developed, and managed for the past five years, a solely owned entity were in progress. It wasn't the way he wanted it, but Oscar had given him no choice. His brother's decision to relocate to the West Coast had come at the worst possible time. And there wasn't a damn thing he could do about it. They'd agreed to split the business financially in the end. In reality, he would now be on his own for the first time in more than ten years with a business that was bulging at the seams with growth. It presented challenge, creativity, and the ultimate in sacrifice. He'd given it a tremendous amount of thought in the past weeks, as well as during the endless drive he'd just completed, and hadn't gotten any closer to accepting it.

In fact, he hadn't felt at all like attending the damn conference. It was absolutely the last thing on his mind. But he also knew that networking could be the most important factor if he was to enjoy his continued success. It was key and, at the very least, he might be able to acquire a couple of new loan consultants. Quite possibly, he could also perhaps develop new business relationships, an absolute necessity going forward, if he were to enhance and make up for his partner's future absence.

"Yes, ten please," Morgan answered. The edge in her voice jarred him back to the present with a jolt. Slightly noticeable but distinctly heard, he dismissed her arrogance immediately. She didn't even know him and was armed with an attitude. Women . . .

Having stepped to the rear of the elevator, Morgan found herself staring at the back of his black jeans, noting the fit, and the Ferragamo shoes he wore. His hair, which waved up at the nape of his neck, was cut very low. His only departure from an extremely clean-cut, conservative look was his

mustache, and it was so well groomed that it enhanced a face
that would still have been handsome without it.

Something about the voice of his fellow elevator occupant
caused Danton to turn around then. She was quietly,
thoroughly checking him out with an unexpected directness
that caused him to laugh. He cleared his throat and held out
his hand.

"Hey, I'm Danton Yearwood. Are you here for the mortgage conference?" he asked, noticing her overnight case and
briefcase.

"Yes, I am. My name is Morgan Collins," she said, offering her hand for a handshake that was firm yet pleasantly
warm.

He let it go quickly, allowing her to pass with her luggage.

"Well, perhaps I'll see you at some of the seminars," he
added as the doors began to close. He hadn't missed the fact
that, although she was somewhat petite, she was extremely
well put together. Her five foot four inch frame was more
than well-proportioned and even in a gray velour sweat suit,
her hair pulled back into a ponytail, she was attractive in a
compelling way. He couldn't put his finger on it, but there
was something about her that made him want to continue
looking at her.

"Probably," she called out as she exited the elevator at her
floor. Her mind was stuck on "black on black in black—what
a combination." The car, the driver, the man—all three in-
vading and occupying a good portion of her thoughts at that
moment. Too bad he was a reckless driver, as well as probably young. It was obvious, by his license plate description,
that he was a mortgage broker. He spelled trouble with a capital T—that was her final conclusion. At the moment, all she
wanted to do was to stay out of his way, get out of her clothing, and take a hot bath.

Two hours and several drinks later, Morgan looked up from
the table she was sharing with several other loan consultants.

She'd found her way to the lobby bar after her manager, Stan Gallagher, had dialed her room informing her that they were all meeting for drinks at 6:00 P.M. and had practically demanded she join the group. It was a good-natured demand and Morgan had agreed to join them. Stan also let her know that they would be taking several specially chosen brokers to dinner later that evening.

Morgan, dressed in an ankle-length dark green suede skirt, matching angora sweater, and brown suede boots, entered the bar, which was now filled with mortgage bankers and other industry types, shortly after 6:00 P.M. Her hair hung loosely about her shoulders, the ends turned under by a quickly applied curling iron. Diamond studs adorned each ear. She looked professional, classy, and definitely capable.

The group had been trading "mortgage" war stories now for the past hour or so including closing problems, title nightmares, and themes of the client from hell.

Those in attendance included two women from a company called The Mortgage Closet, and three men who owned a huge operation called Funding First. Two brothers who were partners in another mortgage brokerage firm had not yet joined them. Stan and Morgan were the only representatives of Town and Country, the dinner party hosts.

Exiting the elevators, Danton spotted the bar, briskly walked toward it, and stopped in his tracks. The bombshell from the elevator, coolly wearing green suede and angora, boots that made her appear a heck of a lot taller, and sporting the face of an angel, was looking right at him. He recognized the challenge in her stare and gave it right back as he approached. Less than two feet from contact, she broke the connection and looked away. He immediately went around the group, ignored her, and shook hands with everyone.

"Hey listen up, I'd like you all to meet Danton Yearwood of First Equities." Stan introduced him to the few who didn't already know him. "Where's Oscar, your partner in crime?" he asked, somewhat disappointed that he wouldn't be presenting the dynamic duo as a team.

"Sorry, Stan, but Oscar couldn't make it this time. It's a long story and I'll catch you up on the latest developments at a more appropriate time," he said smoothly.

"Okay. I'd like you to meet one of our newest team members. She came to us from United States Bank Corp., where she was consistently a top producer for five years running. Meet Morgan Collins."

"I think we already met—on the elevator," Danton explained as he awkwardly shook her hand again. From a sitting position, she looked up at him and smiled graciously. But her smile did nothing to hide her true feelings and Danton, a quick study of people and body language, read her like yesterday's *Wall Street Journal*.

He didn't know if the knot of tension that gathered in his belly was based on dislike or something else. All he knew is that he prayed she wouldn't be handling his account. He didn't want to have to consult with her on anything, for anything, about anything. She seemed self-assured, even confident bordering on cocky, and there was something else about her he didn't quite like but he couldn't put his finger on it.

The group finished the before-dinner drinks and moved to the hotel's celebrated restaurant, First Amendment. Decorated in the spirit of the season, large red hearts, velvet cupids, and pink balloons hung from the ceiling, creating an impressive tribute to Valentine's Day. Few in the group noticed, although Morgan looked up several times, her expression appreciative yet somewhat detached.

Dinner began with mussels, a large Greek salad, and garlic shrimp appetizers, then moved on to honey glazed salmon, river trout, and steaks for the entrée, accompanied by several bottles of both red and white wine. Conversation flowed smoothly, as each person present was a consummate professional within the mortgage banking industry looking forward to the two days of concentrated information as well as the opportunity to network with colleagues and size up any competition that was present.

Dessert was being discussed with only a handful of

attendees willing to order anything other than coffee. Danton watched Morgan as she carefully added brandy to hers. He marveled at anyone's ability to handle several glasses of wine and an after-dinner drink and still hold a cognitive conversation. He'd watched her for most of the night, never coming to any final conclusions, but unable to take his eyes off her.

"So—what do you think of our newest acquisition? She was brought over to cover and develop major accounts, including several in your territory. We were extremely fortunate to be able to work things out, it wasn't an easy negotiation," Stan said, obviously pleased with the company's newest employee and confirming Danton's worst nightmare.

"Well, actually she's not bad at all," he said in a voice somewhat suggestive of shared conspiracy with a fellow male. He knew that Stan would expect him to be attracted to her. He realized then that he actually was and therein lied the problem. "But does she really know her stuff and can she go the distance?" he asked, hoping against hope that something in Stan's answer would somehow let him off the hook.

"You're damn right she knows her stuff. We were able to lure her away from US Bank Corp. with a package that included stock options and an extremely lucrative sign-on bonus. She's the best. Don't let those legs and the body fool you—she's pure mortgage banker all the way, with more than fifteen years in the industry."

Damn, she must have gotten started when she was a teenager, was the thought that ran through his head, but he heard himself saying, "Great, then we should get along just fine, 'cause in Oscar's absence, there will be plenty of room for great service and attention to detail. We're splitting the partnership. I'm going it alone," he announced with exaggerated determination. He wanted to sound resolute. Final. Perhaps it would enable him to accept it, too.

"So that's what's going on. Well, I'm sorry to hear that, but I have no doubt that you can handle it, Danton. You've always been the point man, the one at the front lines. Oscar is brilliant, but wasn't he mainly responsible for the behind-the-scenes operation most of the time? Listen, why don't you and Morgan get acquainted a little. You're going to be working closely together. Your account has always been extremely productive, closing more than fifteen million per month consistently . We are not prepared to lose any of that momentum," Stan said, suddenly all business.

He ushered Morgan, who had been listening to his dialogue intently, into his seat by moving down, which allowed her to sit directly next to Danton.

"Wow, that's a lot of mortgages you're handling. I'm impressed. Are we talking strictly conventional loans or are you approved to do FHA as well?" she asked, taking the seat offered.

The room somehow suddenly seemed too warm for him. The turtleneck sweater and sports jacket he'd worn were both lightweight wool and had, before now, been fine. Excusing himself politely, he stood up, removing his jacket. He then placed it on the back of his chair.

Morgan noticed the well-toned muscles rippling beneath his sweater, although she did everything in her power not to. She forced herself to concentrate on the sounds coming from his mouth, although she managed to avoid looking directly him. His lips were too compelling, and the mustache did nothing to detract from the handsome planes of his face. She kept reminding herself that A, he was a client and B, he appeared to be several years her junior. Those two pertinent facts should be enough to keep things in check—or so she told herself.

"Both, and we have a telemarketing presence on the first floor. Maybe a dozen or so telemarketers every Monday through Sunday are hard at work providing us with our refinance leads. Then originators use those leads to generate business. We also have a real estate operation that drives the purchase business."

"I'm impressed—how long have you been in operation?" she found herself asking, realizing that although he appeared to be younger, his exposure to business, the industry, and general corporate practice had obviously caused him to mature significantly. Or maybe it was maturity that had enabled him to form an extremely successful mortgage business at an early age. Whatever—she found herself fascinated by the man sitting beside her, although she realized that doing business with him would engage her in a constant battle. She'd be damned if she'd back down now, though. First Equities appeared to be the kind of account you worked for all your life in any industry. She would handle it and him; whatever the cost.

"Seven years. My partner, Oscar, who is also my brother, and I started in one room of an office space on Queens Boulevard. It grew so quickly, neither of us could keep up, but we were lucky, made some good moves, and here we are." As he said the word "we," his gut wrenched, realizing that that phase was no longer in effect.

"I'm impressed. Well, here's my card. Call me if you need anything urgently, but I'll definitely reach out to you early next week to set up an appointment," Morgan said smoothly, obviously impressed by his success story.

"Great. Now can I buy you another drink?" he offered, unable to temper his reaction to her. Though everything she'd said had been strictly business, her lips reminded him too much of fresh summer berries, he couldn't help but notice the rise and fall of her breasts beneath the angora sweater, and each time she spoke, her voice sounded like a caress. He couldn't imagine working with her—actually, now he couldn't imagine *not* working with her. The only problem would be which would be more difficult. At the moment, he couldn't for the life of him make that decision.

"No, I think I have reached my limit—almost. I will have another coffee with the remainder of the brandy," she said, noting the remaining contents of the large brandy snifter she held.

"I've never gotten into after-dinner brandy. I think I'll try one myself, though," Danton said, a momentary whim of recklessness gripping him. He wanted to show her that he could match her in anything she chose. Wanted her to know that he could go the distance. In any way, shape, or form on the table.

"Well, you should probably also try one of Stan's cigars. He claims it's the only way to enjoy brandy." The challenge in her voice was recognizable but instead of offending him, it pleased him. And that was unexpected.

"Definitely, it's all or nothing," Stan said exuberantly, reaching into his suit pocket. He was always happy to add another cigar smoking mortgage banker to his circle of cohorts. He quickly withdrew several Cuban cigars and distributed them around the table to the men. The women all declined, some even excusing themselves, not wanting to be present as the immediate environment filled with the pungent aroma of the powerful tobacco product.

"I'd like to ask you a question, Danton, and I hope you won't be offended."

"Go ahead. I don't think you know me well enough to offend me," he countered, wondering where she was going. He hoped she wasn't about to ask him something totally inappropriate, because he knew that he would have no qualms about having Stan reassign a new representative. He'd come too far and didn't give a rat's ass about either her proven track record nor how provocatively she filled out a sweater.

"You passed me earlier today on Interstate 684 and actually, well, you cut me off. Do you always drive like a bat out of hell?" she asked, looking directly into his eyes. He had the same reaction he'd had when he first spotted her in the group—a tightening well below his belt. He was grateful that he was sitting down. He was also glad that the lighting in the restaurant was dim, because his response to her was anything but businesslike.

He smiled slowly, purposely taking his time in formulating his response. "Actually, I was probably thinking of some recent developments at the company. But I find it hard to believe that I was driving recklessly. Are you sure I cut you off?"

For some reason, her question hadn't angered him at all,

and that surprised him. He'd been fully prepared to lash out at her, contact Stan at a later date to have another account executive assigned, and call it a night.

"Yeah, you cut right in front of me. Thank goodness my Saab responds. Rack and pinion steering are only one of its great features. Anyway, it's no big deal. I was just wondering because I noticed your license plates and all. BROKER ONE, right?"

"Yeah, that's right. I see, so you recognized me when we were on the elevator. Is that why you gave me the cold shoulder?" he asked, putting two and two together. He was equally impressed by her obvious knowledge of automobile engineering. It wasn't every day that you met a woman who understood the importance of precision handling and the value of high performance driving.

"I wouldn't say it was a cold shoulder, just a little reserved in case you were some kind of nut case," she said, laughing. He laughed, too, realizing that he probably had been driving as if demons were the inhabitants of his car. It was one of the ways in which he released tension, especially on an open highway.

"Look, I hope I didn't put you in any danger or anything. I apologize, but I did have some things on my mind."

"Don't mention it. It's forgotten. I'm looking forward to working with you, so try and drive a little more conservatively. I need all the accounts I can get," she offered, smiling, which once again caused him to readjust in his seat. On the surface, he appeared quite cool, calm, and very much collected. In reality, he hadn't felt like this since college. He'd obviously spent much too much time in the past ten years doing nothing but building the business, growing the business, and maintaining the business. He felt he was no longer able to control his reactions to the situation, and that was not characteristic of him at all. Hot one minute, cold the next. His mind on everything but what should have really mattered— mortgage banking business.

Two brandies and one cigar later, Danton, Morgan, and Stan, along with several new additions to the corporate party, decided to visit the hotel's bar/lounge, which was named, appropriately enough Last Call. The music, which was so loud that it also reached into the lobby, was pulsing, and included popular hits from rock, pop, R&B, and adult contemporary collections.

The dance floor was filled with people, and the party seemed destined to continue well into the early hours of the morning despite the fact that the first product seminars would begin as early as 8:30 A.M.

Danton, no longer able to camouflage his interest in Morgan but not wanting to seem eager or overpowering, did not ask her to dance. Stan, on the other hand, feeling no pain after having several glasses of wine, brandy with his coffee, and one half-smoked cigar, drew Morgan onto the dance floor almost immediately. And although she tried to decline, attempted to refuse, and actually begged off, it was no use.

Danton watched her move, even under protest, and liked what he saw. She moved effortlessly, without inhibition. And although she held back, not wanting to upstage her partner, who by now was pretty far gone, it was quite apparent that she was in fact a very good dancer.

He didn't remember the last time he'd danced. Yes, he did. It was at Oscar's wedding in the Bahamas two years ago. Well, that was definitely in the past—the wedding, the dancing, and even the marriage. Hence, Oscar's ill-timed move to the West Coast and his relatively foul mood. His brother's divorce was directly responsible for the current state of affairs. There wasn't a damned thing he could do about it but accept the reality of it and handle the business. He realized that, almost at the same time that he decided he would not let the evening pass without attempting to see exactly what Miss Collins was made of on the dance floor.

He continued to watch Morgan as the music gradually changed to a slower tempo. Danton put his drink down, walked over, apparently surprising her, and asked quietly, "May I have this one?" Stan waved them off as he returned to the bar, ready to do battle with either another cigar or a shot of brandy.

No answer was forthcoming as she moved into his arms

and Danton held her loosely, trying to maintain the proper decorum even though he wanted to pull her close enough to feel her entire body along the length of his. Instead, he guided her by simply putting his hand into the curve of her waist. She responded immediately by following his lead, which didn't surprise him. He somehow knew that it would be like that between them.

"So what actually made you leave the United States Bank Corp.? I hear they have some interesting programs as well as decent compensation for the reps," he said conversationally. His attempt to reduce the impact of having her so close that it was wreaking havoc on his senses did not work. Their bodies fit together, as if by design, and Morgan felt it, too, though it was less difficult for her to keep her reaction hidden.

"The bank was great. Nothing in their portfolio was a deficit, but I was working with someone whom I'd developed a conflict of interest with, so it was time to move on," she answered in a way that let him know it was also time to change the subject.

"I'd imagine that with your looks, your brains, and your professional stance, that can happen pretty often," he said, hoping to help her realize that he was, at the very least, on her side.

"Yeah, but you know you're never ready for it and the resolution is always on you. . . . It's nerve wracking sometimes. I don't know what all the fuss is about anyway. I am just an ordinary female, with a better than average track record in the industry for bringing in the business."

"I don't want to burst your bubble, but there is nothing ordinary about you. And on the odd chance that this remark will cause a problem between us in the long run of doing business together, let me assure you that I fully respect your talent, your track record, as well as your good looks." Smiling down at her, his sincerity was obvious and took any perceived threat out of his statement. He wanted to say more, wanted to tell her that with her body and her looks, it was not at all farfetched that she'd wreaked havoc on an alpha male ego, but he realized that the statement would put her on the defensive, and that was not his intention.

"Thank you, I think, for the compliment. I look forward to working with you and your company, so it's important to me that you understand where I'm coming from."

"Don't worry about me. I understand totally and I appreciate your forward thinking approach. If more women were like you, there would probably be a lot more success stories in the industry without some of the scandal."

The music ended and they walked toward the bar rejoining their colleagues, coworkers, and fellow industry mates. It was well past midnight when the party broke up, the reality of the next day's schedule looming ahead.

Danton and Morgan entered the elevator, along with Stan and several other members of the conference.

"Good night," was called out by several members of the group as three bankers exited on the eighth floor.

"Stan, don't forget about the breakfast meeting with the Appraisal Group at eight," Morgan offered as he exited on the ninth floor.

"Thanks for reminding me," he called out, an unlit cigar still dangling from one hand as the doors closed.

Alone now for the first time, Danton and Morgan retreated to opposite sides of the mirrored car. The atmosphere was charged with something that neither was willing to acknowledge or identify.

"Well, good night, Morgan. It was great meeting and hanging out with you," Danton said as the elevator doors opened onto the tenth floor.

"Same here and I'm looking forward to working with you," she said, offering her hand in the time honored tradition of business decorum. Danton took it, raised it to his lips, and kissed the softness of her palm. It was thoroughly unexpected, sinfully sensual, and totally inappropriate.

Morgan drew her hand back quickly as if she'd been singed and put it behind her back. She smiled, pointing an index finger at him in an accusing gesture.

"Mr. Yearwood, you're quite a handful. You should be punished," she said, laughing as the elevator doors proceeded to close.

Quick reflexes at work, even after three glasses of wine, one brandy, and that God-awful cigar, Danton still managed to hit the open button quickly.

"By all means, please, please do." He smiled, a look of extreme pleasure on his face, knowing he'd broken at least one rule and gotten away with it. He felt good, really good for the first time in the past month, or since he'd found out that the changes facing First Equities would most probably become its permanent condition. He knew he was ready to take on the challenges of running the company and anything else that was thrown his way, even if it included a very well-packaged tube of dynamite like the one that had just exited the elevator.

The doors closed and the car rose, taking him to the eleventh floor.

Day Two

Garrett proceeded to the seminar he'd signed up for, "Appraisal Issues and Concerns in the Current Marketplace," which was already ten minutes under way. He'd left the city at 6:05 A.M., making good time due to the lack of early morning traffic, and had arrived just after 9:00 A.M.

His garment bag was being held at the concierge's desk so that he could check in sometime after 1:00 P.M. Wearing khaki pants, a mustard-colored sports shirt, and a brown plaid sports jacket, he made his way toward Conference Room C. Two hours later, he felt the effects of the drive, the concentration, and remaining immobile for an extended period. The seminar instructor had two phases of his research and findings on audio as well as videocassettes available, and many of the attendees were in the process of purchasing these items as the session ended.

Ready for a quick pick-me-up, Garrett headed for the nearest coffee outlet. He figured he'd look for Morgan sometime after that. Actually, he was avoiding reaching out to her just yet, unsure as to how he'd approach the weekend, recent developments, and the uncertainty of their future.

In a small restaurant/café within the hotel's interior, he ordered a cup of coffee and a toasted pumpernickel bagel. He'd already recognized several other mortgage bankers within the corridors who were also breaking from early seminars but wanted to have at least a moment to himself before he was fully vested in the conference atmosphere.

"Is that who I think it is?" was all he heard before he felt his back pummeled with well-intentioned ferociousness.

"Oh, my God, I thought they'd run you out of town a long time ago," he answered when his tormentor came around in full frontal view. "Grant Bartlett, where the hell have you been," he managed to choke out before swallowing the last bite he'd taken of the bagel.

"Man, I moved out to Long Island, closed down the Brooklyn office, and decided to only cater to Fannie and Freddie loans. Of course, I still do some niche products, but mainly it's all vanilla," he offered, referring to the more commonly used products within the industry.

"Good for you. I'm still breaking my ass doing the loans in the boroughs, which you know sometimes require real work. It's good to see you," he added, and realized that he meant it. Really meant it.

"You, too. When did you get in?" Grant asked as he pulled up a chair after ordering coffee and a cheese Danish. His six foot three inch frame didn't fit comfortably into it, but he was used to making do.

"This morning. I had some business to take care of last night and couldn't leave town until then. Did I miss anything last night? I know you and the rest of those lounge lizards don't know how to call it a day and get to bed at a decent hour," he teased, remembering countless numbers of times they had attended parties and conferences. There was an unwritten rule that you absolutely had to hang out until the wee hours of the morning, arrive at the early morning seminars hungover and disheveled, then get a second wind somewhere in the midafternoon right before whatever evening events were scheduled.

"Yeah, you missed seeing me get ripped and make a fool of myself—but since you didn't see it, let's pretend it didn't happen," Grant added, laughing.

"Oh, I'm sure there was someone there to document it and get it all down. Maybe even a little video action, if you know what I mean."

"Shut up, Garrett, you always were a smartass. There are no cameras allowed—you know these bankers have to be able to let loose at some time in their lives, and they sure can't do it at home. These conferences are our only outlet for a little mayhem and pandemonium. I was only getting started last night. Tonight comes the real fun—the pandemonium." Both men laughed, knowing that it was all too true, all too often. Their work required long hours, weekends, and holidays, but paid extremely well. It remained consistent that if you worked hard, you played just as hard—it was an industry truism.

"So, what's next for you today?" Grant asked, finishing off his second breakfast of the day.

"Actually, as soon as I can check into my room, I'm gonna play a round of golf. Did you bring your clubs?"

"You know I did. That was another draw for my coming to this conference, 'cause I sure as hell am not really interested in being holed up in seminars all day long. Send me the condensed version or in a memo," he uttered, sentiments that were shared by many of the veteran attendees.

"Tell me about it . Hey, why don't we meet at the Clubhouse at around two? I'll register us from one of the house phones," Garrett added.

"Okay, but be ready for a little one-on-one action on the basketball court after that, 'cause if I remember correctly, the last time we indulged ourselves, I left without my shirt," Grant laughed.

"Dude, you left without your shirt and your back right pocket. I think I won a C note that day and it was just like taking candy from a baby." The pleasure he'd derived from extracting this small token of championship was clearly visible on his face; Garrett saw it, recognized it, and knew he would do everything in his power to raise the stakes and win next time, even though it was all in the name of sportsmanship, friendship, and pure competition.

"Oh, so that's how it's gonna be. Now it's on for sure. I'll see you around two. My room is 787 if you need to back out. I'll understand."

Garrett shook his head, still laughing as Grant left the small café. He hadn't realized how upsetting the night before had been to him until he'd been able to laugh at the humorous challenges his old friend and competitor had thrown his way. What a mess. That was the only way to categorize his position. He also recognized that any attempt to straighten things out would be difficult, if not impossible. He had no alternative, though, given the circumstances. Although he knew he could not avoid seeing Morgan sometime in the next couple of hours, he was definitely not looking forward to it.

The call had come only three days before. Seventy-two hours. Prior to that, his world had been organized, serene, and predictable; the relationship between Morgan and himself, comfortable and manageable, actually a source of great contentment. He prided himself on dating with a discriminating eye, and Morgan was actually a hell of a catch. Bright, enthusiastic, intelligent, and well on her way to becoming a dominant force in the industry, he'd met her on a blind date set up by a close friend who also happened to be an attorney. He'd called her twice, held a short but invigorating conversation, and they'd chosen the day before Valentine Day for their first date.

February 13 seemed an oddity and probably destined to be a bad omen, but he'd been pleasantly surprised when things had really clicked in the first ten minutes. Dinner, theater tickets to the Broadway performance of *42nd Street,* then a walk through Greenwich Village ending with coffee and dessert at one o'clock in the morning. They'd been together ever since. And he'd been happy, or so he thought, for most of the past months. Having Morgan in his life had allowed him to concentrate on his business with renewed energy and concentration. They spent quality time together most weekends, either at her place or his, doing the things that people in love do, movies, antique hunting, walks in the park, etc. They often discussed the challenges their chosen industry represented and Garrett realized that Morgan had as much respect and commitment to the mortgage banking arena as he had. He liked that.

What he did not like, and seemed unsure of handling, was

the competitive spirit he sensed within her. It oftentimes caused small, insignificant arguments between them although he realized that she probably didn't even recognize the source.

Garrett gathered up his leather case, which contained documents from the seminar he'd just attended, several client files that had loose ends he had to tie up in the next day or so, and the damning piece of paper that threatened to ultimately turn his life around. He'd brought it if only to examine and reexamine it because he'd had such a difficult time accepting its existence, not to mention its ramifications.

He picked up one of the house phones, pressed the button for the front desk, and waited. "Hi, my name is Garrett Stansfield. I'm with the mortgage banking conference. I'd like to reserve a party of two for golf—two o'clock today. Yes, I'll hold on." He waited patiently to be connected to the clubhouse.

Morgan, ready to go back to her room after an early breakfast meeting that had begun at 8:30 A.M. and a Federal Housing Authority or FHA seminar following it, was sorely feeling the effects of the night before. Her throat was dry, her head felt larger than usual, and her eyes stung like small pearl onions encased in a jar of irritating liquid. She had not taken off her sunglasses for the past hour and didn't care if it appeared odd. Dressed in dark jeans, a black blazer, and light blue oxford shirt, accompanied by black boots and dark sunglasses, she looked very much like someone who could handle whatever came her way.

Morgan recognized Garrett as she headed toward the hotel's café in search of any kind of pain reliever. He was on the phone, his back to her. Immediately, her heart beat faster. She walked up, tapped his shoulder, kissed him on the cheek as he spun around, and indicated that she'd be in the café when he'd completed his call. She didn't trust herself to communicate with him without the assistance of something to take the edge off her headache. Especially after she realized that he'd arrived, obviously sometime before, and had not even attempted to reach out to her. He hadn't called her cellular phone, her pager, or her room. She was really glad she was wearing dark glasses now to hide her mounting fury. Something was wrong and she was determined to get to the bottom of it.

"Damn girl, you look good. This outdoors stuff must agree with you. What's with the shades?" Garrett asked casually. She'd caught him off guard, and now he didn't know if he would be able to do what was necessary. And to make matters more difficult, she looked extremely attractive, sophisticated, and somehow vulnerable. Even the sunglasses lent her an exaggerated air of mystery. Garrett realized that the next twenty-four hours would be agonizing. He was not looking forward to it at all.

"Welcome to the world of mortgages, Mr. Stansfield, where some of us are obligated to occasionally wine and dine clients for a living. Anyway, enough about me. I see you were able to tear yourself way from your desk and make the journey," she added. What she really wanted to say was, "You could have at least called to let me know when you were getting here." She continued to stare at him, coolly and without showing her hand, as he, too, weighed his next words.

"Yeah, I finished up most of what I needed to do last night about midnight, threw some things into a bag, and headed out around six this morning. Have you run into any of my cohorts?"

"Not really. I had dinner with several colleagues as well as clients, you know the drill. Anyway, so far, it's business as usual. The showcase starts around two this afternoon and I think I'll try and relax until then. I have a splitting headache." With that admission, Morgan swallowed two Advil, chasing them with a long drink from the large bottle of water she'd purchased. She felt dehydrated, hungover, and awfully irritated.

"I'm going to get in a couple of rounds of golf with an old buddy, play a little basketball, and then see what the nightlife around here brings. I'll probably call you later, okay?"

"Okay, if you want to. I'll probably be at the showcase staffing the Town and Country booth until at least five-thirty

or so. Enjoy your afternoon of sports. It's true that you guys
are really all frustrated jocks, isn't it?" she offered, laughing
as she walked away. What she'd really wanted to say was
something even more insulting, but she didn't have the nerve,
the strength, or the concrete evidence.

Although the conversation had been reasonably pleasant,
bordering on polite, every one of Garrett's instincts told him
that Morgan's behavior was definitely out of character. There
had been no intimate laughter, no small talk, no real connection. "Aloof" was probably the word that best described her,
and he couldn't for the life of him figure out what was causing it. To the best of his knowledge, she was totally unaware
of last night's events, the present circumstances, and his impending future situation. Women . . .

Town and Country spared no expense in creating a booth
that would not only draw attention, but also effectively at-
tract more than eighty percent of the attendees at the
afternoon showcase. Whether they were brokers who were
in the market for new lenders, lenders in the market for as-
sessing the competition, or just the curious gathering
collectibles in an environment that offered something for
everyone, the Town and Country setup was one no one
wanted to miss. Offering unique calculators masked as tiny
silver handheld briefcases, they also had pens, mouse pads
with the T and C logo, four-inch cubes to be used as
notepads, and the requisite spectrum of experienced and
knowledgeable loan officers.

Morgan had answered every question, laughed at every
joke, and provided every assistance she could manage during the past three hours. At almost 4:30 she was looking
forward to packing up and getting back to her room for
some well-deserved rest and recuperation. R&R was the
foremost thing on her mind as she turned to put several
boxes of marketing tools under the table to be shipped back,

along with the entire booth, to their headquarter offices in Lansing, Michigan.

"So this is where you've been hiding all day, Miss Collins," she heard before she stood up and turned around. Actually, she recognized the voice immediately and, though she couldn't figure out why, her heart pounded instantly.

"I haven't been hiding, it's called *working*. For some of us, it's a necessary evil," she responded sarcastically, eager to establish any boundary she could that would draw a line between her and the challenge standing before her.

"Easy, easy. I'm in a delicate condition today. Not a hundred percent ready to fend off the barbs and other weapons you seem ready to unleash. I was only trying to say that I'd missed your presence. I didn't know I was looking for you, but now that I see you, I realize that I've been wondering all day where you might be keeping yourself." His honesty, lack of coyness, and genuine offering threatened to destroy each one of the barricades she'd instantly constructed. They came down in a thunderous heap at her feet as she took in every inch of the six foot two male now looking directly into her eyes.

Danton was wearing the black sports coat he'd removed at dinner the evening before, and his appearance did nothing to detract from the previous day's standard. He looked well rested, amazingly alert, and even more handsome. Cut to perfection, the blazer emphasized his athletic physique. He'd replaced the casual black turtleneck with an open-collared gray knit sweater and was wearing gray wool slacks and the black Ferragamo shoes she'd noticed as they both waited for the elevator. His mustache, which appeared even darker, blacker, more silky in the bright light of the conference center, accentuated the smooth even color of his skin, reminiscent of creamy milk chocolate.

She was in trouble and she knew it. Thank God he didn't, though—that would be her saving grace. As long as she could hold him off, deny him any access to her inner feelings, and portray the stance of a woman who was totally uninterested, she figured she had a chance.

"Well, were you able to accomplish anything in your travels? It certainly looks as if you've visited every vendor here," she responded. She noted that although he only carried one canvas bag, as opposed to many other attendees who had filled several, it was obviously carefully stuffed with literature and other marketing items the display tables held representing each bank, appraisal company, title firm, and credit agency present at the forum.

"Yeah, I am 'tapped out,' as they say. For a while, I thought you might have slipped something into my drink last night. My head felt like a huge sledgehammer had been applied ever so slightly when I got up this morning. The only thing I could remember was you taunting me into having brandy with my coffee," he ended.

The accusation hung in the air like a huge banner. He was teasing her, yet his statement was clearly sexually charged and Morgan knew she was handling dynamite or some other unpredictable explosive.

"You know, I'm really beginning to get the feeling that you don't trust me . Why would I put something into your drink? Is there some information to be retrieved from your psyche that I might somehow benefit from?" she asked, the anger on her face immediate and not at all masked in any way. She was livid. His assertion was preposterous bordering on ridiculous, but it still incensed her.

"You are either extremely naive or just plain obnoxious," Morgan wanted to add. She also wanted to note that his obvious lack of maturity was perhaps due to the difference in age between him and many of his colleagues, but instead remained silent, her stare delivering volumes instead.

Danton didn't want to admit it, but his accusation had even surprised him. Actually, the fact that he'd just damn near insulted her with a verbal slap in the face was as exciting as hell. She looked so gorgeous, her temper aroused but obviously being held in check by a will of steel. He could hardly contain the feelings he was experiencing just standing there looking at her.

She was wearing a peach-colored wool suit with bone pumps and panty hose, her hair pulled up into a French knot. The suit enhanced the warm tone of her skin, enhancing the olive complexion and auburn tones of her hair. Pearl earrings with a tiny gold jacket adorned each ear and she wore no other jewelry save a watch and a gold bangle on the same arm. Danton, normally not one to dive headfirst into any pool, liked what he saw. Morgan had class, style, and a hell of a temper.

"Look, I wasn't serious about your adding something to my drink, but I really did have a hard time getting it together this morning. I suspect you haven't had the easiest day on record yourself. Have you been here all day?" he asked then, turning instantly serious and decidedly compassionate, leaving her without a leg to stand on. She'd been prepared to tell him to buzz off, although she realized that she would be signing her own death warrant with him being a valued client. But under the circumstances, she didn't feel he had the right to harass her. In her mind, if she'd told him to get lost and get a life, she would have been within her rights. And just when she'd been fully prepared to ask him exactly which drug he'd ingested to induce the feelings of paranoia and detachment he seemed to be experiencing, he'd come back to reality exuding calm, no recognizable hostility, and darn near approaching forgiveness.

"Yes, I have, and I didn't have it any easier than you did this morning. Two Advil and a nap after the morning session have kept me going until now. So don't push me, 'cause I'm close to the edge," she said through clenched teeth to emphasize her point.

Danton began laughing with Morgan joining him suddenly. They shared the recognition that after the previous evening of dinner, drinks, and dancing, only the extremely determined would remain undaunted.

The tension broken, Morgan again turned her attention to

the necessary routine of packing up the remaining marketing items as the two other Town and Country account representatives began dismantling the freestanding booth.

Danton turned to walk away and encountered an appraiser whose practice had been sending him solicitations for the past three months. Engaged in conversation for the next twenty minutes, he was within inches from the Town and Country booth and seemed committed to the spot. Morgan assisted her coworkers in wrapping up the session, putting away the remaining marketing materials, and repacking all leftover brochures and product descriptions.

As Morgan grabbed her purse and promised her colleagues that she would meet them for drinks later that evening, Danton, too, ended his conversation. They both headed toward the doors falling in step with each other as if by design.

"If I promise not to say anything else that might piss you off, will you agree to have dinner with me?" he asked suddenly as they exited the conference center.

Dusk was quietly rolling into the mountains, promising a clear, star-studded night. Morgan felt compelled to deny his request, her feelings, and most of all, the turmoil she now felt knowing that Garrett was only within a few feet of where they were now standing. Her indecision also took into account that Garrett had promised to call, although they hadn't made any concrete plans and she'd found that strange at the time. He seemed to take for granted that she would be available for whatever the evening held without even giving her the benefit of the doubt. Once again her instincts told her that something was up, something was brewing, something was amiss. The truth was Danton's offer held some promise. She wasn't sure why for the first time in her life she was willing to sacrifice her professional stance on not mixing business with pleasure. Maybe it was the fresh air, or the mountains, or the fact that she was away from the corporate settings the city imposed. For whatever the reason, she knew within the next instant that she would accept—and let the chips fall where they may.

"Now that's a pretty noble promise for a savvy guy like you—are you sure you can hold yourself to it?" she countered, unable to simply say yes and give in to impulse.

"Not only do I promise, but if you don't have a great time, you can be assured that I will never bring it up again. I'm looking forward to working with you on the account. There's no way that I am going to jeopardize that relationship by having you think of me as some kind of annoying character who is hell bent on harassing you. I'm serious."

"You sound like it. Well, with an offer like that on the table, I guess I can hardly think of turning you down. It sounds like a win-win situation. At the very least, we'll be colleagues who are able to work together, respecting each other's professional stance.

"Yes, and at the other end of the spectrum, we should be able to be friends, too. You have nothing to lose. So, shall we say around seven-thirty? Meet me in front of First Amendment. I'll be the guy with the restrained look on his face," he added, laughing.

"Okay, I see you are never gonna let me live it down that I won't allow you to be the smart-ass you're inclined to be," she returned, not at all sure that he didn't think it was all one big joke.

"Look, maybe this is not such a good idea," she said as they reached the entrance to the hotel's lobby.

"Nonsense. You just need to get to know me a little better and I probably need to stop needling you. I'll see you at seven-thirty. By the way, have I told you that I really like your nose? When I first spotted you on the elevator, it was pointed straight at the sky. I branded you stuck-up, a yuppie princess, and a real pain in the butt. I may have to revise at least two of those descriptions, after all," he added with a mischievous smile.

Morgan laughed, shaking her head. "You've got problems, Yearwood, big problems," she called over her shoulder.

His analysis, sensible and definitive, aside from the nose

business, convinced her once again that he was, indeed, quite mature, capable of handling himself, and perhaps even likeable.

He held the door open for her and then quickly walked away, giving her no additional opportunity for protest or cancellation. Morgan knew she was breaking all the rules, repaving the groundwork that she'd adhered to for all her years in the corporate world, yet she also knew that she would be there at 7:30.

The flashing red light on the telephone beside her bed signaled two messages. Morgan's conscience instantly flared, reminding her that she was, indeed, still very much involved with a man who was somewhere within very close proximity. She pressed the message button, steeling herself for what would probably pull her back to reality, canceling out the impulsive plans she'd agreed to no more than ten minutes earlier.

Stan's voice boomed into her ear, catching her off guard for a moment. "Thanks for being such a good sport last evening and charming the pants off one of our most valued clients. Tonight's dinner won't be half as demanding—just a few appraisers and title people will be there. If you want to blow this one off, don't worry about it. I'll probably see you back at the office on Tuesday morning. Drive safe if I don't run into you again before we leave. And thanks again for being such a good sport last night," he ended, hanging up quickly.

Morgan then pressed the pound sign on the phone, erasing the first message, and pressed the number sign to listen to her next message. Garrett, sounding like he was obviously enjoying himself immensely, spoke rapidly into the phone.

"Morgan, I'm calling from the lobby. I just finished wiping up the court with a couple of my compadres from the past and they're not willing to let bygones be bygones. It seems they want to continue the challenge over dinner. Unfortunately, since I won today I kind of feel obligated to respond in kind and at least buy them a round of drinks. We'll probably be at the lobby bar. Maybe I'll catch up to you later, but I wanted you to know I'm not in charge of my destiny tonight. Hey, I gotta run, 'cause these guys are getting anxious—it seems their adrenaline is running high—too bad it didn't help them any when they could have used it," he tossed in, laughing, obviously for the sake of whoever was close enough to overhear. In the background could be heard several other voices, all male, all obviously on a testosterone high, as they taunted and joked with one another in the competitive spirit that seemed to universally exist between jocks and professionals males the world over.

Morgan's feelings went from guilt to anger in the course of a split second. How dare he. Of all the . . . Now her worse fears were really confirmed. If he hadn't the inclination to spend the evening with her, to even set aside any dedicated time for the two of them after the last couple of days and the space he'd purposely seemed to insert between them, then her suspicions had to be true. And although she couldn't put her finger on any one thing in particular, her instincts were her guide. He'd played golf then basketball all day, now he was blowing her off for the evening. And he hadn't mentioned anything about their upcoming second anniversary, nor Valentine's Day, either. Any thoughts of second guessing her earlier conversation with Danton went out the window with a new found resolve put swiftly into its place. *To hell with you, Mr. Stansfield—I've got dinner plans, too,* she thought as she sat on the bed.

Although she'd only brought two business suits and a few additional pieces of business casual clothing for the conference, Morgan was determined to step out of the box and dress defiantly. Wherein she normally would have felt the need to pull out all the stops and try to make a good impression, her feelings were those of pure rebellion.

Garrett's offhanded casualness along with the prospect of a total stranger's attempt to even marginally bridge the gap left her feeling oddly off kilter. It was as if she were entering a realm wherein she had no significant impact. She did not like the feeling, nor the implication.

Morgan showered and then lay across the bed contemplating the evening before her. No real answers were forthcoming and one half hour before she was supposed to meet Danton in the lobby, she picked up the phone to call him and cancel. Then she replaced the receiver in the cradle. She walked to the closet and chose a light blue flat knit sweater, jeans, and a blue plaid blazer. Ankle boots, which made her significantly taller, were her only concession. That and the fact that she took the time to take her hair down, curl it slightly, and then thread her fingers through it to create a look that was somewhat unorganized yet provocative. She also applied more makeup than she normally wore during the daytime, playing up her eyes with a smoky gray shadow, and then accentuated her lashes with two coats of mascara. She stepped back from the mirror as she applied a nude colored gloss to her lips and actually laughed. Her makeup appeared a bit dramatic, and reminded her of the years of experimentation she and several girlfriends had experienced before perfecting the different looks ultimately achieved by either under-or overplaying its use. The dark and smoky eyes she'd affected with the use of the gray eye shadow emphasized her eyes dramatically, calling attention to every feature of her face.

I really hope that Danton doesn't interpret this as some kind of signal that I'm on the prowl, she thought to herself. She would have to be sure to behave in a manner that would not cause any misinterpretation. And she also felt safe knowing that they were really only colleagues having dinner together at the same restaurant they had been in the night before. Although the resort did have another restaurant, it was more of a coffee shop. She didn't expect Danton to be classless. Up until now he'd expressed a good deal of finesse as well as decorum. Resigned to make the best of it, Morgan sprayed herself lightly with Gucci Rush and looked at the clock.

It was 7:28. She headed for the elevator. When the doors opened, Danton was inside, along with another gentlemen that neither of them knew. Danton looked even more handsome than he had earlier in the day, if that was possible, and smelled better than any man she remembered ever going out with in the past, even Garrett, whose favorite cologne was Paco Rabanne. It made her even more nervous.

"Hi, imagine meeting you here," he said, smiling, thoroughly pleased with the fact that they'd both chosen casual attire, yet had also obviously taken the time to clean up, and change clothes. He especially liked her hair. He'd liked the way she'd had it during the business conference that day also, all pinned up, wearing her suit and pearl earrings. He'd wanted to take it down from the moment he'd walked up to her booth but knew it would have started World War I, as well as a monumental harassment suit if he'd even tried. But he had to admit, there was something to be said for the way she was wearing it now, too, all tousled and unkempt-looking. She appeared to have just rolled out of bed and he couldn't stop his imagination from wandering to places he'd made a pact with himself not to go to.

"Hi yourself. I'm glad that neither of us felt the need to dress," she managed to get out. *Damn he looks good,* was what she was really thinking. The suede blazer he wore only enhanced the deep, rich coloring of his mustache. He also had worn jeans, along with a black open-collared knit shirt that made him look extremely masculine, his physique enhanced by the soft knit fabric of his sweater. Cowboy boots had replaced the more conservative shoes he'd worn earlier and the slight bow of his legs were enhanced by them.

Danton smiled, thinking that her fragrance was something he could definitely get used to—that and the way she handled herself. He realized that he'd have to mind his p's and q's this evening. She wasn't ready for anything more than a casual dinner and he certainly didn't want to do anything that might jeopardize their future relationship, whatever that was to be.

They exited the elevator, headed toward First Amendment, and Morgan stopped suddenly. Danton continued on to the front entrance of the resort and looked back as he realized that she was no longer at his side.

"Where are you going?" she asked incredulously.

"Come on. We are going into town for dinner," he answered, beckoning for her to join him.

Morgan quickly walked to where he stood, a puzzled look on her face. "I thought you meant dinner here at the restaurant," she answered slowly.

"I think it'll do us both some good to get out of the confines of a corporate environment, don't you? And don't worry, I'll still be the same exact gentlemen off the premises." His words, uttered to reassure, were not entirely convincing. But in less than a full moment Morgan accepted the fact that the evening could be filled with challenge and unlimited possibility. He was obviously a man who knew what he wanted. She figured she could handle whatever was to come.

As they pulled out of the parking lot, which was filled to capacity by all the attendees of the conference, Morgan turned to him, a look of curiosity on her face. "How is it that you're so familiar with the area?"

"Actually, I'm not, although I used to ski Hunter Mountain, which is not too far from here. I did pick up a map at the desk earlier today and I got a suggestion from one of the bartenders. There's a popular restaurant down Route Twenty-two in a town called Quaker Hill that reportedly serves great food. I thought it sounded interesting," he ended, eyes on the road as he concentrated on the curves and unexpected cutoffs facing him.

Morgan realized that although he'd appeared to be reckless and possibly given to overestimating his driving ability, he was quite good. She could tell by his handling of the car now that she was in it with him. He drove as if he were one with the machine—and the car responded. All of a sudden she sat up straight as a board, recognition coming to her in an instant.

"So, you knew you were going to ask me to dinner this afternoon, and you assumed that I'd say yes?" she asked, shock and anger apparent in her voice.

"No, I just knew that I wanted to get the heck out of there this evening. My asking you was an afterthought. If you had said no, I'd still have taken the drive, although I am really glad that you chose to come. Relax, you're not as predictable as that. In fact, you've been pretty uncooperative ever since we met; I don't expect you to change overnight." He tossed the comment her way much like a used hanky, and she found herself turning her head to keep him from seeing the smile that spread over her face. She realized that she liked the way he stood up to her, not backing down when she challenged him.

"Well, I sure hope you have eyes like a cat or the instincts of a bat. It's so dark out there that I can hardly see my hand before my face. Here, let me help with the map," she offered, taking the folded sections from him. Their hands touched and the heat generated was instantly felt by both. Morgan quickly began trying to locate any familiar spot on the diagram, as Danton reached over to turn on the overhead interior light.

"Just follow the yellow line—that's Route Twenty-two. We take that to the Village of Pawling. It's right here," he added pointing to a spot on the map only inches from where they were now located.

"Okay, yeah it's right here—we have to take this to Route Twenty-two and then head east. We take that for what looks like maybe ten miles and then exit. Quaker Hill should be right there," she ended, looking up for the first time.

Danton was smiling. "So, you make a pretty good copilot, too," he said. "I like that in a woman. You're obviously quite talented, Miss Collins. The only remaining question is how finely tuned those talents are." The statement dangled in the air like an exclamation point that had been typed above its intended line.

"Well, sir, I don't think you have anything to be concerned about because you'll never know." The glaring reality that this young upstart needed to be taught a lesson was becoming more and more clear to her with each passing moment.

"Never say never. That's been my motto for over twenty years. When I was at Howard, I bet my roommate that we'd never rival each other with girls. So of course we ended up falling for the same woman, going all out to try and impress her, and ragging our friendship in the process."

"You're not in college anymore. This is the real world in case you hadn't noticed. But you don't strike me as the stab a friend in the back type. What happened to the girl?" He now had her full attention. She could just imagine him in college. He probably had been one of the finest brothers on the campus and one of the most popular.

"Oh, you know, she dropped him, then she dropped me, and the rest is history. See, the moral of the story is never say you won't do anything because the day may come when your guard is down, or the stakes are so high that you'll have to eat your words. Trust me, words of remorse make for a bitter fare, " he added, winking suddenly, which seemed ridiculous.

"I'll try to bear that in mind. I went to Fordham University at Lincoln Center and majored in journalism and media studies. Although I was holding down a full-time position with CBS at the time, I still managed to earn a degree with a 3.8 grade point average. There was no time for dating, roommate rivalries, or any of that, so I guess you could say I missed out. But I'm not sorry. I sometimes wonder how I did it, though," she said, shaking her head.

"Wow, I'm really impressed. See, I knew you were extremely talented. You're amazing, Morgan. You look as though you just stepped off a college campus, yet I know from the amount of time that you've been in the industry that that cannot be the case. How do you manage it?"

"How do I manage what?"

"To retain that girlish, almost virginal look when you're surrounded by those who have become tainted by cynicism, the day-to-day rhetoric, and the ups and downs that go hand in hand with what we do."

"I don't know. I guess I just allow things that don't really matter to roll off my back. You know—don't sweat the small stuff. With the move over to Town and Country, I'm hoping I've put myself into the catbird seat as far as programs, pricing, and servicing. I don't think I could have asked for a more smoothly run operation. Every member of the support staff is one hundred percent dedicated to underwriting, closing, and funding loans in a timely manner.

"That's what it's all about and it works for me," she ended, realizing that she'd talked more than she'd planned to and that he'd listened, without interrupting or becoming judgmental. She also realized, with some guilt, that she was unfairly comparing him to Garrett, who most certainly would have interrupted her to point out some flaw in her assessment of life or the overall situation. Sometimes he was right, but oftentimes it was just his way of interjecting his opinion. And most times, his preconditioned attitude created tension between them.

Having reached the exit for the Village of Pawling, they pulled off the highway and began looking for the restaurant. It was only a few minutes before the sign became visible advertising Coach House.

"I thought you said this was a pub," Morgan said quietly as they pulled up to the Victorian style mansion. Painted all white, trimmed in slate blue, its exterior was a mixture of classic turn of the century elegance, accentuated by huge fern plants in wicker baskets hanging from the eaves. Several rattan rocking chairs sat along the porch in clusters, separated by low tables. Weather permitting, the place served as an additional outdoor dining area. It offered a spectacular view of the natural elements and the beauty of the forestlike environment.

"The guy at the hotel said the food was good—legendary, if I remember correctly, and that it represented the best of the area. How was I supposed to know it would also offer country charm, something you ladies appreciate," he offered, the surprise in his voice evident. The old-world elegance was inspiring to see. Someone had gone to a lot of trouble to maintain and restore each facet of the period the structure represented. And they'd done a damn fine job of keeping it historically accurate, yet up to date in terms of the technology utilized. Brass doorknobs and handles, etched glass lighting fixtures, and trims and doors done in real oak beautifully highlighted the turn of the century structure.

"It looks like something right out of a Laura Ashley catalog. I'll bet the food is great here, homemade at the very least," she added as they walked into the main parlor. Several antique pieces adorned a huge mantel creating a room that was both charming and a testimony to the past.

Decorated sparsely, the large room was a study in Victorian charm, its parquet floors buffed to a gleaming finish. Two antique sofas faced each other, with a rectangular glass coffee table, its base comprised of two wooden arches crisscrossed, between them. A vase filled with long-stemmed yellow roses, baby's breath, and stems of pine was its only adornment. Covered in striped mint green silk, the Victorian sofas were trimmed with mahogany wood and matched perfectly. Dark green brocade window boxes adorned each window, sheer eggshell panels hanging underneath. Several large palm trees and an oversized mahogany secretary stood in one corner. The middle of the magnificent oak piece was occupied by a tall pale green glass vase etched with Chinese letters. A sizeable arrangement of white spider mums, yellow roses, and baby's breath filled it.

"Those roses are breathtaking," Morgan commented as they sat down.

"Don't most women like red roses?" Danton asked casually.

"Yes, they can be pretty, but I've always loved yellow— they're so delicate and come in so many different hues—ranging from deep sunny yellow to a delicate butter color, " she added, her enthusiasm obvious.

It was classic, elegant, and old world. It was also romantic. They were shown to a large but cozy dining area, where people were seated at tables intimately separated by wicker plant boxes filled with Boston ferns. Each table held an etched glass candleholder, the panes forming a rectangular box that held and reflected the candlelight beautifully. The atmosphere was extremely intimate. Two couples, a small group of three, and one lone diner completed the clientele that evening. Apparently, only those who were in the know in the area, or who were extremely discriminating in taste, frequented the historic establishment. The huge hearth fireplace that dominated one entire wall of the room gave off a wealth of much needed heat in the cold, February night.

A huge stained-glass window had recently been refurbished and even in the darkness of the night, moonlight could be seen streaming through the panes, accentuating its rich colors.

"This is unbelievably beautiful. I'm really glad that you accepted my invitation. I would not have wanted to dine alone—this should be a shared experience," Danton offered casually as they were shown the wine list. His eyes appeared to be unreadable and black in the subdued lighting. Morgan found herself breathing rapidly for no reason she could immediately identify. She also squirmed in her seat, suddenly unable to get comfortable. The casual business dinner she envisioned was becoming less and less a reality as the charming ambience of the cozy restaurant enveloped her.

"Well, thank you for asking. Actually, I'm glad I accepted. This is much better than having dinner at First Amendment again. And I apologize if I monopolized the conversation in the car . I don't know what got into me. I got a little carried away discussing my career, my past, and my future with Town and Country. Sorry."

"You shouldn't apologize. I found it refreshing. A woman who knows what she wants is rare these days. The fact that you are actually going after it, too, is almost unheard of. I applaud you. Are you, by any chance, a twin?" he asked, the hint of a mischievous smile beginning at the corners of his mouth.

"I could use another partner in my business, and I know you've just joined Town and Country and are geared up to creating a future with them. But if truth be told, you're exactly what I need. Knowledgeable, motivated, and you come with a devoted following in the industry. Damn, I should have you cloned," he laughed.

Morgan found herself laughing, too, enjoying the

evening, the ambiance, and his company more than she'd expected. They ordered a bottle of merlot, thinking it the perfect complement to a chilly night, a blazing fireplace, and good company.

"What do you suppose 'bench bread' is?"

"I don't have a clue. I was trying to figure out what 'braised upstream swimmers' are or 'orange crusted flights of fancy'? I think we need an interpreter," Morgan laughed as they both gave up on trying to decipher several items on the menu. It had been fashioned out of corrugated cardboard and printed in an Old English type. It was charming and original. Obviously, the owners had gone to great lengths to include recipes that were of common occurrence to local folk; they had indeed neglected to include any interpretation on either the inside or the back side of the intriguing menu.

Danton held up his glass in a toast and as Morgan joined him, he whispered, "To great expectations—nothing less is acceptable." They smiled over the candlelit table, each realizing that the evening was offering unexpected nuances as Danton signaled the waitress.

"We're not from around here. Would you please tell us exactly what these items are on the menu. My friend here is starving." He carefully avoided making eye contact with Morgan, who he knew was probably shooting daggers his way at his embarrassing comment.

The waitress was amused. They were obviously from elsewhere, their clothing, their style, and their manner dictated some major city, probably either downstate New York or upstate near Albany. Everybody needed an interpretation of their menu, though. They'd printed it that way for a very good reason; it stood out and made people remember the restaurant, talking about it long after they had returned to their everyday lives in their home cities and states.

"Okay," she whispered patiently. "The upstream swimmer is salmon grilled, broiled, or poached. And the flights of fancy is chicken. Oh, the rustler specials are all steak. Now see, that was pretty easy, wasn't it?" she asked while waiting for them to place their orders.

"Yeah, I should have remembered that people who live in rural parts of the country seem to have the time to have a sense of humor. In a large city, no one wants to interpret a menu. Call it another art form that's been wiped out by modern day focus on business."

"Well, it does make you slow down, that's for sure," the waitress agreed. "I'll be right back with your salads and a basket of our homemade bread."

"So, tell me more about this need for a partner. Why do you feel you really need one?" Morgan asked, eager to know more about his business. She felt a comfort zone discussing business with him, more than when the conversation shifted to personal things.

"Actually, my brother's divorce is what caused all the problems. He was fine until his wife decided to pursue her career in acting. She wanted to be on the West Coast and my brother wasn't willing to relocate. Now that they're already divorced, guess who suddenly decides he can't live here in New York anymore and is, as we speak, moving to California, somewhere outside of Los Angeles to be exact? The guy never gives up, even if his timing is lousy. I'll say that for him" Danton added. "You know, he's always been that way though" he said thinking of the many business situations where Oscar's tenacity had pulled them through difficulty and kept them in the running.

"Your brother sounds like a real trouper. I hope it works out for them even it may look like it's too late. He obviously didn't want to throw the towel in on his marriage. At least he was able to make a commitment and now seems ready to pursue any means necessary to make it work. Most men are so anxious to remain free, single, and able to . . . her voice trailed off as she realized that she was thinking of and speaking of Garrett. Morgan looked down, remained quiet for a moment, and then excused herself.

The women's rest room was reminiscent of a time gone by.

There was even a chain flush commode, with a wooden seat, the walls and the sink's cabinet also done in fine oak wood. Brass accents had been used throughout, including the faucets, handles, and hardware. Soft peach curtains hung at a small interior window that was also trimmed in oak wood. There was a huge dried floral arrangement adorning the countertop at one end. Apricot, peach, and deep auburn leaves filled it, along with several varieties of dried flowers. An oval mirror, also trimmed in oak, hung above the matching basin.

Morgan washed her hands, reapplied her lipstick, and had a good old-fashioned talk with herself in the mirror. She vowed not to allow thoughts of Garrett and their faltering relationship to enter her mind or the conversation. It made no sense and now was not the time to try and decipher it. Bearing that in mind, she made her way back to the dining room.

As she walked toward the table, she realized that her dinner companion was waiting patiently for her return and that the salad course had been served.

"Wow, you didn't have to wait for me. I know you're hungry," she uttered, feeling a little guilty.

"It's okay. Is everything all right? I was a little worried when you bolted from the table so abruptly," he said. Concern was plainly etched on his face. Morgan knew, in that instant, that she would do everything in her power to keep him from knowing just how upset she really was at the state of affairs her relationship with Garrett was in.

"I'm sorry. I had something in my eye and I knew I needed to look into a mirror to remove it. Probably a stray lash or something," she said quickly.

"While you were away, I noticed something. Look," he said, pointing at the windows of the restaurant's front. It had begun to snow lightly and looked very much like the inside of a glass dome when you shake it up, everything standing still and calm, with the swirl of the snowflakes the only real movement until it settled.

Danton almost reached out to take her hand as they both

continued to watch the swirling snow. He stopped himself. He didn't buy her story of the wayward lash for one moment, but knew better than to pin her down on it. Whatever was on her mind, he knew enough not to try and solve her problems. In his eyes, she seemed totally capable of handling them herself.

Their salads, mesculan greens, vine-ripened tomatoes, cucumbers, blue cheese, and balsamic and olive oil dressing, were delicious. Accompanied by the house specialty bread that had been baked with sun dried tomatoes in it, they gave the meal their full attention for the next minutes.

"The salmon with honey glazed pecans smells delicious," Morgan said as they were being served. It looked delicious, too, with a healthy-sized stalk of broccoli on the side. Danton's steak, cooked medium well, was served with thick slices of onion and a mound of garlic spinach accompanying it. Sauteed sweet potato fries were served in a wicker basket to be shared—another house specialty that was as delicious as it had sounded. As they attacked the hearty meal, they continued to discuss both their personal lives and the industry they were challenged by on a daily basis.

They finished the first bottle of wine and Danton ordered another, the night passing in a comfortable relaxed pace. The snowfall forgotten, they continued to discuss mortgage pitfalls and the various nuances of the industry they both loved and shared. Morgan found herself opening up to him in a way that was uncharacteristic and unprecedented. And Danton, who she'd thought would exhibit signs of immaturity, was more capable of handling her innermost thoughts than she'd previously given him credit for. To a great degree, each found solace and acceptance in being able to share thoughts and attitudes they'd assumed would be perceived as radical.

The evening had held several surprises for both and it was close to 1:00 A.M. when Morgan yawned, apologized, and Danton reached over to take her hand. Looking into her eyes intently, he thanked her for agreeing to share his table. "I mean it, I have had an absolutely fabulous evening and I owe it all to you." All of the other diners had since left, with the single gentlemen at a table in the corner the only remaining customer.

Morgan and Danton walked outside to a world that had been changed dramatically in the past three hours. Since they had noticed the first sparsely falling snowflakes, the storm had obviously intensified. There had to be at least four feet of snow that had accumulated on the ground, and it was still coming down. Visibility was greatly diminished, creating hazardous road conditions, to say the least.

"I had no idea it was snowing so hard," Danton said as he looked at the BMW covered with fluffy white flakes.

"Oh, my God! How in the world will we ever get back to the convention center in this," Morgan asked, her mind doing mental calisthenics in an attempt to figure out the situation.

"Don't worry—I can handle this. Wait here and I'll clean the car off," he instructed as he left her just inside the interior of the entrance to the restaurant.

The waitress who had serviced their table came out, shook her head, and said, laughing, "You folks may have to take advantage of our bed-and-breakfast tonight. I don't advise anyone to be out on those roads this time of night— they freeze up really good. You're up in the mountains, honey," she said then. Morgan could not believe what she was hearing. Mountains, freezing roads, B-and-B . . . this was a nightmare. But Morgan knew that she was fully awake, so it must be reality.

Danton came back inside, his face covered with bits of snow, creating a premature gray head and mustache. He looked so damned handsome that Morgan wanted to reach out and warm him up any way she could. She wanted to melt all the snow from him using her own body's heat. She also realized that after two bottles of wine, her thinking had become somewhat impaired with tunnel vision being the main effect. She'd allowed him to order the second bottle only because she felt absolutely safe with him. He had been a consummate gentleman all throughout dinner. He hadn't said one thing out of line during the entire evening.

"Listen, Morgan, I think we'd better leave right now because it's really icing up out there. I apologize for this. I had no idea it was snowing so hard or that it was accumulating this quickly. Come on," he said, reaching for her hand to lead her to the car. Danton had removed most of the accumulation, providing a necessary view from all angles, and had even dug small trenches in front of each wheel, ensuring that they would be able to get out of the snowdrifts that had built up around the vehicle. The ground had become icy as well with the accumulated snow, and Morgan wasn't sure if she was leaning on him for support, or for the sheer comfort of his being there.

They made it as far as the driveway. When the BMW attempted to turn onto the main street, the car spun out wildly. Danton, no stranger to dangerous roads, quickly brought it back under control.

"Damn," he cursed under his breath as he realigned the wheels.

"Do you think it's a good idea for us to try and make it? We have almost an hour's drive ahead of us," Morgan said quietly. The interior of the car had become a soundproof space, the snowfall outside acting as an absorber to everything around them. The intimacy it created touched them both and they looked at each other, speechless for what seemed like an eternity. The night had held many surprises for each of them; the latest creating a bond of intimacy and adventure they'd not anticipated.

"What else can we do? We certainly can't spend the night in the car, and I don't think they'd take too kindly to us sleeping on those sofas in the restaurant, either," he said. It was obvious that he was ready to give it a try. He felt confident in his ability to handle the car on any roadway, but it was the possibility of nighttime freezing road surfaces that bothered him. And he realized that with the high altitude, freezing took place at an even greater rate. If it had been him alone, he would have chanced it. But Morgan was with him and that made a tremendous difference. He marveled at the changes only twenty-four hours could make.

"Listen, the restaurant is a bed-and-breakfast. I didn't realize it but I guess it makes sense. It's a huge Victorian house. There's probably over twenty rooms or more. Why not just stay overnight and make our way in the morning when we can at least see."

"How do you know it's a B-and-B?" he asked, not wanting to believe that the solution to their problem could be that close and that simplistic.

"Our waitress just told me. She also said that the roads will probably be treacherous. Don't you think we should just wait until morning to drive back?"

"I think that's what the smart money would say. The sunlight and rising temperatures of the morning will help get rid of some of the road icing, too."

"Look, I don't want you to get the wrong idea about anything . . ." Her voice drifted off and he sensed her inner turmoil.

"You don't have to say anything, Morgan. We're both adults. We'll get separate rooms." With that statement, she breathed a small sigh of relief, though the realization that she would be spending the night with him, even under emergency conditions, still sent a shiver of excitement up her spine.

They both signed the guest registry, laughing at their unbelievable fate to be caught in a snowstorm that had blown up so quickly and quietly that neither had noticed.

"You know, that sexy little curve at the corner of your mouth had most of my concentration all evening. Your conversation had the other fifty percent. I honestly couldn't keep my eyes on the swirling snowflakes outside. But I do not believe the amount of snow that accumulated in a few short hours," Danton said as they filled out the guest registry.

Morgan's room, at the end of a long and narrow corridor with knotty pine wainscoting running the length and covering more than half the wall's height, was done in all white. The comforter, pillow shams, and curtains all done in a myriad of white cotton, chenille, blended fabrics, even brocade. The walls were painted a creamy shade of antique white with the moldings all done in a more pure, stark version of the same color. It was chic, elegant, and somehow brought to mind the efforts of a decorator who had been trained in modern times, with an eye toward the past. Shabby chic was present throughout the room, with many of the furniture pieces having come from local flea markets and antique shops and refurbished to amazingly authentic condition.

An elegant chaise lounge filled one corner, done in a patterned silk with pale shades of pink and white. Morgan fell in love with it when she saw it. "Wow, I've always wanted one of these in my bedroom. When I get back, I think I'm really going to look for one. It does so much for the room and it looks so comfortable," she said, immediately sitting down and leaning back. "This is really a beautiful environment," she said breathlessly as Danton stood at the doorway looking in.

"Want to see my room?" he asked then, suddenly eager to show her that he would only be next door.

"No, I'm sure it's decorated with the same attention to detail as mine is, but thanks for the offer. Actually, I can't wait to take off these boots and wash my face. And, it is really late," she added, noting the time. She also realized that she was trying to avoid any awkward situation that might arise. If it was at all possible, she wanted to keep things on a really positive note. The fact that they'd have to spend the night would be enough to handle when tomorrow's sun rose. She didn't want to have anything else to deal with.

Morgan felt her stomach flutter and realized that she was unsure of her next move. They were alone, really alone now, and she could no longer deny that she was attracted to him. Whether or not he felt the same way was still unknown to her but most men didn't have to have much of an excuse to jump bones. And he was definitely a man.

"You know, you're probably right," he said, almost as if

he'd read her mind. "I don't trust myself with you, either. You big city professional women have a way of turning things around on a man. I am going to say good night now," he added, quickly closing the distance to his room. She could hear him laughing; his voice floating down the empty corridor actually eased some of the tension, allowing her to laugh also.

Morgan entered the room and quickly washed her face in the adjoining bathroom. There was no television but the fireplace had been lit, the logs burning brightly. It was cozy, warm, and intimate, and for a fleeting moment, she yearned for someone to share it with. She allowed herself the luxury of imagining Garrett sitting beside the fire, their conversation, their laughter, their smiles, their kisses. But Danton's face kept getting in the way, which made her even more anxious and confused.

Her imagination made the quantum leap that her heart would not allow for. After all, they would have to work together in the coming months, and now was not the time to put that working relationship into any mode of jeopardy. She counseled herself for a few moments more, finding no easy answers or conclusions, removed her shoes, and lay across the bed.

It seemed that only a few moments had passed when she heard a distinct knock at the door.

"Yes, who is it?" Morgan answered, rubbing her eyes.

"It's Darcy—from the restaurant." Morgan opened the door, surprised to see the young woman holding a tray containing two brandy snifters.

"Excuse me," she said, then knocked lightly Danton's door also. "Compliments of Coach House. We offer a late night glass of brandy to all guests who stay with us in any weather emergency," she explained as Danton opened his door. His jacket off, shirt slightly askew with towel in hand, he'd continued drying his hair of the accumulated snowflakes.

"Hey, this is a nice, welcome touch," he said as she handed each of them a glass. Walking quickly across his room, Danton picked up his wallet and handed her a bill.

"Well, good night. I hope we don't get too much snow. It looks like it'll probably taper off tomorrow morning," she added, as she approached the stairway.

"I certainly hope you're right," Morgan called out, her voice echoing down the long corridor. It seemed they were the only victims of the fast-moving storm or that everyone else who had dined earlier lived within close range of the bed-and-breakfast.

"I see you took off your boots," he said, his gaze lowered to Morgan's feet, which were clad in navy blue plaid socks.

"Yes, and washed my face. I feel a lot better," she laughed. Taking a long swallow of the brandy, Morgan sighed and leaned back against the wall. She felt relaxed and sensuous, the brandy glass in one hand, the other tucked behind her. It was as if she'd erased several layers of tension when she'd washed her face, and kicked off her professional stance along with her boots.

Danton, instincts guiding him fearlessly, crossed the distance between them and gently kissed her. He'd wanted to do that all through dinner but had kept a tight reign on his feelings. Now his pulse was racing and he knew he had a huge task ahead of him in trying to resist this enigmatic, elusive, charismatic creature. The contact was electric. Morgan placed her hands against his chest to push him away. But that only created more contact as she realized that her hands had become useless in aiding in her own defense. She uttered, "No, no" as he kissed her so softly, so gently. He began at the temple, then at her brow, then on the high curve of her cheekbones. His kisses felt like warm wishes but left heat and desire in their wake. As Danton kissed each of her eyelids softly, her body became more languid with every touch. He repeated her utterance in a questioning utterance—"No?"—then placed tiny kisses at the far corners of either side of her mouth, softly and slowly. There was no answer as Morgan felt the warmth of desire spread throughout her body, much like the fiery brandy she'd sipped only moments before. She wanted to utter her previous protestations again but no longer had the strength nor the willpower.

She found herself waiting impatiently for his next touch, felt him before her and pressed her lips against his firmly, initiating the contact that she'd only moments before dreaded. Emboldened by his allowing her to take the lead, she reached up and wound her arms around his neck, and relaxed her body into his softly. He needed no other encouragement. Danton molded his lips to hers, exploring the inner caverns of her mouth as she complied and aided in his quest. He continued to hold her, his hands gently molding her waist, her hips, and then securing her into his arms again. The heat that engulfed them spread rapidly, and Morgan moaned lightly as she responded to him.

He pulled back and looked down into her eyes, which were filled with desire and confusion.

"Let's get out of the hallway," he said gently taking her by the hand and leading her into his room. She wanted to resist, knew that she should, but she didn't have the emotional, physical, or spiritual strength.

Danton's room, done in blue with gray accents, was an exact replica of Morgan's, except the walls were covered in a subtle gray striped wallpaper. In place of the settee was a large overstuffed chair covered in dark gray velvet. It looked sumptuous, inviting, and all inclusive—the kind of chair a grandfather would have sat in with several small children on his lap. Morgan wordlessly walked ahead of him, climbed into it, and felt her body relax into it. She felt comfortable in the surroundings—not at all intimidated or unsure of herself, and that surprised her somewhat. He had a fireplace also. The logs ablaze gave off such abundant heat that it could be felt throughout the room.

"I think your room is great. It's just done in a different, more masculine tone."

"And I think I'd like to pick up where we left off when you damn near attacked me in the corridor," he said as he leaned over her, lifted her up and out of the chair, pulling her once again into his arms. It felt right. Like she had been there for a very long time. Morgan found herself respond to him in a way that she'd never experienced before. She no longer had the ability to restrain herself. His kisses left her breathless and languid. His lips moved down her neck and to her earlobes. Whispering phrases of encouragement to her, he removed the brandy glass from her hand.

"I don't want you under any influence other than the one that is operating here, passion," he whispered. When she tried to protest and to give explanation, he hushed her with more kisses. "Let yourself go, Morgan. Trust in how you feel, don't think about anything but what is happening right here, right now," he added as they sat on the four-poster bed.

Morgan felt as if she were on a roller coaster that had somehow escaped the track.

"Danton, I really like you and all but I think we should take things a little slower. After all, we hardly know each other. I've been involved with someone for the last two years and I don't think this is the right thing to do." Her speech delivered, she somehow felt the summation did not sound as convincing as the counter-argument, which was playing itself out in her mind.

He looked at her then, stepped back, and picked up his glass. After taking a sip of the brandy, he offered the snifter to her. Morgan took it between hands that were surprisingly calm and turned it up. She finished the fiery liquid, feeling it burn its way down, and relished the sensation. It quieted her but also allowed her to focus.

Danton sat beside her on the bed, taking one of her hands in his.

"Look, if you really don't want this to happen, I understand. But in reality, the fact that you're here with me says more than you realize. If you and I had been together for the past two years, I really cannot imagine you being so unattached to me that you'd accept a dinner invitation with another guy, go off into parts unknown with him, and end up in his bedroom at two A.M.," he ended candidly. "Now, I don't know about you, but I think there's something going on—or maybe not going on—in that relationship that you're perhaps not yet willing to discuss or acknowledge."

"Look, please don't try to second guess things that you couldn't possibly have a handle on. I didn't plan any of this, neither did you, for that matter. The snowfall was beyond anyone's control, and we were simply two colleagues having dinner together. All the rest just happened," she insisted, looking innocent yet incredibly sensual at the same time. He wanted her, but he wanted her to know that this could very well be the start of something long lasting. And he didn't believe for one minute that whoever it was she was involved with was a solid element in her life. The only thing he was unsure of was how much effort it would take to effectively railroad the remaining shreds of that relationship.

"Okay for argument's sake let's just say that the dinner meant absolutely nothing to either of us. Can you honestly say that you don't feel the energy that's been flowing between us all night? That you don't feel the heat that's being generated right now?" he asked, looking into her eyes.

She couldn't bring herself to answer, so she did the only thing that mattered.

Morgan moved toward him, placing her hand on his forearm, her forehead against his, unable to meet his eyes. The softness of her tone was in direct contrast with the emphasis she wanted to put on what she was saying. She really wanted to utter it, shout it, have it heard from the highest rooftop—but that would have to wait until another time.

"I know I'm being a pain, but this has never happened to me before. And I honestly don't understand why I'm here with you right now. All I know is that I can't think of anywhere I'd rather be."

Morgan lifted her eyes to meet his and leaned into the kiss that was waiting for her. Their lips meshed and she breathed a small sigh of relief—or was it a sigh of resignation? She touched his finely chiseled back, gathering strength from the firmness and solidity she found there. His response was immediate. Breathing calmly, he touched her in places she'd long since forgotten existed. The cleft of her shoulder, the spot exactly in the middle of her shoulder blades that was acutely sensitive to any touch. The spot just beyond her waist, as if he were measuring her for an exact fit. Morgan drew breath deeply, and boldly pushed Danton down onto the bed. He laughed then but it was laughter filled with anticipation

"I suppose you think you're in charge now," he uttered, smiling up into her face above him.

"That's right, and I mean to keep it that way," she responded, leaning over him and kissing him recklessly. She climbed over him then, placing her knees on either side of him, her hair hanging over them both. Her hands, which had somehow developed a mind of their own, knew no boundaries as she pulled his shirt open, spreading kisses along his firmly muscled chest. His response was immediate.

"What a little hell cat. I think I unleashed a monster." He laughed, then quickly turned the tables. Flipping her over, he then gave himself the advantage point and the space to quickly remove his shirt. His chest was a complex web of finely chiseled muscles, and even in the subdued lighting of the firelit room, Morgan's eyes greedily took in as much as she could.

Danton looked down at her and smiled. "My turn," he said as he leaned over to once again kiss her quickly. The next kiss was longer, allowing the heat between them to once again build to a temperature that scalded them both. Morgan felt as if her entire body was liquefying, melting like chocolate-covered caramel exposed to the heat of the summer sun. He continued to press soft, enticing kisses along her body, stopping once to savor the skin just under her chin and neck, then carefully unbuttoned her sweater as he kissed his way down the center of her body. His hands sought her breasts and caressed them slowly, gently molding, teasing each peak until it stood at full attention.

"Beautiful," he murmured under his breath as he continued his exploration. Morgan reached up and put her hand behind his head, pulling his head down to her. His lips felt even softer than before and she could detect the distinct Gucci fragrance on his face. He kissed the other breast then, teasing the nipple until it hardened in response. She gasped as he continued his exploration, back and forth, until she was gasping in anticipation.

Danton's caresses moved lower, holding one of her hands gently in his as he explored her body with the other. He lowered the zipper on her jeans and slowly, tantalizingly, eased his way into her panties. Morgan, fully present but somehow encased in a timeless chasm, felt as if molten lava was slowly making its way throughout her body. The heat threatened to singe her and her lover as well, but it was a welcome fire. Danton quickly removed her jeans. When he carressed her in light, feathery strokes, the sensation it evoked was so overpowering that Morgan almost bit down on her hand in an effort to stifle a natural urge to cry out. And when she felt the first wave of release roll through her body, she could only murmur his name softly into the night.

Articles of clothing were hastily removed and left to collect in whichever corner they landed. Removing a tiny foil packet from his trousers, Danton kicked them aside. Never one to take lovemaking lightheartedly, he wanted the experience to be memorable for Morgan. No matter what happened after they returned to civilization, he reasoned, he wanted to be sure that Morgan never forgot this night.

And he went about the business of making sure of that. When he entered her, after protecting them both, Morgan felt as if she'd evolved to another dimension. They complemented each other perfectly with a fit that was as if by design, and Danton began to move slowly. He waited for Morgan's body to adjust to his, allow him full entry, then he raised the stakes. They moved in perfect unison and Danton held back, waiting until he knew she was approaching the edge again. He took his time, savoring the fit, the feel, the fervor of making love with her. Sheathing him like a boby glove, her heat was an inferno, which he found scorching, yet immensely pleasurable.

Morgan felt the promise of another release just beginning and they both experienced the ultimate in sweet satisfaction simultaneously. He continued kissing her, his lips caressing hers softly now, the flames of desire now reduced to burning embers.

Danton, perspiration glistening on his finely chiseled body, gathered her into his arms whispering, "We make love like it's forever," and kissed her softly. He reached down and pulled the forgotten bedclothes over them both, the chilliness of the winter night suddenly apparent. He turned on his side and cradled Morgan spoon style, whispering, "Spend the night with me," before turning out the bedside light.

They made love again just as dawn crested, slowly and with a growing need that was fueled by the impending reality they both knew would soon have to be realized. As Morgan tried to fight off the urge to drift off to sleep, Danton whispered into her ear, "I can't seem to get enough of you—you're like an addiction," and pulled her close again.

Morgan smiled and curled up tightly against the warmth of his body. Despite her resolve, she fell asleep almost immediately, thinking of how incredibly good it felt to be there with him. She'd wrestle with the monumental issues awaiting her at some other time. The last thought she had as she drifted off filtered its way through a haze akin to a blinding snowstorm. *How the hell am I going to work with him now,* threatened to bring her back to full consciousness but she shook it off, lapsing into the deep slumber of a woman who is both emotionally and physically fulfilled.

Danton lay awake long after Morgan had fallen asleep, cradling her gently in his arms. In the past twenty-four hours, he'd met a woman he found utterly irresistible, unconditionally accepted the challenge of running First Equities on his own, and endured a major snowstorm. Instinctively though, he knew that the next twenty-four hours would offer even greater challenges. He also knew at that moment that the woman in his arms would hold a substantial key to his living up to and ultimately overcoming each and every one of them.

Day Three

Garrett was thoroughly pissed. He'd stayed at the bar for most of the evening, swapping stories, sharing experiences, and trading secrets with his colleagues and fellow mortgage gunslingers until well past 2:00 A.M. Then he'd dialed Morgan's room from one of the house phones, gotten no answer, and the realization dawned on him quite suddenly that she was nowhere to be found. Feeling hungry and somewhat abandoned, he'd stopped into the restaurant, ordered a turkey club sandwich and a beer, and eaten most of it alone. It was tasteless and dry. Inwardly, he acknowledged that though he was not looking forward to the conversation he needed to have with Morgan, he also wasn't entirely comfortable with prolonging the agony of it, either. He really wanted to get it over with it. Let the chips fall where they may.

Stan Gallagher had spotted him, joined him, and wound up hanging out with him the remainder of the evening. He wasn't altogether sure of it, but for some reason, he got the impression that even Stan didn't know Morgan's whereabouts.

"The last time I saw her was in the elevator after the showcase this afternoon. She said she'd probably see me sometime this evening and went to her room. Are you sure she's not asleep and just not answering her phone," Stan had responded when Garrett initially asked about her. He really didn't have any idea where she was but she was part of his team and he'd be damned if he would allow himself to be caught in the midst of a lover's quarrel, even though he respected Garrett's position man to man.

"Well, she'd have to be out cold not to answer a phone that rang almost twenty times. I don't know—maybe she decided to leave and go home early," he added, wiping his hands on the napkin almost as a gesture of finality. He'd tried to reach out to her to no avail. If he didn't know better, he'd think that she already knew some of the things he wanted to say to her. But that couldn't be the case, because even he was unsure of how to put the situation into words. He'd always prided himself on being able to think on his feet, and that's the way he'd decided to play it. Just come out with it and be done with it.

"I did suggest that if she wanted to leave, I'd have no problem with it. After today's showcase, there was really no compelling reason for her to stay. We did all our client schmoozing last night," Stan said. In his mind, her job was done already. He figured she'd done the smart thing and headed for home early in the evening as he'd suggested.

"Well, maybe she did take you up on that, 'cause the girl is nowhere in sight. She could have at least tried to reach out to me and let me know she was headed back, though."

"Hey, haven't you learned yet that we can't figure women out, not matter how intelligent, successful, or level-headed they are. My wife is a dentist and even she has days when I think she's some kind of nutcase," Stan offered, laughing at the memory of the exchanges that oftentimes took place between them.

"I envy you that, though—the ability to make that commitment and go forward from there. I've been trying for years. Morgan actually was able to influence me a lot in that regard because she's like this great partner—both on and off the court, if you know what I mean," Garrett said intimately.

"Yeah, I do."

"Anyway, I guess I'll catch up with her one way or the other."

* * *

Morgan awakened confused, a little angry, and most of all, unable to figure out her next move. She was totally unprepared for her continued feelings of ambivalence. One minute she felt extremely rebellious with a devil may care attitude, and the next her thoughts raged out of control with remorse, even bordering on self-loathing. *I've worked too long and too hard in this industry to allow my professional reputation to be destroyed by one night's miscalculation—even if it was in a damned snowstorm,* she thought as she attempted to pull herself together emotionally.

Danton was already busy digging the car out after borrowing a shovel from the manager of Coach House. Awakening alone, Morgan sighed in relief, thinking it had either been a dream or the product of an overactive imagination. But one look out the window at Danton's vigorous efforts to free his BMW from its snow-encrusted existence confirmed that every recollection she'd managed to bring forth this morning, had more than likely occurred. She could feel it in her body, even now as she watched him. She warmed to the thought of him and realized that she wanted him even now, despite the fact that her emotions were doing a huge see-saw between yes and no.

She showered, dressed quickly, rinsed her mouth with the miniature mouthwash found in the bathroom toiletry basket, and pulled her hair back into a ponytail with a rubber band she found in her purse.

Morgan made her way out to the porch, sorry that she hadn't worn a pair of higher, more weather friendly rubber boots.

"Good morning. I thought I'd offer whatever help I could," she called to Danton, who was more than halfway clear to freeing the BMW from its snow shelter. The motor was running, helping to warm up the entire circumference the car occupied.

"Thanks, you don't have to do that. How did you sleep?" he asked, ceasing his efforts to release the vehicle from its snowdrift. He looked over at her for the first time that day and her heart beat faster. He was so handsome, even with snow clinging to his outerwear, his face, and his hair. He stood there looking very much like a protector, and Morgan knew that her feelings were in a quandary. Not only did she feel unable to control her response to him, but what the hell was she supposed to do about Garrett? Although she knew that things between them were less than perfect, they did have a history together. The past two years meant something, even if it wasn't exactly what she'd come to expect in her life. She knew, without a doubt, that the events of the night before would carry consequences. She realized then that Danton had asked her a question and was looking at her oddly as he waited for her to answer.

"Fine, thanks. Listen, it's no big deal for me to help you— it's just that these boots are suede and I don't think they'll take too kindly to all the wet snow."

"Don't worry about it. Listen, why don't you go inside, see if you can get us something to take on the road, and I'll be finished by the time you return. Just coffee and some toast or a Danish or something for me," he added, as he reached into the car to turn on the windshield wipers.

When she came out some twenty minutes later, he'd removed most of the snow from the car and was dusting himself off. Unable to stop herself, Morgan reached down, fashioned six quick snowballs from the powdery stuff that had accumulated on the porch and let them fly in rapid succession. The first one hit the car, the second his head just as he was turning to see where they were coming from. He ducked, laughed, and shouted, "You're really asking for it," before he picked up enough snow to form his own return fire.

Morgan laughed and ran back inside, the shelter and warmth of Coach House offering the best refuge in the world. She waited for a few moments and then took a look outside. Danton was nowhere in sight. Feeling safe, she edged her way slowly into the entranceway. As she stepped outside, a strong pair of arms embraced her, a cold rush of air and wetness pushed into her face.

"Oh—oh—how could you," she screamed as the snowball's full impact of coldness reached her. Danton was laughing so hard, he couldn't respond for the next few minutes. "I told you that you were asking for it," he said, helping to wipe her face with his handkerchief. They both laughed then and he gathered her close, kissing her quickly. The kiss warmed them instantly and desire replaced the playfulness they'd started with. The bulkiness of their coats and the public space they occupied called reason into play as Danton quickly stoked the fires of passion they'd only hours before put to rest. Breathless from laughter and his kisses, Morgan put her hands on his chest and looked up, her eyes liquid pools of emotion.

"I am having a good time—even though none of this was supposed to happen," she offered.

"I know, I feel the same way. It would be great if we could continue this wonderful interlude, but we both have to get back and check out," he said soberly, while gathering up the breakfast they'd ordered.

They headed toward the main roads just after 9:00 A.M. The drive was pleasant, though quiet. They were wrapped in a blanket of thought related to their immediate circumstances and present company. Morgan's concerns were with a business relationship that she'd quite possibly put into jeopardy. She knew that it would be difficult for Danton to treat her with the same detachment, business acumen, and levelheaded approach necessary to transact the business of mortgage approvals. And why hadn't she thought about Garrett during any of this? It was the first time in her entire life that Valentine's Day would represent a quandary between two men, even if one of them did turn out to be a one-night stand.

Danton for the most part appeared to be calm and resolute, though he'd managed to throw a couple of unreadable glances her way. Nonetheless, she'd felt her heart beat faster, her pulse quicken, and her mind fixate on the vivid memory of all that had transpired between them only hours before. It was as if it were imprinted indelibly on her brain; she only had to glance in his direction for it all to come rushing back in full color and imagery. The snowball fight had eased some of the tension but in reality, they both knew that some very important things had occurred between them.

They rode in silence, each wrapped in a cocoon of thought and feeling, unwilling to unravel or share them for fear of reprisal, rejection, or renouncement. It was a silence born of reflection and each knew that it was best to endure it, regardless of the outcome.

Villa Novella was wrapped in a blanket of snow, the roads slushy and wet from the bright morning sunshine doing its part to reverse the effects of the overnight snowfall.

Danton pulled up to the front entrance of the conference center, allowing Morgan to avoid the walk from the parking lot. The six inches or so of snowfall had made what was planned to be a short, uneventful quick trip into a hazardous trek. He was mindful of the ill-preparedness the sudden change in weather had subjected them to. But he was also undeniably glad for the unexpected turn of events. And he was smiling as he parked the car in its space.

By the time he'd parked and walked to the entrance, she'd gone inside, which was the smart thing to do. Unfortunately, it was at the same time that Garrett was in the process of checking out and he was stunned to see her saunter into the lobby.

They eyed each other warily for a quick moment, then Garrett stepped forward, took her arm, and firmly pulled her to the side of the reception desk, well out of earshot of the hotel attendants.

"Well, you've finally surfaced. I've been calling you all morning, last night, and was just about to check out. Where the hell have you been?"

"Actually, I didn't know I had to check in with you regarding my whereabouts. You've been here since yesterday and didn't seem to feel the need to set aside any specific time to get together. Don't play that 'where have you been' non-sense with me, Garrett, 'cause I could say the same thing to you about the last few months," she retorted, suddenly an-grier than she realized she could be with him.

"Listen, Morgan, you know the last few months have been extremely busy, with all the changes in mortgage rates and everything. I thought you understood. If this attitude of yours has anything to do with that, you should have spoken up before now. You don't wait until a week-end away to bring up all kinds of underlying problems and expect to be taken seriously," he practically spat out. His mounting anger was evident but he couldn't be sure who he was angrier with, Morgan or himself, for not realizing that it had come to this.

"Look, we need to talk. I had meant to set aside some time during this weekend but it never seemed to happen. That's my fault, though, 'cause yesterday was the ideal time after your showcase. I got caught up with seeing some of the old crowd and one thing led to another. I apologize for not set-ting up a more specific block of time, Morgan, but let's move forward. Are you checking out or are you planning to make this your second home?" he asked impatiently. His curveball of a real estate joke was not lost on her but she didn't find it funny. Not his joke, not him, or the fact that he was definitely putting her on the spot.

Morgan felt more like cursing than laughing. His superior attitude caused her to renounce any feelings of guilt she might have entertained. But before she could muster up the strength to answer him, her immediate dilemma was put on hold as Danton walked up to the two of them.

Morgan's heart beat faster, her mouth became dry, yet on the surface, she appeared relaxed and calm. She realized that the next moments would most certainly spell disaster if han-dled incorrectly. Without ever having to be told, she recognized that keeping her wits about her would be her best asset in this unanticipated encounter. Smiling graciously, she turned to exchange introductions to the two men who were suddenly, inextricably, interwoven in her life.

"Danton, this is Garrett Stansfield of East Coast Capital. Garrett, meet Danton Yearwood, First Equities Inc." She sounded breathless but calm. Inside, the triangle she'd found herself in was threatening to close its clearly defined parameters as the two men looked at each other, sizing up the situation. Finally, recognition settled in. They were both professionals on the same playing field. Somehow they'd never met, which was unusual, but they were aware, vaguely, of each other's existence. Industry events, trade publications, and mutual legal and title company representatives created a professional foreground in which anonymity was impossible.

Garrett spoke first, obviously somewhat uncomfortable and unsure of the circumstances he now found himself part of.

"Good to meet you, man. I've heard some good things about your operation. Don't you have a partner or something that also heads up the operation?" he asked quickly, eager to pigeonhole his competition. He vaguely remembered having heard something about their company. The industry was a large one, but you could count the black owned, successfully run mortgage operations in downstate New York on the fingers of two hands. He'd heard nothing but positive accolades about this one and was surprised that its owner appeared to be much younger than he'd imagined. Obviously successful, he reminded Garrett of himself maybe ten years earlier.

"Actually, my brother was my former partner. We recently restructured the business. I'm now the sole owner. Miss Collins has been kind enough to agree to act as tutor in the policies and procedures of Town and Country, for which I am eternally indebted."

The tension in the air was palpable, both men squaring off in undefined corners, waiting for the bell to ring. Morgan held the control switch, the key to the equation, and the resolution to any conflict.

Turning to Morgan, Danton looked into her eyes, willing

her to understand his position. His natural instinct, even aside from any competition involving her, was to distrust Garrett. The almost immediate reference he'd made to his partnership told him that Garrett was willing to drudge up any conflict, any negative he suspected might lead to weakness. And that minute deduction let Danton know that Garrett had already correctly concluded he was not talking to a friend. Business competition was one thing, but Danton didn't want him to know there was anything else to be considered until he was sure he had things more under control, and he suspected that it would take more than just one night with Morgan to secure that.

"Please be sure to contact me by Wednesday. I'd like to set up a meeting as soon as possible. You can meet my staff then and we can all become more familiar with the banking programs at Town and Country," he added formally.

Danton was determined to do all that he could to keep this "joker" off balance. He didn't like him, didn't feel that Morgan should be with him, and knew for sure that their relationship was not all that it was cracked up to be. It had only taken him sixty seconds to gauge the depth of Garrett's character, his lack of commitment to Morgan, and his apparent deficit in being able to gauge his woman's worth.

Shocked at Danton's obvious flexibility in adapting to a situation that was totally unexpected and uniquely uncomfortable, Morgan quickly followed his lead, thanking him silently for being considerate and extremely fast thinking.

"I'd love to and I'll definitely call you. Thanks for everything," she uttered quickly, sounding much more calm than she felt. Her heart was pounding, and though she was eternally grateful for it, she was indeed stunned by Danton's ability to act as though absolutely nothing was going on between them.

Garrett looked on, a little disturbed that he'd been unable to handle things the way he'd set out to, but ultimately satisfied that he was still in control. Now all he had to do was find the right time and place to unravel the most recent events in his life so that Morgan would somehow understand his predicament. He hadn't meant to leave this to the tail end of the trip but had not really figured out how to effectively relay his dilemma and still walk out of the room alive.

Morgan watched as Danton calmly walked toward the elevators. She knew without a doubt that he'd purposely put their newfound relationship on the back burner for her sake. She silently thanked him, knowing that a major scene had been avoided. No matter what happened, she admired him for being able to handle himself in the face of adversity.

"Look, I'm almost checked out and I suspect you want to get out of here, too," Garrett said nonchalantly as he walked toward the reception desk to complete his checkout. He obviously wasn't giving Danton a second thought, which allowed Morgan to sigh a breath of relief.

"Yeah, I just have to bring my things down," Morgan said quickly. "You go on ahead, I'll catch up with you later." She needed time to think, alone and unencumbered. Life had just become very complicated.

"Okay, why don't we do this then—meet me back at my apartment tonight for dinner. That way you can get home, unpack, relax, and catch up on whatever for a couple of hours."

"Okay. Garrett, is there anything wrong?"

"No, not really. We need to talk," he added softly, figuring that it made sense to at least offer some form of cautionary warning. He didn't know how she would respond to what he had to tell her but knew that he needed to offer some cushioning if at all possible, because it had certainly come at him like a Mack truck.

"Okay. I'll see you later this evening then," Morgan called over her shoulder as she made her way toward the elevators. A warning bell went off inside her head and she wanted to ask what had been wrong for the past month, wanted to ask if he remembered that tomorrow, Valentine's Day, was their second anniversary. But something told her to leave well enough alone, let bygones be bygones, and not to address anniversaries or any other milestones at that particular moment.

And what had he meant by the "need" to talk? Morgan's earlier feelings of anger, guilt, even confusion were now solidly replaced by curiosity. Tonight would reveal, once and for all, exactly what Garrett Stansfield had on his mind.

Morgan's pager went off just as she pulled her key out of the lock, pushed the door open, and dropped the suitcase, briefcase, and package of groceries on the floor. She'd picked up dry cleaning, had her nails done, and even stopped at the local Food Emporium for a couple of items she knew she was low on.

"Who the heck is paging me on a Saturday afternoon?" she uttered aloud, figuring it must be either a mistake or one darned serious emergency. It was highly unusual for any of her clients to call on the weekends.

Morgan put her groceries away, leafed briefly through the mail that had accumulated in the three-day span, and played her personal messages back before answering the page. As she dialed the number, she realized that it was totally unfamiliar, which aroused her curiosity once again. The phone was picked up on the fourth ring.

"Hi, this is Morgan Collins from Town and Country Mortgage Bankers returning a call," she said crisply. Inwardly, she really hoped it was an error, as she had only four hours to unpack, unwind, and get ready for her date tonight with Garrett.

"Hi yourself. I was just checking that you'd arrived home safely," he said. It was the voice she'd least expected to hear on the other end.

"Danton, hi. Actually, I was just walking in as my pager was going off. I see you got back in record time. Still driving like a madman," she laughed, liking the fact that he'd reached out to her well before their intended business meeting scheduled for the coming week.

"Yeah. I'm probably guilty of at least exceeding the speed limit, but this time I was totally focused and I'd like to attribute that clarity of mind to you. You know, not only did

I drive with exaggerated calm, but I thought about you during the entire drive. I don't know what you did to me but it seems to have been very good." His double meaning was not lost on her, his voice warm and enticing, wrapping her in a cocoon of sorts.

"Wow, well that's a very nice compliment. And here I was thinking that the age difference between us would probably cause me to have to play tutor most of the time," she responded. What she really wanted to say was that she'd initially questioned the time she'd spent with him, thoroughly analyzing it during most of her drive back to Long Island. Unfortunately, she'd come to no real conclusion; indecision still plagued her every thought wherein he was concerned.

"Morgan, sweetheart, I'd be the first to say that you most certainly do have skills. But baby, I promise you that there is very little that you have to teach me. As a matter of fact, I think I can offer you some tips in a couple of things. Just give me time," he added. The seriousness of his statement outweighed any playfulness she might have interpreted.

"I see. You're really something, Danton. You know, I was a little concerned that it might be difficult to work with you after what happened between us," Morgan said, sitting down on her bed as the conversation took on a deeper level of intimacy.

"I know. I sensed that on our way back to Villa Novella, but I don't think you have to worry. We'll find a way to make it work regardless of what decisions we make. I personally intend to make you mine." His revelation sent a shock wave through the phone.

Morgan laughed then, flattered and intrigued with his persistence. "Danton, you're incredibly sweet but I can't tell you how any of this is going to turn out. I was honest with you. You know there's someone in my life right now, although we have some definite issues." As she spoke, she realized that she'd managed to place herself smack in the middle of a relationship triangle and knew that no matter what happened, she'd never again allow anything of a similar nature to occur.

"Morgan, that guy, Garrett or whatever his name is . . ." His voice faltered as he cautioned himself. "Look, I didn't want to get into the middle of anything so I just played it off when we were at the conference, and it's probably none of my business, but something is not right. My guess is you're just not ready to face it yet. Hear me out. Keep your options open and your eyes focused. I'm a guy and I know what I'm talking about," he ended. He'd neglected to say that he wanted to be there for her, at any time day or night, feeling that it would sound self-serving at the very least.

"Okay, that's fair. I'm not going to discuss it because I already feel as though I've somehow betrayed him because of everything that's already taken place between us. I'll never forgive myself for thinking that I could go out to dinner with you, keep it all business, and not allow anything of a personal nature to occur between us. That was underestimating you, big time."

"I think you overestimated yourself, too, sweetheart. You obviously weren't able to override your natural instincts, which is a good thing. Believe it or not, you did the right thing. No matter what happens, I'm looking forward to working with you, getting to know you a lot better. I'll see you on Wednesday morning, right?"

"Yes, ten-thirty at the offices of First Equities. And thanks for the guilt-erasing pep talk," Morgan added.

"You're very welcome. I can't wait until we have the 'I told you so' conversation," he teased. He hung up before she could offer any form of protest.

Morgan washed her hair, blew it dry, and curled the ends under before applying rollers the size of beer cans. It would create a softly falling page boy, which she knew would complement the black dress she intended to wear. Black suede pumps, sheer panty hose, and white gold accessories would complete her attire. She organized the mail, wrote out a couple of bills, and then straightened up her bedroom. It was always a disaster after unpacking from any trip. At 7:30, she lay across her bed and decided to take a catnap.

She had dozed off and slept for about forty-five minutes when her doorbell sounded. *Who the heck is this?* she wondered groggily as she pulled herself up and made her way to her front door.

"Yeah, who is it?" she asked, unable to focus but making out the image of a man with a huge white box in his arms.

"FTD, m'am. I have a delivery for Collins—68 Charing Cross Way."

"Yes, that's me. Just a minute." She proceeded to unlock the door, wondering who would be sending her flowers. Garrett could just give them to her in the next hour or so, she reasoned as she searched her handbag for a few dollars to tip him with.

Two dozen long-stemmed yellow roses, with a small card, were contained in the fifty-inch long box. "Oh, my God," she gasped, opening them. *Garrett just wanted to surprise me. Our anniversary does mean a lot to him after all,* Morgan thought as she unwrapped them. The roses were two different shades of yellow, much like those she and Danton had admired in the sitting room at Coach House. As Morgan opened the card, her heart beat faster.

On the eve of great promise, on the eve of much love, on the eve of St. Valentine's Day—to the woman of my dreams— Love, Danton. P.S. West Hempstead is a pretty small town—but there's only one Morgan Collins listed!

Morgan quickly put the roses into a large vase, placing it in the living room on the glass coffee table. The white leather sofa, pale yellow carpet, and sunshine yellow and light blue accessories were strongly complemented by their addition and she remembered mentioning yellow being her favorite color.

Morgan wanted to pick up the phone and dial him, but didn't trust herself to handle the conversation. She dressed slowly, thinking of the evening before her and of all that had transpired in the past three days. Confusion and indecision were at the forefront of her mind. "What if's" and recrimination also weighed heavily in her thoughts. *I really stepped into it this time,* she thought, applying her makeup.

The telephone's ring, insistent and loud, caught Morgan as she slid her foot into one shoe. Her bag and keys lay on the bed, her black cashmere coat beside them. The caller ID registered "unknown" and she wondered if it was another tele-marketer, a wrong number, or Garrett, whose number was blocked from identification.

She picked it up as it rang for the fifth time, Garrett's voice tinged with impatience booming into her ear immediately.

"What took you so long? Never mind, I'm glad I caught you."

"Okay, I was almost out the door," she responded, her curiosity aroused. "What's up?"

"Nothing really. It's just that I thought about it and decided we should go out for dinner. Why don't you meet me at Houston's in Carle Place. It's close to us both and you always rave about the food there," he added.

"Are you sure? I thought you wanted to stay in and have a romantic dinner . . ." Her voice trailed off, her confusion evident.

"Well, I figured we'd do something a little different." Silence ensued.

"Okay, so what time are you picking me up," she asked quickly. If Garrett didn't think it was important to pick her up on their way to dinner, anniversary aside, then the relationship was obviously unraveling faster than she'd imagined. She waited patiently for his response. In all the sales and marketing training she'd been exposed to, Morgan knew the first one to speak was always at a disadvantage.

His hesitation was telling, damnable and painful. "Listen, you know I would but it's a long story. Just meet me there, okay?"

She was puzzled by his response but knew that now was

not the time to seek answers to her unanswered questions. It seemed that the evening's agenda would be full—with issues coming from both sides.

Morgan, now thoroughly at odds with everything and not at all sure of anything, decided to just give in.

"Listen, I can be there in about fifteen minutes. Don't you even think about being late," she cautioned sternly, the beginnings of a headache vaguely filtering through. She hung up the receiver wondering what the heck was going on.

The darkened atmosphere of Houston's lent itself perfectly to the intimacy of the evening. Although the silence throughout much of dinner could have been cut with a distinctly dull knife, it had served a very real purpose. Thoughts had been gathered, points had been focused upon, and resolution was within reach.

Morgan pushed the remains of her grilled tuna around on the plate, her concentration keenly out of focus as she tried desperately not to become upset.

Garrett had hardly eaten any of his prime rib, something she found immensely strange. He'd been more quiet than usual all throughout dinner, even as they ordered champagne in honor of their second anniversary. The waiter had poured each a glass and its bubbles were eagerly escaping into the emotionally charged atmosphere.

"Morgan, I don't think either of us could have anticipated how well things would have gone this past year. When I think back on some of the times we've had, the things we've shared, I am amazed that we get along so well most of the time," Garrett said, keeping his eyes on the rim of the glass he held between two fingers.

"I know that we've had some ups and downs. We don't always fight fairly, and being in the same field of work hasn't always been easy for us either," he added slowly.

Morgan couldn't help but smile, but there was real anger

simmering just below the surface. He did not sound at all like a man who was celebrating the second of two fantastic years, ready to go on to the next however long it would be. He sounded like he had recriminations that were a mile long, and she found herself desperately resenting him for that. *Hear him out,* she had to tell herself over and over again, quietly holding her most immediate response in deep check.

"What I mean to say is that, although I think you're terrific, intelligent, and a hell of a mortgage banker, it's a little of all of that which keeps tripping us up—getting in the way, if you know what I mean," he added, finally meeting her eyes.

Morgan was unable to speak. She had known that the evening would probably hold some surprise, known that there was something lurking just beneath the surface of the relationship, but she hadn't realized how deeply ingrained nor how significant Garrettt's feelings on the subject were until now.

She spoke slowly, her voice wavering slightly from the pent-up emotion she could not, would not, allow herself to express. "I'm not sure I agree with you and, actually, am a little surprised that some of this is coming up. Where are you going with this, Garrett?" she asked then, suddenly eager to get it all out and on the table.

"Hear me out Morgan," he said then, his facade of gentleness and timidity suddenly falling away. "Look, we needed to have this talk. It's been off track for quite a while, but you have to know that I did not plan any of this . . . it just happened. You know a man has to feel that his woman has his back, at all times. There have been times, and you're well aware of them, when I wasn't sure if you were in my corner or on the other side," he ended defensively.

"Just what in the hell are you saying, Garrett? Let's be really clear on this, because I don't have the faintest idea of what you're referring to. Since when have I not had your best interests in mind?"

He looked pained as he gazed into his glass once again,

quiet descending upon the table as each sought the next words carefully.

"All right. Remember the Alcott loan that I lost and how it meant the termination of my relationship with the Remax office in Bayside? You knew how much that meant to me, to my office, to my operation, and yet you still expected me to go about my normal routine and squire you to that damned play the very same weekend. When I tried to cancel, explaining that I really wasn't up to it, you screamed bloody blue murder and damn near hung up the phone. That's the kind of stuff I'm talking about," he said, justification evident in his voice.

"Garrett, we'd waited for over two months for those tickets, paid almost two hundred dollars. I also felt that it would do you good to get your mind off a deal that had gone bad. Essentially, we all have to face the ups and the downs in this business. It happens all the time. And why're you so upset about that anyway—you didn't go and I wound up giving the other ticket to my processor, Mona," she offered, the memory still fresh in her mind.

"Because that was the weekend that it all came apart, Morgan," he said, looking at her directly.

"What are you talking about, Garrett?" she asked, fearing his answer but at the same time coming to the realization that she had to know.

"After you performed and made me feel like such a loser about not going to the play with you, I got a phone call."

"A phone call from whom?"

"Lisa."

"Lisa was still phoning you?"

"Not often, but sometimes she'd pick up the phone to say hi, or whatever."

"I see. So what happened? I mean what did you two talk about?"

"Everything. I told her what had happened at the closing table, the clients walking out, the attorneys arguing, and the subsequent blackballing of our firm with the real estate office. She was totally sympathetic, even started to cry a little.

That really got to me. I mean, your reaction had been so different and you were supposed to be my woman, care about me and such."

"Garrett, I did care about you, still do care about you, very much. I have to say, though, that I think your approach to the fluctuations in business we experience is a lot different than mine. If those differences cause problems between us, then I'd say we should address them rationally and not allow other people to come between us just because we have different coping mechanisms," she ended calmly. The silence was palpable as Garrett thought out his next comment.

"That sounds good, Morgan, but to be honest with you, it doesn't always work out that way in life. Lisa came over, talked with me until I felt better, and I guess things got a little out of hand," he added softly, his embarrassment coated with a thick layer of defensiveness.

"What do you mean out of hand, Garrett?" Morgan's voice was almost a whisper, her breath coming in short gasps as she braced herself for whatever was next.

"Well, before either of us knew what was happening, we were in bed. I'm sorry, but the truth is the truth. I didn't want to tell you about it but that's what happened."

"So you slept with your old girlfriend months ago and now you're telling me about it on the eve of our second anniversary. Isn't that a little self-serving, especially as you also practically issue a performance review at the same time," she said, anger apparent in her every word.

"Morgan, I'm sorry and I know I was wrong, but I don't think I'm wrong about us. The truth of the matter is that I haven't felt very positive about the relationship for a while. Maybe it took Lisa's insistent meddling to show me that things were not *all that* with us. Anyway, that's not all of it," he said, squaring his shoulders as if he were readying to take on a physical blow.

And in that instant, Morgan knew. The distancing, the unexplained differences she'd felt, the change in his behavior. It all added up.

"Okay Garrett—so what is all of it? Come out with it, don't hold back, because I suspect that this conversation is probably long overdue. Right?" she asked, heat suddenly rising throughout her body like steam being let loose in a ventilation system.

"Yes it is, but not quite the way you're thinking. Yes, we should have talked this out before, but I just found out that I was *really* going to have to talk to you the other night."

"You mean the night when you couldn't leave for the conference with me because you had so much work to do," she asked, putting two and two together and coming up with more than the combined total.

"Yeah, and for the record, I want you to know that I recognize the timing is horrendous—the day before Valentine's Day, the actual day of our anniversary. But I couldn't allow another day to pass without this being resolved." He took a deep breath, looking away from her for a moment and then began slowly.

"Lisa actually came over that night and we had a very long talk. Morgan, she's pregnant. I didn't know any other way to tell you, so I wanted to do it in person. I know you're probably—"

He didn't finish because he saw the look on Morgan's face and knew he'd inflicted a great deal of pain. She looked crushed, as if all the air and life had been pumped out of her in the quick span of an instant. And he realized in that moment that he bore the sole responsibility of delivering that blow.

"I'm sorry, Morgan, really sorry, but you know I take care of my obligations and she really wants us to try for the sake of our unborn child. I know it sounds a little trite but because I've never been a father before, I'm taking this thing very seriously. I'll not have any of that secondhand fathering stuff going on."

"And so you went through the past two days at the conference, avoiding me and keeping me on ice so to speak, because you knew that our relationship was over anyway,"

Morgan uttered, when she finally found her strength, her voice cracking. "You are either extremely cold-blooded or decidedly cruel," she practically spat.

"I deserve that—and more probably," Garrett responded. "But at least I am honest. I didn't have to tell you, Morgan."

Morgan felt herself vacillating between anger, then fear, then sorrow—tears welling up inside her threatening to spill over. Yet she somehow managed to contain it all, her emotions much like a tightly coiled spring. The dimmed lighting of the busy restaurant offered the perfect cover for the less than joyous dinner in progress at table twenty-nine.

Suddenly it dawned on Morgan that Garrett had known about this, known about all of this when he'd phoned earlier to change the location from his apartment to the restaurant. And that he'd chosen it with clear-cut precision in mind. He'd known the busy enclave would sustain almost any reaction save one of pure outrage and Morgan had never been one to favor public displays.

Quietly arranging and rearranging the artfully sliced pieces of tuna, salad leaves, and other greenery on her plate, Morgan wondered when the annoying buzz in her head would quiet itself. Wondered when the damn would burst, the feelings rush forth, and the torrent begin. She felt stuck. Immobile, both physically and mentally, afraid to change her structure or position for fear she'd crack.

Garrett watched her carefully, the tension he'd felt earlier diminished substantially by his heartfelt admission. He hadn't meant for any of this to happen. He'd meant that part sincerely. But he'd also told the absolute truth when he'd shared his feelings on the importance of raising a child. He himself had been reared in a single-parent household, his mother never discussing her husband or marriage of only six months. Garrett had grown up lonely, with no siblings and no real male role models. As a result, he'd never really formed attachments easily, feeling that it would be his lot in life to wage a one-man crusade to foster independence, strength, fortitude, and the right to go after one's dreams unilaterally. Somehow Lisa had caused him to rethink that mantra and, with her vulnerability and the next generation of Stansfield already in progress, he was feeling a lot more positive about everything. He hadn't meant to hurt Morgan. He, in fact, did care a great deal about her, but they were more like competitors or business partners than lovers. He'd never felt that it would work long-term.

In fact, it hadn't been working for the past six months or so. He didn't have the heart to tell her of his many late night liaisons with Lisa or of their burgeoning relationship even while he had continued to see her. And when she had come to him practically hysterical about the pregnancy, he had known immediately what he had to do.

"Morgan, I am deeply sorry about this—especially since it is taking place on the eve of what would have been our second anniversary. But honestly, don't you believe that it's better for us to have gotten it out in the open than tiptoe around it?"

"Tiptoe around it, is that what you call what you've been doing all the time you've been sleeping with two women?" she asked, unable to hold it in any longer. Morgan wanted to add that he'd made the biggest mistake of his life but realized that it was a subjective statement—an opinion that she obviously was entitled to. She also realized that anything else she could have said to him would fall on deaf ears. None of it mattered in the scheme of things because everything that had existed between them was over. She looked at him and smiled slowly, revealing nothing of her innermost thoughts or feelings. If he honestly thought that she would be compliant enough to actually help him feel better about the mess that he'd made of everything, he had misjudged her immensely.

"Garrett, I wish you and Lisa all the happiness that you and I never had a chance to experience." Morgan then picked up her handbag, reached for her coat, and made her way toward the restaurant's entrance. Garrett did not follow.

Inserting the key into the lock of her car door, she realized her hands were shaking. She slid into the seat heavily, emotion overcoming her in waves. Tears clouded her eyes and she leaned over the steering wheel, finally letting it all out. She remained in that position for the next forty-five minutes, unable to move, unable to see through the tears clouding her vision, and unable to control the spasms which wrenched her body.

Morgan awakened early from a dream-filled night in which she'd tossed and turned throughout. Her head pounding, she took two Motrin, drank a glass of water, and watched the sun rise. It was close to 7:30 when she drifted back to sleep, her chest heavy with emotion. Garrett's admission, his analysis of their relationship, and his subsequent destruction of all that they'd shared weighed heavily on her. It also made her give second thoughts to her feelings of guilt about what had taken place between her and Danton.

I should have been doing any and everything I wanted all along, she thought, admonishing herself for her attempt at fostering a one-on-one relationship, when clearly she was being duped on a regular basis. The whole ex-girlfriend thing was just his way of somehow categorizing each of them, continuing to see them both, and creating as much havoc and turmoil as any one individual could.

She silently thanked God that she'd always been extremely diligent about birth control, making sure that she kept up with her diaphragm and also following up with insisting that Garrett use condoms. *Pregnant,* she thought to herself, wondering if Lisa had set out to purposely end up that way, or if it had all been a huge mistake that they were now simply attempting to "deal" with. Whatever the case, it was an equation that she was no longer part of.

Garrett had his work cut out for him and so be it. It was what he deserved. Having tossed and turned for over two hours, finally she slept, only to be awakened by her pager going off. It was 9:00 A.M. on Sunday morning. *Now what,* she thought as she pulled her purse over to the bed to retrieve the pager. Recognizing the number from the day before, she realized it was Danton. She also realized that she was in no mood to talk with him. She felt as if she'd been thrown from a horse—getting back on one would take some time.

She showered, made a light breakfast of one scrambled egg, half a grapefruit, and coffee, and decided to attend the late session of Allen A.M.E. Church. She'd been a regular there since the age of nine, when she had joined the choir at the insistence of her mom.

Church always made her feel better—no matter what was occurring outside those doors, once inside, Morgan always felt as though the solution was within easy reach. As she joined the choir and congregation in singing "Amazing Grace," tears trickled down her face and she knew the pain she was experiencing would pass. The healing hands she'd always known within God's house created a haven for her. And within those moments, Morgan knew she could withstand whatever was to come.

By the time she returned home, the Sunday newspaper under one arm, and a half pint of Häagen-Daz raspberry sorbet in the other, she felt considerably better, though she doubted the night would bring a restful sleep.

The telephone rang just as she finished changing into a navy blue sweat suit and slippers, comfort wear.

"Hi. Obviously you don't answer your pager on Sundays or holidays."

"No, I didn't have it with me. Who is this?" she asked, suddenly recognizing the voice but wondering how he'd gotten her home telephone number. Then it dawned on her that he'd also been able to send flowers to her home only the day before. He obviously was an extremely resourceful and determined young man.

"It's Danton. I hope you don't mind but I didn't want the day to pass without speaking with you. It's Valentine's Day."

"No, I just wasn't thinking about it," she answered, the pain she'd managed to hold off all day suddenly becoming acutely noticeable and not willing to be ignored.

"Well, we'll have to do something about that now, won't we?"

"Danton, thank you for the absolutely lovely roses. I wanted to call you but things have been anything but normal around here. That was very thoughtful of you."

"Hey, I just wanted you to know that I was thinking of you. Actually, I haven't been able to think of much else since I met you. I know you have some things to work out. Please say something if I'm out of line, but would it be possible to see you tonight?"

"I don't think that would be a very good idea. My mind is like one huge blank right about now. You have no idea. Anyway, I am really not in the mood to do anything. Probably just gather my thoughts and put some things into perspective, you know . . ."

"Yeah, I do," he answered quickly. "Look, how about this—what if I just stop by for a quick visit. We can do whatever you want to, we can do nothing if that's the plan. I just want to see you face to face for fifteen minutes."

The intensity of his plea tugged at her heart, somehow pulling the pieces together.

"Fifteen minutes—you're actually willing to drive to West Hempstead from somewhere in area code 201 for fifteen minutes?" she laughed, grateful that he had in fact made her do so.

"Yeah. Remember, I love to drive. I just really want to spend some time with you. I know it sounds corny, but it's true."

"It sounds very sweet and awfully compelling to me. Just don't expect too much from me, I've had a very stressful day."

"No problem. You know, I knew you'd be smart enough to know when someone is being genuine," he added.

"Okay, well, do you need directions?"

"Actually, yeah. I have an idea of the general vicinity, but it'll take me less time to get there if you give me the most direct route."

"Okay, where exactly are you coming from?"

"Ocean Township, New Jersey—Asbury Park, to be exact. Just give it to me from the Belt Parkway because I know how to get into Queens from there," he added.

Two hours later, when her front doorbell rang, Morgan had changed into jeans and a white oxford shirt tied in front. Hair pulled back into the same ponytail he'd first seen when he spotted her on the elevator, she looked relaxed and comfortable—at home, so to speak. Danton presented her with a small red bear and a bottle of cabernet sauvignon. Kissing her cheek softly, he stepped in and was immediately impressed by his surroundings.

The ranch style home, though somewhat small, was a study in subdued elegance. The living room, painted a pale shade of yellow, was outfitted with a long white leather sectional sofa and glass coffee table. The roses he'd sent, contained in a large crystal vase, created a wonderful presence amidst the surrounding pieces and sat squarely in the middle of the table. Alongside it were three aluminum shapes, a cube, a square and a triangle. A large chrome etagere with glass shelves filled one corner. Its display of black and yellow, porcelain abstract figures, as well as several chrome artifacts, was a distinct feature in the well-thought-out room. Hardwood floors gleamed brilliantly. Several oversized pieces of artwork adorned the walls, each with a different theme, yet solidly reinforcing the yellows, white, and silver/gray displayed throughout.

"Hey, this place is really nice. Did you do the decorating yourself?"

"Yeah. I guess it's pretty obvious that yellow is my favorite color. By the way, you're a madman. The roses you sent yesterday were more than sufficient," she exclaimed, truly surprised, impressed, and pleased that he'd gone to the trouble to make such a big deal out of a holiday she now found severely depressing. The red striped bear was holding a red velvet heart and Morgan held it gently in her hands, unwilling to put it down.

"Because I want you to remember this day. It's the first holiday we're sharing and it's one of the most romantic days of the entire year. It's the perfect opportunity for me to make a good impression on you. Not that I don't plan to spoil you after this, but today is the first day of the rest of our lives," he stated with all the stature and deliverance of a Shakespearean trained actor.

Danton, dressed in a black leather jacket, black courduroy pants, and a gray cashmere turtleneck looked casual, comfortable, and very relaxed. He felt that the two-hour drive had been worth it each time he looked at her.

Morgan laughed. "I think I'll go into the kitchen and prepare something for us to snack on," she responded, unsure of her response. She opened the bottle of wine, suddenly realizing that Garrett's revelations of the night before made things between her and Danton a lot simpler. Now whatever happened need not carry negative implications, nor the terrible weight of guilt she originally felt. Silently she whispered, "thanks, Garrett" and realized that perhaps he'd inadvertently done her a favor.

She made a double batch of popcorn while Danton sat browsing through her CD collection in the living room. And though a nagging feeling of rejection, the pain of being suddenly "uncoupled," and unceremoniously slighted lingered in the back of her mind, she also knew a small degree of happiness knowing that he was in the next room.

As the sounds of Smokey Robinson's "Tears of a Clown" wafted throughout the house, Morgan felt herself losing the battle with the emotions she had been able to keep under control for most of the day. Tears threatened to spill over from her eyes as she struggled to maintain her composure.

"Hey, what are you doing in here? I need some company," Danton complained as he entered the kitchen. Morgan quickly pulled herself together and handed him the bowl as she gathered their drinks in hand.

"I was just finishing up. I see your taste is similar to mine in the classics," she added.

"Definitely. Smokey was the king of love songs and he still is, in my book."

"Yeah, mine, too," she added, and then her voice caught. Tears flooded her eyes, clouding her vision for the moment. Danton, who'd allowed her to pass him into the outer area of the living room noticed the sudden change in the timbre of her voice. He'd also picked up on her subdued demeanor when he'd arrived. There was definitely something different about her. And then, in a flash, he knew. There was no other explanation for her being free on Valentine's Day night and, although it made him incredibly happy to be able to spend this time with her, he realized that he'd truly lucked out.

"You can talk to me if you want to, Morgan. I'm here for you," he said softly as they both took a seat on the leather sofa.

Morgan took a deep breath and shook her head. "No, I'm fine. Listen, you didn't come here to hear my tale of woe. I'm really glad you called and convinced me that we should get together. It's been a rough day," she added.

" I don't expect you to feel comfortable talking with me, but if it will help you to feel better, go ahead. It's not anything that I haven't heard or experienced before," he said.

Morgan looked at him, then smiled slowly and looked away. "Not for anything, Danton, but I don't really think it would be a good idea for me to give you the blow by blow details of my breakup with Garrett. Suffice it to say, it's over."

"Okay, I didn't know that's what was going on. I mean, I don't know what happened, but I'm not going to front and say that I'm sorry. Actually, I think it's the best thing that could have happened. In time, you'll no doubt feel the same way."

Morgan's feelings at that point were a bottleneck of contradictions. Anger, frustration, disappointment, and feelings of being duped were at the forefront. Tears welled up again and she had to fight back the sobs she'd experienced frequently throughout the night when she'd been alone and miserable.

Danton, sensing the turmoil she was experiencing, reached out to her and drew her close. And although he'd spoken the truth when he'd admitted that he was glad it was over between them, he'd never wanted her to experience the pain she was now in.

Holding her near, feeling her body tremble with restrained rage, and knowing the depth of emotion she was dealing with, made him feel closer to her. When the sobs subsided, when the tears seemed to stop their endless flow, he continued to hold her, rubbing her back gently, soothing her with soft, unintelligible phrases.

Danton pulled back. Looking into Morgan's tear-streaked face, he kissed her lightly on her lips. They tasted salty, sweet, and unbelievably delicious. The kiss was tender, meant to console, to reassure, but the chemistry between them fanned the flames of desire.

He placed tiny kisses at either end of her mouth, then kissed each eyelid closed, drew her close, and pulled her into a protective embrace. "This is going to be complicated, isn't it?" she murmured softly.

"All indicators point to a yes," Danton answered, realizing that the words carried more truth than either had originally been willing to acknowledge.

If truth be told, he'd made the trip from Asbury Park to Hempstead in record time anticipating a moment just like this one. He'd known that the roses he'd sent the day before would arm her with some hint of his intentions. But he had no idea of the past evening's upheaval and therefore had not anticipated Morgan's emotional vulnerability or its impact on him.

His suspicions confirmed, Danton restrained his natural inclination to shout, "I told you so, I knew it, and thank God almighty, you're free at last." He concentrated, instead, on offering Morgan all the support she needed. He was more than happy to do so, knowing he could not have orchestrated the demise of her former relationship any faster if he'd tried. He was also acutely aware of what he suspected was genuine emotional pain and silently vowed to be there for her, no matter how long it took and in any capacity.

They continued to cling to each other, she being comforted, he glorying in the feel of her being within the circle of his arms.

"Just because you've become a young man now," the first verse of the Miracles' 1960's hit "Shop Around" filtered through the room, its beat enticing and uplifting. Danton took both of Morgan's hands in his, pulled her to her feet, and said, "Let's dance."

"What—wh . . ." she sputtered.

"Come on, sport," he commented as they began moving to the '60's beat. Danton pulled her into his arms then and began to lead her in the hustle. Morgan, a quick study and excellent dancer, followed easily and competently.

Almost an hour later, they had danced their way through the Temptations, the Supremes, and Luther Vandross.

"Okay, you're a certified dance maniac," Danton said then, laughing. "Hey, are you hungry? I'm starving," he added.

"I suppose you're trying to tell me that you've worked up an appetite."

"Yeah, all that dancing has definitely had an impact. Look, I know I said that we didn't have to go out or anything, but why don't we just pick something up, or go someplace local?"

"Okay. Let's see, it's only eight o'clock. Are you familiar with Westbury—there's a lot to choose from," she said.

"Yeah, my brother and his wife used to live not too far from there. I like the area—that's a good choice."

"Okay. Well, I guess we're going out after all. "I'm just going to change out of these jeans," she said, excusing herself. "Make yourself at home," she called out as she headed toward the bedroom located toward the back of the single-level home.

When Morgan emerged some twenty minutes later, Danton had changed the CD rack to jazz, and was calmly leafing through the past month's edition of *Black Enterprise* magazine.

He looked up as she entered the room, let loose with a low whistle, and stood up.

"Wow, you look incredibly delectable—like something right out of a magazine," he added, walking toward her.

"Thank you very much," she said quickly, not wanting to focus on herself at that particular moment. The black suede dress was simple, but definitely made a statement. Sleeveless, its scooped neck and high waistline accentuated her body, the natural curves filling it like the sand in an hourglass. She'd added black patterned hose and suede pumps with a T strap. Her only jewelry was a watch and diamond studs in each ear, her hair pulled up and in a hurriedly applied upsweep. Although she'd only taken twenty minutes to dress and apply minimal makeup, the effects were impressive.

"You're making it very difficult for me to keep several of the promises I made to myself and the 'Male Honor Society' on my way over here," Danton said, a smile playing about his mouth.

Morgan laughed then. "Don't make promises you cannot keep—there's a lot of that going around." The double meaning was not lost on him, but he knew it was a good sign that she was able to refer to her situation in a lighthearted manner. Time would certainly heal all wounds; he'd be there to assist in any way, shape, or form.

"No, I'm not going back on anything, just letting you know that you're really putting me to the test with that sexy black suede outfit. Baby, I swear you look good enough to eat," he added.

"Come on, let's get out of here. You sound like your hunger is getting the better of you," Morgan said as Danton helped her into her coat.

* * *

P. F. Chang's was crowded, the Valentine's Day clientele made up primarily of couples celebrating the holiday of love. Morgan and Danton sat the bar, ordered seltzer and lime, and talked about mundane things related to the industry for well over an hour before they were called to their table.

"This place is one of my favorites. Everything is so fresh." Morgan looked the menu over quickly. "I usually come here for lunch when I'm shopping at Nordstrom or Saks nearby."

"I've passed it many times but never been inside. The decor is great. And this menu offers some interesting alternatives to traditional Chinese food," Danton commented as he scanned the exotic dishes offered.

"I think I'll have a lettuce wrap. All of a sudden, I am kind of hungry," Morgan said, suddenly realizing that she hadn't eaten any dinner, only popcorn.

"Well, I'm starving. I'll have that and some steamed vegetables, too."

"Sounds like you're health conscious, which is really interesting because most guys don't really care or watch the what they eat."

"I think it's important for a lot of reasons. My brother is a vegetarian and I try to watch what I eat also."

"Yeah, so do I. After you reach thirty, everything changes and your metabolism just doesn't burn calories the same way. I work out on a regular basis to maintain my current weight. With my height, I have no choice," she added.

"I think you look fantastic. I like the fact that you're somewhat shorter than I am. It makes me feel protective. And as for age, let's just say that I've already come to the conclusion that you've got skills you could only have acquired with time. I don't foresee any problem with whatever the age difference is between us because I value what you've been able to accomplish. Not to mention that I've always been accused of being an old soul in a young body."

"Danton, I wasn't really talking about that, but now that

you've brought it up, I have never dated someone younger. Listen, we're colleagues and perhaps we can even become good friends, but let's not jump the gun to assume anything else. I've already been through enough emotional turmoil in the past couple of days. Let's just leave it at that for now—please," she ended, her emotions threatening to overcome the calmness she'd managed to arrive at in the most recent hours.

"Morgan, my intention is not to upset you or to create emotional turmoil, but let's be clear. What happened between us in the past seventy-two hours was not routine, or run of the mill for me. Now, I can only speak for myself, but I plan to build on what we started in the Catskills. I don't want to scare you away, but honey, you are everything I ever wanted, needed, and didn't have time to find. The only glitch was your liaison with Garrett. Obviously, the mere fact that we are able to spend this evening together tells me that he is history and I cannot tell you how happy that makes me because I really thought I was going to have to sit on the bench strategically building my next move. He has obviously fouled, probably in the worst way possible, and believe me, that's a good thing. It's good for you, it's good for him, and it is most definitely good for us. Now we can go forward without having to look over our shoulders for his shadow. I don't think you were prepared for how committed I was from the moment we spent time together at the Coach House," he stated, looking directly into her eyes.

Danton reached across the table, covered her hand with his, and turned it over slowly. He stroked her palm gently, then raised her hand to his lips, pressing them against each fingertip.

"Listen, don't say anything right now. Just know that fate must have played a huge hand in all of this. It brought us together in the right place and at the right time. We couldn't have orchestrated it any better had we used synchronized watches," he laughed.

"How did you know that Garrett and I broke up?" she

managed to ask, her voice filled with emotions ranging from happiness to surprise and curiosity.

"I knew something was up from the time I met him. Men size one another up pretty quickly and I just knew something wasn't right. I still don't know the details and you don't have to go into anything specific, but if he couldn't be with you tonight, then he's got some real problems. A woman like you should not be left alone unless it's at your request. Now, I'm not overbearing or anything, and am usually quite busy doing my own thing, but I certainly would not let any major holiday, event, or occasion pass without spending significant time with you in my company. Even if we were doing nothing but listening to CDs, eating popcorn, and chasing each other around the house, we'd be together. That's the kind of commitment I'm talking about." Sincerity was plainly etched on his face and could be heard in his voice as he continued to hold Morgan in his direct gaze. She knew then that he was doing his best to convince her of his intentions, although he realized that her skepticism was probably at an all-time high at the moment. The food was delivered then, delicious aromas filling the air and exacerbating their appetites.

It was after midnight when they returned to 68 Charing Cross Way. Danton killed the engine and turned to Morgan.

"Look, I hope my little speech at dinner didn't make you uncomfortable but I was just being honest. I don't believe in playing games and I felt it best to put my cards on the table. I hope I didn't scare you off," he added.

"No, not really but I was definitely surprised by your sincerity. Most guys want to play games, never really committing to anyone or anything. And we hardly know each other," Morgan reminded him.

"You're right. We haven't spent years getting to know each other. But in the time that we have spent in each other's company, I can honestly say that I've witnessed characteristics that I've come to respect and cherish in a mate. Not to mention that making love with you is off the charts," he admitted. He wanted to add that he'd thought of nothing else all evening, but knew now was not the time or place to press that particular issue. "You know we have a business meeting set up for Wednesday morning, and I cannot imagine going that long before I see you again." Danton was carefully watching her reaction, waiting for her to show him some sign that she felt as energized, as positive, and as committed to going forward as he did. "And just how do you expect me to sit across a conference room table from you, liking what I see, remembering what I like and wondering when we'll be together again," he asked playfully.

"Like the consummate professional you are, Mr. Yearwood. I'm sure you didn't get to where you are today by being hotheaded, impulsive, or without self-control."

"You're absolutely right, but where you're concerned, the normal rules go out the window. Do you know how much self-control I've had to maintain all evening in keeping my hands to myself?" He leaned over slightly, grazing her lips with his softly. Morgan's body responded despite her inner conflict of emotions. The boundaries she'd set up earlier in the evening seemed to be diminishing with each passing hour, and in its place, a mounting feeling of raw sexual tension grew. She felt herself becoming aroused by his kisses, unable to deny her reaction to the nearness of him. He kissed her brow, her temple, her cheek, and her mouth again, while slowly drawing her against him. Their kisses deepened as their passion mounted. Danton found himself wanting to touch more of her, and his hands found their way inside her coat, caressing her breasts slowly and enticingly as he murmured her name into her mouth.

"Morgan, I can't help it . . . I want to make love to you," he whispered softly, his kisses becoming more insistent. And although she had absolutely no intention of becoming involved with anyone so soon after a catastrophic ending to her most recent relationship, she found herself responding in spite of all that she knew and valued.

One hand found its way to her knee, smoothing the suede of her dress, raising it as he caressed her thigh slowly. Unable to stop himself, Danton stroked her boldly, wanting to feel the heat he remembered only too well. When he touched the heart of her, Morgan gasped. Even through her panty hose, he realized she was already preparing for him, her body bathed in silky moisture.

"Let me come in," he whispered against her lips. "Just for a little while," he pleaded, although they both knew the fires they'd ignited would take more than a short time to extinguish.

Struggling to regain her composure, Morgan managed to pull away from him, smooth her hair, and rearrange her clothing while attempting to collect her thoughts. She looked shyly at Danton, realizing that she wanted him physically despite any misgivings she'd had earlier. She also knew instinctively that now was not the time for them to connect on that level, and she struggled with her next words.

"You're really pushing it you know, Yearwood," she said, speaking in a voice heavy with passion, yet attempting to interject humor to cut through the sexual tension present. She felt that if she didn't get a handle on things in the very next minute, she would most certainly be flat on her back and even more confused in the morning. The 750 IL's intimate interior had become steamy from their exaggerated breathing and the pure heat being generated.

"Let's just say that I know what I want and how to get it. But I'm also very patient. I had a wonderful evening and I suspect you did, too," he added, becoming businesslike, almost formal. "I'm looking forward to seeing you on Wednesday morning in my office," he said, tweaking her nose playfully. "I'll be the perfect client. I don't know what your schedule is like during the week, but let's have dinner. How about Thursday evening?"

"Danton, are you sure you want to do this? Look, we don't have to take this any further. We can chalk it up to an interesting conference, a great Valentine's evening, end of story. After all, I'll be working with you on the First Equities account. I really don't want to add the extra pressure of a personal relationship, not to mention that I am in no shape to commit to anything. Are you absolutely certain that you want to continue?" she asked, concern clearly evident by the expression on her face.

"I already answered that question. I know exactly what I'm doing. And yes, it was an interesting conference, a great Valentine's evening, etcetera. But I also know it has the potential to be a lot more than that if you'll just give it a chance. I mean it. Now, you go on inside and get your beauty rest. I'm already anticipating Wednesday morning. You in your corporate attire, fully in charge, taking over your newest account. You can commit to that, can't you?" he asked, fully knowing the answer.

"Yes, but that's because I know how to handle business. I'm good at it and I love it."

"You most certainly do. Boy, I really love an assertive woman," he laughed, coming around to open her car door.

"You're amazing. Your imagination knows no boundaries."

"Yeah, just remember that and also remember that it only took seventy-two hours for me to persuade, convince, and deprogram some of your preconceived notions."

"Yeah, seventy-two hours to do all that," she acknowledged as he walked with her toward her front door.

"Um-hmm, and I'm counting the time until I see you again," he said, lowering his lips to hers once again in a kiss that was filled with passion, promise, and longing. When they stepped apart, both were breathing heavier, and the naked passion on Morgan's face told him everything he needed to know.

"Look, I'm going to be a gentlemen and head back to New Jersey. We have a lifetime to catch up on all the things I would like to do to you tonight, but I think it's best that we take it slowly. Dinner on Thursday," he reconfirmed.

"Sure, that's when I'll starting counting," Morgan replied, smiling as she realized that time was on their side, no matter it happened.

TO MY READERS

To all of you who have shown me the kindness of your undivided attention, I'd like to offer my most sincere gratitude.

It is your attention and growing expectation that now drives me to to create complex characters, a plot that twists, turns and thickens, and above all, characters that live with passion.

It's all for you.

Thank you for the opportunity to do it!!

Linda Walters

More Sizzling Romances From
Carmen Green

__Now or Never   0-7860-0327-8   **$4.99**US/**$6.50**CAN

__Keeping Secrets   0-7860-0494-0   **$4.99**US/**$6.50**CAN

__Silken Love   1-58314-095-6   **$5.99**US/**$7.99**CAN

__Endless Love   1-58314-135-9   **$5.99**US/**$7.99**CAN

__Commitments   1-58314-226-6   **$5.99**US/**$7.99**CAN

Call tool free **1-888-345-BOOK** to order by phone or use this coupon to order by mail.

Name_____

Address_____

City_____ State _____ Zip _____

Please send me the books I have checked above.

I am enclosing $_____

Plus postage and handling* $_____

Sales tax (in NY, TN, and DC) $_____

Total amount enclosed $_____

*Add $2.50 for the first book and $.50 for each additional book.

Send check or money order (no cash or CODs) to: **Arabesque Books, Dept. C.O., 850 Third Avenue, 16th Floor, New York, NY 10022**

Prices and numbers subject to change without notice.

All orders subject to availability.

Visit our website at **www.arabesquebooks.com**.

More Arabesque Romances by
Monica Jackson

More Sizzling Romance From
Leslie Esdaile

__Sundance	0-7860-0320-0	**$4.99**US/**$6.50**CAN
__Slow Burn	-8760-0424-X	**$4.99**US/**$6.50**CAN
__Love Notes	1-58314-185-5	**$5.99**US/**$7.99**CAN
__Love Lessons	1-58314-186-3	**$5.99**US/**$7.99**CAN

Call tool free **1-888-345-BOOK** to order by phone or use this coupon to order by mail.

Name_____

Address _____

City_____ State _____ Zip _____

Please send me the books I have checked above.

I am enclosing $_____

Plus postage and handling* $_____

Sales tax (in NY, TN, and DC) $_____

Total amount enclosed $_____

*Add $2.50 for the first book and $.50 for each additional book.

Send check or money order (no cash or CODs) to: **Arabesque Books, Dept. C.O., 850 Third Avenue, 16th Floor, New York, NY 10022**

Prices and numbers subject to change without notice.

All orders subject to availability.

Visit our website at **www.arabesquebooks.com**.